NOVEMBER'S
MISSING

NOVEMBER'S MISSING

Valerie Power

This one is for the lost.

Lizzie met her at the gate
Full of wise upbraidings:
"Dear, you should not stay so late,
Twilight is not good for maidens;
Should not loiter in the glen
In the haunts of goblin men."

—Christina Rosetti, *Goblin Market*

Prologue

DAY OF THE DEAD

Vivian Johnson was not prepared for what she would find that first morning of November 2007.

Her head pounded and her back ached, unfortunately not from drinking and dancing at some raucous Halloween party, but from a pointless night of hard metal chairs, burnt coffee, and never-ending questions from agents Bill and Ted at the DEA field office in Encantadino.

Did El Blanco get away? Are you sure? Where is Brian Bartley? Have you had any contact with him since the fire?

The questions, and her denials, seemed endless.

The coffee was unfortunate. She could've used something a whole lot stronger.

And Bill and Ted (their actual names, believe it or not, although Bill insisted he was William whenever she called them that) were their same old humorless selves.

So near dawn, when her handlers finally decided to have mercy and take her home, she asked them to drop her at the old woman's house instead. She needed her horse.

Recalling Deirdre Boyd's description of how to get there, she directed them down the twists and turns of Old Dairy Road. When it dead-ended at a huddled old cottage in the trees, she spied the horses out back and knew she was in the right place.

It took some doing to convince the dynamic duo—scowling skeptically in their identical suits—that this was a fine and dandy place to leave her, at an abandoned shack in the middle of the woods. She watched the black

SUV retreat, willing them away with her mind.

And at last, she was rid of them.

Trembling from lack of sleep, lack of alcohol, and sheer relief, she ran towards the overgrown pastures behind the house. She paused at the fence, and put a hand to her chest. This was the first time she'd seen Apache since that night on the mountain in the fires, and it felt as if her problems were over now. He was alive.

Apache's head was deep in grass. Next to him grazed Scarlet, Deirdre's chestnut mare. And beyond them was a rickety old white horse, who lifted her head to look at Vivian.

Apache noticed her, and lurched his head up, pausing mid-chew on an overstuffed mouthful of grass.

He grunted a throaty greeting and trotted to her. Tears welled up as she touched him, his beautiful grullo hide shining like tarnished silver, his coarse black forelock falling over his liquid brown eyes that seemed to form a question, looking her over to make sure she was unharmed, just as she was doing to him. She hugged his neck, just smelling his scent, feeling his blood pulsing, the heat of his body, the in and out of his breath. He sighed, and blew a relaxed snort, then began chewing again, the grinding of his molars a comforting, familiar rhythm.

He was alive. She hadn't truly believed it until now. She hadn't allowed herself to have hope.

Certainly not during those terrifying minutes—hours?—on the burning mountain after she'd lost him. Not during those strange limbo days after the fire. Not even after the gut wrench of Deirdre's creepy little girl saying the horses were alive and safe at Mrs. Fey's.

However, the creepy little girl was right. Here he was.

Miracles do happen.

(But also, as she was yet to discover, the opposite of miracles.)

She looked around to find her tack, saw it against the fence, and led him over to it.

Now she didn't want to take him home, not yet. Despite the call of the liquor cabinet housing her dad's cut-glass decanter of whiskey, somehow the thought of going home to her faux-Victorian on the hill in the southwest corner of Fairy Glen filled her with dread. The dark downstairs, cavernous yet crowded. And the upstairs, hollow as a jack-o'-lantern in the yellow morning light.

She suppressed a shiver as she lifted her cavalry saddle, undamaged except for a few scuffs, onto Apache's broad, dorsal-striped back, and put his bridle on. She led him out of the pasture, and with shaking hands, closed the gate behind her.

He spun around and called to Scarlet, and the mare called back to him, but Vivian led him away, got on, and pointed him east into the bosom of the scrubby foothills. She thought she heard something on the other side of the creek, saw a shadow, a movement.

Just a deer. The wildlife returning to normal after the fires.

She breathed deep, trying to ignore the apocalyptic sky, trying to forget most of last night, trying not to cry, still trying to believe that he was here, beneath her, alive. All that mattered was she had her horse, and she had her freedom.

That is, until she heard a whinny, and Deirdre Boyd's dog-summoning voice calling her name. "Vivian!"

"Dear Lord," she muttered.

Deirdre must've arrived at Mrs. Fey's just minutes after her. She cursed Bill and Ted for keeping her so long, and cued Apache into a trot, trying to get further up the creek. She was almost at the nature preserve, where multiple hiking trails branched off. Maybe she could escape, pretend she hadn't heard.

But Apache defied her, turning in a big circle, back towards her unwanted company. "Traitor!" she said, disbelief coloring her words. He'd gotten attached to Scarlet, even in their short time together in the pasture...what had it been, less than a week? Pathetic.

He went towards the two women on horseback, who were waiting for her on the bank of the creek, the creek that she'd been trying to cross to get away from them.

Deirdre. Good old, do-gooder Deirdre. Her arm was in a cast, and her frizzy auburn hair sticking out from under her helmet matched her chestnut Arab. As much as Vivian hated to admit, they shared a bond now, after that crazy escapade. But the last thing she wanted was to spend more time with that woman.

And Sally—the petite, icy blond, on her older sorrel Tennessee Walker mare. She was so confident in her sunglasses and endurance gear, so sure of herself, so proud of her new man, Sheriff's Detective Tom Goodwin. But she knew so little about him. Vivian was the one who had spent part of last night with him.

She could count the days until that little tidbit of information circulated Fairy Glen. She thought of the word *neighbor*, how the root implied they were all gossipy horse-faced herd animals. Vivian squinted to see if there were any more neighbor ladies lurking in the woods.

When she didn't see any, she sighed in resignation, and put a hand on

Apache's neck. She would indulge him. He was practically glowing with energy now that the other two horses were here. She'd go a little ways on the trail with them, then politely excuse herself.

Deirdre started babbling about actually keeping the horses at the old lady's place permanently. Screw that. Apache was coming home with her, right after this trail ride was over. And Vivian told her so.

Sally interrupted. "We're going to ride over to see the fire damage and have lunch at Gorda's."

That actually sounded...not too bad. A cheap tequila margarita, heartburn in a glass. Nothing compared to Dad's scotch, but hey. You take what you can get.

They fell in line, traveling up the switchbacks, under the eucalyptus trees. To the top of Mount Richardson, where the high reservoir that served their community lay shimmering in the thick smog. Crossing the dam, they all stopped to look down the sharply carved valley towards the Pacific in the distance.

To the right, beyond the creek, Fairy Glen lay untouched by fire, nestled safely in shaggy greenery.

But everything on their left was black. Everything, from the high plateau where Paraiso had been, down the steep hillside, to the line of trees along Hidden Creek, had been destroyed.

That could've been her. It could've been Apache. It nearly was.

Those could've been his bones, instead of manzanita branches crumbling to ash.

All three riders were eerily quiet, even Deirdre, the normally unstoppable talker. She looked at the devastation, then looked at Vivian, knowing the two of them had seen things that shouldn't have been seen, things that probably shouldn't even *be*.

Silently, they continued, hushed by the reality that this fire could've taken everything from them. But it didn't. A miracle.

From the high dam, they went down the snaky hiking trail towards Lake Hemingway, which had seen its share of the fire too. The entire hillside they descended was black, all the way down to Del Diablo Highway, where they would cross the highway to get to Gorda's Cantina by the lake.

All at once, the emotion was too much for her, and there was a strange pulling feeling in her gut.

Apache snorted, feeling her distress. She flinched as he took a misstep, but then realized that he was reacting to Deirdre, who'd jumped off her horse, mouthing words. But it was all silence and nothingness.

A ringing filled her ears. It was all she could do to slide to the ground so she wouldn't fall off.

She saw what Deirdre was pointing at, saw what she and Sally were yelling silently to each other about.

A body. A real body, made of charred flesh and bone, not charred wood or leaves or plants. A small, human, female body.

If only Deirdre hadn't been so observant, they could've ridden on by.

If only Vivian had been ten minutes earlier getting to Apache that morning, she wouldn't have been involved.

But she wasn't earlier. *And now she was most definitely involved.*

Remember the opposite of miracles?

Tragedies. Tragedies are the opposite of miracles.

One must pay for the other.

The day before...

Wednesday, October 31

ANGELA MET UP WITH LEXI after school, and they walked along the track.

Cheerleaders flipped into the air across the football field, near the bleachers. It was the first day back after the fires, and it was Halloween, and they had a lot of catching up to do. She hadn't talked to Lexi since last week.

Angela was in costume. Goth witch, the standard. She'd even used semi-permanent dye to blacken her hair this morning. Her mom was on a double shift at work, so she wouldn't have to deal with her outrage until tomorrow.

Lexi was wearing her cheer uniform, but had painted one rivulet of blood coming out of her mouth. "I'm a dead cheerleader," she had said, when people asked what her costume was.

Lexi gave Angela a quick hug, the letters on her uniform crisp against Angela's black lace. *EVH* in orange letters, for Encantadino Valle High, ran diagonally down a green banner on her sweater.

Orange and green, for the orange groves. The Ranchers. Not the most intimidating team name. But thanks to Lexi, the cheer squad had gone to state finals last year.

"Good luck today," Lexi told her as she piled her curly mahogany hair into a high ponytail and tied it with a scrunchy.

"Lexi!" shouted Eric, Lexi's big gay friend, from across the field. "Hurry up!" Eric was the one that would fling her in the air, tiny little Lexi flying up, her arms crossed over her chest like an Egyptian mummy, spinning like a rotisserie chicken, but fast, so fast she was a blur.

Lexi turned back to Angela, talking quickly. "Tonight, before we go out, I'll hypnotize you, bring up that repressed memory. I know it's in there." She touched the center of Angela's forehead. "Okay. Be careful taking that bus. Don't let any pervs sit close to you."

"There's no pervs Lexi. Just old ladies going to blow their social security checks at the casino. But I told you, I can't remember anything."

"I can remember stuff from when I was one year old. I bet you can too. We just need to access it. I've been reading this book—"

"Here comes Jason," Angela whispered. He was walking along the track towards them. Lexi froze and stopped talking.

"Lexi, can we talk?" he called, and stopped about twenty feet away from them.

Jason was big and muscular, he was almost twice as big as Lexi, it seemed like. She turned around slowly, put her hands on her hips and looked at him.

He shot a brief glance at Angela from under his brown side-swept bangs. He looked at her a microsecond longer than usual, pulling his eyebrows down into a straight line. Then he focused on Lexi again. "What are you doing tonight?" His voice was tight. He looked almost—sick?

Lexi let out a laugh like tinkling bells; her fake laugh. "Wouldn't you like to know?" she said, then turned her back on him, and lifted a lock of Angela's hair to examine it. Angela knew they'd been fighting, but not the latest details. It had been a crazy week, with the fires.

Lexi leaned close and whispered to Angela, "I have a surprise for you. You're going to be totally blown away. You know those lessons I was taking down in San Diego over the summer?"

Three more cheerleaders ran by, stopping to pull Lexi with them across the field to practice.

Jen, a willowy girl, looked down at Angela, reached out and touched her hair. "Whoa. Is that like, real dye, not the spray-on stuff?" Her eyes widened.

Angela barely nodded, shyness coming over her, and then Gemma, the bossy one, elbowed Jen in the ribs. "It's a wig."

Lexi said, "The hair does look good, Ang. It suits you."

"What are you doing tonight Lexi?" Gemma asked, ignoring Angela.

"Nothing. Just hanging out with Angela." Lexi smiled, still looking straight at Angela, and winked.

There was more yelling from the rest of the squad in the distance, and quick as a herd of gazelles, Jen and Gemma turned and ran towards the others on the far side of the field.

Angela didn't belong with these people, didn't understand why Lexi was her friend.

"They're impressed," Lexi said, a smile lingering on her deep purple lips. "Takes guts to dye your hair. They'd be even more impressed if I told them where you're going. And on Halloween, no less." Lexi took her hand. "But don't worry, I won't tell anyone about that, not until you're ready. And tonight? I have a BIG surprise for you. Been practicing all summer. You're gonna be blown away."

Jason was still hovering nearby.

Lexi said, "Anyway, you better get going. I'll come by your place at six. Right? I have to shower and change before we go."

Angela nodded.

Lexi gave her a quick kiss on the cheek. "Love you. See you tonight," then turned and ran towards the cheer squad, doing a handspring at the 50-yard line along the way. Jason had faded back against the bleachers, and was just watching Lexi. Angela had become invisible again.

Angela swayed with the bus as it wound its way north through the avocado groves. She reached behind her and tried one more time to open the window, but it was stuck.

She was on regional transit. At the downtown depot, the casino bus driver had taken one look at her and said, "Sorry honey, you gotta be eighteen to ride."

So instead of being in a tall, dark windowed, air-conditioned bus with a bunch of puffy-white-haired ladies, their purses jangling with pennies, she was in the bright, hot, stuffy city bus.

Her foreign feeling hair wafted across her face as someone else successfully opened their window and allowed a cross breeze through.

"India?" someone said. She felt eyes on her, cleared her hair off her face and looked up. Were they talking to her?

An old man sat across the aisle, his eyes bright and black, his face worn and brown, caved in at the mouth from having no teeth.

He said it again, the old man. "Eres indi-haina?" his pointy tongue darting out of his mouth as he spoke, like a snake's sniffing the air. He pointed at her, raised his eyebrows.

She had no idea—he was asking her if she *was* something, but she didn't understand the next word. One year of middle school and one year of high school Spanish was not enough to make her fluent. She tried something anyway, just to not seem rude.

"Estoy...bruja," she said, pointing to herself, then pulling her witch hat out of her backpack and putting it on. She'd used the wrong verb, or had she? Was it soy, or estoy?

The man wheezed with laughter, saying more things she couldn't understand. She just laughed with him. Despite Lexi's warnings, Angela could tell he was harmless, probably someone's grandpa or even great-grandpa, in his old Wranglers, fancy belt buckle, pointy ostrich-skin boots like the ones she'd seen at the swap meet.

He took the stiff white cowboy hat from the seat beside him and put it on over his wispy, slicked-back white hair. "Estoy...vaquero!" he said, and laughed so hard tears wriggled down his face through the ravines of his wrinkles. She laughed too, for real this time. His outfit was no Halloween costume.

The bus lurched to a stop. The old cowboy stood up, nodded to her and said, "*Vaya con dios*," no longer laughing, serious. She didn't know if that was him still playing a movie star caballero, or if he actually said things like that to people. But, oh, this was her stop too—the church. Maybe that's why he'd said it. She scooted forward in her seat, clutching her backpack. Bright yellow. It ruined her costume.

He shuffled off the bus, behind a gaggle of hunched old women in dresses, gray and black hair tied in thick buns at the napes of their necks. It took forever. She waited, letting them all go first, until finally, she descended the steps.

Angela stepped down into a cloud of dirt and hot bus exhaust. The air brakes poofed, and the bus growled slowly away. The old cowboy was shuffling bowlegged down the road to the casino, while the old women migrated across the parking lot to the mission, clucking to each other like chickens.

Long and low, red roof and white plaster, swooping arches down the length of it. Just like the model she'd built in fourth grade. She remembered how patiently her mom had helped her piece it together, getting glue stuck in her long brown hair. Guilt clutched at her and she picked up her pace.

In the courtyard, voices of bustling people rang out, mostly Hispanic or Native looking people, setting up tables with lots of flowers and candles.

She looked for anyone who might be in charge. Maybe there was a church office or something where she could ask?

A big old wooden door stood open to the busy courtyard. Nobody inside, just a desk that looked recently abandoned with a chair askew. On a table sitting under the window set deep in the two-foot thick adobe wall, was a big guest book.

She flipped through the pages. In the front was a map printed on pink paper and slipped into a plastic sleeve. Cemetery sections were listed, with dates. That would at least narrow it down. There. She needed to go to the section north of the church, near the edge of the cemetery. She was good at finding stuff on maps, in books, in libraries.

She'd done a lot of that recently. There was like an itch, something pulling at her, a void inside of her. She couldn't help it. Mom either didn't know or wouldn't tell her. So she'd taken matters into her own hands, with a lot of help from Lexi. And what she'd found had been sad and shocking, but a relief at the same time. The relief of knowing.

And yet, the knowing came with infinitely more layers of not knowing.

Even though the altars in the courtyard looked really cool, ornate and pretty, she walked right by them, not wanting to waste any time. She had less than an hour before she had to catch the bus home in time to meet Lexi. It was already past four o'clock, time slipping away on the late autumn slant of the sun. She headed out to the edge of the cemetery.

The hillside was covered in stubs of short dry grass that crunched under Angela's feet. This section was far from the shady willows and marble headstones near the mission, and it looked, well, low rent. The whole place was yellow; the sky, the earth. A hot wind kicked a cloud of dust in her face.

The headstones were haphazard out here. Not really in rows. Some were flat into the ground, others were slightly raised, but none were the typical tall gravestone that filled the Halloween stores. Some were so old the names were unreadable, the carved letters melted into the stone, like the *Ivory* on her bar of soap after a few showers.

She crested a small rise, and sucked in her breath. The steep hillsides facing her were black. Charred remains of bushes and bare boulders that looked like Homer Simpson's head sticking out of the earth were all that remained. The fire line came right down to the chain-link fence. Even some of the grass on this side of the fence was burnt.

A man in a dark coat was kneeling in the near distance. Two old women, holding on to each other, smiling and laughing through their tears, passed her on their way back to the church, shielding their eyes from the sun. They nodded and smiled at her—they might've been on the bus with her, she couldn't tell.

She turned her attention back to finding the grave. Up and down each row. These looked newer, but generally basic. She was getting close to the end. Maybe the obituary was wrong, maybe the grave wasn't here.

Maybe she was totally wrong about the whole thing.

She kept going, getting closer to the guy in the coat, who was putting black-eyed Susans on a grave. Carefully she walked by him, peeking a glance at the name carved in stone.

Cheryl Sandman. That was it. But who was he?

Her shadow fell on him, and he looked up. She stepped back.

His eyes were lit up from the sun shining sideways through them, golden green. His hair was longish, fine and light brown, like hers.

Her vision shifted. Something like the door to an unused room opened inside her, a room that she now saw was filled with forgotten treasures.

The man spoke. "I figured it was only a matter of time." He stood up. "Angela?"

She nodded, dumbstruck.

He pulled a stuffed Simba out of his black trench coat and offered it to her. She took the plush toy, staring at the grimy matted fur, at its shiny plastic eyes, then up into his.

He smiled, and said, "I think we have some catching up to do."

Thursday, November 1

EL DÍA DE LOS MUERTOS

Deirdre got done with her round of questioning, and crossed the restaurant to rejoin Sally and Vivian.

They were at Gorda y Flaco's Cantina. She wished like crazy Bonnie was here, someone she knew better. Someone more...comforting. Neither Sally, with her go get 'em attitude, or Vivian, the reclusive loner of the neighborhood, were what you'd call soothing.

Deirdre slid into the booth, and Sally got up. She was next to be questioned. Deirdre watched her walk purposefully across the restaurant towards the law enforcement officers.

After they'd found the body, Sally had called the sheriffs, and the women had met them at the highway and led them up the trail, to the scene.

The scene. It sounded so simple and sterile. Nothing like it actually was; the grisly remains of a young girl that they'd discovered on their trail ride into the burned wasteland.

Tom Goodwin, the sheriff's department homicide investigator, was in a booth on the opposite wall, along with another detective. Sally sat down across from them, steepled her fingers together, and looked at them both intently, ready to answer all the same questions Deirdre had just answered.

Last night, Sally and Tom had been dancing together at the Halloween party at the Fairy Glen firehouse. Now they were all business.

Deirdre looked out the window at the horses. They stood tied up under the shade of a giant oak. Apache, Vivian's dusky gray mustang, had his head over Scarlet's withers, staring into the window like he was keeping an eye on them. Sally's mare Giselle stood slightly apart from the other two, sleepily minding her own business.

Beyond the horses, the sky was a dull yellow, reflecting sickly green on the lake.

It must be close to noon. Deirdre's stomach grumbled. She took her eyes off the scenery, focusing across the table. Vivian's thin face was gray, even under the ash.

They shouldn't have come on this ride.

She sighed. But if they hadn't found her, how long would that girl's parents have been waiting for their child to come home?

On the altar near the fireplace, candles burned, dancing slowly among the sun-colored marigolds, making the dead people in the photos appear to live again.

Deirdre remembered the face of the missing girl on the flyers, and how, the last time she was here, the shy busboy with the straight eyebrows had explained that November 1 was Day of the Dead "for the children." Los niños.

Someone had to find the girl, and the sooner the better. She just wished it hadn't been her.

Behind the bar, Gorda, the stout and glamorously made-up proprietress, caught her eye. A flicker of knowing passed between them, then Gorda finished polishing a glass with a flourish of a white towel, and turned away.

Deirdre desperately wanted to wash the ash off her face and hands while they waited for Tom to finish his questioning.

But the thought of seeing the little girl's face on the missing poster in the bathroom was preventing her from moving out of the booth's comforting vinyl embrace.

Three frosty margaritas on the rocks with salted rims landed in front of them, followed by hot oval plates of rice, beans, and something covered with cheese. The two servers disappeared as quickly as they'd come.

Deirdre turned a thankful glance towards Gorda, who was pointedly not looking at her, then turned back to Vivian, who eyed her plate as if it was a black hole, then picked up her margarita.

"Well, I guess we do need to eat," Deirdre said. "Especially you Vivian." She tried a left-handed forkful of beans and rice to test her appetite. Her stomach grumbled again and she dug her fork into the main dish. Tender shredded chicken wrapped in a firm corn tortilla, smoky tomato sauce, gooey cheese, and a hint of cool sour cream. Chicken enchiladas. Perfect.

Vivian let out a quiet groan.

"You don't look so hot," Deirdre said with her mouth full.

"I'm fine. Just had a rough night," she said, sweeping aside her shoulder-length gray hair. "Excuse me." She unfolded her thin frame from the booth and headed across the restaurant for her round of questioning, rubbing her lower back.

Sally got into the booth, her blond ponytail bobbing behind her head while she scooted around to the middle seat. She pushed her glasses up her nose, looking at the plates of food with alarm. "I wish you hadn't ordered food without telling me. And, margaritas? I thought you didn't touch the hard stuff."

"I didn't order it," Deirdre tried to explain, but gave up. "Just try it, it's good." She took another bite of the enchiladas.

"I was supposed to be at work by ten." Sally looked at her watch and sighed loudly. "Almost noon! Maybe I can still make it in, and work til five." She took a sip of her margarita, and the tension emanating from her dampened ever so slightly. She put down the glass, and almost to herself said, "Well, I guess we *do* need a drink, after what we just saw."

"Do you think it's Samantha Austin?" Deirdre asked. She didn't know the missing girl, but after seeing her face on the news and the missing posters here at Gorda's for the last few weeks, she felt an odd kinship to her.

Sally said, "Obviously. We saw it. It was a little girl. Whether she died in the fire or was dead before that, that'll all come out in the medical examiner's report."

After pushing the food around her plate, Sally said, "Why are they taking so long?"

The other detective had gone somewhere, and Vivian and Tom were alone in the booth leaning towards each other, speaking in hushed tones.

"It's not like she'll have anything different to say. We were all there, we all found it at the same time."

Deirdre turned to Sally, reading trouble on her face. Sally was probably getting tired of this routine—after all, she'd discovered the body in the quarry last month. That was how she'd met Tom.

But there was tension between them today. Tom had left the Halloween party early last night, too. Sally pushed the beans around her plate.

Deirdre had eaten half of her food already, but suddenly, she wanted no more of it, and pushed her plate away.

When Vivian came back to the table she just sat, stiffly, nursing her drink.

The other detective returned, and he and Tom stacked their notes together and stood to leave.

"Tom!" Sally called over her head, waving to him.

Tom's eyes locked onto Sally's and he approached the table.

He was tall and slender, dressed in jeans and a long-sleeved plaid shirt, with the slow deliberation and nondescript good looks of an old time cowboy. Deirdre was immune to those particular charms, being happily married to Walt, but his straightforward manner had made her trust him from the first moment she'd met him.

Deirdre scooted around the booth to make room for the two sheriffs, but Tom remained standing.

The other detective, Scott Kobayashi, was a handsome and buff young man of Japanese descent with a military haircut and a silk suit. He said, "Thanks for waiting around. We have your contact info so if anything comes up, we know how to get in touch." To Tom he said, "See you back up there Goodwin." He jerked his chin towards the trail across the street, and headed for the exit.

Tom lifted a hand to him, then looked back at them. "I'm so sorry you all had to see this." His face had softened into something apologetic, but he was strangely formal, and Deirdre detected annoyance from Sally.

Deirdre spoke up. "It's okay. I mean it's not okay—but—I'm more sorry for the parents of whoever it is." She lowered her voice. "I didn't want to ask you while you were questioning me...but...it's that little girl isn't it? The one on these posters?"

She gestured to the glass entry door, where "MISSING" in big red letters shone through in reverse. Samantha Austin, the freckled pre-teen with braces and the friendly face, smiled happily from the poster.

"Too early to say." Tom shifted his weight and straightened his back, stretching out the wrinkled folds in his shirt. "Right now, there's no way to know who it is, not even age or sex. So let's not jump to conclusions."

Sally cleared her throat. "Well, we were all there, so we know it's a her. Hey, wanna share this lunch that I didn't order?" She smiled at Tom.

Tom frowned. "I'll have to take a raincheck. I'm on my way back up to the scene." He started to leave but then turned back. "Oh, one more thing. You'll have to take a different route back home. We've got techs up there doing their work. We've closed the trail. I hope you know another way home." He put his hat on and tipped it to them.

Sally's eyes followed his Wrangled backside as he walked out the door. She threw down her fork. "Well, we've got a long ride home. I'm ready whenever you two are."

* * *

DEIRDRE WAS RUNNING SO LATE she rode Scarlet straight home—or as straight as possible, on their roundabout detour of trails. She didn't have time to stop at Mrs. Fey's and pony Ginny home as she had planned.

This morning, when she'd gotten Scarlet out of the pasture, she hadn't seen either of them—the old mare, or the old lady. A brief vision of Kathleen Fey played before her, her pewter hair set free down her back, her snowman-shaped body bouncing as she galloped bareback on Ginny.

Funny. Mrs. Fey could probably barely reach a horse to put a halter on, much less ride one anymore.

Deirdre's Bronco was still at Mrs. Fey's too, so after she put Scarlet away, she got into the big burgundy F-150 and headed to Clara's school.

It was the kids' first day back. Clara stood waiting on the curb with the rest of her third grade class, who were wild with energy after a week of school being cancelled during the fires.

She hugged Clara tight, buried her face in her tangled, dusty blond hair, and choked back tears.

"What's wrong Mommy?" Clara asked.

"Nothing sweetie, just glad to see you." She wouldn't tell Clara anything about this. Well, it would probably come out, sooner or later. Clara was a newshound, enthusiastically reciting some of the most awful stories, possibly a bit 'on the spectrum,' as last year's teacher had described her (whatever the hell that meant). How could she broach it? She'd wait til later. Her brain wasn't functioning right now.

Next was Justin. By the time she got to Stanton Academy, where he attended seventh grade on a scholarship, she was a little more in control of her emotions.

Justin approached the car with Brian Bartley Jr. In their shorts and polo shirts, the two looked like they were cut from the same mold, just with different coloring—Justin with brown hair and eyes, and Brian with sandy hair and freckles.

"Mom, can we give Brian a ride home?" Justin asked in his usual chipper tone. "He says we can swim in his pool too."

Clara started screaming with happiness at this idea.

Deirdre was glad she'd had the drive time to collect herself, because Brian Bartley Jr. had lived through *way* more trauma in the past week than she had, and she needed to be supportive.

"Sure, hop in," she said.

She wanted to touch base with Stephanie, Brian's step-mom, anyway. She was still uneasy around Stephanie. The rift between them, even though it was manufactured, felt real. When you call someone a psycho, it sticks.

On the drive to the Bartley estate, Brian said, "Cool truck Mrs. Boyd."

She couldn't help but smile. To him, the old beat-up pickup was a novelty. He seemed just as sunny as ever.

"Thanks Brian. How are you doing? Okay?" She steered through the winding streets of Rancho Alto, the richest, most genteel neighborhood in the county, maybe in all of Southern California.

Brian said, "Yep," and explained that he thought it would be easier for him to go back to school sooner than later, to field the questions and the sympathy before it took on a life of its own. "Besides," he said, "everyone's got plenty of their own fire stories without focusing on me." Smart kid.

At the Bartley house, a massive yet tastefully old-school Mediterranean villa, she greeted the lady of the house.

Justin borrowed a pair of Brian's swim trunks, and Stephanie asked him to find one of his sister's old swimsuits for Clara.

Once the kids were out back in the pool, they talked. She told Stephanie the whole awful story of their ride this morning, and the discovery.

"Oh my god, I'm so sorry. Do they have any idea who the body is?" Stephanie cocked her head to the side, her hazel eyes shining with sympathy, her glossy, expensively-highlighted hair falling in a smooth sheet across her shoulders. Not even thirty, she had the composure and wisdom of someone much older.

Deirdre shook her head. "No. But it's probably the missing girl, Samantha Austin." She dragged her hands down her face, shook her full body, and asked, "How is Brian doing, really? He seems just like his normal self."

Steph got up, leaving her walker behind, and hobbled on her titanium femur to the French doors. She looked out at her stepson. "He puts on a brave face, but I'm afraid of what's going on inside. I mean, how can he be coping so well? His mom was murdered, his dad is MIA. His siblings...who knows what happened to them?"

Stephanie sighed. "I keep thinking about Crystal. I barely knew Jeremy, but Crystal lived with us, here, for the first couple of years." She looked at the inside of the living room, as if remembering the past. "That's whose swimsuit Clara is wearing." Then she looked at Deirdre again, her eyes wide. "Oh my God. Do you think—that body you found, could it be her?"

Deirdre stood and went to her. She put a hand on Steph's shoulder. "It's not Crystal." She said it so firmly, she surprised herself, and Stephanie accepted it and seemed to relax. She didn't know that Stephanie and Crystal had actually lived together as a family once.

Now, there was an Amber Alert out for Crystal, assumed to be with her eighteen year old brother Jeremy, who was a murder suspect. But, there was no real way to know if they'd even gotten out of the fire.

Deirdre felt herself shrinking at the memory of the waifish, fierce girl on the rooftop, surrounded by smoke, protecting her brother. She realized just now, it was almost an inverted mirror image of what Jeremy's mom had described seeing years earlier—Jeremy, as a snarling, feral eight year old, protecting his little sister from their raging father, in this very house.

"I know Crystal hates my guts. But I'm her step-mom," Stephanie was saying. "If they find her, she'll always have a home here." She looked down and shook her head. "I know her though. She's like a wild horse. The harder you hang on, the more she fights." She turned to look back out the window. The boys were yelling and splashing, and Clara was giggling hysterically in the warm November haze. "Imagine that. Your entire blood family, ripped away from you in the span of one day." She paused. "Well...technically his mother had already been dead for a few days but—don't tell Brian that, please. He doesn't need to know that gory detail."

Deirdre said, "You're his family too Steph. Don't forget that."

Stephanie's mouth slanted to the side.

Deirdre continued, "And, you're a whole lot better than the family he got from birth. Don't undersell yourself." She looked out the window just as Brian cannonballed into the pool. A vision of him from underwater, getting dropped in the pool at Paraiso played before her. Who had rescued him from the burning balcony and dropped him into the water?

Stephanie saw her watching him. She smiled and said, "Brian keeps talking about how Mrs. Boyd saved his life. He thinks you're a hero."

"Oh, no...he's sadly mistaken." Deirdre laughed, but inside she was hoping Brian *wouldn't* remember now. She didn't want to break his heart by telling him she left him there...no better than what his dad did to him. Speaking of which, she asked, "Any word on your husband?" He was the one who'd caused all this trouble.

"Footage of him crossing the border at San Ysidro, that same night. That's all they'll tell me. I think they only told me that so I would feel safer, because he's not even in the country anymore."

So, Brian Bartley Sr. had fled to Mexico.

Deirdre groaned. That made her think of Día de los Muertos all over again. "I keep thinking about the Day of the Dead stuff at Gorda's, and the missing poster, and how the waiter kid told me November first is for the children. And then, we find a dead kid." She felt her face squinch up. "Those poor parents."

Stephanie said, "My mom's at the mission right now, setting up our ofrenda." She turned and looked at Deirdre. "That church is beautiful. I can keep the kids for a while, if you want to go there, maybe say a prayer with her?"

* * *

THE CHURCH WAS DARK COMPARED to the sunblasted walls of the mission's courtyard.

Deirdre stepped further inside, and the echoing voices from the festival in the courtyard were muffled by the thick walls. A cool silence descended.

It had been so long since she had been to church, real church. The twisted and tortured Jesus. The faded ornate paint on the flaking plaster. The dark wood arches that formed the central dome above her, all twisted and tilted and spun around her. She wondered if she'd burst into flames.

Carefully, she walked down the center aisle, as her eyes adjusted to the dim.

Ahead, countless candles illuminated the altar. The air was so still that the flames stood straight and tall, never wavering.

Teresa, Stephanie's mother, was praying near the front. Her thick dark hair flowed down her back, her shapely figure in a feminine lavender suit with a little flounce around the waist.

Deirdre hesitated, but then got down on the padded kneeler beside Teresa, folding her hands, but not bowing her head.

When Teresa looked up at Jesus on the cross, there were tears in her eyes, but as she noticed Deirdre next to her, a broad smile changed her face.

She silently grabbed Deirdre's hand and squeezed. Then she planted a kiss on the photo she was holding, and showed it to her.

It was a simple black and white portrait of Stephanie's father, Teresa's husband. There was no mistaking who he was. He had Stephanie's perfect oval face. Or rather, she had his.

"He's only been gone three years," Teresa whispered, brushing away a tear. She hooked her thumb towards the side door. "Let's go outside."

They pushed through the big wooden doors, out into a small courtyard with a huge tree. Thank goodness, it was shady and not blazing hot out here. They sat on a wooden bench built around the tree trunk.

Three little girls with painted skull faces ran by squealing. She wasn't sure if coming here had been such a bright idea after all. Could she handle all this death imagery so soon after seeing an actual dead person?

"It's good to see you here," said Teresa, patting Deirdre's knee. "What brings you?"

"Stephanie said you'd be here. I hope I'm not intruding, I just—well, I had a hell of a day, and my mom has been gone for a while, so sometimes I glom onto older women." She was surprised that had popped out. She'd never even thought about it before.

Teresa arched a brow.

"Well, not that much older, but..."

Teresa laughed, thank God.

Deirdre went on to tell her about finding the girl, how she didn't even recognize what it was at first, and then how the horror had rushed over her like a tidal wave when she realized it was a human body.

Teresa's jaw dropped open as she listened.

Deirdre finished her story, and suppressed a squeaky sob.

Teresa pulled Deirdre's head to her chest, and rocked back and forth making soothing sounds.

Deirdre laughed while she cried some more. "Thanks, you're really good at this. I could take parenting lessons from you." She sniffled and sat up.

"I've seen you with Justin, and you don't need no lessons girl."

Deirdre laughed. "Thanks."

Out of the church door came two women, both old, the younger one helping the very old one with a hand on the elbow. As they reached the sunshine, both put their hands above their eyes to shield them in identical gestures.

"Hey, do you have a picture of your mom?" Teresa asked.

"Yeah, sure. Here in my wallet. Why?" Deirdre dug behind the pictures of her kids, her brothers and sister, nieces and nephews, Walt, and Walt's parents, and pulled out a folded photo.

Teresa widened her eyes disapprovingly, took the photo and tried to smooth it on her skirt, then stood up and headed back to the church. "Come on, let's go to the big courtyard out front. We'll put her on our ofrenda."

"Oh—no, Teresa, no. I think you've misunderstood—or more like I've misled you..."

"What is it? You don't want her on our altar, that's okay—"

"—My mom is gone, but she's not dead."

"Oh," Teresa sat back down next to her. "Prison?" she whispered conspiratorially.

"No, no, not that."

Teresa grabbed both of her hands. "Look, you don't have to tell me mija, but—"

Deirdre interrupted before she could chicken out. "She's in an institution."

"Oh. Okay, let's go inside and pray for her."

Deirdre stared. Teresa hadn't skipped a beat when she'd told her.

She took Teresa's waiting hand and let herself be pulled inside.

* * *

VIVIAN NURSED HER THIRD MARGARITA, leaning against the wall at the end of the empty bar, observing the few patrons lingering over a late lunch on the restaurant side of the cantina.

She had listened as Gorda phoned the parents of the missing girl, to tell them a body had been found on the trail west of her bar. Probably better coming from her, with her amazingly smooth voice. Although Detective Tom Goody-Two-Shoes wouldn't see it that way. After all, the body wasn't identified yet. But the sheriff couldn't control everything. People still had freedom of speech. And who else would it be? It was definitely a young girl. That much was obvious, if you'd been there, seen it.

Vivian relived the moment. She'd watched the full range of emotions play over Deirdre's face: confusion, shock, fear. Disgust, sorrow.

Still in the ash of the disaster, with it covering their faces, their noses, their ears, she watched, and time stopped, sounds silenced. Sally sprung into action, throwing a leg over Giselle's back, sliding to the ground. Running towards Deirdre, a comedy in mime as they mouthed at each other, turning to look at the ground, moving their mouths, pointing, shrieking. All of it in slow motion.

Vivian had reached down to touch Apache's neck then, as if she was grounding herself, protecting herself. Finally she dismounted, and walked closer.

She already knew.

Those days of waiting during the fires, she'd done nothing but watch the news. It had to be the missing girl, Samantha Austin.

She set down her glass and turned to look out the window, trying to replace the horrific scene in her mind with the view of the lake. At least she'd forgotten about Bill and Ted. Discovering a dead body was a real mental palate cleanser.

On the television above the bar, the four o'clock news played. The volume was down low, but she could still hear. Something about Prius owners suing the makers of their GPSs for steering them to Seeker's Sanctum during the fire.

An overly dramatic reporter's voiceover said, "Some quirk of wind or topography created a lee of the fire, that surrounded Fairy Glen on the map like the eye of a storm. And by some miracle"—there was that fucking word again—"Seeker's Sanctum, in the center of the eye, was untouched by fire. The religious retreat received and sheltered 428 lost residents of San Amaro Hills, who followed their GPS directions down Sanctum Road..."

Oh, Vivian could just see it. A chorus of synthesized female voices with English accents. Whooshing white Priuses sliding silently down the road, deeper and deeper into the countryside so feared by the teenagers of the surrounding towns. Distracted by little baby Jordan's upchuck, and Kaila in the backseat crying because the DVD player has the same movie on that she HATES, the Prius pilots wouldn't notice that this is a road that maybe *should* scare you; maybe the teenagers had it right. It looks like a set from a movie where any second a hillbilly could step into the road brandishing his pitchfork, blocking your way.

Except, instead of a fictional hillbilly, what blocked their way after a four mile glide, was a gate at the dead end. A segment of the road had been converted, several years ago, into a nature trail, and it was closed to traffic. Except, the GPSs didn't know that.

Vivian looked at the television. The reporter was on-site now, at the gates just outside Seeker's Sanctum. "The spiritual heads of the retreat welcomed the panicked suburbanites with open arms..."

And open palms, no doubt, Vivian added to herself.

"Seeker's Sanctum had plenty of parking and a large auditorium, along with many dormitories. The fire never got to their part of the valley, and they never received an evacuation order."

Really. Vivian highly doubted that. More likely they had ignored it. They'd always acted like they were outside the law.

By the time the news story was over, the Austin family began to arrive at the restaurant.

First the father, getting out of a nameless pale blue Chrysler that he'd parked across the street in the dirt lot near the lake.

He was extremely large, obese, and the car righted itself like a boat as he released it from his weight. He looked like he didn't know what to do with himself, his face stuck between bravery and complete disaster.

Next, the mother, a squat woman in a plain, long dress, surrounded by a minivan full of similarly dressed female relatives.

Vivian turned away. She didn't want them to figure out she was one of the people who had discovered their daughter. No, she was just an anonymous bar patron.

She shook her glass, rattling the ice. "One more," she said to Gorda.

Gorda raised an eyebrow, shook her head, and took the glass from her.

Instead of refilling it, she dunked it in the tiny sink full of steaming water behind the bar.

Vivian opened her mouth to protest, then closed it again.

"Your horse wants you," Gorda said.

In the parking lot, Apache was pacing on his lead rope and calling out. The other two horses had left, and he was mad. She'd told Sally and Deirdre to go on home without her. She didn't want Apache to become herd-bound. They had protested, but she convinced them she was feeling okay by digging into her lunch.

That was two hours ago. She was still full, and still drunk. She didn't want to get on *quite* yet.

"He's kind of being a nuisance," Gorda said. Her button eyes were unreadable.

That was no way to talk to a paying customer.

"You're right, I was leaving anyway," she said, louder than she'd meant to. She stood up. Then froze. To her horror, she remembered she didn't have any money on her. After all, she hadn't brought her purse along to her interrogation with Bill and Ted. So, she was *not* a paying customer.

"I'll come back tonight to pay," she said, more quietly.

Gorda shook her head. "It's on the house."

Vivian didn't say thank you. It was no gift. She hated feeling indebted to people.

She walked to the door, pausing and stepping back to make room for the family that was coming through. More cars had shown up, more people. Balloons, flowers.

Vivian wondered who would show up if she died.

When she finally got through the door Apache nickered to her, and she ran to him.

* * *

THE SUN WAS SETTING WHEN Deirdre finally said goodbye to Teresa and followed her out of the parking lot, where Teresa turned left onto the country highway, back home towards her ranch. Deirdre watched as her little car drove away, beyond the mission and the reservation, deeper into the fertile valley with the steep hillsides sprouting avocado trees.

Stephanie had been right to send her here. She already felt more at peace. Still sad for the little girl, but not as torn up inside.

As she turned right onto the highway to get to the interstate, where she'd join the rush hour traffic, pick up the kids from Stephanie's, and somehow try to get dinner on the table before the whole family got cranky, the gas light came on.

Cursing, she pulled into the casino's well-lit and well-priced gas station. The old pickup definitely sucked up the gas. After tomorrow's dressage lesson, she'd ask Bonnie to help her go pick up the Bronco, and Ginny at the same time.

As the tank filled, she went inside the mini-mart for a coffee to get her home. She was exhausted.

Back outside in the parking lot, a woman was handing out flyers. With a jolt, Deirdre recognized her old friend Cassandra.

Cass shoved a flyer in her hand, not even looking at her. Deirdre glanced at it. Missing. A girl.

A girl just like the one they'd found burned today.

"My daughter is missing. She may have been here yesterday," Cassandra, her long brown hair in a ponytail, bossy and nurse-like, wearing light blue scrubs and clogs, continued handing flyers to every person that walked in or out of the minimart. "Call the number, there's a reward." Cassie said this directly to Deirdre. Then she recognized her.

After a brief moment of confusion, they hugged, and Deirdre said, "Let's sit down for a second. Have a sip of my coffee." Cass looked exhausted, pale and drawn.

They sat on a concrete bench, and caught up. Deirdre hadn't seen her for —what had it been, eight years? More?

Cassandra had fostered Angela as a four-year-old, after she'd been LifeFlighted into the ER one night. She'd officially adopted her a few years later—a closed adoption to protect her from whatever trauma had befallen her. That much Deirdre knew, because Angela hadn't spoken a word for the first few years Cass had her. And as part of exploring ways to help her open up, Deirdre had offered rides on Ginny—informal horse therapy.

Deirdre thought of the sweet, shy little girl, and how her eyes would light up at the sight of Ginny. "I'm sorry I lost touch with you guys."

Cass waved away her apology and continued her story.

Angela had just turned fifteen, started her sophomore year at high school, and Cass hadn't seen her since the morning of Halloween. "Which was only yesterday, I know. But she's not like that."

Deirdre instantly understood. As moody and rebellious as Rebecca was, she knew her well enough to realize that she wouldn't have purposely disappeared last week, right before the fire evacuation.

Cass worked twelve hour shifts at the hospital and had gone to work before Angela left for school that day, but she'd peeked in and saw her, safe and sound, sleeping in her bed at 5am. Then, Halloween night, the ER overflowing with patients, they'd asked Cass to work another eight hours. When she got home at 3am, Angela wasn't there.

Deirdre got a sick feeling in the pit of her stomach. The dead girl today— could it be Angela?

No, no. That girl must've died in the fire, which was over a week ago. But could they be related?

Cass was still talking. "The cops say because she's a teenager, and because it's Halloween, and because they have their hands full with investigations after these fires...they keep telling me not to worry, that she'll show up. But I can't just sit and wait. I know something's wrong."

After spending many hours at the police station reporting Angela missing, she'd gone to the school bus stop this afternoon and asked the kids. They'd seen her get off the bus at the transit station downtown, and transfer to one going 'way north,' like to the casino or something.

"Why would she come to the casino?" Deirdre asked.

"No idea," Cassie said. "I have to keep going, I have to hand out more flyers." She stood up, but then one of her knees buckled and Deirdre caught her before she landed too hard on the cement bench.

"I'm sure she'll be home soon. Do you still live over on the eastern shore of the lake?"

Cass nodded, then sighed shakily. "What do I do next? This was my last hope. The casino says they don't let minors inside. Why would she have come here?"

"Talk to her friends," Deirdre advised, grabbing a few extra flyers from her. She looked at the photo on the flyer again. Angela had matured, but still retained the timid aura that she remembered from her kindergarten days, even in the photo. Something tentative in her eyes. "Who are her friends?"

"Lexi. Lexi is her best friend...her only friend. I've been trying to call her. She's not answering. And their phone is disconnected."

Deirdre thought for a second. "Boyfriend?"

"Angela didn't have one, not that I know of at least. And I kept tabs on her, more than she knows." She tapped her lip. "Well, thanks for the coffee. It was good to see you." Cassie stood up, "Hey, there's the casino bus...I gotta run, I wanna ask the driver if he saw her."

Deirdre almost called after her for her phone number, but she realized she had it, on the flyers in her hand.

She topped off the tank and drove south on the 15 as the sun slipped behind the hills to the west.

Traffic was heavy, and she needed to pick up the kids, but now there was one place she had to stop first. She called Walt and explained what was going on, and apologized.

"No problemo," he said. "I'll pick up the kids, and dinner too."

"You're an angel. A literal angel."

"You've had a tough day," he said.

"See you at home. I love you." She hung up.

Staring at the taillights in front of her, she pondered.

First Samantha Austin, then Crystal Bartley, and now Angela Hernandez. All from, or last seen in, the Lake Hemingway area.

Three missing girls.

And one dead one.

* * *

On Del Diablo Highway, Deirdre slowed and put on her blinker, infuriating the rush hour drivers riding her tail, their headlights making stars in her rearview mirror in the dusk. She pulled into the parking area for the trailhead.

Up there, somewhere in the darkening burnt landscape, was *the scene*. They hadn't called it a crime scene. Not yet at least.

She hoped the little girl wouldn't have to stay out there all night, that they'd taken her body away. Although, what was in store for her body was probably a long stay in a cold morgue while tests were done.

There were still a few official vehicles here, but Tom's brown cruiser was gone, so she merged back into the stream of headlights and continued down Del Diablo. Even from the highway, she could see bright lights at Gorda's, and made the left turn down to the lake.

Gorda's parking lot was crawling with reporters and news vans with their big round dishes on top, cameramen and cables and microphones.

Tom was surrounded by the local San Diego news reporters in their identical pastel suits, peppering him with questions:

"Was it someone that died in the wildfire?"

"Could it be Jeremy or Crystal Bartley?"

Oh God, not that idea again.

But no, she was sure it wasn't her. The body had been much smaller and dark haired, not tall and thin and dishwater blond like Crystal.

"Tom!" Deirdre tried to catch his attention. He held up a finger to her, and said to them, "We'll do a *short* press conference at seven. No sooner."

He moved away as the reporters kept asking questions, one of them yelling "Can't we get something for six o'clock?"

She had to trot to keep up with his long-legged stride as he headed to the restaurant. "Damn it, this wasn't supposed to turn into a circus. I just wanted to get some dinner. Who called the media?" He paused as she caught up. He looked tired, and very old in that moment. "And who the hell told them it was Samantha Austin?"

Deirdre thought it was a rhetorical question, but then realized he was looking for an answer. Looking right at her.

"It wasn't me," she said, putting her hands up and backing up a step.

"There's no room for assumptions in detective work," he said, looking into the distance. He ran a hand down his face.

But what about instinct, and action?

"Hey, Tom? I have a favor to ask," she said, already knowing her request was doomed from the look on his face. She gave it her best shot anyway. "I ran into an old friend today whose daughter has been missing since yesterday. Do you think you could help her out?"

She held out one of the flyers. He didn't take it.

"She says Encantadino Police aren't taking it very seriously. I mean, look at this flyer, she had to make it herself."

"How old?"

"She's fifteen."

"And missing since when? Yesterday?" He sighed, and took the flyer. "I don't usually work missing person's cases, and it's not my jurisdiction." He met her eyes, which were probably beseeching, and softened his face. "But I've got a few friends on the force in Encantadino. I'll look into it." He said it comfortingly, but she knew he was just placating her.

"Maybe you could mention it in your press conference? Or better yet, my friend could go on camera to get the word out, in case anyone's seen Angela."

Tom looked at the massing news media and said, "No, I want to keep this simple. Not muddy the waters. There's enough speculation as it is."

Frustration boiled under her skin, but as Deirdre assessed Tom's steadfast expression, she knew he wouldn't budge. He told her, "The best thing you can do is track down all of her friends. Usually missing teenagers show up in a few days."

Except for the one we found dead this morning, she thought, but didn't say it out loud.

"Fine. Whatever you can do would be appreciated."

Tom said, "I do have one request. Please don't talk to the media about what you found today. This is an active investigation."

She nodded.

"Thanks," he said, and climbed the flagstone steps to Gorda's front door with heavy feet.

Her feet felt pretty heavy too as she walked back to the big Ford pickup. Why was she stressing about this? Because she knew how important it was to act quickly. She'd made so many mistakes with Rebecca. Mistakes she now knew wouldn't have made a difference in finding her. But that was an exceptionally unusual case, being kidnapped by a cartel sicario. And she still regretted some of her decisions. If she'd gone back and looked for the apartment at Copperwood, she might've found Tanya's dead body. That would've at least gotten the cops' attention. Seemed like dead bodies were the only kind they cared about.

Across the way, she spotted a familiar figure among the crowding reporters. It was the fireman she'd seen the day she'd rescued Rebecca, the one that told her to go to Paraiso. The one that had been horribly injured, burnt badly on his chest. He'd made it, he'd survived! She was so thankful.

She walked across the street towards him, then broke into a run. "Hey, wait!"

"Wait!" a woman's voice echoed behind her. "Wait, are you...?"

Deirdre stopped, only because she'd lost sight of the fireman in the reeds by the shoreline.

She turned to find a reporter chasing her. This one was older, more serious looking than the rest, although that could've just been because she was a brunette in dark clothes, so, you know, stereotypes galore. She was running in her heels to catch up, and turned her ankle on the potholed asphalt, but righted herself with a spry leap. "You're Deirdre Boyd, right?" she asked, catching her breath.

"Yes..." Deirdre answered, unable to deny it, but wary of what this woman might want.

"You were involved in the fire rescue on top of the mountain last week."

Oh, that. Deirdre blew air out of her cheeks. "Yep. That was me."

"Would you be willing to do an interview with me?" the woman said, her dark eyes flashing. "I mean, not now, but...soon?" She reached into her pocket and handed Deirdre her card.

"Oh, no...I don't think so."

"What's your connection to this case anyway?" the woman asked.

Deirdre glanced at the card. Jackie Page, Channel 9. "You'll have to ask the sheriffs. I'm not supposed to say anything." *At liberty.* That was the phrase she was looking for. Well, at least she didn't sound like a bad TV cop, like usual.

A light dawned in the woman's eyes. "Did you find the body today?" she whispered. Apparently she was such a seasoned reporter she was practically psychic. And she was whispering because she smelled chum in the water and didn't want her fellow sharks to get it first. "Is it related to last week's events on the mountain?"

"No. No comment. Excuse me." Deirdre said, straining her eyes to see if she saw the fireman. He was gone.

But the reporter was still there, hovering.

"Hang on," Deirdre said, thinking of an idea. She pulled one of Cass's flyers out of her purse. "There's another missing girl. This one's only been missing since yesterday, so it can't be the girl we found today—" *Damn it!*

She'd given it away. Right after she'd promised Tom not to say anything.

The woman, trying to hide her vindicated expression, took the flyer, looked it up and down, and folded it into her jacket. "If you promise me an exclusive about what happened up at Paraiso, I won't tell the others that you found the body," she said, indicating the competing reporters behind her, who were waiting for Tom's press conference, which would give them nothing but the facts. Not the truth.

"You must need some time to...process," Jackie Page added, after Deirdre didn't answer. "What a shock it must've been, to find a body like that."

"What about Angela?" Deirdre pointed to the flyer. "She's the more urgent matter. She needs people to keep an eye out for her. She needs people to help find her."

"I'll try to put something on the eleven o'clock news. Deal?"

Deirdre nodded.

"Call me tomorrow, and we can set up a time for your exclusive." With the look of a well-fed cat on her face, Jackie Page sauntered away, back to the crowding reporters.

"Shit!" Deirdre said. Tom would be furious. But at least she'd gotten some action for Angela. The living are more important than the dead.

If she's still living, the morbid thought popped up again.

As she slid the reporter's business card into her wallet, Vivian's two-decade-old Mercedes coupe pulled in. Vivian, who'd cleaned up and put on a very stylish and pointy-looking pantsuit in a pale gray—went so well with the rest of her—gracefully exited the vehicle and tucked a taupe leather clutch under her arm.

"Vivian!" she called.

Vivian pulled her head back on her neck as she looked around.

Deirdre jogged over, grateful for the sight of a familiar face, even if it was an unfriendly one. "What're you doing back here?" she asked. "Hey, you look like a million bucks. Do you have a date or something?"

Vivian switched her purse to under the other arm and straightened her jacket. "No. I came back to pay for my meal."

"Oh!" Deirdre hadn't even thought of that. Should she have? "I guess I should pay for mine too."

"Allow me. You've got enough on your plate with tearing down your barn."

Yes. Deirdre didn't even want to think about that.

"Well, okay...thanks." She knew Vivian had wads of cash, so she didn't do the false generosity back-and-forth of *No, please, let me pay!* She was too tired.

They walked into Gorda's together. Tom had his head down, writing notes in his folio, next to a half-eaten dinner.

When he looked up to see who'd come in, his eyes narrowed. Deirdre panicked. Did he know she'd already accidentally spilled the beans?

Then she realized he wasn't looking at her, he was looking at Vivian with something like shock or surprise on his face. This must be the first time he'd seen Vivian dressed up.

For some reason, she'd come back to Gorda's looking like she could take over any board meeting; looking fierce and, well, really quite beautiful.

Deirdre looked at her with new eyes. It wasn't just the clothes. She'd seen corporate Vivian before, back when she was still working as VP of a pharmaceutical company. But corporate Vivian had been stressing so hard it sucked all the beauty out of her.

Vivian's eyes lingered on Tom for a moment. "I've been seeing entirely too much of him lately," she muttered, and veered towards the bar, and Gorda. "I'm here to pay our bill from today," she said, and took out her wallet.

"I told you, there's no bill," Gorda said in her low buttery voice.

"I really must insist." Vivian imperceptibly stamped her foot, her voice brittle.

Gorda turned away from Vivian's waving credit card, and started polishing glasses. "Besides, we don't take American Express."

Vivian turned around and walked out, pushing the exit door with enough force that she almost knocked over some customers on the way in. Tom followed her with his eyes, then caught Deirdre and Gorda staring at him, and looked back down at his notes.

Gorda looked at Deirdre. "What's with that one?" she asked, referring to Vivian. "I'm not going to charge a bunch of ladies that just found—" she looked around and dropped her voice to a whisper, "—that just found a *burned body*, for something to eat to bring up their blood sugar so they don't go into shock, or for something to drink to relax them so they're not freaking out about what they just saw. Can you explain that to her? I said on the house, and I meant it."

Deirdre replied, "She's just a thorny person. But good. Basically. I think. Anyway, I like her. We went through some shit together, up on that mountain. She comes through when you need her."

But maybe, just maybe, she'd steal a boyfriend or two along the way, without even trying to.

* * *

ALL SAINTS' DAY

They'd spent last night at a wild Halloween party in the middle of the desert, Angela and Travis, with lots of raunchy old ladies in tube tops, beers and fireworks. Dust and the smell of gasoline and the sound of engines revving and men with motorcycle mustaches hollering.

He'd convinced her to go with him. It actually didn't take much convincing.

When she'd seen his face in the graveyard, she knew he was the one. She looked at it again now. He was in the driver's seat. They were traveling down a desolate road with wispy bushes on either side.

On the right, a sandstone mesa turned dusty blue in the coming evening, and on the left ran a disused railroad track and a line of electric poles. The wire looped up and down as they zoomed past, like it was scanning the profile of his face. The face she recognized as a part of her.

"Starting to look familiar?" he asked with a sideways glance, catching her staring. He pulled a bunch of papers from under his seat and rustled through them, then put them in her lap. Printouts of Google satellite, newspaper clippings, and some finely typed pages of records.

"Well?" He gestured around, and she realized he was talking about the surroundings. She was confused by his question. *He* looked familiar. This place didn't.

"Where are we?" she asked.

Yesterday, as he'd driven her down the freeway, past her exit, she'd sent a quick text to Lexi: *Sorry, can't make it tonight.* But now, twenty-four hours later, she was really worried about what her mom was thinking. There was no cell reception out here, and her battery was close to dead. Her mom would be having a conniption fit.

"You don't remember this road?" he asked.

The setting sun was a splash on his dusty windshield. She looked closer at the side of the road, at the nameless desert landscape as it went by. "Why would I?" She leaned forward. Her back hurt from sleeping most of the day in his car, parked in the shade of someone's carport, in the little trailer park that looked even worse by the light of day.

He caught his breath, then released it in a whoosh. "I thought it would be good for us to come here, to get some...finality."

"Oh." She cast back, but her only memories were little snapshots, buried beneath her new life's HD video.

Was there really such a thing as knowing too much? She wished she could find out. There was a chasm inside her, yearning to be filled with knowing. Everything before the age of four.

He continued. "I didn't have nothing but time. Time to do research. See, I found out..." He ran a hand over his stubble. "Maybe I shouldn't tell you any of this."

"No. Tell me." She had a dying need to know, always, anything about her real mother.

"My partner was the one that killed your mom."

Angela had only just recently learned that her mother was a murder victim, and it still hit her like a wrecking ball, the words. Kill. Murder. "Edward James," she said. Once she'd found her mother's name, the news reports of the trial were only a mouse click behind.

Travis kept talking. "Why would he do that, I wondered? What did she do—or take? And why," he opened his palms to the sky, through the windshield, "out here?"

"Out here?" she echoed. She didn't know any of the details. She hadn't gotten that far in her search.

They pulled off, to the side of the road, onto some sand, where Travis almost got bogged down but gunned the engine and shot them out between some bushes and onto the edge of a wash, where the ground was firm with scattered stones. He parked the car.

"Camping here tonight," he said, and pulled a blanket from the trunk. He put it out on the edge of the sandy little cliff crumbling into the wash. He patted the blanket, and handed her a beer from the cooler.

She'd barely ever drank beer. Only once, one of Lexi's dad's from the fridge in their garage. She sat down and took it.

"I really need to get back," she said. He gave her a face. "Or at least somewhere my phone works so I can tell my mom I'm okay." She was barely fifteen. Not really independent, like Lexi, who went anywhere she wanted without ever telling her parents.

"Oh, didn't I tell you? I told her we were taking this trip." He popped his can open in a spray of foam.

"Really?" It didn't seem believable, but she believed everything that came out of his mouth nevertheless. It was like magic flowed from his lips. It set her mind at ease. She opened her beer.

"Yeah, me and her have been talking, since I got out. Talking about how to...do this."

"This?" She didn't know what 'this' was. Why hadn't her mom said anything to her? It was just like her, keeping secrets. Deciding what was best for her. Anger flared deep inside.

"So, are you glad I brought you here? I didn't even get a chance to grieve for her, you know. I just went to jail, and you two were gone forever. But at least now, one half of forever has ended. I'm with my baby girl again."

They sat, and he had a few more beers, and so did she. He got more talkative as the sun sank further, asking about school, her friends, what she liked to do. Then he told her what he'd been doing the last eleven years. Serving time.

"I didn't go to jail for what I brought home on Halloween. It was for something else, a job I did with a partner. But Halloween, I did that job alone, and it was all mine." He looked at the ground and shook his head. "Never shoulda opened that door Angela." He gave her a sharp look, and she felt ashamed, even though she didn't know what for.

He went on. "So I figure, Eddie knew about the job I was doing. He called me that night to make sure I was home, and tipped off the cops. But then what did he do? He followed you guys out here, and killed your mom. He's still doing time for that." He followed the line of the horizon with his green eyes.

"I don't know anything about this," she said. "I...they didn't tell me much." Her tongue felt heavy. "I had to research where she was buried on my own. That's the first time I found her grave. First time I knew her name even."

"I'm sorry sweetheart." He pulled her close under the sweaty armpit of his faded black t-shirt. "That's why I felt so strongly we had to come here, you understand?" He took a swig of beer, and looked her in the face. "Spittin' image of her, I tell you what."

The sun hit the line of the sandstone cliff in the near distance, stretched, squashed and sank into the earth. It was like the sinking sun had sucked all the orange from the sky, and the landscape turned a cool blue.

The coarse sand beneath her butt was starting to get cold. Her black lace sleeves were worse than nothing, amplifying the chilly dry wind. Most of the makeup was gone, but she still wore the black Victorian dress and boots of her witch costume. She sat up straight and wrapped her arms around herself.

He said, "You know, it makes me wonder what she had, and why she wouldn't give it up. Makes me wonder where the hell my stash is." He looked at her. "Means it's still out there. Somewhere. Possibly somewhere close by." He drew his brows together. "I know she was hiding it for all of us to share, once I got out."

"I need a jacket," Angela said, and stood up. She didn't know where she was—who she was, what she was. She didn't have a clue what her dad was talking about. But it made her scared.

"You cold?" He hopped up and jogged jangly-legged to the car a few steps away. "I've got something to warm you up." He opened the trunk and pulled out a shovel, and tossed it to her. "Start digging. You take the first shift." He popped open another beer from the cooler and pulled out a sleeping bag. "Since you're cold an' all."

"Where am I supposed to dig?"

He tapped his forefinger to his temple. "Only you would know."

"I was only three! Why would I know where it is?" She felt her voice get hysterical.

"You were four. And you were here that night. The night she was killed."

"I was?"

"In the car, it said. Or, in a car seat. Something. She must've hid it, and wouldn't tell him where, so he whacked her." She flinched. "Is it here? Did she bury it? I don't know. I just know it's worth a shot. It wasn't in her car, and it wasn't in the apartment. Eddie didn't have it when he was arrested."

"He might've stashed it somewhere else. Before he got arrested," she said.

"Oh, that's a very bright idea!" He tapped his temple, then said, "You must get that kind of thinking from your mother."

She gripped the shovel tight. His face was half visible in the twilight, hard to see his expression.

There were so many questions, she didn't know where to start, but one superseded them all. "How...how did she die?"

"He beat her to death. Now, you wanna get rich? Start digging kiddo."

She was too stunned to do anything but obey.

Later that night, after he'd asked her over and over if the place was starting to look familiar, if she remembered anything, telling her to dig, anywhere, after her hands started forming blisters and the beer was sloshing in her empty stomach, he said, "Think like your mother. Where would she put it?"

And she *had* remembered something then. She kept digging, putting her head down to hide her face with her hair as she pieced the images together.

She wakes up, cold, in her car seat. Stars outside the window.

Her mother driving, orange glow from the dashboard. Her mother reaches over and adjusts the blanket, tucking it around her.

Bumping down the road. Dust, painted red by the taillights, pluming behind them. Her mother is crying now.

The car comes to a stop.

"You know where it is, don't you now, Angie?" He could read her face. Damn.

She dropped the shovel and ran. She scrambled in the sand, up the wash, in and out of bushes, running blind, tears streaming, finally seeing the place where her mother had pulled her out of the car, climbed the rumpled cliff, and placed her high upon a large flat stone, then draped the blanket over her.

Little Angela had gone to sleep then, like a bird with a sheet over its cage.

She stopped and stood, dazed by her memories, until it was too late and Travis caught up to her.

Friday, November 2

DEIRDRE DROVE THE KIDS TO school Friday morning, all three squeezed into the bench seat of the pickup next to her.

"What happened Mommy?" Clara asked.

Justin turned to Clara. Deirdre gave him the evil eye, shook her head, and put a finger to her lips. But it was too late.

"She found a dead body," he said.

"A corpse?" Clara asked, and turned to look at Deirdre, with awe and wonder on her face.

Deirdre grumbled, "Thanks a lot, Justin."

Rebecca burst out laughing.

When the two younger kids had both been dropped off—Clara running into her schoolyard yelling "My mom found a dead person!"—Rebecca put her backpack on the seat next to her and stretched out, kicking one leg up on the dashboard.

Deirdre had to drive Rebecca to school now, since her bike had burned up on the mountain. After school she was getting rides with her best friend Darius to where they both worked at his father's restaurant.

"How are you Mom?" Rebecca asked. "Really. I mean, that must've sucked, finding that body."

She turned and looked at her daughter, sitting there in the passenger seat, her small body belying the inner toughness, which she tried to project with her teased black hair and eyeliner. She'd gotten a nose ring when she was living with her dad in Hermosa Beach last year, but Deirdre had forbidden her from wearing it, and thankfully, the hole was closing up again.

"I'm doing okay. Thanks for asking honey." But she had slept horrible last night. Or, more accurately, hadn't slept. The thought that the body might've been Angela after all haunted her all night.

But no, it had to be someone that died in the fire. Like Crystal.

"Actually...I slept like shit last night."

Rebecca widened her eyes. "Wanna talk about it?" she asked, and took a swig of coffee from her travel mug. The coffee was a battle Deirdre had long given up on.

"I keep thinking it could be Crystal," she blurted out. She'd been so certain when she reassured Stephanie, but now she wasn't so sure.

Rebecca choked on her coffee. "It's not Crystal," she coughed out, wiping her mouth.

"You're right." Rebecca was so logical. The body had been smaller than Crystal, and her hair was dark. It couldn't have been her.

Although who knows what fire does to a body, right? Or to hair.

As they got closer to the high school, Rebecca shifted in her seat. "Mom, what's the deal with Vivian?"

What isn't the deal with Vivian? she thought. She remembered waiting on the ridge with her, spying on the Paraiso housing development through the gathering smoke, planning their attack to free Rebecca and the other Bartley kids. And how Vivian had known exactly which cartel Hector was working for.

But Deirdre just said, "What do you mean, sweetie?"

"The other night, at the Halloween party, I saw her. She was in a big black SUV that pulled over at the fire station, and Tom Goodwin left the party and got in too, and they took off."

"No kidding?" So she *had* sensed something yesterday between them. Could they really be having an affair? She had been half joking with herself when she'd thought that.

Rebecca said, "I saw the license plate, and it looked like one of those federal ones."

A federal license plate? Well, if that was a date, it was a weird one.

"Oh wait!" Rebecca sat up straight and put her hand out. "Can you drop me off here? I don't wanna go all the way to the front, no, wait, stop. Ugh! Mom!"

It was too late, Deirdre had pulled up to their usual spot. A throng of high school students gathered around the truck.

"I feel like a circus freak," Rebecca said. She got out and slammed the door.

"Have a good day honey!" Deirdre called after her.

Rebecca better get used to being famous. They both better.

Deirdre had canceled her dressage lesson to help Cassandra find Angela.

Over at her house on the eastern shore of Lake Hemingway, across the lake from Gorda's, she sat with her old friend, trying to help her think of ways to track down her daughter. She would've given anything to have a friend to bounce things off of when Rebecca was missing. She'd been a complete wreck. But also there was a wildfire coming her way, and a lot of other shit going on. All of her friends had been equally freaked out.

But Cass already had a plan, was already in motion, and unlike Deirdre, it wasn't the motion of a chicken with its head cut off. She'd forgotten how dynamic Cassandra was.

Cass said, "First stop is Lexi's house. I still can't get a hold of her parents. I've been calling and calling. So we'll have to just go there."

"How well do you know Lexi's family?" she asked.

"Not that well. I'm always working." Cass said it firmly, but there was a kernel of guilt in the middle of it.

They drove a few minutes away into a flat suburb with square grid streets, low modest houses built in the fifties. The smell of smoke was rank. As they got closer, there were flattened burnt lots interspersed in a patchwork with the yellow, white and baby-blue bungalows.

Deirdre's heart hurt, and she put a hand on her chest, remembering the pain of seeing her family's home destroyed by the firestorm eight years ago. The one last month had thankfully spared Fairy Glen and the Boyd family's rented home.

However, she and Rebecca had been in its thundering, merciless path anyway.

But everything was fine now. *Everything was fine.*

"Deirdre?" Cass said. "I said turn left, back there. You missed it."

"Sorry," she said. Fat lot of help she was. Supposedly she was driving because Cass, the mother of a missing child, was too distraught. She had to keep it together.

Making a left at the next street, Deirdre doubled back. When they got to the address, Cass sucked in her breath. Deirdre pulled over at the house, awestruck.

Cass was out of the truck and knocking on the neighbors' doors, while Deirdre just stared at the house—what was left of it. The living room had a huge hole in the roof. The sofa was still in there, half charred, open to the elements. The rest of the house didn't exist anymore. This was Lexi's family's home? No wonder they weren't answering the phone.

Cass hopped back in the truck. "We have to go to the church down the street," she said.

They drove down there.

The church had a big parking lot. In it, there were motorhomes, trailers, and right out front, pop-up tents under which a few people were clearing folding tables of buffet supplies, cleaning up after breakfast.

"What do they look like? What kind of car do they drive?" Deirdre asked.

Cass didn't say anything. She got out of the truck almost before Deirdre had pulled to a stop, and approached the man lifting a steam table tray with the remains of scrambled eggs, and started talking to him.

This was the second Catholic church Deirdre had been to in as many days. Was she supposed to get some kind of message from that?

The door opened and Cass hopped back in. "They're around back," she said, guiding her around the church building, past a long row of porta-potties, and a trailer with showers.

"Wow," she said. There were even more cars, trucks, vans and RVs back here, even tents. A shanty town. Just last week, before Fairy Glen was cleared to return home to, they had lived in one at the racetrack. The difference was, this time around Deirdre had eventually found out she still had a home to go back to. These people must not.

"There," Cassie said, pointing to a burgundy minivan. It was in a parking spot close to the end, so there was a curb and a patch of grass next to it, a few trees separating them from the busy major thoroughfare on the other side. Over the side door of the minivan was a popup shade.

Deirdre parked, and she and Cass got out.

Cass approached a man and woman, about their age, both with dark brown hair, the man tall and broad-shouldered, but turning fat like an ex-football player, the woman shortish and stocky, but tough and strong looking.

"Can I help you?" the man asked.

Deirdre noticed a tent behind the minivan, a cheap Walmart dome tent, half unzipped. A boy's face looked out.

"Are you the Marconis?" Cassie asked, and before they could answer, she said, "Where's Lexi?"

The boy climbed out of the tent. He was maybe ten or eleven. Then another, smaller one, and another, even smaller. They all had curly brown hair and flawless skin. They looked so much alike it was like seeing Russian dolls un-nesting from each other.

"Excuse me, who are you?" The man stepped between Cass and the boys.

"I'm sorry—Cassie Hernandez. Angela's mother? I'm looking for her. Can I speak to Lexi? She might know where she is."

"We haven't seen Lexi since Halloween...the day they went back to school," the woman said. "But she told us she was staying with her friend Angela." Her voice rose into anxiety. "She told us she was staying with you!"

"Oh shit," Deirdre and Cass said, in stereo.

* * *

ALL SOULS' DAY

Little Angela had awoken to the sound of her mother screaming. She kicked the blanket off, and stood up on the sandstone.

Up a winding gully, a windswept wash of perfectly shaped sand currents and tiny bushes waving in the night wind, was her mother, running.

A man ran after her. He grabbed her by the hair. "Where is it, where's my cut?"

She said, "I don't know, he got arrested. Please, don't hurt me."

"Tell me where it is."

"I don't know. Please don't hurt me." He hit her, and blood flew out of her mouth.

"Where is it? Not at the apartment. As you know."

"I don't have it, please—" Then she screamed, struggled.

They fought. The man screamed too. He roared and threw her off of him, then hit her again. "Where did you hide it?"

Her mother didn't speak now. She was on the ground, not moving. The man kicked her. He came back down the wash, but didn't see Angela above. He started ripping the car apart, the seats, the lining, the trunk, the wheel wells. Angela was quiet like her mother had told her to be.

She'd stay quiet, and then this man would leave, and she and her mom would get back in the car and go to grandma's house.

She was good at playing games, at keeping secrets.

Angela woke up, groaning. In the back seat.

He was there, driving. "Don't even think about it," he growled. "You're lucky I didn't leave you out there, you ungrateful little—" He stopped talking to take a corner, and the tires squealed on the pavement. "You know what it's like to die in the desert? You wanna find out? I don't think so." Harsh sunlight spilled in, illuminating the dust on the dashboard, skimming off his shoulder, which pulsed under the black t-shirt as he shifted gears.

She sat up. "I need to go home," she said, faintly.

He ignored her. "Nice shiner you gave me too," he said. Gingerly, he touched his eye socket. "I figured you might be hungry, got low blood sugar rage or something. I'm giving you the benefit of the doubt."

She remembered elbowing him in the eye, a struggle. Then what? Had she been unconscious all night?

They pulled up and parked in a sunbleached lot, next to a low slung building spewing hamburger scented smoke. Her stomach clenched. She was hungry.

"Let's eat. No funny stuff."

Inside, it was dim and the jukebox played. There was a tubular television mounted in one corner of the ceiling. She had seen the antenna on the roof, a giant flying metal monster, with wires descending at angles holding it fast against the winds. Local San Diego news was on.

Her father guided her to a rectangular booth at the rear of the diner and pushed her into the seat facing the back wall. He sat across from her, facing the door. A waitress came. He refused the menus, said, "Two cheeseburgers two fries two cokes," and she went away again.

Angela had been gone for what, two days now? She needed to get home. On the TV, zoo animals played. Giraffes, lions, gorillas. She read the caption. "Exotic Animals Lost to Wildfire." The video switched to aerial footage of a burned hillside.

The waitress dropped off the cokes. Angela stabbed her straw to take off the paper, and the first gulp of the cold sweet bubbly drink made her dizzy. On the TV, she caught a glimpse of the headline "Burned Body Found Near Lake Hemingway," and a shot of the trailhead off Del Diablo that went up to the high reservoir. It was all burned too.

Her dad slouched across the table and looked straight into her eyes. "You know where it is don't you? That's why you tried to run, out there." Now he was scarily quiet instead of aggressive.

She shook her head. "No, I just wanted to see where—where it happened."

"You're lucky I went and rescued you, or you'd be dead in the desert, just like your mom. Why should I take you back home? You haven't done shit for me." He leaned back and took a swig of coke, no straw. He wiped his mouth with the back of his hand.

She looked away, looked up to keep the tears from spilling out of her eyes.

Holy shit. Taking up the full TV screen was her face. Her, Angela Hernandez, in her dorky student ID photo; long, stick-straight, pale brown hair and watery gray eyes. "Missing Encantadino Girl," the banner read.

Missing.

Travis lied. He hadn't talked to Cassandra at all.

She kept her face straight. He was too far back against the wall to get a view of the television. Wasn't anyone else in this dump watching TV? She was sitting right here and nobody had even recognized her.

The news switched to the next story, as the waitress came with the burgers. Angela tried to catch her eye, but the woman just looked in her direction and asked, "Need ketchup?" then left when she didn't answer.

"I have to pee," Angela said, and stood up, making for the hallway right behind her dad in the back wall.

"Okay, but I'm right here," he said. He grabbed her wrist as she walked by and whispered, "Remember what I do when you run from me." The hard lines around his mouth deepened.

In a flash it came back to her. She felt again the yank of her hair, the blow across the back of her head.

She tore her eyes from his and walked down the hallway, into the tiny Pepto-Bismol pink bathroom with the sticky door handle.

In the mirror was a girl who looked nothing like the photo on TV. Her hair was black, frizzed out, mascara smudged around her eyes. Pretty damn goth. Lexi would've been proud.

But no wonder nobody recognized her.

There was a window, up high on the wall. She hopped up on the toilet, opened it, and squeezed through, into the blinding midday desert.

* * *

WHEN CASS AND THE MARCONIS had gotten over their initial confusion and shock, Cass said, "We'll need some pictures of Lexi to make a poster."

Gina looked bereft. "I don't have any photos. Everything burned in the fire. We have nothing. Nothing left." Gina said this with such shame, her voice dropping heavily at the end.

Cass said, "Look, I have a three bedroom house. You're not staying in your car anymore. Follow us back there."

While they planned, Deirdre got back in the truck and called Tom.

"Tom. What if I have two missing girls now—I mean in addition to Samantha? And Crystal. Would that be enough for you to make a statement on television?" She filled him in.

Tom broke in. "It's not my jurisdiction. They're both missing from Encantadino. It's best to let these things run through the normal channels. Especially since they're teenagers, and friends. What makes you think they're not just off together somewhere?"

"Mother's instinct. Just like I knew my daughter was in trouble. Real trouble." She shouldn't have to explain this to Tom. Suddenly her wrist ached, and she clutched the cast and made a sound.

"Are you okay?" Tom asked.

"Yes," she said through gritted teeth. The pain was bone deep. It ached up and down her arm, her elbow, her shoulder. Cass was walking back towards the car. "I gotta go," she said, and hung up on Tom.

Luckily Cass had the high school yearbooks, so they were able to use Lexi's picture in it for the missing poster. Deirdre dropped Cass back home and went to the print shop to put the order in, then took the yearbook to Gorda's, where she was sure she'd find the news media.

When she got there though, there was nobody.

"Damn it!" she said under her breath. Then she remembered, and took the reporter's business card out of her wallet. After she made the call and left a message, she sat down next to Vivian to wait. The posters, even though they were a rush job, would take a couple of hours.

Gorda brought her a Diet Coke, and she sipped it while she waited, tapping her foot as the afternoon sun slipped lower.

When Jackie Page called her back, she got up and paced around while they talked. She told the reporter about the second missing girl. Or third, or fourth, really.

"Can you text me some photos?" Jackie asked.

"Yes, I guess I can—but the camera on my phone isn't that good. Wouldn't you rather come and get the story in person?"

Jackie put her on hold for a couple of minutes while she checked if she could snag a videographer.

Deirdre paced past the Día de los Muertos altar. She stopped and looked closer at one of the photos, but just then Jackie got back on the line and said, "I'll be there around five. Can you get me both mothers? If so, I can go live at six."

"Yes, yes I can," Deirdre said.

She hung up the phone, looked at the photo again. It was the firefighter she'd seen yesterday in the parking lot. She turned to ask Gorda about it, but she was busy with a few patrons who had come in. And now it was time to go pick up the posters.

* * *

ANGELA'S MOM PULLED THE CAR into the parking lot of their apartment building. It was dark outside. "Okay, now we're gonna run upstairs, and pack *your suitcase okay? We're going to Grandma's house."*

"Grandma!" Angela squealed.

"No, wait!" Her mother's splayed hand pressed Angela back against the seat, startling her. She followed the line of her mother's eyesight, up to the apartment door. A yawning black rectangle.

Finally, her mother spoke. "Forget that, we're just gonna go straight there, okay? We don't need to pack, do we?" She turned the ignition back on, backed out, and then drove with her neck craned forward, almost sticking over the steering wheel, onto the freeway, where Angela fell asleep to the engine sound and the lights and green signs overhead, cuddling with Simba.

Angela startled awake, sitting upright. Clutching Simba.

She looked at the stuffed animal. Was this the same one? How could it be?

She looked around. She was in the sleeping berth of a semi-truck. The miraculous semi-truck that had been parked out back of the diner, the engine running, the driver snoozing in his air-conditioning.

He had believed her when she pleaded for a ride, said she was running from an abusive dad. As if he saw it every day. Once they were on the road, he even handed her some brochures with numbers of hotlines, offered to call one up for her.

She said no, she just had to get home to her mom in Encantadino.

The drive was long, and he tuned in the local TV station on the radio somehow. Afraid the news of her would be on, she said, "Can we listen to music?" and he just laughed and changed the station for her.

He'd been heading east to drop off a shipment in Brawley, so once he did that, they headed west again. The drive took hours, but at least in this giant metal beast of a machine, she was safe from her father.

She crammed Simba into her backpack and pretended to sleep again.

* * *

DEIRDRE WALKED ACROSS THE STREET from Gorda's parking lot and stood looking through the reeds at the sparkling lake, the water lit up intense indigo, just like the twilight sky above it. At dark, Samantha's parents and family were going to hold a vigil, and then go lay flowers at the entrance to the trail across the highway.

Hopefully they had reflective equipment, the way people drove at rush hour.

She spun around. She had to keep a lookout for Cass and the Marconis.

Jackie Page was already there with her videographer, setting up for her shot.

Deirdre began walking back towards the parking lot, just as headlights turned off the highway and came down the road. That would be them, she'd bet.

But, it was just a random car, and the guy that got out went into Gorda's. It was Friday, and day two of Días de los Muertos, so Gorda's was starting to fill up with more than just the regulars.

That was good. The more people knew about this the better. Gorda would definitely be playing the news on the TV in the bar.

There was another set of headlights. That must be them. Deirdre started walking over.

Cass and Gina parked and got out, their faces pale and devoid of expression, eyes hollow and dark. Like the little girls with faces painted like skulls that she'd seen at the mission.

Gina's husband wasn't here. Probably home taking care of the boys.

She greeted them and took them over to Jackie Page, introduced them, then faded away to let them talk.

Deirdre had already paid her respects to Samantha's parents. They were strange people, some kind of Mennonites, or maybe Mormon fundamentalists. But they had appreciated her sentiments.

She looked at her watch. Six on the dot. She watched as Jackie listened through her earpiece to an invisible, far-away anchor, adjusting her jacket, her hair, and with one final finger sweep for lipstick on her teeth, looked right in the camera, squared her shoulders, and as the red light went on, said, "Post-fire devastation. A burned body. An epidemic of missing girls. We're live at Lake Hemingway with the latest."

And just like that, the red light went off, and she sagged like a marionette whose puppeteer had just hung it on the wall. Cass looked even sicker now, after the horrifying words she'd just heard.

Jackie looked at the two mothers and said, "We're first up, so get ready."

Deirdre took the opportunity to run over and squeeze Cassie's hand. "You're doing great." She stepped back as the cameraman waved her away. This was the lead story, so it was first up. Jackie's strings lifted her again, making her taller, more animated than real life. Her voice more erudite, words clipped and nasally, enunciating every word just so.

"After the gruesome discovery of a burned body on a trail west of here, and the parents of a local missing girl coming to a tragic and heartbreaking conclusion," she gestured behind her to the gathering vigil keepers, "we're now learning that there are at least two more missing girls."

Jackie indicated Gina. "One family, who lost their home to fire." Then she turned to Cass. "And this mother, who worked tirelessly, saving lives in the ER. Both are now devastated by the absence of their beloved daughters, who join a growing list of missing girls in the North County.

"Alexandra 'Lexi' Marconi is 5'3", 120 pounds, with brown eyes and dark brown curly hair. Her friend Angela Hernandez is 5'6", 125 pounds, with straight, light brown hair and gray eyes. The girls were last seen at Encantadino Valle High on Thursday."

Jackie took a few steps forward and the camera swiveled with her. "Where are Angela and Lexi? If you know anything, call the hotline you see on your screen right now. Anything you can tell law enforcement might mean the difference between life and death. Back to you Bob."

* * *

IT WAS DARK WHEN THE semi-truck got to the outskirts of Encantadino, where the driver stopped for gas.

Angela watched him go inside the truck stop to pay. Under the fluorescent lights, he was talking to the clerk. Talking for a long time, longer than it took to pay for gas, that was for sure.

The clerk picked up a telephone, glanced outside, and started dialing.

That was her cue to leave. She didn't want to get in trouble, involve the cops, or anything like that. She just wanted to get home.

She slid out from the bunk, found the latch on the door, and slipped the long way down to the asphalt, then went around behind the big semi-trailer.

On the far side of the truck stop's vast parking lot, a Jack in the Box shone its garish red lights into the night. She ran towards it.

A single car sat in the drive-thru, a white convertible.

Two girls were ordering food, giggling hysterically as they yelled over the radio into the squawking box, saying they couldn't understand.

She hesitated. She'd never asked a stranger for a ride, and doing it twice in one day was probably pushing her luck. But these were two girls. It had to be safe.

As she got closer, the one in the passenger seat poked the driver, who looked at Angela and said, "Whoa!" and jumped up straight in the seat. They both squealed, then started laughing hysterically again, falling on each other.

"You scared us!" the passenger said. "I thought you were a ghost!"

"The Gray Girl!" they both yelled to each other.

"Wait, are you okay?" the passenger said, suddenly looking serious.

"Can I have a ride?" Angela asked.

"What?"

She stepped closer, and they turned down the radio. "Can I have a ride? Please?"

The girl stepped out and put her seat forward. "Sure, hop in."

Angela climbed into the backseat, her pointy boots catching on her skirt. She rearranged herself, and said, "Thanks."

"Where you headed?" the driver asked her, meeting her eyes in the rearview mirror. "Halloween party?"

"Lakeshores."

"Cool. We can take you."

As they pulled up to the window to get their order, Angela looked behind her. She didn't see the truck driver coming after her. She hunched lower in her seat anyway. She turned back around, and caught sight of the television playing inside the empty dining room of the restaurant.

She almost got out and ran inside to look closer, but she didn't have to, she could see perfectly clearly from here.

Her and Lexi, side by side. On the left, her best friend, last year's photo, her curly hair wild, her golden freckled skin accented by pink lipstick and a bright smile. On the right, Angela. Same dorky photo she'd seen on TV this morning. "Two Missing Friends," said the headline.

Lexi was missing too? That was so random.

"Check it out," said the passenger. She elbowed the driver again. "Good thing we picked you up, huh?" she said to Angela. "There's some psycho out there taking girls."

Angela just nodded and tried to smile.

"Yeah, they found one of them already, that Samantha girl? All burned up. Satanic shit." The driver shoved a fry in her mouth while they waited for their second bag of food.

"And now her ghost is wandering around Fairy Glen!" the passenger said. "My friend saw her a few days ago, when he was driving to school."

"Nuh-uh. Spencer is such a liar...Gray Girl my ass."

Angela tuned the girls out. Was Lexi really missing? She'd stayed out all night before...and her parents only ever grounded her for it. They'd never put her on the news, or reported her missing.

Angela slumped in her seat again. She knew where Lexi had gone, nobody else did. She had to get home and straighten this all out. It had already gone on too long.

* * *

AFTER THE NEWS SHOOT, DEIRDRE told Cass and Gina to go home and get some rest, she'd man the table with the flyers for the rest of the night. She hugged them goodbye, and watched as they drove away.

A few other cars left the parking lot, but more showed up. And soon, Gorda's was full of the usual Friday night drinkers.

Inside, the altar was ablaze with candles, and the spirits of Gorda's ancestors. She felt pulled towards it. It looked so beautiful, like the one at the mission yesterday, with the flames dancing, the marigolds, the fruit and sugar skulls.

Deirdre thought of her own father, long dead, then her mother, not dead but perhaps living a fate worse than that, and long fingers of guilt stabbed at her heart.

Gorda's family photos were from many different eras. The older ones had a metallic sheen to the dark parts of the photo's surface, and deep cracks in the thick, aging paper. She'd seen them when they'd ridden over here before the fires.

But now she looked more closely at the several photos showing a tall and slender man from more recent times. A close up of him at twenty-something; dark, glossy hair cut short around the sides with a thick lock on top that swooped rakishly over his long face, softening the straight and heavy brows. Another photo of the same man with a slightly thinner and much younger Gorda, a baby in her arms, both of them looking on adoringly. Another photo of the man with two others, all dressed in yellow fire pants, red suspenders, and dark blue t-shirts, smiling huge smiles, arms clasped around each others' shoulders in manly camaraderie.

She recognized him now. That same fireman that told her that Rebecca was trapped at Paraiso, the one she'd seen across the street at the lake last night.

"Gorda, who is this?" She called across the noisy bar.

Gorda was busy serving and didn't hear her. She noticed the old man at the end of the bar, Sheffie. He saw her too, and got up and walked over to her.

"Fancy seeing you here!"

"So, you survived the fires okay then?" she asked.

He nodded. "Seen tons of 'em in my day."

"Where do you live, Mr.—uh..." She realized she only knew him by Sheffie.

"Sheffield. I live nearby. You look like you seen a ghost again," he said with concern. "Let me buy you a drink."

"Oh, I really shouldn't, I'm supposed to be at the information table for the missing girls."

"Well, suit yourself." He walked back to the end of the bar, and squeezed into his usual place.

Deirdre went to the other end of the bar. Gorda was still busy, so she decided to wait for her. She wanted to ask about the man in the photos. From her vantage point, she could still keep an eye on the front door and the table with the missing flyers and the sign that said, "Please help bring them home."

But the only people coming in now were headed straight to the bar and didn't even give it a second glance. "Oh well. One drink won't hurt," she told herself.

When Gorda finally had a break in the action, Deirdre called her over and ordered.

"Who's that fireman in the photo?" she asked, after she got her drink.

"That's Flaco," Gorda said. The young waiter swooped behind her to place some empty glasses in the bar sink, and suddenly it all came into focus. The boy's straight eyebrows and narrow brown face.

"That's Flaco?" she whispered. "And is that," she pointed to the waiter, "your son?"

Gorda nodded. "Little Javi."

"Flaco saved me—he saved us! He told me where to go to find Rebecca."

Gorda stopped for a second, looked down, then nodded and said, "That's what he does."

"Another Corrrrrrona, Pore Fave-or," a rowdy college boy said in an insulting parody of Spanish, and Gorda rolled her eyes before turning around to serve him.

Deirdre took a sip of her margarita. Her eyes wandered the bar, until they came to rest on Sheffie's whiskered face.

His eyes peered out at her from under all the hair like a sheepdog, with a sharp glint, like fool's gold.

She looked again at the photo of Flaco and his buddies. There was a copy of it framed behind the bar, right under the liquor license and business certificate for Gorda y Flaco's Restaurant and Cantina. Why had she never noticed it there?

There was a smell like a wet sheep, but not unpleasant, and she jumped as she realized Sheffie was sitting right next to her now. "This is the time of year that the veil between the spirit world and ours is the thinnest," he wheezed. He took a sip of his whiskey. "All cultures believe that. Yours does too."

"Mine?"

"You're Irish right? There's really no hiding it. I can tell an Irish girl when I see one, boy howdy." He sipped again. "Like Maureen O'Hara, just look at you!"

Oh boy, Sheffie was flirting with her again. She wished Lina was here—she had actually seemed to enjoy it.

"So Sheffie, tell me again about this Kathleen you were in love with."

"She was beautiful."

"Yes, I know, but what else was she?"

"She was amazing, poetry in motion, could ride a horse like nobody's business, put all the men to shame, but then, like I said—"

"Yes, her mother..." She'd heard all this before.

"Her mother was a witch. Got 'em all burned. All burned." He was near tears now. How could she ever get anywhere with this guy? She held a finger up to Gorda for another margarita.

"You sure?" Gorda asked her.

"Well...make it a virgin one."

Gorda nodded.

Meanwhile Sheffie was sniffling into his glass. She looked away, to the muted ten o'clock news, where there was an aerial shot of the safari park, its boundary breached by a black section of burnt hillside.

From her periphery she saw a man enter the restaurant and glance at the information table. She should be there, he actually looked interested. But he took a few flyers and ducked out again. Damn. Dereliction of duty.

With her fresh margarita, she headed back to the information table. Maybe if she was holding a drink people would talk to her, get interested in the search for the girls.

Outside, Samantha's family was still holding their candlelight vigil. Maybe the man who'd come in was part of that.

As she was threading through the customers in the busy bar, she spotted the fireman again, outside, looking through the glass door. She rushed over, but by the time she got there he was gone.

She looked back at Gorda, whose face had drained. The beer she was filling overflowed, and she snapped back to attention, wiped her hands on a bar towel, and placed the beer on the counter with a shaky hand.

Deirdre went back over to her. "I saw him here yesterday, too," she said. "Flaco. Out in the parking lot, near the reporters."

Gorda sighed, and tears came into her eyes. "He's never been a quitter. I just wish he could move on."

"How long have you two been split up?"

"Hey, turn up the TV por favor!" The same obnoxious college guy yelled from the end of the bar. "I need the sports scores."

Deirdre looked at her watch, and shot a look at Gorda that they'd continue their conversation some other time. It was getting late, and she needed to get home. She said goodbye to Sheffie and left.

Outside, Samantha's family was still singing. She wondered if they would stay there all night.

* * *

THE STONER GIRLS DROPPED ANGELA off on Lexi's street.

As she walked on, her feet got heavier. Her mom would be so mad. She'd gone on this quest to find out who she was, but she wasn't any wiser now, just in a whole lot of trouble, trouble that her mom had warned her about. She was a complete fool, a nobody, the bastard child of a complete bastard. The product of a criminal and a victim.

As much as she wanted to see her mom, be in her own bed, she also couldn't face her.

Lots of these houses were burned, this whole side of the subdivision. Even on her own street, houses had burned. Hers had been spared. She got to Lexi's house and stared at the gaping hole in the living room, the blackened sofa.

She reached for her phone, but realized it was gone.

Well, once she was home, she could call her in the morning, commiserate about their punishments. They'd never live it down at school, "Two Missing Friends."

Did Lexi go home with one of those boys, one of the rich boys she'd talked about? Had they gone off on a long trip somewhere? Were they still filming at the asylum?

Lexi was tired of being poor. She was always saying she was going to 'shoot out of here like a rocket' when she turned eighteen, maybe up to LA, Hollywood. She was the most determined person Angela knew, and that was saying a lot, because Angela's mom was not a person to mess with either. Adoptive mom, she'd have to say now.

She thought of her mom again. She would freak out about Angela dyeing her hair, and be *soooo* mad that she had taken off without letting her know. How could she explain what she'd done? Her father's appearance had changed everything. She'd found her birth mother and her father in one day.

She started walking, faster, towards the street that led to her house. But just then a car turned in at the end of the street and sped towards her.

It was him. He pulled up right in front of her and rolled down the window.

"Angela. I found you again. Imagine that."

She froze, then started running towards the turn in the road to her house, wanting nothing more than to be home again, but he cut her off, screeching his tires as he blocked the road.

She backed away, turned and ran, as fast and as far as she could. To the end of the road, past where Lexi used to wait for her, balancing on the white wooden blockade with the red reflectors, doing handstands on it. Past where she'd probably waited for Angela on Halloween night, tapping her foot and finally leaving without her.

His headlights lit up the reflectors, and she dove under the blockade, scrambled up and began running by heart, not sight.

She stumbled down the rocky path in the darkness, blinded by a watery curtain of tears, deafened by her panicked breath. The trail descended sharply and she lost her balance and fell on her side, scraping her palm. Scrambling to her feet, she stepped on her skirt and fell again, on her knees.

Almost went headlong over the edge there Ang. Keep it together.

She lifted her head and saw the dam in the distance, lit by faint streetlights on the opposite shore. Water, tons and tons of water, just pressing; pushing against a massive amount of gently curved cement.

Lexi had described the secret way through. They'd meet at the end of the dirt lane, where the houses started to peter out. "We'll go through the dam and meet the guys, who'll be parked on the other side, then drive up to the gate at Paraiso, and hike from there down to the asylum."

Angela looked behind her, got up again, and ran. She at least knew this part, she'd been playing here since she was a kid.

The homes she passed down here were older, next to the eastern shore of the lake, and they'd been there way before her subdivision was built. They were all spread out, and all different, at least what you could see of them under the shaggy eucalyptus trees.

Angela ran past some horses sleeping at the edge of a pipe corral. One horse startled awake, and blew a big snort.

As she ran, she tried to remember what else Lexi had said.

"There's this tunnel, full of the most amazing art you'll ever see. And it's all hidden, it's like a secret just for special people. I don't even think Jace and the rest have been there. It'll just be you and me."

"Isn't it locked up?" she'd asked. "If it's part of the dam, couldn't someone go in there like James Bond and blow the whole thing up?"

"Well, it *is* locked," Lexi said seriously, then a grin twisted her mouth. "But there's a hole in the fence."

Angela saw the dam closer now, water lapping at the curved wall of concrete, metal handrails running along the top, razor wire and chain-link.

She stopped, listening for footsteps behind her. Nothing but her own breathing. Maybe he hadn't even followed her down here. She listened again, and thought she heard singing this time. But then it was gone. She'd imagined it.

She kept going, following what looked like the most beaten path, as she wove in and out of the trees. She was getting closer. She heard the singing again. It was real. Across the lake, points of light floated in the darkness.

The trees opened up, and here was a trail. It led down a very steep switchback to the front of the dam, the part with no water. She couldn't see what was at the bottom, but started down anyway, gathering her skirts around her so she could watch her feet this time. She'd never been a brave hiker, and this was the worst footwear she could imagine—a pair of thrift store boots from the eighties, black lace like Madonna wore, with tiny pointed heels.

Lexi was the one that had told her to dress goth, because they'd be making a movie. And, Lexi would be unleashing her surprise.

If they'd been together, maybe Lexi would be home now. Maybe they'd both be home now. Angela started to cry, but made herself stop.

When she got to the bottom her boots sank into mud. A frog ribbitted in protest and she flinched as it hopped away. Reeds and grass and muck surrounded her as she plodded through.

She looked up, and vertigo took hold as she tried to take in the height and expanse of the structure. On this side, it looked like some strange skyscraper on another planet, alternating columns of concrete pierced by rectangular holes like windows up the height of it.

She focused on the ground again, and moved forward. She had to scramble up a series of giant steps, obviously not made for people to walk on, but made for water to flow over. Then there was a ramp, slippery with algae and a trickle of running water. No way to get up that.

Except—her eyes adjusted—except for this plank that someone must've left here.

She walked up the plank, her arms out, balancing her.

At the top she had to scramble up some girders and onto a flat platform. There was a chain-link gate set in the wall, and she could see the tunnel through it. She looked around, kicking the fence here and there, and there it was, a flap cut in the chain-link, the one Lexi had told her about.

She squeezed herself through, her black lace getting caught in it. It was so dark here, but she thought she saw little lights ahead. With her hand against the rough wall, she stepped forward, deeper into the tunnel. Her boots echoed on the concrete. It smelled of mildew and moss, the tang of fresh spray paint.

She was so hungry now she couldn't even think. She wished she'd asked for something at Jack in the Box. She hadn't had anything but that coke this morning in the desert.

A string of Christmas mini-bulbs lit the tunnel, and illuminated in the pink, green, and blue light, the walls were covered in graffiti. But not the calligraphy-style gang tags she was used to. This was...it really was art, like Lexi had said.

The first panel showed a woman, elongated into a mighty goddess, while tiny happy people danced at her feet.

Next, was a war, with a huge angry face in the clouds above the battlefield.

Then, fire. She looked at this one longer. There were hills, and behind them glowed giant yellow and orange flames licking up and around to the top of the rounded tunnel ceiling.

The longer she stared, the more they seemed to move. Sleep deprivation and hunger. And possibly a head injury, she thought distantly. She couldn't remember anything after Travis had caught up to her last night.

She better get going. He could be catching up to her now, reaching out to grab her by the hair...

Continuing through the tunnel, she came out into an elevated walkway with a wall on one side, and a handrail on the other. Something skittered on the floor, and she jumped, her heart thumping.

Rats?

But no, it was just something she'd kicked with the toe of her boot.

She felt around with her foot again, and bumped it. Something small. She reached down and patted around til her hand hit it.

A lipgloss. She peered at it in the dim light. Could've been anyone's, the random bits of humanity that end up as trash, but it wasn't. It was still shiny, intact.

She pulled the applicator out of the tube and held it up to the closest mini bulb on the string. Midnight Rose. Lexi's favorite shade.

Lexi would never willingly leave behind a lipgloss. And she wasn't one of those people who was constantly losing things, dropping a trail of breadcrumbs and cell phones and keys and hair ties behind her.

Although, she'd come through here alone, probably pissed off and late because she'd been waiting for Angela, trying to get to the boys before they gave up on her.

"Oh *Angela!*" Travis's voice reverberated through the tunnel like a church chamber. It wasn't even a yell, just a casual call, like someone saying, "Yoohoo!"

She dropped the tube of lipgloss, and it bounced and made more noise than should even be possible. Shit! She grabbed it off the floor, crouching and listening.

"Angela. I can hear you. Come out and we can talk about this...I'm really, really sorry." His voice was gravelly, twisted.

She flattened herself against the wall. All she heard was dripping, her heart beating, her breathing. She looked left and right, not knowing which way his voice came from.

Then there were soft, sneakered footfalls on a cement floor. She peeked over the handrail. He was directly below her, in a large chamber.

She stepped back and squeezed herself tight against the wall. She looked up. Could she climb somewhere? Above, cavernous dark space loomed.

She tiptoed a few feet to an opening, where a metal stairway descended a few steps into mucky water. Maybe she could hide in the water, possibly? But then she'd be trapped if he saw her.

She kept going, farther from his voice, further through the dam. This walkway continued a little longer, but at the end there was a heavy metal door, lined with rivets. She checked the handle. Locked.

His footsteps thunked as if he was coming up stairs. *Oh no!* She squeezed her eyes shut.

Soon he'd get up to her level. And she was trapped. She backed up a few steps and saw another door opening to the side of her, with metal stairs, going up this time instead of down.

She took the stairs on silent feet. After three stories she was panting, trying to catch her breath, trying not to breathe too loud, pulling herself up by the cold pipe hand-railing, her backpack heavy on her shoulders, like hands trying to pull her down.

And here the steps ended on a landing. Feeling with her hands in the dark she felt another locked metal door. Nowhere to go. It was so dark up here she didn't dare take a step without holding the banister.

"Angela!" His voice was sharp now, and close. She gasped. "You're all over the news, Ang. You and your little friend. Does she know where it is? Did you tell her?"

A flashlight pierced the darkness below. It was enough to see by. She looked left and right. To her right, she could just barely see a big square hole.

There was no way to get to it from here, except—there was a rope tied to the banister and it went across diagonally to the opening. She tugged it. Shards of wire poked her fingertips and she jerked away. She felt it again—it was actually made of metal, twisted like rope and almost as thick as her arm. It was secured around the handrail, and the rest of it stretched through the square opening in the wall.

Feeling in the darkness, she pushed on it, testing it with some of her weight. It was a little slack, but definitely tied to something on the other side.

She'd never been coordinated or athletic like Lexi. But she had to get away from Travis. She'd seen a murderous glint in his eye last night. And now she had run from him, again, and made him even angrier.

What was he looking for? Whatever it was must be valuable. And apparently, she knew something about it.

She wished she could remember. She wished she could hear anything over the pounding of the blood in her neck, her raspy, panicked breath, in and out.

And then she did hear something—someone moving. Then she heard something else, and she realized it was her own whimpering. She stopped it. She just had to get away.

"Angela!" The voice raised an octave, and the flashlight swung upwards. "Are you up there?" Under his voice, he said, "You're a sneaky little bitch, just like your mom."

She swallowed a sob. There was a soft clang as he stepped on the metal grate stairs.

He was coming up here.

The rope was her only choice.

Something took over to help her, something made her brave, Lexi's voice in her ear, telling her how to move her body, where to step.

She climbed up on the pipe railing, balancing with her hand against the cold concrete. Thank god she couldn't see down. She didn't remember how many flights she'd climbed.

Below was the flashlight, bobbing as Travis climbed the steps. At each landing he'd swing the arc of the light around the stairwell.

"Don't look down," Lexi told her. "Walk across, like you're just walking on a curb. Keep your hand on the wall." She did. The metal cable lurched and she squeaked. The beam of light shot up, blinding her, as she splayed her feet out, both hands on the wall now, nothing to hang onto but sheer concrete.

She couldn't do it, she'd fall, her feet were coming out from under her.

Only a few more feet to the opening but her brain froze in fear.

But her feet kept inching along, without her brain, and soon she was near the opening, and as the footsteps, pounding faster now, skipping stairs, came higher, she hurled her upper body into the opening, and somehow—Presidential Fitness Test results be damned—she pulled herself up and onto the ledge.

She laid flat on it for a second, hyperventilating.

It was one of those windows she'd seen from the outside...and through it she could see lights of the places downriver, Rancho Alto and beyond. She was near the top of the dam, ten stories high, nothing to stop her fall.

Everything spun as he pointed the flashlight right in her face. They were only ten feet apart, and if he was brave enough, he could come get her, and then they'd both fall.

She heard his ragged breathing. "Why are you running from me? I just want something, something good, for both of us."

"I don't remember! I don't know how to help you!" she screamed at him.

"But *I* can help *you*, Ang. I'm sorry. I did it wrong. I don't have much practice being a father. We could—we could go anywhere we want. We'll be rich, I can buy you all the clothes you want, and we can live in the Caribbean..."

"Okay," she said. "Just, stop shining that light in my face for a second."

When she could see again, she noticed that the metal cable came through the big window she was sitting in, and around to the outside, where it was hooked to a ladder enclosed in a tubular cage of metal.

She looked up. The ladder went up the extra fifty feet or so to the very top of the dam.

Inside the dam, Travis reached for the cable, pulled on it, doing his own bravery test.

The ladder on the outside of the dam was too far away for her to reach. But about halfway between her and it, a big bolt, as thick as her arm, stuck out of the concrete.

She could do it. She took off her backpack, and swung one strap over the big bolt.

"Don't you dare!" he said. "It's too high! What are you doing?"

She hesitated. He actually sounded worried now.

She'd been blocking out his platitudes, knowing now, a couple of days too late, that he was just manipulating her.

But now, he sounded like he cared. He didn't want her to die.

Then she remembered why. Because if she was dead, she wouldn't be able to tell him where his treasure was hidden.

Grasping the other backpack strap with all of her strength, she swung into the emptiness of the night.

Saturday, November 3

ANGELA LANDED ON THE OUTER cage of the ladder and hung tight like a baby monkey. Now, if she could just—she wiggled and pulled the backpack, jerking on the cable where it was looped over the bolt, and just as Travis said, "I'm coming after you Angela, hold on!" the cable came free of the bolt, and she heard a strangled yell, a thump, and a clang.

Her heart was pounding, her palms got slick with sweat and she readjusted her grip on the cold metal.

"Don't look down," Lexi's voice urged.

Her eyes were pulled downward, against her will.

"DON'T. Look. Down. Start climbing."

She contorted herself inside the cage, hanging over nothingness. Once her feet and hands were on the ladder, she took a deep breath, and rung by rung, pulled herself up.

At the top of that terrifying ladder climb on the sheer face of the dam, Angela reached another opening.

She climbed inside and collapsed in relief, panting to catch her breath with her cheek on the cold concrete of the tunnel floor.

All the while, she listened intently for sounds that her father had followed her, and was about to jump in and grab her.

She rested there in that tunnel, slipping in and out of half-sleep, full of nightmares. Nightmares of a lithe, reptilian body sweeping by on the other side of the concrete wall, as if she could see through it, like glass in an aquarium. Nightmares of the water pushing against the other side of that concrete. All that water...

When she couldn't take the claustrophobia anymore, she crawled the rest of the way out on her shaky legs, and came out on the other side of the lake. She felt with her hands in the darkness for someplace to rest, until dawn came.

Now, the world was turning gray. There was enough light to see by, and she'd have to get moving. She didn't want her dad to find her. That is, if he wasn't dead, splattered on the concrete spillway below the dam, or dead inside of it, fallen down the center of all those flights of stairs. Had she killed him? She covered her face with her hands.

How had her world gone so wrong in the span of a few days?

The pain hit her in the stomach—her father's cruelty to her, the way he'd tossed the shovel to her, snatched her phone from her, yanked her hair. The way he had something he cared about more than reuniting with her—some kind of treasure he was looking for.

She dug through her backpack, her hand hitting the Simba stuffed toy he'd given her. He hadn't taken that away, the way he'd taken her phone.

She looked closely at it. This was Simba as a cub, young and vulnerable and gullible. He'd been tricked by his evil uncle.

If only the man she'd met and escaped from wasn't her dad, but an evil uncle.

Maybe he was! If she could only remember what her real dad looked like, some beauty mark or scar that would set him apart from the man she'd encountered these last couple of days.

She tried to remember more about him, from long ago, but couldn't. Mostly she remembered her first mother. Her slim body, her animated brown hands always doing something—chopping vegetables, baking cookies, brushing Angela's hair, doing macrame or crochet or whatever it was she liked to do, decorating things with hot glue and gemstones. But her face was blank.

Little bits of memories surfaced; the kitchen, the brown corduroy couch, Angela's bedroom, decorated with Disney princesses.

Where had that been? Where had she lived? The harder she tried to grasp it the more it just escaped her.

It wasn't until a few weeks ago—just before the fire in fact—that Lexi, in a stream of afternoon sun on the floor of her bedroom, had hypnotized Angela, and she had finally remembered the shape of her mother's name, written in gold script, a necklace on a short chain she wore at the base of her collarbone. Shiny gold against brown skin. *Cheryl*.

Lexi had been preparing for this 'memory regression' as she called it. She'd studied all the books in the high school library that had to do with hypnosis, psychology, neuroscience. She called it digging for treasure. Lexi was a natural detective.

Maybe Lexi could help her find this treasure her dad wanted so bad.

Then, she could just tell him where it was, and he'd leave her alone.

She had to find her.

The gathering warmth from the rising sun was finally unfreezing her knees and elbows, her fingertips. All of a sudden she felt the clawing of thirst. All she could think about was that lake, that water.

But was it drinkable?

She pictured herself balled up in agony, little worms making their way through her intestines.

But the thirst was a thing of its own.

And, people drank this water. This was a reservoir. It got piped into their homes.

She pushed herself up, stepped down an eroded embankment, and waded into the shallow water, near the reeds. She couldn't feel any part of her body, it was so cold and stiff.

She scooped some water with her hands, swished it around her mouth experimentally. Then she swallowed, and scooped up more, and drank and drank.

The water's surface was still and dark. All she could see was a murky reflection of herself.

She'd heard stories of Ernie, the lake monster, but didn't believe it. This lake was way too populated, way too small. There was no way a mythical creature could live in it undetected.

But, what about those dreams she'd had last night?

She got out of the water as fast as she could.

At least now she could think about a plan, now that the overpowering thirst was quenched. She was hungry too, but it was a distant feeling.

Angela looked to the west, away from the rising sun. Across the highway a wall of granite rose. The big hill between here and Fairy Glen. Somewhere over there was the road up to Paraiso.

Barking traveled on the wind, from across the lake.

She'd have to get going, she didn't want to be found. At least not without Lexi.

If they came home together, they could put up a united front. She'd start by finding the asylum, even though she had never been there before and was terrible at navigating.

She climbed through the weeds and up to the highway, where she could cross and go up the other side. She had to go up and over the mountain, because the only thing she knew was that the asylum was in Fairy Glen. Everyone knew that.

When she got to the dirt pullout next to the dam, she made sure nobody was around.

She took a deep breath and dashed across the empty highway while it was still shrouded in fog.

But which way was the road? She went to the right, and kept in the small weedy ditch between the mountain and the highway, until she came to a small parking lot.

There was a trail entrance here. The parking lot was empty. She guessed nobody was in the mood to hike when the place was all burned up.

Set back in the parking lot, near the entrance to the trail, was a roadside memorial.

Someone probably died here in the fire. That girl Crystal Bartley was missing, and she'd been in the fire up at Paraiso. Lexi knew her. Maybe this was for her.

She looked closer. The flowers were fresh, like they'd been put out yesterday. There were also stuffed bears, balloons, a cross made of filigreed gold plastic. On the cross was the name "Samantha." That was the one the two girls that gave her a ride had talked about. Burned up, in a Satanic ritual, they said.

Judging by all the bears, she must've been young. Angela said a prayer for Samantha, and then scurried through the metal posts that marked the beginning of the trail.

But then, she heard the sound she was dreading. His car, with its rattly muffler.

She started running again, and scrambled up the trail, between bushes turned to charcoal by the fires, her heart pounding as she scaled the steep terrain.

* * *

JACKIE PAGE HAD FULFILLED HER end of the bargain, and the story on the local news last night had brought about something good. Volunteer dog searchers showed up at Cassandra's house early Saturday morning.

There was also a team of other volunteers that would be showing up at Gorda's. Bonnie and Sally were hauling the horses over to meet up with them, and Deirdre would join them when she was done here at Cassie's house.

Cass gave each dog handler an item of Angela's dirty clothing to lock onto her scent. "The sweatier the better," said the woman in charge of the team. Her dog was an extremely active female beagle. Among the other dogs were an Irish setter, a shepherd mix, a black Lab, and a Cairn terrier.

The Marconis didn't have anything of Lexi's to give the dog searchers. They'd lost everything. They said she'd worn her cheer uniform as a costume on Halloween, because that was one of the few things she had on her when the house caught fire. That, and a few other clothes—black leggings and a red t-shirt, which she'd taken to school with her, in her gym bag.

"I hope this works," Cass said to Deirdre outside on the driveway. She cocked a worried eyebrow. "It's been—what—two days since she's been here? Three?"

Deirdre didn't know anything about how old a scent these dogs could track, so she just squeezed Cass's arm.

Gina Marconi was inside, struggling to make breakfast for her three boys in an unfamiliar kitchen.

Burt, the father, insisted Lexi was just "gallivanting," she'd done it before, and that she'd come home any time and be "grounded til the end of time." He was staying at the church, sleeping in his truck, in case she returned. "It's the only place she knows to find us," he had said gruffly, after Cass offered to let them stay with her.

At first the dogs just milled around and jostled each other, zigzagging aimlessly around the street, noses to the ground, tangling leashes.

It was a gray morning, with fog over the lake, and the blackness of the peak up to Paraiso beyond. Gorda's place, and the houses along that small area of shore, were lucky to have escaped the blazes.

A cool breeze picked up off the lake, as an Encantadino squad car rolled down the street towards them.

"Oh great timing," Cass said. "They're interviewing us, now that there's a connection with the two girls. I hope they take me seriously this time."

"I'll let you know if anything happens with the dogs," Deirdre said. She gave her a quick hug and got into her car. She was heading back around to Gorda's to meet Bonnie and the horse trailer, but she could stay and see if the dogs went anywhere first.

Cass went inside with the policemen. Deirdre rolled slowly away, braking for the dogs criss-crossing the street.

At first one, then another, then the rest of the dogs pulled down the street, all aligning now, as if to a magnetic pole.

Three blocks along, where she was supposed to turn right, one of the dogs let out a howl, and all of them ran to catch up.

Deirdre turned left and followed them to end of the road, where she got out of the car and trailed behind.

They went down past the barricade, down into the ramshackle neighborhood on the flood plain on the eastern shore of the lake, then down a twisted rocky path to the dam, where the dogs clamored and clawed at a locked chain-link gate leading into the innards of the dam.

"Oh my God." Deirdre prayed the worst wouldn't be discovered.

"It's like she was just here!" one of the searchers said.

They were stuck waiting for a dam employee to come unlock it, but in the meantime, Norah, the leader, picked half her team to drive around Lake Hemingway to the opposite shore, and continue the search from there. They would meet at the dirt pullout off Del Diablo Highway.

"We can meet you there with the horses," Deirdre said.

"Okay good," said Norah. "We've got some other mounted patrol coming too."

Deirdre watched them go, and then looked up at the sky, where silvery clouds billowed.

After all this drought and fire, she found herself praying it wouldn't rain, so the scent trail would be preserved.

Her phone rang. It was Bonnie.

"I just got to Gorda's with the horses. Where are you?"

* * *

AFTER THE LONG CLIMB, ANGELA got to the top of that hulking mountain that stood between Lake Hemingway and Fairy Glen. Her breath whistled in her lungs, and she stood, just panting.

Her father hadn't followed her. Hopefully he hadn't even seen her.

Below, on a flat part carved out of the mountain, were the remains of Paraiso.

Beyond that, the shapes of the mountains and canyons receded into the distance, folding and crumpled in dark green.

When she could finally breathe again, she descended the hill, into the burned housing development.

It was eerily quiet in the morning light. She walked past a burned house. Just the foundation remained. In the backyard was a swimming pool, full of a slurry of ash and debris. And, one dead raccoon. She pinched her nose and walked faster, away from the smell.

This was the place that Crystal Bartley had been during the fire—her dad built it. Had she died up here? Nobody knew.

What if she had?

Angela started looking at the piles of burned debris, wondering if any of them were human.

Surely they'd searched the whole place up here?

She kept looking for a way down. Hadn't Lexi said they were coming up here to Paraiso first, and then hiking down into Fairy Glen?

She was getting closer to another house, which hadn't burned completely —there was still a structure to it, made of metal. Maybe there was a way down on the other side of it.

She stepped carefully inside, the heels of her boots clicking on the ash-covered cement floor.

Wait, who was that? Movement—a shape, walking between the houses, a human male shape. She crouched behind a charred masonry wall. Shit. Was he here, still on her tail?

Shaking, she made herself smaller, and watched as the dark figure traversed the yard.

It wasn't her father, as she'd thought. This man was wearing a tight navy t-shirt, and his shape was all different. Muscular, but compact, not big and rangy like Travis. His pants were bulky, held up with suspenders, and had a reflective strip around the bottom. Fireman's pants.

Her heart beat in her throat. She didn't want to get in trouble for being here, didn't want to be found. Not yet, at least. Not without Lexi.

She waited until he left, peeking out occasionally. He didn't drive away— there was no car or firetruck nearby. He was all alone, no other firemen around that she could see. He seemed to melt into the morning haze.

When she'd held still as long as she could stand it, she fled the house.

But where was the way down? *Was* there a way down? She scurried along the perimeter of the plateau, looking at the drop off.

The heavy vegetation that had covered these hills was completely burned away, not even skeletons of bushes left.

Maybe she'd just have to go straight down.

She took a few steps down the hill. It was so steep she had to fall back on her hands, and finally sit on her butt in the black soot. While she sat there, trying to work up the nerve to go down, she looked out and tried to get a lay of the land.

The asylum was near a creek, she'd heard talk of that, but which creek? Hidden Creek was the main one, but there were other tributaries, little streams that joined up with it.

Like that one, hundreds of feet down the burnt slope from her. It had been stripped naked by the fire. No bushes or trees, just boulders spilling down the slight grade through Rancho Alto and out to the ocean. She traced it the other way, towards Encantadino, but didn't see anything useful.

She looked into the distance, towards Fairy Glen.

There was a stark dividing line where the burn had stopped, and beyond was all green.

It looked like a beautiful place, a place she would like to spend time in. It didn't seem spooky at all, not like the kids at high school said, *Fairy Glen is full of ghosts and witches.*

But the asylum, *that* was somewhere that sounded scary to her.

She'd never been afraid of ghosts. Man was capable of much worse. What kinds of terrible things had happened in that place?

From the descriptions she'd heard, the asylum was a good place for a party. That's all she knew.

Where would it be? She took a deep breath. There was only one way to find out.

The journey of a thousand miles begins with a single step.

It was one of Lexi's favorite quotes.

Angela gave herself a pep talk. "Okay. If I have to slide down on my hands and my butt, I will." She started down the bare dirt slope.

But the ground gave way, and she was sliding, face down, mouth full of dirt, falling, tumbling away into nothing.

* * *

BACK AT GORDA'S, DEIRDRE PULLED in near Bonnie's trailer. There were only two horses tied up to it—Gatsby, Bonnie's big bay warmblood, and Scarlet.

Bonnie, her longtime friend and dressage instructor, was tacking up her horse. She saw Deirdre and smiled and waved.

With her silver-blond waves cut short around her face, Bonnie was a natural beauty at sixty plus years old. Her angelic demeanor and positive outlook created a benevolent aura around her that never failed to soothe Deirdre's harried mind.

"So Lina didn't come?" Deirdre asked, approaching the trailer. "Why not?"

"She's going through some stuff," was all Bonnie said. She lifted her saddle onto Gatsby's back.

"Do you mean, going through stuff, like in the garage? Or *going through some stuff?*" she asked, but before she got her answer, she heard a metallic clank and the rumble of a diesel engine.

Sally pulled up next to them with her truck and trailer. Vivian was in the passenger seat, looking uncomfortable, and Apache was in the trailer next to Darkling. The horses were touching noses, contented as two friendly geldings can get.

Bonnie smirked at Deirdre.

"Sally and Vivian, now that's an unlikely pairing," Deirdre said.

She filled them in on the dog searchers' discoveries, and the plan to meet at the dirt pullout by the dam.

When they were all saddled up, they rode south on the lakeside trails.

But before they got far, the dogs all came down to the lakeside, sniffing in the water, and following footprints in and out of the muddy bank.

Norah said, "Angela must've been here recently, they're going wild."

After a while though, the dogs didn't pick up a trail again. It was like it dead-ended at the lake.

"We can ask a boat team to drag the lake," Norah said.

Deirdre's stomach lurched. That made it sound like Angela had drowned.

Norah continued. "But that'll take some time. So the rest of us, we'll divide into three teams. This will be a quick search on the main roads and trails, the path of least resistance, so to speak. The most likely routes that a person might travel. One group will go south and another north, and one up the trail where the body was found. Let's go."

Bonnie and Sally volunteered for the group that would go up the trail.

Deirdre and Vivian went south. Deirdre had no desire to revisit that trail where they'd found the body unless absolutely necessary.

As she and Vivian and the rest of the group progressed down the side of Del Diablo Highway, a truck towing a long stock trailer pulled in and parked at the turnout by the dam.

Two horses, already tacked up in Western saddles, were being unloaded by their riders, who were wearing orange vests and cowboy hats.

They joined up with the group, which crossed the highway, heading up the road to Paraiso.

The dogs stayed in the lead, although from what Deirdre could overhear, they weren't really picking up a scent.

The higher they climbed the winding road set deep in the canyon, the more Apache and Scarlet began lagging, stopping, and snorting. Scarlet even pulled a couple of 180 spooks, which Deirdre could feel coming. She was starting to understand this squirrelly little mare.

The other two riders turned around and came back to them.

"Now I know why you wear that helmet!" said one cowboy-looking guy to Deirdre. He even had a handlebar mustache.

"I wear a helmet because I'm fond of my brain," Deirdre said.

He may not have heard her, because he continued on. "Couldn't ever get me on one of those Ay-Rabs," he said, looking at Scarlet. "But that horse there..." He looked at Apache. "That's one fine looking mustang." He called to Vivian. "Let me ride him for a day, and he won't ever pull nothing like that again."

Vivian gave him a withering stare. "Are you speaking to me?"

Deirdre was pissed. "You know, there's a good reason they're acting like this," she yelled at the cowboy as he rode away.

The nicer, older man said, "You could do the sheriff's mounted posse training. Be real good for her." He smiled at Scarlet. "You don't know what your horse is capable of until you push them a little. Kind of like people." He tipped his hat, and then turned and trotted to catch up with his buddy.

"You have no idea what these horses are capable of," Vivian said, boring her eyes into the man's back. "*Or* these people."

"Should we make the horses go up here?" Deirdre asked. "It was so traumatic."

Vivian looked at her. "I'm not letting *them* get the last word." She tilted her head towards the cowboys.

Deirdre smiled. "Damn straight."

It was a long way up on the asphalt, and they were left far behind because of the horses' reluctance.

Scarlet may not be brave, but she was smart. Deirdre didn't blame her for acting spooky and nervous now. The closer they got to Paraiso, the more she saw visions of the wall of flame coming at her.

When they rounded the corner before the gate, Deirdre indicated to Vivian to take a right onto a little dirt trail. It was the path that she'd used to get out of Paraiso, the night the Colombian man had shot at her.

As they climbed, the gates into Paraiso came into view below them. They were locked, of course. Horses, dogs, and people were stuck in the steep-sided canyon with no way around.

Deirdre called down to them, and pointed out how they could get onto the same trail she and Vivian were on.

The searchers all backtracked and got on the trail, which led them to the plateau where the construction site, or what was left of it, sat.

Deirdre sucked in her breath, awed by the devastation she'd lived through.

The tall house had partially survived, but on the half that stuck out over the edge, the steel beams were twisted and deformed.

"Feel weird to be back?" Vivian asked her.

"You can say that again," she murmured.

The dogs began baying. They were onto a scent, but then lost it again.

They continued calling Angela's name, but the dogs seemed to be stymied when they reached the edge, where the steep hillside dropped off below the nightmare tower house. She got off Scarlet, and peered over the edge.

Far below was where the natural clearing had been, where she'd been shot at, the night the black rider had come to her rescue, and led her straight up this hill. Now it was completely barren. Nothing, no trees, just a black slope.

She moved away from the edge. The swimming pool that had saved their lives was full of ashy water. A dead raccoon floated in the center.

But the house it used to belong to was burned flat. "So much for fireproof. What are they gonna do with this place?" she wondered out loud.

The dogs were confused now, sniffing here and there, not knowing where to go next, running along the cliff edge.

From the ridge above them, she heard more calling. The other group had made it up here. There were Sally and Bonnie and the other dogs. When they got down to the plateau, they said the dogs had been tracking Angela up that trail.

The trail the burned body was found on.

But now, all of the dogs just milled around. The dog handlers in their group had looked through all of the hiding spots in the construction site. Angela wasn't here anymore, if she ever had been.

Suddenly, a siren whooped behind them.

Sheriff's Deputy Harvey and Wilma Wagner, the Fairy Glen Fire Chief, parked and exited their respective official vehicles.

Wilma was a tiny but fierce woman with short curly brown hair, dressed in her smart blue fire uniform. She crossed her arms and gave the deputy a disapproving look. "That was totally unnecessary," she said to him. "You could've spooked the horses."

"No, our horses are trained to deal with that," the young cowboy said, giving Scarlet a sideways sneer.

"We got a call that you were here," Wilma said to everyone. "I'm sorry to say, we cannot allow any civilian searchers up here. This is a hazardous materials zone, and it's dangerously steep. With no plant matter to hold these cliffs together, it's in danger of a landslide."

"But Wilma, Angela may have just come through here...we have to at least try," Deirdre told her. "Vivian and I know the way down, it's just over there—"

Wilma was shaking her head. "Listen, the fire changed everything. I wouldn't even let my firefighters do it, unless someone was in desperate need of rescue."

"But someone *is* in need of rescue!"

Wilma just set her jaw and walked back to her red truck. "You all need to leave. The deputy will make sure you can get out, and he'll lock up behind you."

Vivian pulled Apache closer to Deirdre. "Maybe we need to start from the other side," Vivian said. "In Fairy Glen."

Deirdre looked out over the innumerable canyons and hillsides, fading into the distance. If Angela was somewhere out there, they'd need to cover a lot of territory to find her.

"Let's ride tomorrow," Deirdre replied. "We'll meet at Mrs. Fey's."

* * *

ANGELA CAME TO, STRUGGLING TO breathe.

Ash filled her nostrils, her mouth. She gagged and tried to spit it out, but choked instead. She panicked, coughing and hyperventilating.

Where was she? She put a hand out, and felt smooth, cool rock. She sat up, and looked around. She was next to a huge boulder. Gasping, she thought back.

She had fallen down that terrible burnt hillside. There weren't even any bushes or branches to hold on to, just all burnt away. Her stomach lurched, thinking of the ground giving way beneath her feet.

She dragged herself upright, stumbled, still trying to work up enough spit to get the ash out of her mouth.

There was the tiny stream she'd seen from above. She scooped up what little water there was, swished out her mouth, and then drank greedily.

It had to be cleaner than the reservoir water, right? Well, maybe. But it tasted good, fresh and clean and active, even in the midst of all this ash.

She drank some more, then splayed against a rock, panting.

Her head hurt. She put a hand to the back of her head, and felt crusty dried blood, and a swollen lump. She pushed on the lump experimentally, and winced.

Covered in ash, she was gray, as gray as the world around her. The light was leaving the sky. Overhead, a white owl circled high in the haze, higher and higher, until it disappeared.

She stood up, making for the trees, for the part that hadn't burned. She could camp for the night. She knew how to camp, she'd been a Girl Scout.

Little currents of ash kicked up under her feet as she stumbled the rest of the way, imagining what kind of shelter she could build with sticks.

But when she got to a dry grass meadow before the trees began, she was so tired she just found a soft place on the ground, curled up into a ball, and fell asleep.

Sunday, November 4

VIVIAN ARRIVED AT MRS. FEY'S before the rest of them.

Bonnie and Deirdre would meet her there with the trailer, but Vivian had chosen to ride here, along the creek in the cool foggy morning, peaceful with Apache.

Mrs. Fey, a plump, very old woman who was dressed like an extra from Little House on the Prairie, came out to greet her.

She invited her in for tea, but Vivian refused. "I'll stay out here with my horse. Thank you for taking them in after the fire. I suppose I owe you something for his feed."

"Feed?" Mrs. Fey waved her hand dismissively. "All he had was grass, and that grows for free."

Sure, free, if you don't pay a water bill, Vivian thought.

The strange little boy, the grandson she supposed, was there and said hello to her. He was—not quite an albino, no. He had extremely white-blond hair, but his eyes were green. He introduced himself. "I'm Peter. What's your name?"

"Ms. Johnson," she said.

He then started telling her about something she had no interest in whatsoever. "We're looking for our cat. She's been gone since Halloween..."

His speech was very articulate, and there was a touch of....something about him. She couldn't put her finger on it, but it made sense that he was friends with Deirdre's youngest, the strange little girl.

Vivian ignored him and moved away, feigning that Apache wanted some grass. The kid left, looking dejected, but Mrs. Fey followed her.

"You and that horse have quite a bond," the old woman said.

"Yes, we do." She left it closed-ended, but the old lady kept talking.

"I used to ride horses. When I was younger."

"Ah." Vivian was grateful to her for keeping the horses safe, but she didn't really want to hear this woman's entire life story.

Mrs. Fey reached out a hand to Apache's neck. She was so short, Vivian was afraid Apache would step on her, but instead he rested his forehead on Mrs. Fey's bosom, while she gently rubbed the base of his ears with her gnarled fingers. She whispered something, possibly in another language, then said, "They sure enjoyed their time here. He and Scarlet and Ginny."

Vivian used the reins to pull Apache's head back to her, an irrational jealousy coming over her.

"Can I help you with something else?"

Mrs. Fey shook her head and looked around, saying, "I do hope Deirdre gets here soon, there's a letter I'd like to show her."

"Yes, well, we'll be busy. We're searching for a lost girl." Where was Deirdre anyway? Couldn't she just not be late for once? Did she remember the time change last night? "Two lost girls, actually."

"Oh. I didn't realize that." Suddenly Mrs. Fey's face filled with worry. She grilled Vivian about the details. And with each revelation, she looked a few years older.

"Oh dear," she muttered to herself. "Falling down on the job."

Apache whirled around and trumpeted. Bonnie's big white Chevy and three-horse trailer rolled around the corner. Scarlet whinnied from inside.

Vivian looked at her watch. Only fifteen minutes late. Not unforgivable. But they'd have to get going if they hoped to make the most of the day.

Bonnie parked, and the horses were unloaded, saddled and made ready.

"Mrs. Fey!" Deirdre greeted her with a hug, as if they were old friends. "There's room in the trailer for me to take Ginny home today."

Mrs. Fey looked confused. "Ginny? Why, she hasn't been here since you took her and Scarlet home, a few days ago."

"No...I thought..." Deirdre's face dropped, her mouth opening and closing. "...when I came to ride Scarlet on Thursday morning, she wasn't here. And neither were you...I just thought she was in a different pasture." Deirdre's voice was getting higher, more hysterical.

Vivian thought back to the morning that she'd come here, after her long night. There *was* an old spindly white mare grazing alongside Deirdre's horse. But, she wasn't here now.

Maybe she died, was lying in all that tall green grass. Vivian didn't voice that prospect out loud.

"Come on, she'll turn up," she said. "Let's ride."

They all started off into the trees, searching for Angela and Lexi.

* * *

TODAY, ANGELA WOKE UP WITH the sun and kept hiking, fueled by the one crumbled granola bar she'd found in the bottom of her bag. She had to find Lexi.

Who, if she'd stuck to her plan—and she always did—had last been at the asylum. Angela realized how unlikely it was that she was still there, but pushed that to the back of her mind.

The witch hat made a good sun hat. The smoke was clearing out of the sky day by day, so the sun was getting more powerful, once the fog burned off.

She hitched her backpack up and trudged along, seeking the shade of the trees that stood over the creek.

As she got closer, she could hear the bubbling, feel the moisture rushing off from the movement of the water.

What was that on the other side—a coyote? No, a gray fox. It froze, staring at her with bright, black eyes, kind of like the old man on the bus.

She watched it for a second too, but then impatience moved her onward, and it skittered into the undergrowth.

She got to a spot where what looked like a beaver dam created a little calm pool of water. She looked down at her reflection and didn't recognize herself. She looked like a zombie.

"I'm the Gray Girl," she said. Like the Jack in the Box girls had said.

She splashed some water on her face, trying to wash away the ash.

When she stood, she swore she heard giggling. She looked left and right. The branch of a bush on the other side of the creek was waving as if springing back from being pushed. That's probably where the fox had gone. Maybe it had babies to protect. Puppies? Maybe they sounded like children, the way coyotes sound like—what *do* they sound like, crazy people yelling? Or the way cats make themselves sound like babies crying so we'll take care of them, long after they're kittens.

Kits! Yes, that's what baby foxes are called, kits.

But, there was another giggle...her heart raced. Her eyes scanned over the far side of the creek again. Boulders, a thick carpet of oak leaves on the ground, a canopy of trees overhead...that was all. As she turned, a flash of red popped in and out of her peripheral vision. A terrified sound, an exhalation of fear, came out of her against her will.

What was that? She was on high alert now. If it was people in the woods —and she would've welcomed that at this point—they would've just been talking to each other. This felt like someone purposely messing with her.

Playing a prank, trying to get her scared.

A vision came to her, of the last time she thought she'd been the victim of a prank.

Lexi had brought over a Ouija board one night when her mom was on graveyard shift at the hospital. Lexi made her turn out the lights, set up the candles, and place both their hands on the Ouija thingie. Angela had at first thought nothing of it, humoring Lexi. Until, the thing moved.

And it had spelled out *Sandman*.

She had laughed, and said, "You mean, like the Metallica song, *Enter Sandman*? Come on, Lex."

Lexi said, "I didn't do that—I don't even like Metallica! I don't know what the hell that was." And then Lexi had shivered, crossed herself, packed up her board and gone home. She hadn't spoken about it since.

But, when Angela had entered 'Cheryl Sandman' into Google, that's when everything had become clear. That's when she knew. Her mother was trying to contact her.

Behind her, another *crack!* and this time she screamed. She turned to see an acorn bounding into the creek. It had just bounced off the rock next to her, making that sharp sound.

She put a hand on her chest. Her heart couldn't take this.

But that *had* been a giggle before, and not a human sounding one. Not animal either.

"Oh God," she said, feeling the blood drain from her head, her face grow cold. "I need to sit down."

"Come sit with me," Lexi said into her ear. She whirled around.

It was the same thing she'd said to her the first day of school last year, when Angela stood, a lost and confused freshman in a sea of orange plastic picnic tables, too hot to touch in the Encantadino September sun. She had looked around to see who it was. And over in the shade, Lexi was sitting with a few friends, patting the bench beside her.

But this voice was real, not a memory.

"Lexi!" she yelled, ecstatic. She'd found her!

No answer.

"Lexi!" Still no answer. "Stop screwing around!" She turned in a complete circle, but didn't see any sign of her friend. "Lexi! We're in big trouble! Both of us are missing!" She waited. "You have to come home with me!"

Nothing.

"Lexi, stop scaring me!"

"Boo!" The voice in her ear again. Her knees buckled and she almost fell.

"Goddammit Lex!"

"Oooh, taking the Lord's name in vain, are we now?"

Angela looked up. Lexi, wearing black pants, a red t-shirt and a black jacket, was doing a handstand on a ten foot high boulder behind her. She put her feet back down and stood up, twisting a spiral of her eggplant-tinted hair on her finger.

"There you are!" Relief flooded Angela's veins, relief and anger, and pure joy of seeing her again. "I'm not damned to eternal brimstone, or whatever you Catholics believe. So I can say whatever the hell I want."

Lexi laughed, her real laugh. A sound less like tinkling bells and more like a roaring fire. Angela was always proud of her ability to make Lexi laugh.

Lexi sat down on the boulder and crossed her legs. "I found these," she said, pulling a handful of something out of her jacket pocket. "Wow. Check you out," Lexi looked her up and down. "Ever heard of the White Lady?"

Angela, out of breath, just shook her head.

"She was a Victorian lady—or maybe older, I can't remember—but anyway, her kids got washed away in the flood a hundred years ago. *La Llorona*, en Éspanol." Lexi had a perfect accent. She got straight As in Spanish.

"What does that mean?"

"Weeping woman. Look around. Check out these weeping willows. That's probably what they're named for too, because they lean over the water."

"Lexi, come on," Angela was tired of this. She just wanted to go home. For them both to go home.

"So, nooooow," Lexi said, "instead of the White Lady, you can be the Gray Girl. I'm going to start my own urban legend. The Gray Girl of Fairy Glen," she said, looking up and spreading her hands, as if reading letters on a movie marquee.

"Hate to tell you, but you didn't think of that," Angela said. "These two girls gave me a ride—"

"I know," Lexi interrupted Angela, undeterred. "But that one, she's just a sad ghost of a pioneer girl that got crushed by a wagon wheel. *You*, now you would make a much better Gray Girl. Give it some style, some pizazz. Come on, say it like you mean it. *I'm the Gray Girl of Fairy Glen*."

"No, Lex..."

"I know you hate Drama, but that's just because you're too shy. You'd be so good at it. Say it! Once more, with feeling!"

"Okay, fine. I'm the Gray Girl of Fairy Glen."

"Louder."

"I'm the Gray Girl of Fairy Glen!" Angela yelled, then coughed. "Ow. That hurt my throat."

"You need to practice talking loud," Lexi said. "It shouldn't hurt."

"It's only because of all this ash!" Angela bent by the bank of the creek, and drank. The water activated her stomach, and all of a sudden she was starving. "Hey, got anything to eat?"

"Try these." Lexi held out her bounty again, and Angela could see what it was now—mushrooms. Lexi dropped them down on the ground.

Angela was so hungry she didn't say no, it's dangerous, what kind of mushrooms are those, she just picked them up and shoved them in her mouth.

Lexi laughed, widening her eyes. "Impressive, once again. Like my dad says, it's always the quiet ones."

"What does that mean?" Angela said.

Lexi didn't answer.

"Are you camping at the asylum?" Angela asked.

"Um, for a little while, yeah. Until I can figure out where to go next."

"Maybe I'll stay with you," Angela said. "Can you do some more hypnotism on me? I have to try to remember where something is... something my father is looking for." She looked up at Lexi. "I met him by the way. He's a real asshole."

There was a sound across the creek; a footfall, a twig snapping. *Was that him?*

She turned and looked, then looked back up at Lexi, panicked.

Lexi wasn't worried. She looked in Angela's eyes. "Come on, you have to check this out. Walk around the other side of this rock. You'll be safe here."

When Angela came out on the other side, she couldn't believe what she saw. It was a magical glade surrounded by standing stones; pink bushes, pink trees, pink grass, pink rocks, like a little girl's candy land.

She spun around and looked up at the rock. "Lexi?"

Where did she go?

* * *

REBECCA RODE HER BIKE ALONG the side of the road.

This part of Fairy Glen always made her claustrophobic. The further east you went, the closer the trees bent overhead, blocking out even the brightest daylight.

She biked perilously between the occasional speeding car and a mossy drainage ditch full of jagged rocks, wobbling along the white line.

It was her day off work, she had an extra hour because of the time change last night, and now she was heading for the trailhead at the end of the road.

Rebecca had used that extra hour to buy *yet another* BMX bike at a garage sale—like this was getting to be a recurring theme with her, losing her bike—and with her newfound freedom, she was going on a quest of her own. Her mom and her friends were searching on horseback for the missing girls. So she figured she'd go on her bike.

She was relieved when she turned off the main road with its speeding cars, into a neighborhood.

The houses were less ranch or farm-style and more suburban than the ones near her house. One acre lots, it looked like, and all greenly landscaped, not full of dusty animal pens or rows of citrus trees or greenhouses.

She'd been here before. There was a popular entrance to the Mount Richardson trails at the end of this long street.

But that wasn't the only way to get to these trails, she had other choices. She had chosen to go down this street on purpose.

Up ahead. There was the address. 45609 Orfila.

For better or worse, she had a photographic memory. It was like she was reading it off that IRS form in Mr. Fariz's office.

Why did her heart skip like that? It was just a house, and she was just a teenager riding her BMX past it. An anonymous teenage girl.

The deep grinding sound of a garage door opener shot to her core. Now the garage door was slowly opening, revealing a woman from the shoes up.

Rebecca slowed down to get a glimpse. Off-white pointy-toed pumps, peeking from beneath cream polyester trousers with a perfect crease down the front...a pink nubbly jacket...straight dark hair with bangs. An older woman, about fifty.

That had to be Jeremy's mom.

She didn't look anything like Jeremy, but there was something about the way she flipped her hair as she opened the car door that Rebecca recognized right away.

It was then that Jeremy's mom caught Rebecca staring. Her face changed, mouth opening. She scurried out of the garage, heels clicking.

"Wait!" she called out, but Rebecca was already pedaling, accelerating towards the trail at the end of the curving road, feeling like she was being pursued by a ghost.

When she got to the trailhead, she stopped and looked behind her, panting. Jeremy's mom had sounded...almost plaintive. She wasn't expecting that. She should be more careful in the future. And definitely take a different route home.

The sound of feet pounding on the dirt came from the forest, and she whirled around to face the trail.

A couple of little boys were running out of the trees. But they didn't look right—they were pale, no expression on their slack faces. Fear in their eyes.

They saw Rebecca and skidded to a stop, tumbling over each other.

"Hey, what's up?" she asked them.

The younger one started babbling. The older one chimed in. "There was a girl, she was all gray. She said, 'I'm the Gray Girl of Fairy Glen'."

"She was a ghost!" the little one said. "She was mad!" and he started crying. She could tell he wasn't fooling with her. His shorts were all wet in the front. The fear was real. They had seen something.

"Go home," she said. They stood up, and for a while they just stood there, the little one whimpering and snotty, even the older one forming tears in his eyes.

"It's *okay*. Go home," she repeated, trying to sound more comforting. "I'll check it out. I'm sure it wasn't a ghost." More likely, it was one of the missing girls. The boys started to leave, but she said, "Hey, which way?"

The older boy pointed down the trail. "Near the castle stones."

She got back on her bike and continued down the wide trail with trees on either side.

She wasn't familiar with the castle stones, but she guessed they were big, and perhaps looked like a castle. At least if you were eight years old.

There were lots of giant boulders around here. Big, smooth, granite gray, rusty red or pale buttery colored, scattered and embedded into the dusky green mountainsides, tumbled into the creek and the subsidiary streams. Like the mountain god had spilled his basket of eggs.

Hopefully she could find the stones the little boys were talking about.

This was a trail that only the locals knew about. This wasn't part of the nature preserve farther east that usually got inundated with hikers from all over the county every weekend. She had no idea who this part belonged to, if anyone. Maybe the government.

She paused her biking to listen and look. Thick trees surrounded her, so there wasn't much to see, except a strip of hazy sky above her, along the path the trail cut through the woods. A few birds twittered here and there. At least they hadn't all died in the firestorm.

But no other sound.

When she was about to start pedaling again, she heard a shriek...was that laughter or screaming?

Her heart began to pound, realizing how vulnerable she was here. What if there was a psycho killer in these woods? A serial killer that was taking these teenage girls and vanishing them into thin air...but what was he really doing to them? It would be horrible—grisly bloody torture, rape and all kinds of other things she didn't want to imagine. She about whipped the bike around and booked it out of there.

But what if someone needed help? One of those girls?

She listened again, trying to block out her pounding heart. "Hello?" she shouted. Weak. She tried again and put some oomph into it. *"Hello!"* This time her voice was almost as loud as her mom's. Not quite. If only she could do the whistle with two pinkies in her mouth like her mom, too.

Silence. Even the birdsong stopped.

She would've even welcomed Jeremy's mom right now, stumbling down the trail in her heels and Chanel.

"Well, here goes everything," she whispered, and started pedaling again, listening like a bat with sonar ears.

"Hahahahahhahahahhahahahah!" A crazy jackal laugh came from the other side of the trail.

"Shit!" She ground to a halt, twisted around, and said, "Who's there?"

Nothing.

Then, a flash of red in her peripheral vision. She whipped the other way, trying to see what it was. A part of the bushy undergrowth was waving like something had just run under there.

"That's it!" she yelled, throwing down her bike and crashing into the undergrowth. "You wanna scare me? Do it to my face!"

Then she heard other voices in the distance. Hoofbeats. Behind her. Thank god.

"Mom!" she called at the top of her voice.

And once again, her mother came to her rescue on thundering hoofbeats.

* * *

WHEN DEIRDRE HEARD HER DAUGHTER yelling for her, she kicked Scarlet into a canter, swerving her around the other horses to get in front, racing to where she heard her daughter's voice.

But Rebecca was okay. Thank God.

She was standing on the trail, her bike off to the side, visibly trembling. But in one piece.

"There was someone here. Somebody was laughing at me," Rebecca said, and explained what she had seen and heard.

Deirdre decided instantly to leave the rest of the day's searching to the other women, and take Rebecca back to Mrs. Fey's to wait for them.

To her surprise, Rebecca didn't protest. She rode her bike behind Scarlet as they returned to Mrs. Fey's. Deirdre checked behind her often, making eye contact with her shaken daughter.

She was sorry to miss the search, but they couldn't really do the typical grid search anyway. Fairy Glen was so three-dimensional that even though it covered a handful of square miles, the actual surface area when you accounted for the steep terrain was much more than that. Some areas were completely impassable, they were so vertical and brush-choked. Part of that heavy brush had burned away, but a lot of it hadn't. So the search was limited to trails, and even though she hated to admit even a whiff of defeat, it felt almost hopeless.

But her daughter was more important to her. She would take no chances with Rebecca.

Inside the little cottage, Deirdre could see that Rebecca was intrigued by the dark, old world, hobbit-esque look of the place, although she tried to hide it as she took a seat in a rocking chair in the corner of the living room, wrapping her arms around herself.

"Dear, let me make you some tea," Mrs. Fey said to Rebecca. "You've had quite a shock, it looks like." She wrapped an afghan around Rebecca's shoulders before going into the large, bright kitchen at the back of the house.

Peter, Mrs. Fey's towheaded little grandson, came in from the garden, and she introduced him to Rebecca. He started chattering to her.

Deirdre followed Mrs. Fey into the kitchen. Now that Rebecca was safe, she wanted to know what had happened to her old mare.

"Kathleen, where is Ginny?"

"I don't know love. I'm sorry...I was out that morning. Looking for my cat."

After scanning the living room for the cat, Deirdre said, "You found her right?"

"I haven't seen her since the day after Halloween."

"Cotchee? Cotchee is missing?" Deirdre said. "Black cats should never be let out on Halloween night."

"I know that," Mrs. Fey said.

Deirdre said, "Do you think someone took her?"

"More like some*thing* took her." It was Rebecca, speaking from the corner of the living room. She was itching her arms, which were starting to break out in welts.

Peter's green eyes went wide as he turned to look at Grandma Fey to see if that was true.

"No," Mrs. Fey said firmly. "Nobody and nothing took her. She has a mind of her own. But she'll come back."

Mrs. Fey obviously didn't want to talk about it, especially with Peter around. It was too upsetting for a young child, to lose a pet. Maybe she'd found...parts of the cat.

When Peter wasn't looking, Deirdre looked straight at Rebecca and made a zipping motion across her mouth. Rebecca looked at the floor. She knew she shouldn't have said that.

Mrs. Fey took Rebecca's tea out to the living room when it was ready. Rebecca took a tentative sip, and the color started to return to her face, as Peter babbled happily away to her about something he and Clara had done at school, a book they'd found in the library.

Mrs. Fey gestured for Deirdre to sit at the kitchen table. She poured two cups of tea.

"Now, tell me about these missing girls." She looked at Deirdre intently, and Deirdre told her the details.

* * *

LEXI HAD LED ANGELA INTO a strange world.

Under the hazy yellow sky, there was a salmon colored meadow, with partly burned bushes, rocks all covered in pink, and black crunchy dirt underfoot.

But Angela couldn't keep up with Lexi, who kept scampering ahead, turning back, and giving her meaningful looks. But she didn't speak again.

Things shifted, stretched, pulled.

Among the pink, a white unicorn had appeared, then ran away in a spray of rainbows. The sky fell apart, and she spun in circles until she fell down laughing.

I'm the Gray Girl...in a pink world.

And then, everything melted away.

When she woke up hours later, she was sunburned, and realized it wasn't a magical candy land.

This was where the airplanes had dropped that pink stuff, and it was still stuck on everything. There hadn't been any rain yet, and all these plants that were saved from the fire still looked pathetic, like they would die.

They probably would die, suffocated by all that pink.

She got up and tried to follow the path of the creek as best she could. As she walked, the creek widened out, into a shallow pool.

Now it was getting dark, and Angela was exhausted. Maybe she could find a soft, safe place to lie down.

Like...there.

There was an ancient, dead oak. Its bare, gnarled limbs were twisted into infinitely branching shapes. Holes and knots in the trunk looked like mouths and eyes in a spooky cartoon tree.

It hadn't burned—it was dead long before the fire. The tree had grown, branched out, and died, but it still stood. Trees were amazing that way. What if people did that? They die but they're still just standing there? She shivered, imagining it.

At the base of the tree was a little hollow, the roots circling like a mother's arms, where she could lie, with broad, green leaves from a running vine as her mattress.

In among the green leaves were small orange orbs. Pumpkins.

That made her smile. She moved one or two pumpkins out of the way and lay down in the leaves, and curled into a ball, hugging her legs to her. Her eyes closed. The sound of slow moving water lulled her, and she fell asleep.

Soon she heard her mother speaking.

"We have to take a little trip honey. Get dressed, right now."

"No, I wanna wear this!" She loved her Halloween costume.

"Okay," her mother sighed, then smiled at her.

They got into the little car.

Angela brought Simba. She brought him everywhere.

They went through the dark night, fingers of trees overhead like a tunnel.

After a bunch of curves rocked her back and forth, Angela started to fall asleep.

But then she woke up with a start. "Where did they take daddy?"

"To jail honey." Her mother was a dark shape, a disembodied voice.

"What does that mean?"

"It means he did something bad, and he has to spend time there. Where is it...where is it..."

She was looking for something. The blinker went on, then the car slowed, and turned.

It was very dark outside, but her mom turned off the headlights, so even the inside of the car was dark.

The engine got louder, and the car hit some bumps and dips.

At last the car stopped and her mom got out. She opened the trunk and then slammed it again. Angela looked out the window but couldn't get out of the car seat.

A light bobbed, getting farther away. Then, her mom set the light down and Angela could see her. She was hunched on the ground, bending over like she was praying, pulling away at something with her hands.

Angela clutched Simba in the dark. She stuck her thumb inside the little hole in his chest. Sometimes she hid things in there, but this time, it was empty. No candy. No toy.

The door opened, letting in the cold night air. Her mother got back in the car, and they turned around and went home.

She was lulled by the branches overhead, and she looked out the window through sleepy eyes.

The lions and tigers of the forest were burning bright. They ran alongside the car with her. All of the animals were there—the monkeys hurling themselves from branch to branch, gazelles springing in rhythm, wildebeests in a lumbering gallop. They were all wearing tuxedos and tiaras.

Little Angela fell asleep, sucking her thumb.

* * *

DEIRDRE WENT TO BONNIE'S HOUSE for their Sunday wine night.

They were in the kitchen waiting for Lina and Sally to show up.

"I feel like a failure," Deirdre said, taking a sip of her chardonnay. She was purposely steering clear of the red wine, she was too prone to tears already.

"Honey, none of this is your fault," Bonnie said, sweeping her silver and blond waves away from her face before giving one last concentrated effort to open the inner bag of a box of crackers.

"No, I'm not talking about Angela," Deirdre said. "Or any of the other missing girls. I'm talking about Ginny. Where is she? Mrs. Fey wouldn't lie about her being there. But there's something she's not telling me, I can feel it."

The bag of crackers exploded, sending multi-grain crisps into the air, clattering down on the kitchen island. "Son of a—" Bonnie said, and blew a wave off her forehead with a puff of air.

Lina walked in, all dressed in black head to toe, with red lipstick and her new shiny black bob. She looked less like Cowgirl Lina and more like Natasha the Spy every day. Maybe a reflection of her marital woes.

"Hi Lina," they said.

"Good evening." Lina's Bosnian accent made her sound like Natasha too. Or Bela Lugosi.

"We're talking about Ginny," Bonnie said, and turned back to Deirdre.

"Didn't Vivian say she saw her in the pasture too?" Bonnie looked at the pile of crackers, shrugged, then swept them off the counter onto a plate. "What now? Oh, cheese." She stuck her head in the fridge and pulled a couple of rounds and wedges out.

Lina popped a cracker into her mouth and chewed. "Vivian drinks like a fish. She probably left the gate open."

Deirdre and Bonnie looked at each other. "You think?" Deirdre asked.

Bonnie said, "It's a plausible explanation. Leave it to the scientist here." Bonnie winked at Lina and handed her a glass of wine, then added the cheese to the platter. "If Ginny is out there, she'll come back."

"Who else we waiting for?" Lina swiveled on her bar stool to look outside as she chomped another cracker.

Deirdre tuned out her friends' voices as she wondered if Lina's theory was right. Vivian could've been careless and left the pasture gate open.

Especially if she'd been with government agents late into the night, like Rebecca had told her.

Sally walked in. She took a big huff, and planted her fringed leather purse on the counter before mounting the bar stool like a horse, except sidesaddle because she was in a skirt. She was too short to just sit on it.

"Wow, you look nice," Bonnie said. "Going out with Tom later?"

As Bonnie and Sally started talking, Deirdre turned to Lina. "Do you really think that? About Vivian and the gate?"

"Probably," Lina said, with an apathetic shrug.

"That doesn't explain where Mrs. Fey was that morning though...she wasn't there either."

"What. Is she not allowed to leave her house?" Lina asked.

"She doesn't have a car!"

"Maybe she was walking the kid to the school bus. Her little, what is he...? Grandchild?"

"Peter. Yes, you're right. It *was* the first day back." Deirdre blew out a breath. "You're so logical. Well, I guess we'll just be on the lookout for Ginny, in addition to the missing girls." She put her chin in her hand.

If Ginny was out gallivanting, the same word that Lexi's dad had used, she knew the way home. It was only a matter of time.

Speaking of gallivanting..."Mrs. Fey's cat is missing too," she said.

Lina said, "Have you read all the Fairy Faxes about the missing cats and dogs? Just in the last week?"

"And it was a black cat right?" Bonnie asked.

Sally said, "If you let your cat outdoors here, you're just asking for it to become a coyote's dinner."

But, Deirdre thought, *Cotchee*? That cat was almost as big as a coyote herself.

"Besides, it was Halloween!" Sally said. "Sickos take them and do things to them."

"I hope not." Bonnie said. "Come on, let's go into the living room."

While Bonnie and Sally were shuttling the appetizers into the other room, Deirdre turned to Lina. "How's it going with Mike?"

"We're...talking." Lina said. Did that mean they were *talking,* like about their relationship, how they could improve it, what happened to it? Or just that they were on speaking terms?

Lina was intensely private, and she was in a lot of emotional pain, so Deirdre didn't push. She held out a hand to Lina and Lina took it, and smiled at her, a genuine smile. There were tears in her eyes.

Sally came scooting back into the kitchen, clicking on her heels. "Lina, you haven't been riding, you need to get those horses out soon." She opened the fridge and rustled around.

Lina made a noncommittal sound.

"They'll just get barn sour," Sally warned in an echoey voice from inside the fridge. She turned around and cocked a hip. "Playing nice little wifey at home won't get your man back. Believe me, I know."

"Hmmphhh," Lina said, and went into the living room. Deirdre followed.

"So what's the plan?" Sally asked, coming back with a teeny tiny splash of white wine in her glass. Saving herself for dinner with Tom.

Deirdre said, "Let's keep searching. It's the least we can do, it's right in our own back yard. Those dogs smelled Angela at the dam, and it was recent. And, it seemed like they picked up something at Paraiso. I have no idea why Angela or Lexi would be in Fairy Glen, but if we keep searching, maybe we'll see something, or find something. It can't hurt."

"Unless you tamper with evidence," Sally said.

"I hope you're not implying that we're looking for more bodies. I'm looking for live girls!" Deirdre protested.

"Sorry, I guess Tom is rubbing off on me," Sally replied. There was apology in her voice, but also a bit of smugness. Lina very audibly cleared her throat. Or hawked up a loogie.

Deirdre was dying to ask Sally if she knew where Tom had gone on Halloween night, but something stopped her. Something to do with Vivian. She sensed something between Tom and Vivian. Now that she knew they'd been together that night, it made sense why Vivian and he were acting strangely the next day, after the gals had just happened to stumble across a dead, burned body.

Boy, you'd think the chances of Sally being there to find a dead body two months in a row were just too low.

All this tragedy in Fairy Glen was frazzling Deirdre's nerves. A piercing headache suddenly jammed through her eyeballs like a knitting needle. "I need to lie down. I'm going home guys. Good night."

She walked home in the dark. Back at the house, before she went inside, she visited the stalls, which they'd have to start tearing down next weekend, just to move them ten feet over the property line and rebuild them again.

Scarlet stuck her head out the stall door and looked at her.

"Where did you guys go that day?" she said, putting a hand on Scarlet's velvet nose. "And where is Ginny?" she whispered, tears choking her.

The guilt she felt for the old lost mare was hard to swallow. How she could've left her to be consumed by flames, she didn't know. Sure, Mrs. Fey said she was certain she'd been there with the rest, but did she really trust the old lady's grasp on reality?

Through her tears she said to herself, "Don't think about it. You got Rebecca back."

Yes. That was the important part.

And now she needed to help Cassie get Angela back.

* * *

THE SCREAM OF AN ANIMAL woke Angela up, her heart beating, her breath coming hard.

She couldn't see anything, it was pitch black. She listened and listened.

What kinds of animals...what kinds of animals stalk the woods at night?

No, she wouldn't let herself think about that. This was the middle of Southern California, she was not prey.

Except to her father.

She kept listening for his footfalls, following her. Stalking her. Twigs cracking.

Her eyes couldn't stretch any wider. Everything was crackly; her skin, her clothes, her hair, her eyes. She couldn't tell if she was the one making noise, or something else.

If she got up, she might reveal herself. She stayed on alert, not sure if she was hallucinating the sounds she heard.

No—she heard something, something real.

Pulse pounding in her neck, she stopped breathing to listen.

Another crack, and then the sound of something sliding through the bushes across the creek from her.

Ears straining, she heard the rhythmic in and out...breathing. Close, it was so close. She listened through the darkness.

Something big.

Something not human.

Monday, November 5

LONG PAST THE MIDNIGHT HOUR, deep in the forest, in the uncharted parts where natural spring waters swirled, fairy ferns grew high and verdant, and wildfire never touched, the old woman finally spotted her prey.

Ahead, in a small clearing ringed by sycamores, next to a bubbling brook with mossy banks, where starlight glimmered off the curled fronds of the giant ferns, Ginny, the white mare, glowed in the ghostly light.

Mrs. Fey stopped outside the clearing to catch her breath, then stepped toward her, extending a hand, revealing a fat, freshly pulled carrot from her garden.

Ginny looked at her slyly. Once she'd assessed that Mrs. Fey didn't carry a halter, or rope, or anything of that nature tucked behind her, Ginny took a step towards her and nuzzled the feathery carrot top. But she didn't eat.

"Why don'tcha come home love," Mrs. Fey said with a sad lilt. "Give the lass a chance to see you once more."

Ginny's eyes reflected like the moon, a blue orb encircling her rectangular pupil. She blinked once, and turned to go deeper under the giant ferns. Slow enough that Kathleen could follow if she wished.

"Damn," she said, but pulled up her heavy skirts and trudged into the undergrowth after her. "Will ya not come home?"

Ginny turned to face her.

No. I want to live free. Get to run again. I never get to run. I want to live free before I die.

"Can't fault you for feelin' that way," Kathleen said.

Ginny blinked. *Why aren't you riding?*

"Well, that's a long story, but, let's just say I'm having transportation issues at the moment."

I have something to show you. Someone who needs help. Try to keep up.

Then she turned, bolted, and vanished completely into the dark trees.

Mrs. Fey sighed, shook her head, and hitched up her skirts again.

As dawn lightened the sky, she followed Ginny into the woods.

* * *

TINKLING BELLS RECEDED INTO THE forest. The sound sent fingers of alarm into Angela's slumber, pulling her awake.

She shot her eyes open.

It was daylight, but high clouds covered the sun.

She must've fallen back to sleep at some point last night, despite her terror.

Disoriented and groggy, she scrunched up her eyes and opened them again.

In front of her sat a bundle, wrapped in a rough cloth dish towel. She rose on her elbows, eyeing it. Who'd been here, while she slept? She looked around, scanning the trees.

She didn't see any movement, or hear anything other than the occasional caw of a raven, the closer tittering and whistling of songbirds.

Had that creature in the dark been just a nightmare?

Curiosity got the better of her. Inside the bundle was a hunk of yellow cheese, and a half loaf of crusty brown bread. She bit off a hunk of bread, shoved some cheese in her mouth.

Also, there was a green glass bottle with an old fashioned stopper top. She popped it open and sniffed it tentatively while she chewed. It smelled like apple juice, and she took a deep swig.

It felt like it entered her veins, branching out and bringing her muscles and sinews back to life. She ate and drank, not caring who watched her, who had left this here for her. This was the best food she'd ever tasted. She ate it all.

After all this time not eating, the food filled her belly, weighing her down. She lay back down to rest, her hands laced across her tummy, eyes closed against the ashy grit that filtered through her eyelashes.

A voice. "You know, bread and cheese make you fat."

She opened her eyes. Lexi was sitting on a tree branch, high above her. "Lexi!"

Lexi did a flip, and was now hanging upside down from the branch. Her dark hair descended toward Angela in spirals.

"What happened to you?" Angela said, but Lexi seemed annoyed now and didn't answer for a while. Was she mad?

"I could ask you the same question," Lexi finally said. "You stood me up on Halloween." She *was* mad. She'd been so upbeat when Angela first found her, but Lexi's moods were fickle, shifting like the colors of an opal.

"I'm sorry," Angela said. "So you decided to ditch me to get me back, is that it?"

Lexi, still hanging above her, took something out of her pocket. Glitter, gold glitter, fell over Angela.

"God you're such a diva Lex," she said. "Are you trying to hypnotize me again?"

She remembered how Lexi had gotten an old pocket watch of her grandfather's. "What if you're some princess, with a giant estate waiting for you to claim it?" Lexi had said. "We have to find out." So, on one of the last summer afternoons before school started, in Angela's room, she made her lie on the bed, while the watch swung back and forth like a pendulum.

Angela had drifted into a very relaxed state, riding on the currents of Lexi's voice, suggesting she slip deeper into her subconscious. "Remember your faaa-ther," she'd breathed, and Angela had woken up then, laughing, because it sound like Darth Vader.

But now, as Lexi swung on the branch above her, Angela remembered that pocket watch, swinging, swinging, back and forth, as the gold glitter fell over her, bright reflective spots, dazzling her...

Bright gold, glittering in her hands...

Angela was counting. Counting gold pieces.

In the kitchen, her mom was making her favorite, pumpkin pie.

She lay back against the brown corduroy, watching her stir the ingredients, moving busily back and forth, talking on the phone that she held against her shoulder, dusting the small kitchen with cinnamon and nutmeg. Soon the air would smell warm and spicy.

She went back to counting her chocolate gold coins, Snickers and Krackles and Butterfingers, Smarties, Skittles and Starburst, pairing the good ones with the lesser ones. Two pieces a day. How long would that last? Time was a huge stretching thing. Getting to Christmas took for-ever.

The front door opened and in a burst of chilly air, a man dressed like a robber rushed in. "Get off the phone Cheryl! Hi sweetie," he said, and holding a pillowcase full of his own Halloween loot, rushed through the living room.

Her mom whirled around, and set down the bowl. "Daddy's back from trick or treat!" Angela squealed, and got up to follow him down the dark hallway.

"Daddy," she called out, running farther down the hallway.

Finally she got to the door. "Daddy?" she said as she pushed the door open to her parents' room.

But the room was not her parents' bedroom. A huge pile of gold almost touched the ceiling. She took a step forward.

But there was nothing, no floor to catch her.

She fell, tumbling and spinning, down into nothingness.

* * *

BY MONDAY, THE VOLUNTEER SEARCH parties from the weekend were gone —people had to go back to work after all. Gorda's had a few lunch patrons and that was it. The bar area was empty except for Deirdre, Vivian, and Gorda herself.

Deirdre was keeping an eye on the information table about the missing girls while also acting as hostess, since Gorda was short-staffed. Sally had to work, but she'd promised to come by when she got off, as long as Deirdre promised to pick up her daughter from school that afternoon.

Cassie was at home, with Gina and the rest of the Marconis.

Hope was hard to come by as the days wore on. So far the tips on the tip line had been mostly crackpots, news junkies, and psychics.

Outside, under an overcast sky, still yellowish from the fires, the sheriff's department boats were searching the lake.

The sad truth was that people lost interest as the trail grew colder and chances of finding a kid alive grew smaller. The only ones left after days, weeks, months, and years in some cases, were the parents—waiting, hoping, and grieving all at the same time. It sounded like hell, or actually purgatory. Deirdre thought she could deal with hell, she liked excitement. But purgatory involved waiting, which was the worst possible thing she could imagine.

Something had to happen, and soon.

The bell over the front door tinkled, and she turned to greet the customer. But it was Cass.

"Can we just sit for a bit?" Cass said, and Deirdre took her to a booth where they both sat down. She could keep an eye on the front from here.

"How are you?" Deirdre asked her.

Cass looked pale, and took a few breaths before answering. "We had to call our dentists today."

"Why?"

"To get X-rays. To give to the coroner's office."

In case the dead body was Angela or Lexi. The thought was like a kick in the stomach.

"I had to get out of that house," Cass said. "Let me buy you lunch?"

Over tacos, Cass told her what was going on. She had her hands full with the family staying with her, and she needed an outlet, someone outside to confide in.

When Deirdre gently pressed her about why she'd never met Lexi's parents before now, she scoffed and said, "Oh, I've spoken to them, on the phone. But I'm always at work, I don't have time to socialize with the PTA."

Cass must be paying an arm and a leg for her mortgage. And nursing paid well, but the hours were long and stressful. You had to hustle, and that's what Cass did.

"Besides," Cass said, "Lexi is trouble. I hate to say that, but she's too mature for her age. She calls me by my first name, like we're friends or something. Angela is totally in awe of her. I try to get her to be more assertive, but she's still like this shrinking violet."

Deirdre could see that bothered her. Cass was a boss, plain and simple. She took the bull by the horns, took the world by storm. She ate lunch like she was in basic training. Her two tacos were already gone.

The bell on the front door tinkled again, and Deirdre hustled over to greet the customer, a young man with black hair in a sort of pompadour.

"One for lunch?" she asked, pulling out a menu.

"No." He took off his sunglasses. His eyes were a yellowish green, like grass on the verge of becoming hay, under straw-colored eyebrows. He held out a folded newspaper. "I want to apply for this job."

There were a few circled ads on the classified page. Deirdre noticed him looking at the missing flyers, and handed him one before she directed him to talk to Gorda at the bar.

Cass was at the door now too. "I have to go. Thanks for listening." Deirdre squeezed her hand.

Deirdre sat back down at the information table.

Vivian came and sat beside her. "Who is that?" she asked, about the guy that had come in.

"Some guy looking for work."

Vivian turned to check him out. Gorda took out an application and gave it to him, and he sat at the end of the bar, swinging aside a wallet chain attached to his studded belt. He started to fill in the application, a crease forming between his eyebrows.

"Vivian, why are you here?"

Vivian smiled. "Well, you can't blame me. The scenery is pretty nice." She waved her arm towards the guy at the bar.

Deirdre turned back to the table, hoping for a miracle. Nobody else came in until happy hour.

* * *

WHEN ANGELA WOKE AGAIN, IT was late afternoon.

She'd had a crazy dream, where Lexi hypnotized her. The food had definitely been real though, not a dream, and she still felt the nourishment coursing through her, felt the fullness in her belly. But the towel and the bottle were gone.

Lexi playing tricks again.

She turned over, moving her stiff arms and legs. Something crackled beneath her. She reached under her to pull it out, and in her hands were the crushed pieces of a decaying plastic jack-o'-lantern. How funny. A fake pumpkin next to some real pumpkins.

What had she dreamed? Something about an inheritance. A hoard of treasure.

That was the same thing her dad had told her, the same reason he wanted to find her. If only she could remember.

She stood up from the pumpkin patch on aching legs and moved again.

Her boots were giving her blisters, but she couldn't take them off. The ground was too rocky. Her sleeves had torn and were covered in gray. Her hair felt like burnt straw.

But she kept going. From what everyone had said, the little snatches of conversations she heard from the older kids after their weekend parties, the asylum was next to a creek, not like the rushing creek she walked along now, but near a wide spot where the water swirled and pooled. She'd heard talk of tire swings, people jumping off them into the water.

She came to a place where squares of concrete lay in the grass, then a decaying cement bridge, with rebar sticking out, crossed over the creek.

On the other side, she had to climb over tree roots and boulders. There was no path, so she had to make her own way, feeling like she was Rambo in the jungle. She kept heading up the creek.

It was already getting dark again.

How on earth did Lexi think they were going to get to the asylum and back in one night? She'd been walking for days now. Although, she was completely lost, she admitted it. Lexi wouldn't have gotten lost, that was the difference. Probably when you go straight there it doesn't take any time at all.

Where could she spend the night? She needed someplace protected. She didn't want to have to lie awake all night listening for—whatever. She pushed aside a crackling bush that disintegrated as she walked through it.

Finally, she came to a huge pool. Across the water was a dilapidated barn. Her heart sank. That definitely wasn't the asylum. It was the old dairy.

Surprisingly, she wasn't thirsty. The water looked so clean though, reflecting the sky above but showing the boulders under the surface. Trees, marvelously green trees, bent over the water on all sides. She wanted to dive in. And if she swam across, maybe she could shelter overnight in the barn, get an early start in daylight.

She stepped into the amazingly cold, wet water. Ash flowed away from her. She dunked her head, then again and again, washing her face, running her hands through her hair, blowing her nose.

There was a crack behind her. Breathing sounds, heavy snuffling.

She crouched, flattening herself against the bank.

Out of the bushes pushed a shiny black nose, like wet leather...the nostrils flared. Snorting out. A bellowing, like a cow, lowing.

A sound tore through the air. Something bestial, low and throaty, like thunder. Then a sharp ripping sound, like a woman's scream.

She stopped breathing. So did the cow in the bushes.

Then, Angela went deeper into the water, moving quicker than she thought she could. She waded across to get to the other side, to the abandoned dairy, where she could spend the night in safety.

Dark was coming fast. And there were big cats roaming.

Tuesday, November 6

AFTER SHE GOT OFF WORK at noon, Sally went to Gorda's to help out. The place had become the de facto headquarters in the search for the missing.

Nothing was happening though. Everyone that came in was oblivious, only looking for their next taco. She shoved flyers into their hands anyway.

Outside, she saw Tom's unmarked Crown Vic pull into the parking lot. She walked out to greet him.

He was talking on his phone, saying, "We got Lexi Marconi's cell records unlocked. I'm going to the address of the last call she made. Okay. Let me know how it goes with Sam's parents. Bye." He hung up and turned to Sally. "Sorry. I just came here to tell you I can't have lunch. Just got a lead." He put an awkward hand on her shoulder, smiled, and started to get back into the car.

"I'll come with you," Sally said. He said nothing, and he made no move to stop her. As she ran around and got in the passenger seat, a reporter was setting up for a live shot. The light on top of the camera turned red.

"Four missing girls, and one burned body. We're live at Lake Hemingway with the latest."

"So, what is this about?" Sally asked as they drove.

"I'm leading the homicide investigation."

"Homicide?" Sally said. "You're sure?"

"Yep." Tom nodded sadly. "Just got the test results. She, and it is a she"—Sally already knew this, since she'd seen the body—"didn't burn in the wildfire. The lab found traces of an accelerant. So, most likely, someone murdered her, and they burned the body. Probably to make it look like she died in the wildfires last week."

Oh no. Sally thought of her daughter Emily, who was safely in class at Stanton Academy, right this minute. "Who would want to murder a little girl like Samantha?" she said.

"It's not Samantha." Tom looked at her. "They eliminated her as a possibility."

She was silent as she slowly came to the conclusion that the body being burned meant...it could be someone who'd been alive and well after the fires came through. Maybe one of the other two missing girls, Angela or Lexi.

Tom echoed what she'd just thought. "We're pretty sure one of those other missing girls is our victim."

"Do Samantha's parents know? They must be relieved."

Tom just nodded. "My partner went to their place this morning to let them know. But, that means their daughter is still missing, so it's not all good news." Tom paused. "Encantadino PD is working with us now. Even though Lexi lives in their jurisdiction, the body was found in my jurisdiction. This is my investigation now." He tapped the papers on the seat next to him, keeping his eyes on the road, as they followed the street that ran around the lake.

She pulled the phone record printouts out of his folio as they drove, and he didn't stop her from looking. The call was made at 6:35 pm, 10/31/07. It had been just under two minutes. What could be said in that amount of time?

The address was a double-wide mobile home in the most downtrodden part of Del Diablo. They parked under a pepper tree, out of the blazing midday sun.

"Wait here," he said, unbuckling his seatbelt.

"Hi, I'm Detective Goodwin," she heard Tom say, when the door opened a small crack.

Sally looked around. In neighboring yards, cars on blocks, trash, broken plastic toy cars and Barbie dream houses. In this yard, there were a few items. A hospital commode sat leaning against the rotting wood of the carport.

Tom was inside now. She couldn't just sit here, it was ridiculous. She got out to stretch her legs. Suddenly, she saw eyes. A woman's eyes. An old lady in a wheelchair was sitting in the deep shade of the front porch overhang. Staring out at the dried-up lake.

Sally walked toward her. The woman just kept staring into the distance, deep in the chasms of dementia, Sally could tell from here.

Still, sometimes they saw, and remembered. It was worth a shot.

"Hi," she said softly. She heard two male voices inside.

She pulled Angela's missing flyer from her back pocket, unfolded it, and placed it in the lady's hands. "Does she look familiar?" The lady didn't look down, so Sally took the flyer and held it in front of her. No reaction. Sally pulled out Lexi's flyer. "How about her?" No reaction.

But then, her eyes flew open, she started to cry, and her wails reached a high pitch. Sally, for once, didn't know what to do.

The man flung open the front door. Sally had already folded and slid the flyers into her pocket again. Tom looked out, gave her an exasperated look like *I told you to stay in the car*. He came outside on the porch. "This is Sally. She's one of the volunteer searchers."

The man, his early balding head covered in a comb over, his belly straining against his dingy white t shirt, came out. "Grandma, it's okay. It's almost time for your tea." He said it with such tenderness. "Here, we can sit out here and talk," he said to Tom.

Tom perched on the edge of an Adirondack chair of questionable integrity.

Sally remained standing, in the yard. John sat next to his grandmother, holding her hand in his.

"Could you bring some flyers Sally?" Tom said. Was he really ordering her around like some kind of assistant?

She walked back to the car, her face flaming, and retrieved two unfolded flyers of the two girls.

When she got back, Tom was saying, "...so, some kind of wrong number. Maybe she was trying to call someone else in the neighborhood." He sat back in the chair, putting a lot of faith in the old split wood, and looked out at the lake. "Two minutes is a long wrong number though."

The man said, "Yeah, if there was a phone call--"

"Oh, there was a phone call," Sally interrupted. Tom shot her a look.

The man continued, "Yeah, like I was saying, maybe my grandmother picked it up and didn't know what to do. Forgot to hang up. She's done it before."

Tom said, "Yes. And if Lexi was trying to call someone else, she would've immediately hung up and dialed the correct number, not waited for your grandmother to hang up." He said it almost to himself. It wasn't quite a question, and it didn't reveal whether that's what Lexi had done or not. "Okay," Tom slapped his knees and stood up. "Thank you for your time."

The old woman started to wail again, then she yelled at the top of her lungs, "There was a fire! A fire!"

"Yes, Grandma, there was a fire, and we're fine now," John patted her hand and glanced accusingly at Tom.

When they got back in the car, Tom turned to Sally. "You know," he said, "I'm going to have to deputize you if you don't stop interfering in this investigation. There's a science to these things. You don't want to scare the suspect, or even let him know he *is* a suspect."

He was chiding her, like a little girl, and it chapped her hide. "I'll have you know I'm a student of criminal law."

Tom laughed, and she melted a little bit inside. He had the greatest laugh, the handsomest face, the sexiest voice as he said, "Law and human nature are two very different animals."

She sat back in the seat and folded her arms.

His phone rang. He said a few words, then hung up and turned the car back toward Gorda's, his mouth a hard line.

"What was that?" Sally asked.

He turned and put a hand on hers. "Sorry, I can't tell you. Not until we release a statement."

He pulled into Gorda's and parked. She knew he was right, but she was still peeved by the brush off. Not to mention, he'd done the same thing to her Halloween night. She was thinking of an appropriately icy goodbye, but then someone banged on the window and she jumped.

Tom rolled it down. It was his partner.

Scott said, "Come on. Before you go notify, the boats pulled something up. Let's take a look."

Tom gave him an awkward look, and Scott leaned down, saw that she was in the car, and said, "Oh, sorry Sally. I didn't see you there."

She just waved.

Tom unbuckled his seatbelt and got out without saying a word to her.

Sally got out of the car. From the steps of Gorda's restaurant, she had a clear view as the two men strode down to the boat ramp, where a small rubber dinghy with an outboard motor came buzzing into shore.

The techs were already there, in their dark blue pants and t-shirts. They crouched around a black gym bag. One of them had unzipped it, and with a purple gloved hand, pulled out something long and red.

Sally gasped, thinking it was internal organs or something, until she got herself under control and really looked, saw what it was.

The tech kept pulling, and she was reminded of magicians or clowns pulling never-ending scarves out of various orifices, as the black bag disgorged an almost endless length of soggy red fabric.

* * *

Rebecca's Tuesday shift at WokChikaBok!Bok! started at 4pm.

"Rebecca!" Mr. Fariz called. He was sitting in the dining room. No other customers were there, except the woman he was chatting with. He was in jolly spirits and waved her over.

"Rebecca, come and meet our new favorite customer." He laughed, his round face reflecting joyfully as she approached.

As soon as the woman turned around, Rebecca froze.

"You must not work Sunday or Monday right?" the woman said through a mouthful of whatever she was eating, pointing at her with her fork.

"Uh, Mr. Fariz, I have to start my shift—"

"Oh Rebecca, have a well deserved rest. You're the best employee I have, oh, besides Darius of course." He smiled at Darius behind the counter, who looked bored and unamused. "I'll cover the register, so our best employee, and our...only customer, can relax." To Rebecca, he whispered, "Hey, she's keeping us in business so far this week." He lifted his eyebrows like, *Let's humor her.*

When he was gone, Rebecca said, "How'd you find me?"

Jeremy's mom said, "Well, you're not that hard to track down. I just had to eat twice my yearly allotment of Chinese food to do it. And I have to say, not bad!" She twirled a dainty forkful of noodles into her mouth.

Rebecca just stood and stared at her until she swallowed and said, "Rebecca. Sit down."

Well, let's just dispense with the formalities, shall we? That suited her fine, she only had seven minutes until her shift started, no matter what Mr. Fariz said. She hastily itched her arm where the poison oak rash was. "How'd you know it was me that day?" she asked. The day she'd ridden by on the bike.

Jeremy's mom knew what she meant. She smiled and looked a little too closely at Rebecca's face. "You look just like your mother," she said, with a tinge of what sounded like affection in her voice.

That one was a surprise. "Don't know how you figure that, but...thanks?"

Awkward silence.

"I'm Laura White."

"I know your name."

Laura's eyebrows raised.

"My mom told me about you," Rebecca mumbled, trying to soften her edge.

Laura put her fork down, covered her plate with a napkin, and said, "Were you and Jeremy...?"

"Uh, no," Rebecca said hurriedly. "No, not really. I mean, I really only knew him for a few weeks."

Laura smiled. "That can be a long time when you're a teenager."

Rebecca didn't say anything. *Did she want details? Hell no.*

Laura said, "Did he ever talk about me?"

"Not much. He said that you love him, and want the best for him, but that you made him get this job to learn responsibility." *Even though he already had a job*, she didn't say out loud. "Look, I don't have a lot of time. What is it you really want to know?"

Laura White didn't answer, so Rebecca continued. "I'm pretty sure it's this: Is he alive, and if so, where is he?"

"Yes, to boil it down. That is what I want to know," Laura said, patting her mouth with the paper napkin.

"You guys kicked him out. I mean, that's what my mom told me. She said that you kicked him out on his birthday." His birthday, when they'd lain on the Paraiso rooftop looking at the stars. Their first time on that roof. The second hadn't ended so well. "So why would you even care where he was?"

"You're judging my worth as a mother? Is that it?" Laura's voice turned steely. "Don't think you can judge me any more harshly than I judge myself, little missy."

Rebecca's eyes widened. She must've looked scared, because Laura's face softened. "Listen. He wasn't even living with us, barely ever came home. Kicking him out was...a formality. And the police won't tell me *anything*—" Her voice broke a little, but she regained control, "—precisely because he's eighteen."

Laura took a moment, then said, "Do you know anything about a mother's love? He's my only child. I need to know that he's safe."

Rebecca sighed. "Okay...I did hear from him afterwards. I know he made it out of the fire, and that's all. I hope that gives you some peace of mind." She scooted to the end of the bench, but Laura shot a hand out, a hand like an iron vice, like a handcuff, encircling her itchy wrist.

"How?"

"How did he make it out of the fire?" She twisted out of Laura's grip. "Hell if I know lady, I barely made it myself—"

"How did you hear from him?"

Oh. She sat back down again, took a deep breath, and started in. There was no reason not to tell the truth. Most of it anyway. "I got a text. It was dated the 28th, but I didn't get it til Halloween. You know, it was delayed, because cell reception was all screwed up from the fires."

Laura stared at her, forcing her to go on.

"It was from his phone number. But he said he was going to ditch that phone, so I shouldn't bother replying. He was with Crystal, so I know they both made it out of the fire. I was just glad to hear from them."

Laura whispered. "Where are they?"

"That's all I know. Promise!" Rebecca crossed her heart. "He didn't say where he was."

Laura sat back and folded her arms, but Rebecca was done.

Jeremy was wanted for a murder he didn't commit, and for the kidnapping of his younger sister Crystal, who more than likely was the one calling the shots. Rebecca didn't want anyone finding him.

There was no way she'd rat him out.

Even if, in that single text, Jeremy *had,* in typical stupid fashion, given away his location.

Because what happens there, stays there.

* * *

ANGELA HAD BEEN WALKING ALL day. The going was slow, with her blistered feet and her empty stomach.

But she kept going. Now it was almost dark, and she was still following the creek.

She had taken a turn up a tributary, through a steep walled canyon, because she remembered the kids talking about the 'Y', the place where this smaller creek joined up with Hidden Creek. You had to go through a big tunnel, but once you did, it looked like a rainforest up in there.

So, she had found the tunnel, and walked through it, and now she was certain she was on the right track.

The fire had come through this part. It was pretty devastated, trees all burned so they looked just like a jumble of burnt matches on a giant scale.

Above the rushing water sounds, and the wind through the blackened the trees, she heard what sounded like a mermaid's singing. But then it was gone again.

She couldn't even be sure what she was hearing anymore.

She kept struggling ahead. Stars were starting to show up now in the early evening sky. And, was that really straight lines, blocky shapes in the darkness?

She came into a clearing. Ahead of her was the asylum. *Yes!*

A two-story stone building with a collapsed roof. Part of the second story walls were gone, but most of the second floor was still intact. Where windows had been were now just holes.

She climbed the steps on the front terrace and stepped carefully through the empty doorway.

The place was big. She walked through, noticing the different rooms.

This one might've been a kitchen, there was a fireplace with a hearth in there.

Next to it, a big long room. Dining hall? She pictured insane people yelling and throwing their food, or orphans begging, "Please sir, can I have some more?" and getting a big ol' slop of porridge or whatever.

That sounded good actually. She was so hungry she could cry.

She kept walking back into the darkness, holding her fear at bay.

Down the hallway, in the back, there was a staircase. So far there was no sign of Lexi.

She looked up the stairwell and saw the night sky. Fluttering shapes flying crazy outside in the blank sky. Bats. The staircase was stone, but she wasn't going up there...well, maybe just up the stone part. She wouldn't trust the wooden floor up there.

She took some tentative steps, then hurried up the last part while there was still light to see by.

The treetops here on this side weren't burned, although the whole canyon reeked of fire. She looked across the bare joists, and saw some rope wrapped around one. It was brand new.

Inside the huge old house, there was a sound. She turned and looked down the stairs.

Adrenaline coursed through her. Was her father here? She sank to her knees.

But then, a small figure darted past the stairwell, long dark hair flowing behind, wearing a long dress, or a robe.

"Lexi!" she shouted. She *was* here!

Angela ran down the stairs, and out the front door. "Lexi! Come back!" her voice echoed into the dark forest.

But she didn't.

Angela wouldn't play that game again. She'd let Lexi have her temper tantrum, or play her prank, or whatever she was doing.

She went inside to find wherever Lexi had been sleeping this whole time, and lie down and put up her aching feet until Lexi decided to come back.

* * *

THAT NIGHT, THE FAIRY GLENNERS gathered at the firehouse for the town council, held on the first Tuesday of every month.

As Deirdre looked around the big meeting room, she counted heads. There were more residents here than usual—even more than last month's meeting, when they'd all come to hear about the car at the bottom of the quarry.

And possibly even more than the emergency town council a few weeks later, where Wilma had prepped them, both practically and psychologically, for fire evacuation.

Now, community spirit was high after surviving a natural disaster together.

But so was the tension.

Deirdre noticed quite a few worried-looking mothers and fathers in the crowd. An epidemic of missing children—in addition to more missing cats, dogs, chickens, and even a goat—had them on edge.

Wilma was at the front podium now, glancing at her watch, and had already silenced everyone in the big echoing room. She started the agenda.

Sally came in late and sat next to Deirdre in the second row. "I have news for you," she whispered.

"What is it?" Deirdre said, a little louder than a whisper.

Wilma stopped talking and glared at them. Even the A students can't get away with talking in class. She continued, "As I was saying. We're still looking for a council members. But we can't hold an election until we get some nominations. Anyone?" There was silence. "Come on, I get tired of leading these meetings all by my lonesome."

Everyone laughed and elbowed their friends, but nobody raised their hand.

"Hey, you're not all alone," Deputy Harvey spoke up. "I do the meetings with you." He sounded a bit hurt to be left out.

"Yes, Deputy Harvey and I get tired of doing these meetings. Okay, no takers this time." Wilma sighed, and with the air of a disappointed schoolteacher, took her time shuffling her papers.

Finally, she started on the main agenda. "First we'll start with the post-burn report. Congratulations on surviving the biggest wildfire complex in the history of California. There were others who were not so lucky, as you all know."

Deirdre thought of the burned little girl. Sally's leg twitched beside hers, and she inhaled audibly.

Wilma pulled the map of Fairy Glen over on its wheeled bulletin board. With her laser pointer, she pointed out the housing developments of San Amaro Hills. "One good thing about having all these tract homes surrounding us—maybe the only good thing—is that the fire didn't come around our north and west. Not enough vegetation to sustain anything serious."

Next she pointed to where the fire had swept around Lake Hemingway, up and over Richardson Peak, and down through the valley where Hidden

Creek and all of its tributaries ran towards the ocean—the wild, chaparral-choked canyons separating Fairy Glen from Rancho Alto and Paraiso. Or what used to be Paraiso.

"We all know the story of some of our residents happening to be up here during the fire," Wilma said in Deirdre's general direction, as she put her red dot directly on the plateau where Paraiso's homesites had been. "And I guess it's no big secret anymore," she looked at Deputy Harvey in the front row with raised eyebrows, and when he didn't object, she went on, "that there was a meth lab right about here." She put a searing red dot on the spot where the construction trailer had stood on a clearing on the steep slope.

"On Wednesday, October 24, as the fire got closer, CalFire's C-130s were strafing the canyons, dumping retardant to create firebreaks. They get a majority of the credit for stopping the fire from crossing Hidden Creek into our side.

"However, there were other factors in play. The canyon where the meth lab was situated is practically inaccessible, as some of you know," Wilma looked right at Deirdre. "It's too deep, too steep, and the smoke was too thick by that point for the pilots to get a good angle of attack. What the investigators have since determined, is that the explosion of the meth lab and the fire it caused, which raced straight up that steep, steep hill to Paraiso, actually created a backburn that stopped the fire from jumping to the next hill, here," she pointed to the tall central hill that Vivian's house was on, "stopped it from coming over that hill and right into our neighborhood. So, the very thing that was threatening our little idyllic enclave—Bartley and his housing development and associated crimes—was in some ways the thing that saved us too. Ironic, huh?"

Everyone shuffled and breathed out, taking in the near miss.

"What will happen to that land?" someone asked, finally.

"Paraiso? Well, right now it's condemned. It's too dangerous, with the burnt structures and the hazard of the meth chemicals, not to mention the instability of those steep hillsides now that all the vegetation is burned. And without a builder around, I don't think we need to worry about that road cutting through, at least not for some time to come."

"I hope not," Deirdre said. She thought of Stephanie, who was the VP of the Bartley Development Corporation. Would she pursue building Paraiso? She had been against her husband's plans, saying they had no money to build—or they shouldn't have had it. It was soon discovered where he'd been getting the money to pay his workers, eking by payroll to payroll.

"Okay, Deputy, it's your turn." Wilma sat down in the front row.

Deputy Harvey got up and took over her place at the podium. He was a young man with an older, paunchier, almost old-fashioned look, his face plain and folded like a basset hound. His voice was deep and rolling and gentle as he spoke.

"Hello folks. As you mostly know, I'm Deputy Charles Harvey, with the San Diego Sheriff's Department."

So, Charles, that was his first name. Deirdre made a mental note of it, and decided to try to say something nice to him tonight, even though he hadn't believed her last month about Bartley being a bad guy.

"I see some new faces here tonight, so I thought I'd introduce myself again. I'm assigned to community outreach in Fairy Glen and Pleasant Hollow. I do these safety reports each month. As you all know, there was a burned body discovered last week, over near the lake."

He held up a stack of flyers. "And there are also several girls, teen girls all around the same age that are missing."

As the deputy listed the names of each girl and where they were last seen, and handed stacks of flyers to everyone assembled, Sally whispered in Deirdre's ear. "I was there today when they pulled something out of the lake. I think it was evidence. And, you didn't hear this from me, but," she looked around, "there was an accelerant on the body. Someone burned her on purpose. It was a murder."

"Oh, that's terrible!" Deirdre said. She passed the stacks of flyers to the next people. She had enough of her own. But wait, where was Lexi's flyer? "Deputy Harvey? Charles?" she raised her hand. "Where are the flyers for Lexi Marconi? I have some in my car if you need extra—"

The look from his hound dog eyes stopped her. A feeling of dread washed over her. She knew what he was going to say next.

"The coroner's office has determined the identity of the dead girl." Deputy Harvey said to the crowd, taking his place back at the podium. "Unfortunately, it was Miss Marconi."

There were gasps all around the room. Deirdre put a hand over her mouth. Sally grabbed her other hand.

Wilma came to the podium. "There will be a vigil for Lexi tomorrow night at sunset, near Gorda's cantina on Lake Hemingway. We can pray that her soul will rest in peace. And we can pray the other girls are still alive."

Wednesday, November 7

ANGELA NEVER FOUND ANY KIND of bed, but she found Lexi's bag, and her cheer sweater. She was wearing it now to fend off the morning chill.

Last night, she decided she felt safer upstairs, sleeping at the top of the stone steps. Which was uncomfortable, and cold, but preferable to the vulnerable feeling of being on the ground. In her dreams, Lexi descended from above, dropping down from the latticework of tree branches overhead, like a spider dropping down by a silken thread.

But once again, she said nothing.

Angela had barely slept. Now, the sky was getting light again. She got up, stretched, and went downstairs and out onto the stone patio in the back yard.

Up against the wall on the side of the house was another hearth, a fireplace for an outdoor kitchen.

Her throat caught. The white shapes of a ribcage protruded up from the hearth.

She stepped forward. The thing was dead. But too big to be human.

This was freshly killed, some kind of deer.

But it didn't look like a human had killed it. The flesh was ripped away.

She walked closer, and saw that it was very large. It was white, and brown, and black, and had straight horns that twisted and spiraled. Weird.

The eyes looked at her blankly, like big black olives. "Poor thing," she said.

There was still meat. One hind leg was still mostly there, and barely attached to the body. She was hungry.

She went into the forest to gather unburned wood, brought it back, started a fire with a lighter she found in Lexi's bag, and cooked up the leg.

It was the best tasting meat she'd ever had.

It didn't occur to her until after she'd eaten, and the synapses were firing in her brain again, that this hadn't been here last night. Whatever had killed it was not long gone, and it might come back for another snack.

She'd better get the hell out of here.

* * *

ONCE THE SUN ROSE ABOVE the hills enough to see by, Angela left the asylum.

Obviously, Lexi wasn't coming back. Maybe she was already back at home, with her parents.

Then she remembered. Lexi didn't have a home anymore.

What was going on with her? Sure, she was a little mischievous, sometimes moody. But the Lexi she knew wouldn't play games like this.

Angela started walking. She still had a home, and that's where she intended to go.

She was no longer afraid of Travis—he could tap into her brain for all she cared. She didn't remember anything. And no matter how much she searched, or how much he threatened, she wasn't going to find it.

Apparently this sneaky little bitch, as he had called her, was so sneaky she even hid things from herself.

Let him come get her. She had nothing to give him.

Up ahead was the old dairy. She could stop by the pool of water to try to wash up a bit. Her hands and face were covered in meat juice and blood, and it was starting to gross her out.

She heard the breathing in the bushes again, and a *moo*, and looked around for the cows.

But instead of cows, a giant head emerged. The head of a—wildebeest? *What the hell?*

She was terrified, trapped in place by fear.

It swung its head towards her. It let out another huge, bellowing *moooo*, and took a step toward her on its cloven hoof. This thing was huge, thousands of pounds. It could trample her, kill her with one swipe of its horned head.

It stepped into the water and started drinking.

"Oh my god," she breathed.

Other animals emerged. She couldn't believe what she was seeing. A type of monkey, long hooked arms fringed with black fur, round brown eyes, circled with white, staring at her.

A gazelle of some sort, no—two of them...

She started trembling, realizing she'd eaten part of their relative.

This was not right. It was like her dream had come to life. The dream within the dream, the exotic animals in formal wear that she had imagined, on that dark drive, with her real mother.

Then she realized—the news report she saw in the cafe in the desert. The zoo animals. This was them.

They weren't wearing tuxedos and tiaras. They were real, breathing animals. Blood thumping in their arteries, just like hers was thumping in her chest, her jugular.

Across the pond, something tawny slinked down towards the shore.

A lion. Or rather, a lioness. There was no mane around her neck. Her shoulder blades slid past each other with each confident step she took towards the water.

Angela froze as the lioness's head swung around, and their eyes met.

The wildebeest froze too.

The lion's mouth was hanging slightly open. It looked around, before plopping down on its belly like a house cat and lapping up water with its huge tongue.

She backed slowly away. The lion followed her with its eyes. She froze again.

All of the animals had stopped to stare at the standoff.

Could she climb a tree? Can lions climb trees? She was pretty sure they could. Where could she hide that the big cat couldn't get her?

Then, there was a high, trembling whinny.

In the shadow of the trees, at the mouth of the creek, an ancient white horse appeared.

The horse whinnied again, directly at her.

"Don't ask me," she said under her breath.

The lion turned to look at the nag.

It whinnied a third time.

"*Shut up,*" Angela told it, but then the horse whirled around and disappeared into the woods.

The lion looked after it with curiosity, and slowly rose from the water and slunk into the trees after the horse.

Angela backed away from the bank of the creek as quietly as she could, letting the other animals drink in their uneasy peace.

She backed away from the water and started walking west, resisting the overwhelming urge to run. She knew she'd eventually get to Fairy Glen Road, maybe some houses first, if she just kept going.

But, then she heard a crack. A jostling of bushes. She froze. Then she ran, as fast as she could.

She just wanted to go home. As bad as she had wanted to remember her real mother, she couldn't. Even after all her searching, she couldn't remember who she was, and she never would.

It didn't matter anyway. She'd had a good life. Cassandra was a good mom. The best mom. If the lion ate her now, she at least knew she'd been loved. Tears streamed down her face.

She veered to the right, pushed through some bushes, and climbed a hill, out of the forest.

At the top of the ridge, she looked down.

There below her was a big compound, full of grass and trees and tropical landscaping, lots of buildings, it looked almost like a school, except there were no kids, just adults. The lawn was full of people dressed in white.

She breathed a sigh of relief. She dropped her backpack and loped down the rocky slope, dodging boulders. She could get to them, she could scream and be heard, someone would come help her.

She rounded a boulder.

Wham!

Something hard hit her across the ankle. There was a sharp pain, and a rattling sound filled her ears, and she knew what had happened.

She hopped back a few steps as the snake squiggled away, looking as surprised as her.

"Aw shit." Now, she was well and truly screwed. She'd never get back home, unless she could get to that big church camp school-looking thing before the snakebite took hold. Do people die from rattlesnake bites? Yes, they do.

Unless they get to a hospital.

She thought of Cassandra, how she'd love to be wheeled into the ER right then, to see her mom. She could see it so clearly, her mom's face above her, feeling for a pulse, barking orders at the doctors.

But she was fantasizing, she needed to get real, and fast.

"Help! Help me!" she screamed, as the burning traveled up her leg and she limped along, her heart speeding up and up and up. "Help!" it turned into a desperate shriek.

The building was so far away, the parking lot and the other buildings looked like dollhouses, and the people, all dressed in white, looked like insects. But it only took one to hear her.

She saw a man turn, as if he heard her, but then he kept walking.

"Help me, up here!" She screamed, but her voice was too weak. He'd moved on and was joining some other people now, then they all went into the big building, totally focused on themselves. Unaware of anything outside of their bubble.

Her hope was draining away. She cried, choked, tried to yell louder, but tripped, and fell, the pain coursing through her like electricity.

She'd never ever felt pain like this. She wondered if this is how much pain her real mother had been in, when she died.

The sky above her was a clear blank blue.

Was this how she'd die too? Alone, in the wilderness? So close, so close to civilization.

But not close enough.

A silent, white-feathered, winged shape descended around her, surrounding her.

She couldn't see anymore, everything was white. But she felt herself lift away, going higher.

Into the heavens.

* * *

REBECCA MOVED THROUGH THE CROWD gathering along the shores of the lake for Lexi's vigil.

A chill pierced through her hoodie and she zipped it up and stuffed her hands in the pockets. She felt invisible, a side effect of being short and wearing dark clothes. She hoped to use that to her advantage tonight.

Rebecca's mom had forbidden her from helping with the searches for Angela after what happened on Sunday. But that didn't prevent Rebecca from gathering information, AKA eavesdropping. She felt sure Lexi and her death held a clue to where Angela was.

She wondered how many people would show up.

A woman was passing out candles with little paper circles around them to keep the wax from burning your hands. She said they'd light them at sunset.

The wisdom of this in a fire-prone wooded area was questionable. Along with the fact that Lexi was burned. But it was a nice gesture, and besides, everything that could burn probably already had. Rebecca took one.

What was the deal with candlelit vigils? Was it some sort of primal instinctual thing, a throwback to the times when people were afraid to go into the woods in case the big bad wolf got you? When cavemen crowded around a blazing fire to keep out the night?

And were they supposed to mourn, or pray, or what? Maybe both.

Samantha Austin's parents and family were here, along with a few other families, like church friends, because they were all dressed strangely, in long blue dresses.

They must be relieved that their daughter wasn't the burned one. But, then where was she? Still missing. They'd re-printed missing flyers with a new, higher reward for any information leading to Samantha's return. It was over $100,000 now. They really didn't look rich. She wondered where they got the money.

As she walked by, all she heard were Bible verses. She wouldn't count on overhearing any hot gossip about Samantha, then.

Maybe it had been better for them before, to believe the worst, than to go back to not knowing anything, being in limbo, waiting. She thought again of Jeremy's mother's face, desperate to know what happened to him. She wiped the image away, not quite able to name the feeling it brought up in her.

Nearby, Rebecca's mother stood with Cassandra. Lexi's family wasn't here yet, if they were coming at all.

Not only had the Marconis found out that their kid was dead, but now they were under investigation too. "Just a formality," she had overheard Sally saying. But because they hadn't reported Lexi missing until a few days after she had disappeared, it threw suspicion on them.

Over in Gorda's parking lot, Vivian pulled up in her old gray Mercedes. She got out, took one look at the crowd, hugged herself and looked almost sick, then went up the steps into Gorda's, awkwardly skirting around Tom and Sally, who were looking over the crowd from their high vantage point near the front door.

Tom caught her eye, and she shrank into her jacket.

Thankfully, his view of her was soon blocked when a shiny white short-bus emblazoned with pictures of tropical plants and scripty letters spelling out *Enchanted Gardens Retirement Community* pulled into the official asphalt parking lot in front of Gorda's.

It was blocking everyone that was parked there, but she guessed the oldies couldn't dismount the bus into the dirt because of their brittle bones or something. Was it Field Trip to a Mexican Restaurant Day?

About ten old men and women eventually got off the bus, which then drove away. They made their way across the street to the dirt lot after all, took candles and started talking to each other, and a few others that had gathered, in hushed tones. They were here for the vigil.

Rebecca moved closer, wondering what the connection was. Lexi's grandmother maybe. At the thought, she felt the sharp pang of missing her grandmother. Not the one in LA, Abuela Lupe, although she was cool. But she saw her at all the holidays. No, her other grandma. Her mom's mom.

One tall, sharp-eyed old lady zeroed in on Rebecca. "Were you two friends?" she asked, sternly.

For a moment Rebecca was disoriented, still thinking about her grandma. Yes, she had been friends with her grandma.

But then she realized the old lady was talking about Lexi, asking if Rebecca was a friend of hers. Her eyes were sparkling, expecting a positive answer.

"Uh. No, I didn't know her," she said, but the woman kept looking at her, questioning her with her eyes. "My mom...found her."

"Oh, poor dear." The woman's powdery, wrinkled face changed into an expression of understanding and sympathy. "How is your mother?"

"She's uh. Fine." She realized all the oldies were looking at her now. Some were tall, some short, some thin, some not so thin. "How are you related?" Rebecca asked.

One man puffed up his chest. He wiped some tears away, eager to talk instead of cry. "Lexi worked at our retirement home. We saw her every weekday afternoon. Served us dinner," he said, in a dry wheeze.

"Except for when school started," shouted a short, deaf old lady.

"What?" the man yelled.

"Except for when school started," the lady said, right into his face. "She wasn't there every day!" The deaf lady was a stickler for details.

"Oh, right," he said, and rolled his eyes when she turned away.

"She knew all of our orders, our favorite drinks..." another lady with a fluttery voice and hands said.

Then they all started in.

"Hot water with lemon. With a whiskey chaser, she'd joke."

"Buttermilk? Can you really drink an entire glass of buttermilk?"

"She was a hoot! Don't even get me started when one of us ordered prune juice. Especially if we asked her to nuke it a little."

Rebecca's nose wrinkled but then she quickly unwrinkled it. Nobody noticed. They were all in rapture about Lexi.

"And then of course we'd grill her—about her friends, her family, her boyfriends, her dreams for the future..."

They all stopped then. One woman in the back let out an awkward sob.

"I don't know how to explain it," the first tall woman said. She'd had a severe look at first, like a strict English teacher, but her personality was actually warm and friendly. "She was just, extraordinary. She could make us laugh at ourselves without making us mad, keep us entertained with her exploits." She dropped her eyes, and tears slid down her face. "We all knew she would do great things. It's a real loss to the world."

Rebecca didn't know what to say, and even if she did, she was surprisingly choked up. After all, she didn't even know Lexi. Thankfully, the organizer woman who'd been passing out candles started talking over the PA system.

"We're here tonight to honor the life and legacy of someone taken from us too soon."

Rebecca looked around. The group had grown to twice the size while Rebecca was busy yakking with the oldsters.

"Lexi Marconi was just sixteen years old, an enthusiastic sophomore at Valle High School. A cheerleader. A peer counselor. A devoted daughter"— Rebecca looked around but still didn't see Lexi's parents—"sibling, and friend." At this, Angela's mom let out a small yelp, like someone had stepped on her toe, then put a hand over her mouth. Rebecca's mom wrapped both arms around her, like she was helping her stay upright.

"Sunset tonight is at 4:51," the woman leading the vigil continued.

Except it had already gone down behind the looming mountain of Paraiso to the west. Rebecca shivered again and pulled her hood up. Across the lake, a coyote howled.

"At that time, we'll light our candles one by one, in a chain, and have a moment of silence. Then, we'll sing one of Lexi's favorite hymns."

Hymns? The girl went to church too? She was too good to be true.

"After that, we'll pass the mic around for anyone who wants to share memories."

The news crews were there too. One of the reporters pushed her cameraman into place for a better angle.

The lady leading the vigil looked at her phone screen for the time. She might've been a teacher at the high school? She had that vibe.

A couple more cars showed up. A bunch of chirpy teens got out, and immediately stopped talking, realizing they got here at exactly the wrong time, the silent time. They hurriedly grabbed candles and looked serious.

"The sun has set," the woman with the mic said somberly, and lit her candle with a Bic lighter that took a few tries to spark up, which was less than ceremonial. She then lit the nearest person's candle, and that person found someone else's to light.

Lexi's parents arrived and got out of their minivan, followed by her three little brothers.

A few more people throughout the crowd let out strangled sobs.

It took about eight minutes before everyone's candle was lit, because more people showed up and got into the semi-circle that people had naturally formed, and then of course they needed candles.

The last ones were two boys, who'd pulled up in a subdued but still totally bank BMW. They definitely weren't Valle High students. Rebecca's antennae perked.

One of the boys looked at her, a smile spreading to the side of his face.

She moved around the perimeter of the crowd. Why weren't there more cops here, besides Tom? She guessed they had officially done interviews of Lexi's friends and family, but here was a treasure trove of information, all in one place. Everyone who cared about her.

And probably her murderer too.

She gravitated to the Valle kids. There were boys and girls, mostly juniors and seniors from their looks and the fact that they drove here. A tall girl with a wavy ponytail down her back was talking. "It's too bad Jason didn't come."

"Yeah," the boy next to her said. "He's broken up."

"Well that, plus the cops are asking him all kinds of questions. Of course he's the number one suspect."

"Jen! Don't say that."

"Well, you know they had broken up."

"Really? No, I hadn't heard. God, there's so much I don't know."

The large guy said, "God, I can't believe she was burned. Do you think she was alive when she burned?"

"Eww. Eric, why. Don't, just don't. I'm already nauseous. Gemma, why is your candle going out—here, light it again."

"Do you think it was a cult? I mean Halloween night, burned up? It sounds Satanic to me," Gemma said. "Acchh. Stupid candle, it went out— ugh! What's wrong with this thing? Jen, light me up again. Please."

"I don't know," Eric said. "I just know that over summer vacation she got in to some kinda weird shit."

Rebecca got closer and listened to the volley of gossip delivered in earnest stage whispers.

"I don't even want to be here. This whole place is spooky. Fucking Fairy Glen is spooky."

"We're not even in Fairy Glen."

"Close enough! Have you heard all the ghost stories? The Black Witch, The White Lady, The Gray Girl?"

"Gray Girl? That's a new one on me."

"Some friends of one of my friends say they saw her running across the road in Fairy Glen."

"When? Recently?"

"Like, before the fires."

"And now, Lexi shows up dead and burned, in Fairy Glen?"

"Not really in Fairy Glen."

"Close enough!"

"Where was she going Halloween night?"

"Nowhere. She said she was staying home, just hanging out at Angela's house."

"She left practice, and took the bus home like always."

"You know what that means. Maybe Angela killed her."

"Angela? No way. The girl couldn't kill a spider."

"Look, isn't it suspicious? They had plans, now Lexi is dead, and Angela is missing. She's probably on the run."

"That's not fair. What about Jason? They'd been fighting. It's always the boyfriend."

"Jason wouldn't kill anyone."

The two boys from the BMW were awkwardly keeping at the edge of the circle, like her. Social niceties weren't her forte.

She kept her radar attuned to the boys, while approaching the group of popular kids. She just needed a way in.

"Damn it! Stupid freaking candle," the one girl said. There it was.

"Here, let me help you," Rebecca said. She took the girl's candle, lit it again with her own, then held it upside down to let some wax run off. "Here ya go. The wick was too short." She handed it back.

"Thanks," the girl said. "I'm Gemma." The candlelight reflected in her wide pupils as she snuck up and down looks at Rebecca with her big mascara'd eyes. "Did you know Lexi?"

"Uh, yeah." Rebecca lied. "We went to nursery school together." She hoped to god that they didn't know she was full of it. She was starting to sweat. She was okay with lying, she just didn't like doing it on the fly, without a net. "I can't believe this happened to her." That last part at least was true. And it was a good pivot of subject.

"Yeah," Jen, the tall, less talkative, yet subtly more dominant girl said, pausing for a long time before almost whispering, "Crazy."

A male voice from behind Rebecca made her jump. "What do you think happened?" It was the rich boys, or one of them at least. She looked him up and down like he was the outsider, trying to cement her new insider status with these Valle kids.

Jen and Gemma turned around. They also looked this newcomer up and down. Eric was back at his car, bending inside doing something. His back was shaking. Oh. He was crying, and trying to hide it.

"Did you know Lexi?" Gemma asked the BMW guy.

"Uh, no. Yeah, yeah I did. A long time ago."

"You mean, like nursery school?" Gemma asked, sarcastically, while looking straight at Rebecca. Uh oh. Was she busted?

The guy shuffled his topsiders, blushed a little, and laughed. "Actually, yeah."

He was really cute, even though Rebecca could kick herself for thinking so. She noticed Gemma turning to look at her, about to ask why *they* didn't know each other if they all went to nursery school together, but the guy started talking, saving her.

"They're saying it was Satanic?" he half-whispered, his face glowing orange in the light from his candle.

Gemma pshawed, even though she had said the exact same thing five minutes ago, while Jen said, "Yeah, they *are* saying that. I won't believe it unless I see it in a police report." She turned her back to him. To Rebecca, but loud enough for him to hear, she said, "There's enough fucking gossip in the world dude. This was our friend. Show a little respect."

He backed away.

Rebecca said to the girls, "I don't remember him from nursery school. What a liar. But, you know, it *is* hard not knowing what happened, or why. Did she seem different lately?"

"Lexi?!" Jen said. "Lexi was the *definition* of different." Rebecca laughed, as if she knew. "But, I know what you're saying," Jen continued. "She was changing. We used to cheer together, Freshman and Sophomore year," Jen said, pointing back and forth between Eric, Gemma, and herself. "This year, she didn't even try out. We begged her to stay on until we found another flyer, that's the only reason she was doing it. Because we asked her." She broke into a small sob, then recovered and said, "She was the best."

"Was she still doing Drama this year?" Rebecca asked, trying to keep them talking. She was eyeing the rich boys out of the side of her vision. They were still lurking nearby, talking to each other over their lit candles. Everyone else in the crowd was singing now, "I'll Fly Away." The cute one threw a glance her way.

"Yes, she still loved Drama," Jen said. "Drama Queen, always was. And all her other activities. It wasn't like she lost interest. We only had one class together this year, and since school started, I only talked to her in Algebra. I mean, you know she got all goth, but that was more like a fashion decision for her. That's why Gemma was all looking at you weird, she connected you to Lexi's new look. No offense."

"None taken."

The singing ended. People were milling around. One of the old ladies had taken the mic and was talking about how great Lexi was.

Rebecca was bothered by the fact that nobody seemed to care about Angela, still missing.

She wondered if Angela hung with this crowd, if she was cool enough to have friends a grade or two above her. Or if she was more like Rebecca. An invisible.

Rebecca was late for work already, and she didn't want to be here anymore. She hadn't found out anything useful.

She kept thinking about Crystal, and Jeremy, and how his mom was so desperate for any little news, any little crumb.

Walking over to the Bronco, she smiled at Eric, who was still sitting in his car, and gave him a half wave. He smiled back, grimly.

As she pulled her bike out she saw the BMW boys, walking backwards away from the vigil, up a hill. One was filming with a tiny camcorder, the view screen flipped out to the side. They were trying to get a better overview of the crowd.

Eric looked up, and saw them too. He dropped the smile and a crease formed between his brows. He got out of the car, and walked towards them quickly, a hulking figure in the dark.

As she was mounting her bike, soft crying caught her ear. She pulled out her cell phone and turned on the flashlight.

Sitting in a pile of leaves on a small embankment under a tree, a little boy with dark curls was kicking stones near him. He was crying, and his face was all red.

Gosh, was she just a magnet for sobbing little boys? She had wanted to see what Eric was going to do, maybe ask him to follow that BMW to see where it went, but she had to do something. What if this little boy was lost too?

Remembering how she'd scared the two little boys in the forest, she flipped her hood off, swept her hair back from her face, and tried on a smile. In her softest, most feminine pitch, she said, "Hey, what's wrong?"

"Lexi called me a snitch. So I can't tell you."

"You know Lexi?"

"She's my sister." He looked up at her, pouting.

"Ah. I understand all about that. I have a little brother too," she said. He looked down. "But he's not as cute as you."

He smiled a tiny smile. She put down her bike and crouched down near him.

"If I was your sister I wouldn't call you a snitch."

"You wouldn't?" he asked, looking up at her face.

"Nope. I'd call you..a responsible sibling. What did she tell you?"

"She didn't tell me, I just heard her. On the phone. I eesdwopped."

"And what did she say?" Rebecca's thighs were cramping, but she couldn't move now, she couldn't spook this kid.

"She said where she was going."

"And where was that?"

"She was saying they would go shoot at a silo."

"A silo, huh?" So Lexi was more of a hick. Going to farms to shoot guns, that was a total aggie thing.

But a silo? That didn't make any sense at all. Silos were like a midwestern thing, grain storage or something. There were none of those around here. Disappointment flooded her, and she put her hands on her thighs and pushed herself up. The kid was probably just babbling.

"When she saw I heawd her, she got weal mad. She said, 'Don't you dawe tell anyone. Snitches get stitches.' But, should I tell? Is she in twouble? Will I get in twouble?"

Poor kid was too young to understand what *dead* meant. She'd have to tread lightly here.

"No, of course not. You're not in twou—trouble. She wouldn't care if someone knew she was at the silo."

"NO, not THE silo. *A* silo."

"Jeffrey!" She heard a woman's voice calling. "Jeffrey!" She sounded panicked.

Rebecca stood up and looked around. It was Lexi's mother, her head on a swivel, walking through the dark crowd by the shoreline.

"He's over here!" Rebecca called out. "Come on Jeffrey, go back to your mom." She herded the little boy in the direction of his mother.

"There you are! Thank God. Jeffrey, don't ever do that!" Jeffrey started crying as his mother picked him up.

Suddenly, Rebecca understood.

She rushed into Gorda's.

Sally and Vivian were both there, sitting at the end of the bar with her mom. She followed their gazes, to find they were all staring at the cute new barback, Zachary, who was bringing liquor bottles out from the back room.

Disgusted, she let out a guttural sound. They turned and looked at her.

"We have to ride to the asylum," Rebecca said.

"Does anyone really know where it is?" Sally asked.

"I thought the asylum was an urban legend," Vivian said.

"We could always ask Sheffie," Gorda said. "But he's not the most reliable."

Rebecca's mom said, "We could ask Mrs. Fey—or maybe Clara knows—

she was trying to show me on an old map, in one of her books. I could look on Google satellite, and figure out how to get to it."

"Or you could just ask a teenager." Rebecca said.

"You've been there?" her mom asked, mouth agape.

"We've all been there. It's like a rite of passage. If you want to search tomorrow, you can trailer the horses to the nature preserve parking lot," she said.

Her mom said, "We'll ride at sunup."

* * *

VIVIAN HAD MEANT TO GO to yoga, but found herself instead driving all the way around the dark mountain to Gorda's to partake in the candlelight vigil, and she was still here, hours later.

She was starting to enjoy drinking in public. It felt...unapologetic. And besides, if Gorda wouldn't let her pay her debt directly, she could pay it in profits from her bar tab.

"So, any news on the missing girl?" the bartender asked. "I mean, the one that's still missing, not the dead one."

Vivian was nursing her drink, and she looked up to see who was talking. It was the guy, the cute new guy that Gorda had hired, leaning down near her. She looked at his face, took her time answering.

"Not really *news*. We're doing another search tomorrow."

He tilted his head a little, focusing on her, then looked at her glass. It was close to empty, and she was planning to drive home soon, so she was basically drinking melted ice, waiting to be sober enough she wouldn't get a 502. She shook her head.

"Where you looking this time?" He stood up straight and started polishing a glass.

"The asylum. I don't really know where it is but the kid does."

He turned around from stacking the glasses. He was tall with broad shoulders and a slightly curved back, like a swimmer, and his face was hard. His jeans hung a little low but not too much, a studded belt kept them respectable enough. He had two full sleeves of tattoos, and more tattoos peeking up from the neck of his t-shirt.

"Not many folks in here tonight," he said, looking around. "Those vigil people aren't big drinkers. I don't think Gorda would mind if I joined you."

Vivian didn't normally like tattoos—or men, for that matter—but the way the muscles of his arms slid underneath them as he poured the tequila shots...now that was interesting.

"Where is Gorda anyway?" she asked, realizing she still had a while to wait before she could drive home. And this shot of tequila would reset that clock again.

"Night off," he answered, setting a small white plate of lime slices next to a salt shaker on the bar.

"So," she said, sitting back, relaxing, enjoying just looking at him. He was young, and strong, and...while the black hair didn't really suit his complexion, it did set off his eyes. He certainly had a style.

He noticed her looking. That was fine. "Tell me about yourself," she said.

As the shots flowed, the night melted into silence around them. He waved goodbye to the last customers, the door banging open and then swinging closed as they left.

Now nobody was here, and the jukebox had stopped playing. The barback was telling her his life story. He was a local boy, had been a skater, gotten in trouble. "Did a little jail time. That's why I was lucky to get this job."

"So Gorda didn't do a background check?" she asked teasingly.

"No, she didn't have to. I was straight with her. Told her I knew my job and that I was a hard worker. She said she understood, and she'd give me a chance."

"How very kind of her."

He hit some buttons on the cash register, then ducked into the room behind the bar and turned off the lights. The only illumination now was the rope light glowing underneath the liquor bottles.

"So." He came back out and jangled his keys. "Wanna take a walk and look at the stars?"

Thursday, November 8

VIVIAN SAT IN A BLANK room, entirely made of stainless steel, while Bill and Ted's voices came over a scratchy, too-loud intercom in a barrage of questions. The words were warped, impossible to understand.

She tried to cover her ears, but her hands were tied behind her chair.

"Jeremy and Crystal—I think they got away," she said. "Have you heard anything? Do you know if he's safe?"

"We're not interested in them. Where's Bartley?" the warped voice said.

"I have no idea. I told you that."

"Under the terms of your deal—" It was Ted's slow drawl.

"I told you, I don't know!" she shouted. She had absolutely no clue where that bastard had taken off to, leaving his son tied up on a half-constructed balcony in a wildfire. "I know more about the other guy. The Colombian."

"Really. How?"

"I knew him. Before."

Suddenly, she was on a rooftop. Rio de Janeiro, Carnival, 1987.

She was there on business for PharmaCutix. Costumed festival goers, expats, disco lights, an open bar. Feathers, laughter. Across the dance floor, she saw him. They locked eyes.

Now, he was next to her. They began to dance. He whirled her around, held her from behind, put his cheek next to hers as they swayed.

The music got faster.

She held onto his hand and he spun her around and around and around, but it was too fast, they were too close to the edge.

He leaned out, over the street full of revelers, three stories below, and now she was falling, falling with him...

Vivian lurched awake. A pile of bedclothes, a hot, heavy arm across her stomach...her bare stomach! Where were her clothes?

She wriggled and stuck her head out of the covers, and was shocked at the squalor.

Where was she?

All at once, the night before came flooding back, like water from a burst dam.

She and the bartender had walked along the lakeshore, discussing lord knows what. At some point he'd leaned over and kissed her, which had surprised her.

She was no stranger to one night stands. But this man—Zach was his name—was a good twenty-five years her junior. It had been about a decade since she'd gotten that AARP letter in the mail, the one announcing your old age, your one foot in the grave.

Her head was pounding, her back ached from the uncomfortable mattress, her mouth was dry and her brain felt like it was stuffed full of cotton. It might as well be. This had been an airhead move.

He felt her wriggling and mumbled something. He pulled her back under the covers. She'd been trying to slip out without waking him, find something to cover her, and get out of this tiny, falling apart camper with its peeling, faux-wood laminate.

This is where they had returned to, after their lakeside stroll—although it hadn't looked nearly as shabby in the starlight. It had looked like a treehouse, a little cabin in the woods. And he had slowly undressed her, and she him, in the dark.

"Don't go yet," he said, and kissed her. A full kiss on the mouth. In the morning. Which was glorious, and intimate, and melted her heart, just a little.

But the camper was warming up, and she felt her bladder expanding painfully.

She pulled away from him. "I really should go," she said, thankfully finding her shirt on the floor, draped over his boots. Then her pants.

"You sure? I can sneak into the kitchen, cook you breakfast. Hmm?"

Her phone rang. It was Deirdre. She answered. "What is it?"

"Where are you? I'm at your house with the horse trailer."

"I got...waylaid." She couldn't help but smile. At least she hadn't said *Something came up.* "Go ahead without me. I'll ride down and meet you at the nature preserve."

Deirdre said, "That'll take way too long, and you won't be able to find us —" but Vivian closed her phone.

She said her goodbyes to dear, young Zach, and stumbled out of his camper—which was on stilts no less—in the overhang of trees behind Gorda's restaurant, down the uneven asphalt lane, and to her car, sitting all by itself in the parking lot, the first rays of morning sun accenting its age. The faded paint, the worn upholstery.

But it was still a damn good car. She took the curves down Del Diablo at well over the speed limit, enjoying its German-engineered handling.

* * *

DEIRDRE COULDN'T BELIEVE SHE'D FAKED a sick call for Rebecca.

That had to be a new low for her, but she needed to get to the asylum, and Rebecca was the only one who could lead her there. In all her years of exploring the trails through Fairy Glen, she'd never run across it.

They met Wilma at the parking lot of the nature preserve, a small hushed place at the base of the hiking trails that zigzagged up the northern face of Mount Richardson. The fire had ripped through here, and there was a locked gate closing off the parking lot, but Wilma, with her giant ring of keys, unlocked the padlock and opened the gate.

"Watch out for trees coming down," she said, as Deirdre pulled the trailer past her. "Don't make me regret letting you guys in here."

Only a few of the oaks that had surrounded the parking lot remained. Some were half burned. The fire had taken what it wanted, picking and choosing. She saw the trees with new eyes, as potential widow makers. Or rather—she thought of Walt—widower makers. "Thanks Wilma."

Once she got Scarlet ready and tacked up, Rebecca led the way down the trail, commanding the little BMX bike. Deirdre was impressed, she'd never really seen her daughter ride before, other than down the street. Maybe they should do more of this, once this was all over. Scarlet liked following her. It meant she didn't have to think too hard.

"You know, everyone calls it an asylum, but it was a sanitarium," Rebecca said over her shoulder.

"Yes, how many times has Clara told us that?"

"She comes in handy sometimes," Rebecca said with a smile.

"How often have you been here?" Deirdre asked. "And when?"

Rebecca had only been back since last May. When she'd lived here before she was too young, wasn't she?

"A long time ago Mom. I rode my bike here, during the day." She stopped her bike and turned around. "It wasn't a party. But I saw plenty of beer cans and stuff. It was a teenage hangout, even back then. Everyone knows about it."

She picked up the pace again, and Deirdre asked Scarlet to trot to keep up.

They went through some unburned trees, on one of the easier trails that didn't go up the mountain. It was a flat loop that anyone could hike, with the native plants marked on little plaques. But at a point along the trail, Rebecca ducked away behind a hip-high boulder, on an invisible path. They went through some undergrowth, and on the other side of it, the path became clearer.

"It gets kind of rough here Mom. Can you handle it?"

"Of course dear." Deirdre didn't know if Rebecca could hear the sarcasm in her voice. Her daughter hadn't witnessed Scarlet taking her up the burning mountain to rescue her. Everything else seemed easy by comparison.

Down an embankment made bare and black by fire, a little trail first followed along the creek a good ways, until it widened out into a shallow pool.

There was no sound except the creak of the saddle and squeak of the pedals, and the water gurgling and rushing over the rocks. The stifling heat was made worse by the overcast sky.

There was a wide place with a waterfall in the creek, tiny rapids, a fallen tree over it.

"This all looks a little different since the fire," Rebecca said. "But I know we're going the right way."

Deirdre glanced at her phone, but there was no signal. They were too deep in the bends of the valley.

She felt more uneasy the further they went. This felt like unknown territory to her. She'd never ridden farther east than the nature preserve and the Richardson Reservoir at the top of the mountain. Up ahead, against the gray sky, shaggy feathered shapes were circling.

Vultures.

"Do you see that Rebecca?"

No, please no. Please don't let me find another dead girl.

Scarlet felt her tension and flattened her back, humped it up, and tried to turn and go, but she put the opposite leg on her and didn't let her turn.

When she'd caught her breath, Deirdre said, "I hope Lexi's parents have closure. I just hope...I hope we can find something that will help. You know, one way or another."

"I know Mom."

"I mean, I keep thinking about Stephanie—"

"—Who?" Rebecca said over her shoulder.

"Stephanie Bartley. And how she's stuck in limbo, not knowing what happened to Crystal."

Rebecca stopped her bike so fast she had to pull Scarlet to a halt before she ran her over.

"Why would *she* care about Crystal?" Rebecca asked.

Deirdre said, "That's Stephanie's step-daughter. Crystal lived with them for a few years. Not to mention, little Brian is missing both his siblings."

Rebecca looked down, turned, and started pedaling again. "Hey, Mom..."

On the bank to Deirdre's right, the bushes rustled. "Hush! Did you hear that?"

"No, what..."

"Ginny! Is that you?" Deirdre called.

Scarlet looked around, head high, nostrils flared. She started dancing in place.

"Vivian?" Deirdre yelled, back the way they'd come from. Rebecca's eyes were wide.

"Mom. Don't freak me out. I don't hear anything."

Deirdre put a finger to her lips, but as the seconds ticked by, nothing else moved. "Okay." She cued Scarlet to walk on.

Finally they got to a place where they had to cross the creek.

Rebecca got off, rolled up her pants, put her bike over one shoulder, and waded in. Deirdre followed on Scarlet, who had her job cut out for her, navigating over the rushing water and rocks. It never went past her knees, but it was still tricky. Rebecca was like a water sprite, leaping from rock to rock, effortlessly carrying her bike.

Once they were on the opposite bank, Deirdre looked up. The were down below Fairy Glen Road now. She heard the whooshing of cars above.

"It's through here!" Rebecca called. She stood at the opening of a huge corrugated steel drainage tunnel. "We're lucky it's not the rainy season. It's totally dry. Will Scarlet go through this?"

Deirdre got closer. It was about eight feet in diameter. She'd get off and lead Scarlet through. Hopefully. She slid off, nervous about how echoey, how long the tunnel might be. What if Scarlet freaked out inside of it?

The floor of it was lined with silt and leaf debris from former floods. Peeking into it, she saw light on the other side. A good sign.

"Come on Mom, it's not that far. She'll be fine."

Scarlet perked her ears and took a step in, following Rebecca as she pushed her bike through. Deirdre took a deep breath and did the same.

On the other side she came out into a deep, steep sided canyon full of trees. She'd never seen this before. Most of the trees were black from the fire.

"This was so pretty in here," Rebecca said, sadly.

They followed the dry creekbed up the little canyon.

Deirdre was sorry she hadn't ever seen this before it burned.

Up ahead, through the black trunks, was the face of a stone building. It looked like the ruins of a castle.

"There it is!" she said.

"Yep," Rebecca said. "We're heee-eere." She said it all sing-songy, like the little girl in *Poltergeist*.

"Don't do that Rebecca," she snapped.

Rebecca just laughed. But the unease settled back onto Deirdre, dropping over her like a black lace veil. They approached the building, and it seemed to get taller, looming in the gray sky. The circle of black birds still spun above it.

She slipped off Scarlet, suddenly overcome with vertigo.

"What did they do here?" she asked.

"Who, the sanitarium people?" Rebecca dropped her bike into an overgrown patch of grass and stepped high through it to get to the crumbling terrace steps. "It was just a place sick people would go to recover. They needed fresh air and sunlight, to get over their lung diseases."

"So, there were no crazy people locked up here?"

Rebecca just scoffed at her, and rolled her eyes. "You're as bad as the teenagers, Mom."

They had to go up some wide, crumbling steps, through a narrow green gate flanked with ivy and grass. She heard the distant squawking of ravens.

The front of the asylum would've been beautiful back when it was still intact. It was made of gray stone cut into big blocks, which had been covered over with white plaster that was mostly crumbled away. Huge windows were just blank holes, like empty eyes.

How did people get here back in the old days, she wondered. Was there another road in from somewhere to the east? And where had they cut all this stone? Maybe the old quarry. But that was a long way from here.

"Come on!" Rebecca said, and ran through the front doorway into the hall.

Deirdre looked for a place to tie Scarlet. Finding a fallen log, she wrapped the lead rope around a thicker branch, hoping it would hold.

"Stay," she said solemnly, more as an incantation than a command she expected would have any effect. Scarlet eyed her and gave a soft snort, then shifted and bent to look behind her the way they'd come, worried wrinkles forming above her eyes.

Deirdre stroked her neck. "Easy, girl."

Going back in, she called out for Rebecca. Her voice echoed.

"Rebecca!" she called again, venturing further into the dim interior.

To her right was a long, high-ceilinged room that went from the front of the house to the back, like the ballroom in the Haunted House at Disneyland. The walls were covered in graffiti. None of the windows had survived, except, as she took another step into the room, she saw there was one rosette of stained glass, high and centered in the back wall. She shivered. Like a church, a cathedral.

The stained glass was beautiful, and how it had survived was a miracle.

Was it stronger than the other windows, so storms and fires and tree branches didn't break it?

Or was it just so beautiful that no vandals had wanted to destroy it just for fun by chucking rocks through it?

She called again for Rebecca, stepped back into the hallway, and ducked into each room she passed. It was impossible to tell what they'd been used for. There was no furniture, no fixtures, just empty rooms. Among the graffiti, there seemed to be a common theme. Pentagrams.

And there, tucked in a corner of one of the smaller rooms was a gym bag. Carefully, she opened the zipper and looked inside. There was a white and green pleated skirt. Was this Lexi's cheer uniform? And was that blood on it?

And, now, she caught a whiff of something unpleasantly familiar.

She left the little room. "Rebecca where ARE you?" The hallway became a long, twisted, vertigo-inducing corridor.

"Mom!" It was Rebecca's voice, coming from the back of the house.

Deirdre ran the rest of the way. The farther she got, the more destroyed by time the building was. Roof gone, rafters exposed, stone walls tumbled, like London after the Blitz. The circle of carrion birds spiraled overhead.

She burst forth onto the back terrace.

Stench assaulted her nostrils; roadkill, meat rotting in the sun, shit. The smell of death.

In an explosion of flapping wings, dark shapes ascended into the sky. All except one.

Rebecca. Her small black-clad frame faced away from her, stock still. The crows and blackbirds landed in the nearby trees, scolding angrily from their branches.

"Honey?" she said, her voice quavering. "Rebecca? What are you looking at?"

She got closer.

Please don't be another dead girl, please don't be another dead girl.

Deirdre breathed in, and pain pinched her side, the stench even worse. Strange sounds, like pigs grunting, a wet smacking.

"Mom?" Rebecca finally spoke. Terror made her daughter's voice weak. She didn't turn around. "Mom, what is this?"

Peering over her shoulder, she saw what Rebecca was looking at. Once again, her eyes and brain could not meet in the middle.

Grunting and hissing, the vultures hunched around something, their naked heads jerking in an out of...

White rib bones. A carcass.

Oh no, don't be Ginny.

There were hooves...but they were small and cloven like a deer. She breathed out in relief. But the rest of it was all wrong, not a deer...reddish-brown and white and black fur..."What in the hell..."

"This is why I don't eat meat," Rebecca said, her voice thin. Then she gagged, and ran into the bushes to throw up.

Deirdre checked her phone for signal. She had one bar. It was enough to call Tom.

The rest of the day was taken up with leading first the patrol sheriffs, then the detectives, the crime scene techs, animal experts, and dog searchers back to the site. Rebecca left, saying she had to get to work. By the time Deirdre got home that evening, she was exhausted, but she had a plan for tomorrow.

* * *

LATE THAT NIGHT, VIVIAN AWOKE to a shriek echoing off of the bare walls of her upstairs bedroom.

She opened her eyes and looked around, startled by herself. Then embarrassed.

How loud had she screamed?

She looked at Zach, still sleeping next to her, his muscular, tattooed back to her.

When she had finally gotten to the nature preserve this morning, hoping to miss Deirdre's expedition (and she did, thank *God*) she had spotted him, driving slowly down the road, as if looking for something. Turns out, he was looking for her.

He told her she looked like a goddess on horseback, and she had invited him to come back to her place when he got off work later.

Luckily, screaming her head off from a nightmare hadn't woken him up.

But clearly, if she was screaming in her sleep, she wasn't fit company.

Hopefully she hadn't done it when she'd stayed with him at his place last night.

No wonder she was having nightmares. Being interrogated by the DEA was not the most pleasant thing she could imagine. Especially when they were trying to extract information that she just didn't have. They only wanted to know about Bartley. And nothing she'd told them about Hector —the White Ghost, El Blanco—had appeased them. After all, he was dead, wasn't he? He'd fallen from the roof, into the fire below.

Another shriek. This time from outside, on the hillside. A cougar.

She got up, put a robe on, ran downstairs and grabbed her big flashlight.

Outside, Apache whirled around his corral. She shone the flashlight around the perimeter of her property, wishing she had a dog. They were way too needy though, she wouldn't be able to put up with that.

"Apache!" she whispered. He stopped, threw his head over the fence, snorted, then trumpeted a whinny so loud it deafened her. But he wasn't talking to her, he was looking to the north, over the hills and homes.

She stood still, waiting, listening. "Who are you talking to anyway?" she said.

His ears were still pricked, eyes nailed in the direction of Deirdre's house. After a minute or two he let loose with another volley of high then guttural calls, and from a few blocks away, the pealing of another whinny carried over the hills.

Then, there was a third shriek. It echoed through the foothills.

It came back to her then. The day of the fire.

She'd seen a huge white shape, felt the explosion, seen Jeremy's sister fall over him to protect him. Somehow Deirdre had gotten tangled up with Hector, and they had both tumbled over the side.

Vivian had run to help pull her up, and then—then what?

She'd looked briefly over the edge after pulling Deirdre up, and below, in the smoke on the steep slope far beneath, a tawny cat-like shape had crawled away. Then, she'd turned around to find Jeremy, but he and Crystal were gone.

Had they gotten away?

Vivian grabbed a halter and Apache inside and closed the stall door, to protect him if a particularly ballsy mountain lion came calling. After one more sweep of her flashlight over the hillside above her house, she trudged back up the stairs.

The light in the bedroom was on.

She heard the toilet flush, and Zach walked back into the room, completely naked.

As her eyes took it all in, her heart spun, and her brain processed how lucky she was. She was not even looking for this, for a relationship, and here it...

She gasped and jerked back.

Right there, on his upper left pectoral, was a swastika.

She backed up, clutching her robe around her. "What the hell?"

He saw what she was looking at. "Oh." He sat down on the bed, ran a hand through his hair, and sighed. "Jail. They make you declare your allegiance."

She stared, prompting him for a better explanation.

"White boy that I am, I didn't have much choice. When I earn enough at the bar, I'll have it covered up, and turned into something else. Tats are expensive."

"Sooooo, you're not a Nazi." She couldn't believe she was in this conversation.

"Nope. Some of my best friends—"

"Don't say it!" She held up a hand. Sweat pricked her forehead, her underarms. "I thought you'd been in county jail or something, not prison." Her voice turned shrewish.

"It's all the same. For me, getting this tattoo was life or death. I'm not violent. I know I look tough, but I'm not a fighter." He looked down, shame coloring his cheeks. "I didn't wanna get shanked."

She was still speechless. He looked back up at her, and said softly, "Haven't you ever done something you regretted?"

Regrets.

Yes, that's something she could fully identify with. And self-preservation, too.

She was still doing time, in her own way.

She sat down next to him, brushed the black hair away from his eyes, assessing his face. She laid her head on his shoulder, and he put his arm around her, and they laid back down.

Maybe she wasn't lucky. Maybe they were meant for each other.

Friday, November 9

VIVIAN FELT LIKE SHE'D JUST gotten back to sleep when she was awoken by a persistent banging at her front door.

Taking her time, she slipped into her silk robe and slippers and went downstairs. The pounding came again, this time at her back door.

She entered the kitchen, squinting against the harsh sunlight. She really should remember to close the shades at night.

Through the glass she saw who it was. Big surprise. Since Jeremy disappeared, Deirdre Boyd was the only one who ever came to her door.

She opened it. "What is it?" She looked around to see if Deirdre's mare was with her, but instead it was Deirdre's Bronco parked in the driveway.

Deirdre looked particularly frantic this morning. Her dark red hair was swept back haphazardly, and her face was pinched. "There was an animal—it wasn't any animal from around here. It was like a sacrifice."

"Context please?" she said, squinting against the sun, but her heart started beating faster. Was that the scream she'd heard last night?

"You stood me up again! I could've really used you at the asylum, because we found something, and Tom takes you more seriously than me." Deirdre set her mouth in a challenge.

"What's your obsession with searching for these girls?" Vivian desperately needed coffee, and didn't want to think about Tom. She backed up into the kitchen and Deirdre followed.

"I know Angela. She used to ride Ginny. We can't give up."

"Who is this 'we' that you keep referring to?" Vivian asked as she filled her coffee machine.

"You don't have time for coffee," Deirdre said, and actually, physically, pushed her out of the kitchen into the living room. "Get dressed—I'll get Apache ready and load up your tack."

"What are you talking about?"

There was a horn honk down on the street below her house. Vivian went to the window and looked out.

Deirdre said, "That's Bonnie. She's got her trailer, her and Lina, and there's room for one more. You need to go with them."

"Let's get one thing straight," Vivian said. "I'm not a member of your little Wine Night Posse." Then she asked, "Wait, what do you mean *I* need to go? Where are *you* going?"

Zach walked down the stairs. He'd put a shirt on, thankfully, but was running a hand through his messy black hair, yawning. "Everything okay down here babe?"

Deirdre's mouth dropped open. Zach looked at her. "Oh, hey! How's it going?"

Vivian put her finger out to him. "I'm fine. Please." She flicked her eyes upstairs.

He stepped slowly back up the stairs.

"Vivian," Deirdre hissed. "What the hell?" She shook her head and raised her arms. "Anyway, I'm late, I have to go. Get ready and go with them."

"Wait—" Vivian said forcefully.

But Deirdre was already out the door.

Vivian sighed, and went upstairs to change. She kissed Zach goodbye. "Sleep in if you want. See you tonight?"

He smiled, and nodded.

As Bonnie drove the trailer to the staging point, she filled Vivian in on the latest.

Tom Goodwin and the sheriffs had done a complete search of the asylum premises yesterday. Despite Deirdre's superstitions, Tom said the pentagrams didn't mean anything. "It's a teenage hangout, they're practically required."

After that, they called in forensics. There was lots of real blood, not just near the animal, but inside the asylum. It would get tested to see if it was human or something else.

The "animal sacrifice" as Deirdre had called it, would have to be analyzed to tell what had caused its violent demise.

And to that end, a member of the biology department from the local university, along with a representative from the wild animal park, were consulting with the forensics department to analyze the exotic antelope's remains.

"They're thinking now that instead of burning up in the fire, some animals might've escaped the safari park." Bonnie said.

"Bizarre," Vivian said.

Lina piped up, "You think they could've warned people about that. I suspect a coverup. I mean if you don't find bodies, why say the animals are dead, unless you're hoping you can find them before anyone notices wild predators roaming all over North County?"

We already had predators, Vivian thought. "Don't you have a job, Lina?" She didn't know the girl well, or what her interest in this search was.

Lina turned in her seat and appraised her coolly. "Yes, I do. Do you?"

Bonnie said, "She's working four tens now. Fridays off."

Bonnie caught Vivian's eye in the rearview mirror. Not an unkind look, just inquisitive. She knew all of her neighbors viewed her as an oddity. And frankly, she didn't care.

Bonnie continued, "They also found what they believe is Lexi's bag with part of her cheer uniform in it. And a whole lot of fake blood, like bottles of it, and some type of climbing rigging, carabiners and such."

"What were they doing, a prank, a...*Halloween* prank?" Lina asked. She waved her hand disdainfully when she said Halloween. Guess they didn't celebrate that where she came from.

Bonnie ignored Lina. She said that now that the search dogs had some clothes of Lexi's, they tried to track her from the asylum. But they couldn't —probably too long of a time had passed. She had apparently been there, if the clothes were any indication, but where had she gone from there? How did her body end up on the other side of the mountain, burned?

No, instead, the dogs were picking up more intently on Angela's scent around the asylum. And they followed beyond the asylum and across Fairy Glen Road, to the north, but had lost track of the scent.

"So that's why we're searching there today. Can't hurt to check every area at least once," Bonnie said.

She pulled the trailer over and parked in the dirt turnout on the north side of the road, past the nature preserve parking lot, and they tacked up the horses.

A skinny trail led up a steep yellow grass hill. At the top, they looked down into Seeker's Valley, which spread out in a vee from the dead-end at the gates to Seeker's Sanctum. The same dead-end that all those yuppies had been caught in when their GPSs told them to evacuate along that road.

Before them was a long gentle downward slope of mostly dry grass with some small boulders peppering it, ending in a high fence at the retreat's property line.

Beyond Seeker's Sanctum were other large properties and ranches scattered over the rolling hills, and beyond that was the sea of Spanish tile in San Amaro Hills.

Vivian rarely rode over here. She'd ridden the nature trail below them plenty of times, but never come up on this hill. She liked the view from up high.

Bonnie said, "Let's spread out here, since there's no trail. We can weave back and forth and cover the whole hillside."

It wasn't long after that Lina said, "Look!" She got off her horse and knelt near a rock, as Vivian and Bonnie trotted over to her.

She lifted a yellow backpack into the air, and had opened it and started digging through before Bonnie could say, "Don't touch it!"

"Why?" Lina looked back inside and rattled off the contents as she pulled them out one by one, and dropped them back in. "Trash. Witch hat. Stuffed animal."

Vivian cued Apache around the other horses. If the backpack was there, maybe something else was further along...Bingo.

"Hey!" Vivian said. "There's a whole bunch of blood on the ground over here. And..." What was she seeing? It didn't make sense. "...and feathers. Big. Ass. Feathers."

Snowy white feathers as long as her arm.

* * *

DEIRDRE WAS HEADED TO THE mission for the second time in two weeks. Was this becoming a habit?

Cass was too upset to drive, she said, which was strange for someone so strong, but hope was running thin.

Deirdre definitely would not tell her anything about the discovery at the asylum yesterday—there was no way to know what that all meant, and it would just freak her out.

Dead animals, pentagrams, blood, and cheerleader uniforms. That was the stuff of a girl parent's nightmares. Better to wait, let the officials figure it out, and decide what to tell her.

Deirdre had been planning to search on horseback this morning, but when Cass called her for moral support, she thought of the perfect substitute to go in her place. Vivian.

Who, despite her protests, loved searching for things. At least, she loved looking through her binoculars, ostensibly at hawks. And apparently, sleeping with young men who looked like they walked off the cover of a bad boy romance novel. She smiled at the thought.

On the drive north on the 15, which was short-sightedly undertaken during morning rush hour, Cassandra explained why they were headed to the mission.

"I checked the search history on my computer. She'd been researching someone named Cheryl Sandman. I think it's her birth mother." Cass blew out a big breath.

"So, her birth mother is at the mission? What, is she a nun or something?" Deirdre tried to make a joke and immediately regretted it, because Cassie looked so pained.

"Cheryl Sandman, she's buried there. In the cemetery."

"Oh."

Cassie went on, "I saw that she'd looked up the church's address, and how to get there." She sighed. "I should've noticed what she was going through. She asked me a few months ago what I knew about her real parents. I was prepared. We never kept it from her that she was adopted. I mean, she was old enough to remember. But I didn't know anything to tell her. It was a closed adoption. All I knew was that she had some trauma before she came to us. They told us, don't be surprised if she has nightmares. That's why we thought riding horses would help her, and it did. She never did have nightmares. Other than the not talking, which she grew out of, she was such a happy little girl." At that, Cassie broke down.

Deirdre was taking the exit off the freeway. She turned right and pulled off the road to let Cassie cry, hugging her awkwardly across the seats.

Cassie regained control and said, "Thanks, I'm okay now. Let's just get there."

Deirdre started driving again. They were only a few miles away now, but the going was slow because of how twisty the road through the valley floor was; riverbed and fields on the right, cliffs and steep hillsides on the left. When the road straightened out, the giant casino was visible ahead.

Cass said, "When I searched the name...Cheryl Sandman...when I searched that name, I found she'd been murdered, her car left in the desert, and a small child had been found nearby."

"Angela?" Deirdre said in a hushed voice.

Cass nodded. "I think so. Poor thing. I can't believe that's how she started her life, and now? Where is she? Is she in danger? Is she...dead? I thought she was trying to go to the casino, and I had no idea why. Now I know she just wanted to ride the bus up here to go to the mission. But she couldn't, because she couldn't pass for eighteen. She must've taken the city bus."

"But we know she was back near your place more recently," Deirdre said. "She must've returned safely from the mission—"

"I know. But maybe what we find here will shed more light on why... and where..." Cass choked up again. "Maybe someone saw her? Clergy, people at the bus stop. Anyone, anyone."

Deirdre pulled into the nearly empty parking lot. They parked close to the mission and went into the courtyard.

They talked to all the clergy. Nobody had seen a girl like the one in the picture. But Halloween had been a busy day they said, everyone setting up altars, people milling about.

Cassie's energy visibly drained with each apologetic 'no'.

Deirdre shuddered to think that she herself had come here seeking Teresa's comfort, just one day after Angela had been here. It felt like crossing paths with a ghost. Someone walking over your grave.

No—she put thoughts of ghosts and graves out of her mind, even though that's partly why they had come, to see Cheryl's grave, just like Angela had done.

What did Angela find that day that made her not come home?

Deirdre suddenly wondered if Teresa had been here that day, too. While Cassie was asking around, she called Stephanie, got Teresa's number, and asked her. She said no, she'd only been there on November 1. *Damn.*

Cass joined her again. She'd found out where the grave was.

They walked the long, treeless way out to Cheryl Sandman's plot. It felt like they were the only ones there. Nobody around to ask if they had seen a young, lost girl.

There it was, a plain stone, flush with the ground in the dead grass, only her name and the dates.

"1969-1996. She didn't even make thirty," Cass mused.

"It's so tragic," Deirdre said. She felt sorry for saying it, but it was true. Hopefully Angela would come home, and make it a happy ending.

Both of them cried and put their arms around each other.

By the time they got back to the parking lot, it was creeping up on noon.

"Have you been eating? Sleeping?" Deirdre asked.

"I took a leave of absence from work," Cassie said, not answering the question. "But, I'm thinking of going back to work next week. I'm so glad you came and helped me today. I needed to get away, get out of that house. I would never say anything to Gina, but...I'm so pissed at Lexi! Even though she's dead! That's fucked up, isn't it?" Cass looked at her with tears in her eyes.

"No," Deirdre said, and put her arm around Cass. "No. It's understandable."

"I mean, did she make Angela run away with her? The more I get to know that family, the more questions I have. They swear up and down Lexi didn't have a boyfriend. But it turns out, she did! And she was always out 'gallivanting' as they say. They say she always did that. And, how could they let their sixteen year old stay out overnight, much less for nights at a time? Plus, her little brother was so scared of her that he didn't want to tell on her, even after she was dead?"

Deirdre thought of her older brother, the respect and awe and fear that she had for him. "Older siblings can be pretty intimidating. You know how kids are. They don't always know the right thing to do."

As they got back in the car, Cassie's phone rang. She answered it before the first ring stopped. "Hello?" she asked, tension stretching her voice into a tightwire.

The searchers had found a backpack, and the sheriffs were asking her to come ID it.

* * *

Tom DROVE AROUND THE LONG road through San Amaro Hills, down a ghost street full of empty, brand new houses, to where the road to Seeker's Sanctum branched off the very end of one of the cul-de-sacs. The color of the asphalt changed from deep black to dirt-colored, potholes riddling it, showing the earth underneath.

The religious retreat (some would say cult) was the closest structure to the blood and the backpack they had found. Cassandra Hernandez had identified the backpack as belonging to Angela. When she had seen the stuffed toy, she started crying and said, "She was dressed as Simba, for Halloween. The day she came into the ER."

The lab techs had taken the giant white feathers, along with blood samples from the ground. The biology department at the local university was going to help analyze them.

Were there abnormally sized birds here, in addition to exotic antelope? He knew Fairy Glen had a reputation for strange things, but he found the antelope much easier to explain—one of them had gotten out of the safari park, escaping the flames that had killed so many of its herd mates. The feathers...not so easy to explain.

He followed the winding valley road deeper into the trees, doing a maximum of 25 mph since there weren't any warning signs for the sharp curves.

At about mile seven the road dead ended, with the gates of Seeker's Sanctum to the left. He got out to stretch his legs and have a look around.

The road was gated here, with an opening to the side only wide enough for people, horses, and bikes. Beyond the gate it was dirt with trees lining either side, a nature trail that had been reclaimed from automobiles when they decided to close off through-access several years ago.

He stared down the trail for a while, seeing where it turned and disappeared into the trees. It'd be a nice ride to do with Sally sometime. Alas, not today.

He went to the intercom on the gate and pushed a button.

A crackly voice said, "Welcome. How can we help you?"

"I'm Detective Tom Goodwin from the San Diego Sheriff's Department. I'd like to ask a few questions."

There was a long pause.

"What is this concerning?" came the staticky reply.

"There are two missing girls, and we're canvassing the areas they were last seen." He didn't mention the third girl that was dead.

"And, who do you need to speak to?" the man's voice said.

"Whoever's in charge." Tom tried to keep the growl out of his voice. Seemed like they were stonewalling, which raised his hackles, and his suspicions.

"Please hold on a moment," a woman's voice said. He pictured a gaggle of cult members crowded around the intercom, desperately trying to make a decision. He could always come back with a search warrant if it came to that.

But after half a minute, the woman's voice came back on. "Please drive through, you can park next to the administration building."

He got back in his car as the gate slid open.

He pulled through, and followed the winding driveway past birds of paradise and palms, other tropical plants that made it feel like you were in Hawaii, not Southern California. He passed a big assembly building on his right, and pulled into a spot labeled "Visitor," near the well-marked administration cottage.

A white haired man, dressed in a white tunic and loose pants, and probably in his fifties although he could've been a well-preserved seventy, came out to greet him.

"Hello. I'm Raymond Bower." He shook hands with Tom, and they went inside the small building, where Mr. Bower ushered him past the open area, full of xerox machines and typewriters and a few staffers—he guessed the intercom talkers—who had stopped work to look at him with curiosity, into his office and closed the door.

"Now, what can I help you with Detective?"

"As I said, we're investigating a missing person's case."

"*A* missing person. I thought you said two girls?"

"Well, yes," he said, but left it hanging as he pulled Angela's missing flyer out of his notebook and handed it to Raymond, watching his face carefully.

The man took the flyer, tentatively, not looking at it, instead looking at Tom for further info, his tan healthy face creased with concern.

Tom waited.

Finally the man looked down, and in a split-second, Tom saw relief on his face before it vanished again into the appearance of concern. He read the flyer.

"Oh, poor dear. But this says she was last seen at the mission. Is there a reason you're searching this area?"

He tried to hand the flyer back to Tom, but Tom waved it away.

"Keep it. In fact I have extra, if you'd like to post them around."

"I'm sorry, but I haven't seen this girl. If you'd like to ask some of our staff members, we're about to have afternoon prayer. I could summon them here first. But I thought you'd said there were two missing girls? Do you have a flyer for the other one?"

Tom thought how best to proceed. There was something this man was hiding. Whether it was just his strange pseudo-religious practices, or something else, he couldn't be sure.

"We found Angela's backpack up on the hillside." Tom tried to find a window to get his bearings and point, but there was no window nearby, and the others were blocked by shrubbery, so he just pictured the map in his head. "To the east of you."

"Ah." Raymond sat back in his seat.

"We have reason to believe she's injured, so time is of the essence here. I'd like to search your place. She may be hiding somewhere." Tom stood up, trying to force the flow of the back-and-forth in his direction. "I'll call my men in, and we'll be able to cover the entire grounds in very little time." He looked at a map of Seeker's Sanctum on the wall, an artistic version that showed the various buildings much larger than they really were. "How many acres is your property?"

Raymond stood and walked around his desk. He was hale and hearty, and his skin was so smooth and reddish tan that it almost glowed. "I'm sorry, but that will be very disturbing to our seekers."

"Your seekers?"

Raymond smiled. "Our guests. We are a retreat, for anyone seeking spiritual guidance or healing."

"Well, this girl needs healing, and we have to find her." Tom lowered the pitch of his voice, as if he was sharing confidences. "There was a large amount of blood, farther along from her backpack. It seemed like she was heading in this direction. She can't have gone far, and with the blood, it's imperative that we find her soon, you understand."

Raymond shaped his clay face into an expression of deep concern. "I do understand, but I can assure you she's not on our property. We perform complete security rounds, day and night. May I ask about the other girl you mentioned?"

"Then what will it hurt to search again?" Tom said, ignoring his question, letting some aggravation creep into his voice, hoping to out-alpha Raymond.

"I'm sorry, but I can't allow it," Raymond said. "I assure you, we will call you if any kind of information comes to light."

Tom faced off with him. "Are you really going to make me get a search warrant? Because I will. All you're doing is killing time, time that could be spent saving a little girl."

He thought of the dead animal at the asylum. How close it was to this place. The thought that maybe they really were doing Satanic rituals, like Deirdre Boyd had said, flitted across his mind. But that was ridiculous.

Raymond cleared his throat. "And, have you gotten search warrants for all of our neighbors also? As you can see on this map"—Raymond pulled out and unrolled a 16 x 20 color aerial photograph, with yellow lines computerized onto it indicating property lines—"we have many, many neighbors, some of whom have much larger properties than ours, and most likely don't patrol them as thoroughly as we do. While I can tell you with certainty that this girl," he held up the flyer, "is not here, can our neighbors do the same?"

"You're not really gonna do this, are you?" Tom asked.

"I'm afraid so. You see, we are...misunderstood, for lack of a better word, and you're not the first person to come here wanting to snoop around. We have freedom of religion in this country. Freedom from unreasonable search and seizure—"

"Enough!" Tom was surprised at his own anger. He flung open the office door. "We'll do it the hard way. But you're only hurting a little girl."

The young woman in the outer office opened her eyes wide in alarm.

Raymond said, "It's okay, Susan."

Tom walked past her, not bothering to stop and question her, even though she seemed unreasonably jumpy. It would've been pointless. It felt like he'd dropped into a dysfunctional, abusive family, and all the kids were afraid to say anything. He'd seen it so many times.

As he left, he pictured trying to get a search warrant. Normally it was pretty easy, but the key was probable cause. Were a nearby dead animal and the rumors of a small community enough to get one? The man was right, there were lots of other properties around.

But whenever he encountered resistance to searching, there was always a reason. It was a paradox. Innocent people let you look anywhere. Ones with something to hide did not. In his opinion, the mere act of invoking your constitutional rights proved your guilt.

And time was running out. If Angela was somewhere here, hurt and bleeding, they'd need to act fast.

He picked up his phone to call Sally.

* * *

SALLY WAS AT THE COURTHOUSE'S tiny library when her phone vibrated. It was Tom. She couldn't answer it in here, so she told the clerk she'd be right back and left the files she was researching with him, Post-it notes and bookmarks carefully preserved, then went into the echoey hallway and called Tom back, as serious, dark-suited men and women clicked by in their dress shoes.

"Sally, what do you know about Seeker's Sanctum?"

"Well, hello to you too," she said.

He apologized, and explained his urgency.

"So, they wouldn't let you search? Doesn't surprise me," she said.

Of course there had always been rumors about that place. It's a cult, they're Satanists, they're Mormon, they're waiting for UFOs to take them away.

But Morgan, her yoga teacher, had gone to a few weekend events there and said they're fine, just victims of the rumor mill that thrives in and around Fairy Glen. Sally told Tom as much.

"I know for a fact they wouldn't let us in on horseback. Deirdre Boyd messed that *way* up last year, riding on their trails through the olive groves. Someone confronted her and told her that it was private property. The campus, or whatever you want to call it, is fenced, so we can't sneak in. I can ask Morgan if she has any connections there. What can we do in the meantime?"

Tom said, "I'm going to ask for a search team to canvas this whole area, get the dogs back out here. Hopefully the other property owners aren't as secretive as Seeker's Sanctum. I'll put in for a search warrant but I'm racking my brain for probable cause."

Sally said, "Okay, good luck. I'm in the middle of researching Angela's birth mother—or the person Deirdre says Cassie thinks is her mother. Cassie said something about Simba too, that Angela was actually dressed as Simba when she was brought in on the LifeFlight, right?"

Tom was silent.

"I think there's more to that," Sally continued, "I can try to get the adoption records unsealed, but that'll take me some time. In the meantime I'm going on the assumption that it's probably her—"

"What does her birth mother or The Lion King have to do with anything?" Tom asked. "Angela could be lying somewhere bleeding—"

"Just listen, will ya? Her name is Cheryl Sandman. And guess what? She was a murder victim."

There was silence on the line. "Solved?" he asked finally, in a gruffer than usual voice.

"Yes. One Edward James. The motive was never determined, but it didn't matter, he was caught the day after the murder, evidence galore, a no-brainer conviction."

"Well, that's interesting. But not necessarily relevant. Right now, we need to prevent Angela from becoming a murder victim herself. I'm calling in a big search in Seeker's Valley. Can you get a horseback group together to help comb the hills? I figure if we harass the retreat enough, they might relent and let us in. Let's shake the tree and see what falls out, eh?"

"Oh, so now that you need me, I'm not jeopardizing your investigation, is that it?"

He was silent. The clock on the wall ticked loudly in the now vacant lobby. He didn't answer.

"Fine," she breathed, and hung up.

* * *

BY LATE AFTERNOON, THE LADIES joined the search effort on the hills surrounding Seeker's Sanctum.

Deirdre, Bonnie, Vivian, and Lina rode from their houses and took the nature trail that went north from Fairy Glen Road, which was spooky enough in the daytime, with its tortured-looking trees overhanging the trail, much less on a darkening, windy and cloudy late fall afternoon.

Deirdre listened with hyper-alert ears to every noise—birds in the trees overhead, the bushes and small wildlife darting in and out next to the wide trail and the little stream that followed it.

By the time they got to the end of the nature trail and the gates to

Seeker's Sanctum, it was almost dark. A line of cars was entering the gates.

They turned right, hopping over a fallen-down split rail fence, and followed the fence line of the property, and although, no doubt, the other searchers had already done the same, they called Angela's name every few minutes, stopping the horses to hear any response before continuing.

When they came out of a stand of eucalyptus, they could see over the fence to the main open area of the retreat center. Good thing about horseback, you can see over most fences.

People dressed in white were gathering, setting out chairs or blankets to sit arranged in a semi-circle on the lawn. A large, meaty man in all white was in the center. He was holding them all rapt with his magnetism. Deirdre could feel it from here.

Sally had told them that Tom was absolutely sure they were hiding something, and that they hadn't allowed a search. He'd get a search warrant, but it might take some time. And that would give the Seekers time to move whatever, or whoever, they were hiding.

She called out, in her loudest voice, "ANGELA!"

A male voice just behind her said, "Please stop!"

Scarlet jumped ahead, but Deirdre gathered her and turned to see who it was.

"Please, can you lower your voices? You're upsetting the ambiance. We're going to get very bad Yelp reviews," a tall, pudgy man with a baby face was saying to her over the fence.

"We're looking for a missing girl, I'm sure you've heard," she said to him. She handed him a flyer from her saddlebag.

He took it and looked at it, sympathy welling in his eyes. "I'm sorry, I haven't seen her," he said, and she believed him.

She blurted out, "What's the deal with you guys anyway?" It sounded so rude, but she was dying of curiosity.

The rumors about "the cult" as some called it were sometimes unbelievable, but there was no denying they were secretive. Even she and Bonnie had run afoul of them last year riding on the hills on the other side of the road from them, which apparently they also owned.

And by run afoul, she meant that a very nice and peaceful person had reminded them politely that they were on private property.

The young man seemed not to take offense. "We're a community of people who find God in nature."

"Oh. Okay." She was startled at his honesty, his relatability. After all, wasn't that why she rode trail?

"I hope you find her. We'll pray for you. God Bless," he called after her, as she urged Scarlet onwards to catch up with the other women, who were still calling Angela's name.

The volunteers—hiking, horseback, and canine—were now spread out along the hillside were they'd found the blood. There was no crime scene tape in the spot, and she wondered if that was normal. Maybe they hadn't found anything else. They'd taken a sample of the bloody dirt and feathers to the lab. Hopefully it wasn't Angela's. Hopefully it wasn't human. But lab results, she'd learned, were slow. And if there was any chance Angela was nearby, they had to pounce.

She joined the other women. "Anything?" The question was, of course, pointless. If there was anything, the searchers would've been yelling and gathering around.

She looked down the valley. She could see Seeker's Sanctum Road, see the blue and red lights of sheriff's vehicles traveling up and down it, stopping at each ranch. A breeze ruffled her hair, and crickets started chirping. The air felt wet and cool.

The terrain here was tricky, and she had to look back down to guide Scarlet. She'd brought a headlamp with her, might have to pull it out soon.

Dark clouds were gathering to the east, as the last rays of sunlight hit her back from the west, squeezing in a flattened line under the cloud layer, like someone trying to peek under a closing garage door.

Scarlet's front foot sank into a gopher hole, and she turned and hopped uphill in indignation. While wrestling her back in the direction she was supposed to be canvassing, Deirdre's eyes caught the movement of a small light on the black hillside across the road from the retreat. Then it was gone.

"Hey," she said to Vivian, who was closest. "I saw something."

"What?" Bonnie heard and rode over. Gatsby blew out a big snort.

"Shhh. Wait...There! See it?" she said. "It's like a flashlight, someone walking the Sanctum trails over there."

Thunder boomed through the valley, then spots of rain dampened her sleeves.

"I saw it," Bonnie said, over the last rumbles of thunder.

"Me too. Two people," Vivian said, lowering her binoculars.

"Should we go check it out? That part's not fenced." Those were the trails they'd gotten busted on.

"Yes, let's do it," Bonnie said. "I heard the searchers say they were about to wrap up here. Dogs didn't pick up anything, except where the blood and feathers were found."

So, Angela had been here on this hill. But aside from the path where they'd found her backpack, there was no scent trail. It was as if she'd disappeared.

No, it was like she killed a gigantic chicken, and then vanished into thin air, like some kind of magic trick, leaving behind blood and huge feathers. Deirdre started to imagine little Angela as an old-time medicine show barker.

They were almost back at the gates into the retreat. Of course, from down here on the valley floor, the perspective was all different, and she couldn't even be sure which arm of the folding hills she'd seen the light on. But, there was only one route that went that direction, she figured. Unless the person with the light was off trail, which was practically impossible in the dense chaparral, they would eventually cross paths.

They pulled out their headlamps and put them on over their helmets.

They went through a stream crossing that Deirdre was dreading, having ridden it many times on surefooted Bowie, but never on Scarlet.

They had to walk in the rocky falls of the little stream, as it snaked back and forth through some particularly impenetrable tall trees. Once through the trees, they had to hop out of the stream bed up a two foot muddy clay embankment onto the trail.

Scarlet did okay, despite Deirdre's tension.

"Let's be quiet from now on, we don't know if she's being held captive—anything could happen," she said.

"You didn't tell me this would be dangerous Dee!" Lina hissed at her. "Maybe I should go home."

"Yeah right," Vivian said snidely, "through those woods, Little Red Riding Hood?"

They traveled single file along the trail carved through solid ten foot tall manzanita and scrub oak. It was like traveling down a hallway, with no visibility beyond what was directly in front and behind. It gave her the creeps; she and her fellow riders lined up like little marching soldiers, easy to pick off.

Bonnie was leading, holding a battery powered lantern that might as well have belonged to the guy that ran the ferry across the river Styx, for how frickin' creepy it made this bushy passageway.

Every now and then, Bonnie batted away a spider web that stretched across the trail, but some would be left behind for Deirdre to desperately wipe from her face.

They were very quiet. She felt as though something would happen, any time.

It did.

A figure in head-to-toe white came around the bend in the trail, striding very quickly, and almost ran into them.

The horses jumped. He screamed.

He was a Seeker. After they'd all recovered, they told him they were looking for the source of the light, and he said, "Well, that was me," and they said, "Where's the girl you came up here with?" on the off chance that he'd blurt something out.

"What? Look, you have to leave, you've been told before, this is private property. These are not public horse trails, and we forbid you from easement on our land!"

"Well what if we just said," Bonnie paused, "that we're going anyway, so screw you." Gatsby pushed past the man, and Deirdre followed on Scarlet, scooting by, followed by Lina and Vivian.

Bonnie held her lantern in front of her as she allowed Gatsby into a hand gallop, looking behind her, and finally letting out a *whoop!*

The man was yelling at them, running after them, but quickly fell behind as all four horses galloped up the gentle but inexorable slope, until they got to a part of the trail that was carved into the bare face of the mountain.

It was narrow, and treacherous. A fall off the edge, straight down, was perfectly plausible.

At a walk, they followed Bonnie up the nightmarish trail as she called, "Angela honey, are you here?" She continued calling, then turned back and said, "Once we're at the top, we can go home over the hill and back down our side, so we don't have to face that guy again."

"I can't believe you Bonnie! This is the second time you've busted a blockade," Deirdre said, trying not to look over the edge to her left.

"Hey, it was *one* guy," she said. "Now quiet, let's go back to calling."

"I can't believe we're doing this! I'm going to die!" Lina said. Deirdre looked back at her. She had covered her eyes with her arms. Walker, her extremely patient and bomb-proof Paint gelding, was plodding along.

"Lina, you'll be fine. Suck it up," she said irritably. "Walker can take care of you *and* himself."

Scarlet on the other hand, would probably relish the drama of stepping off the edge of the cliff.

They progressed in fits and starts through the drizzle, which was getting heavier by the minute. Every time Bonnie called, they would stop and listen for at least fifteen seconds, their headlamps slicing the darkness as they each cocked their heads to listen.

Deirdre looked behind her a few times, not to check on Lina, but to see if Vivian was still back there. She'd been so quiet this last part of the ride. "Vivian, any sign of them?"

"No."

The Seeker must've decided to go back for reinforcements. The women would be able to get up and over the ridge to their side before anyone could get up here anyway, even if they did take their time searching for Angela along the way.

The drizzle became an honest-to-God rain, and gusts of wind threatened to push her off the edge. Freezing drops pelted her face. She hunched closer and closer over the saddle, both from fear and from cold.

They rounded a sharp outside corner switchback. Up ahead was a hand-built stone sitting area a few steps above the trail, a place where people could rest on their hike and enjoy the view.

There was a sound, an electronic bird call, carried on the wind.

"Someone's phone!" Deirdre whispered.

Bonnie dismounted, and Deirdre did the same. Bonnie got closer to the rock viewing area, listening for the phone again, but instead, they heard a voice, talking. It sounded like a young girl's voice.

They put their finger to their lips and signaled for Vivian and Lina to stay put. Creeping higher on the trail, they followed the sound of the voice, their movements muffled by the steady rain.

Through a hallway cut in the head high scrub brush, there was a small stone house. Deirdre handed her reins to Bonnie, clicked off her headlamp, and went through, not knowing what she would find. The tin roof sounded like machine gun fire under the assault of pelting raindrops.

Windows without glass, square holes in the stone structure, emanated a faint blue glow. Deirdre crept closer, unsure whether there would be a captor with the girl.

She heard singing, lovely lyrical notes. She got close enough to peer inside. A white face, eyes downcast into the glow from a phone screen. A young girl was thumb-typing, completely entranced, singing to herself.

"Angela?" Deirdre said.

The girl screamed. So did Deirdre, a sharp squeak of adrenaline, the sound swallowed by a clap of thunder.

Then the girl turned and ran.

"Angela!" Deirdre yelled, going inside. Forgetting to turn on her headlamp, she was totally blind in the dark. She reached for it, and when it came on it bounced off the walls and back into her eyes. "Damn!" She pulled it off her head and held it in her hand, feeling for the door out. The structure was only about 8 x 10 with a rough dirt floor, and soon she found the back door and ducked outside into the rain again. "Angela! Come back!"

She looked around, took the only path, one leading away and up the hillside to the peak. A small figure in a long dress scurried uphill. Deirdre dug her boots in and blasted up the slope, gaining on the girl, who was now on her hands and knees in the mud. Deirdre grabbed an ankle and held on. "Angela, honey, you're safe, we're here to take you home!" she yelled.

In the struggle, she got a muddy sneaker kick to the mouth, that made her let go in sharp pain.

Grunting, she shone the flashlight right at the girl's face, full of ferocity and fear. A face Deirdre had memorized, weeks earlier than the one on Angela's Missing poster.

Her mouth formed a grimace, lined in shiny metal gleaming in the headlamp's beam. "I'm not Angela!" she screamed "Leave me alone!"

Samantha Austin shoved Deirdre again with her foot, and fled uphill.

"Samantha! You're alive!"

After recovering from shock, Deirdre followed her, again. "Come back! Please!"

Samantha pulled her skirts up and ran faster, then cut to the right, along a trail just under the very top of the hill. A narrow, dangerous pathway along slick rock, that led to the west. Eventually it would go down a gentle slope towards the abandoned, wild, unsuccessful olive groves. But here, it was steep and slippery, and with the wind now pushing at both of them, one bad step could be catastrophic, could send her plummeting into the impenetrable brush below.

Deirdre didn't want to follow her, didn't want to spook her. She knew from catching loose horses that running at a terrified creature was not the way to get it to come to you.

"Samantha!" she tried one more time. The girl stood straighter, seeming to realize where she was, turning slowly around.

A bolt of lightning flashed across the sky, illuminating a man's outline on the top of the hill.

Deirdre and Samantha both screamed.

Bonnie caught up to her. "What's happening? Are you okay?"

Deirdre shone her headlamp up the hill. The figure above them was gone.

But when she aimed her light back down at the trail in front of her, so was Samantha.

"LISTEN, I KNOW WHAT I saw!" Deirdre proclaimed, as the rain beat a tattoo on the metal roof of the fire station.

Sally sat back and looked at her watch. It was after midnight now. She and the other riders were all sitting in hard metal chairs in the empty meeting room at the fire station, being debriefed by Tom, while the firefighters were still out there beating the bushes so to speak. In the middle of the night in a thunderstorm.

By the time Sally had gotten home this evening and saddled up Darkling to join in the search, the fire department was already mounting a rescue mission on the hillside between Fairy Glen and Seeker's Valley, near the old olive groves. Sally had followed them up the hill to help. But there was no sign of Samantha.

I should've been on the search all along, instead of researching at the library, she thought. *I wouldn't have let a missing girl slip away.*

Tom said, "Okay. Just settle down, have some cocoa, and we'll go through this step by step."

"Seeker's Sanctum wants to press charges for trespassing and assault?" Lina cried. "I told you guys we shouldn't have gone up there! We almost ran over that man!" She put her head in her hands. "I don't want to go to jail!"

Bonnie patted Lina's arm.

"You're not going to jail," Sally said. She was so irritated with them all that she refrained from adding anything else.

Deirdre said, "Right! We won't go to jail. That land has had trails on it for longer than they've owned it! We have the right to use those trails—it's grandfathered in." Deirdre turned to Tom. "But, since *technically* that property does belong to them, now you have a reason to search the place. The girl I saw, it wasn't Angela. It was Samantha. And you have an eye witness. Me."

Sally laughed out loud. Deirdre looked like a wild woman, her arm in a splint, whites of her eyes showing, red hair and mud and blood from her busted lip everywhere. Nobody would take her seriously.

Zach handed Deirdre a steaming cup of cocoa. He had poured hot cocoa for them all from a thermos, served in the fire station's styrofoam cups. Why was he here? Who'd told him about it, and what was his interest in this? And why were his jeans all muddy up to the calves?

When Zach handed Vivian her cocoa, his hand grazed hers, they locked eyes, and then he whispered something in her ear.

Oh. That was his interest.

Tom, whose voice had been a calming bass counterpoint to Deirdre's soprano litany, momentarily trailed off as he lost concentration. Or rather, his concentration shifted. To Vivian and Zach.

"Okay, listen, everyone," he said, breaking his gaze away from the couple. "And listen carefully. I appreciate your efforts, but let's not sacrifice the credibility of this search. What I want you to do is go home, and leave this alone for a bit, okay?"

While Deirdre argued, Bonnie stood up, and Lina slumped her way to the door. Zach and Vivian had already disappeared.

Finally, when they were all gone, Sally confronted Tom.

"Hey. You're blowing hot and cold. This afternoon, it was all about urgency. In fact, isn't there something in your code of ethics about relentless pursuit of criminals? That's what my friends were doing, relentlessly pursuing! And not a criminal, but a lost, at-risk girl. They didn't know what was up there, just that too many little girls are missing around here, and you're trying to block us from finding them! You're treating this more like a crime scene than an active live search, more worried about your precious evidence."

He looked stunned. "Sally," he said, "You of all people know how precious evidence really is. It's the only thing that brings criminals to justice. It is important."

"If Emily was missing, would you act like she was dead? I hope not."

"It's procedure."

"I'm sick of your gaddamn procedure!" She didn't usually swear, and when she did her Chicago accent came out. Her face was flaming hot.

Tom's eyes stretched open and he backed up a half step. While she had his attention, she might as well go for the gold. "And I'm sick of you staring at Vivian!"

He laughed and tried to look surprised. "What?"

That pissed her off even more. "Oh, don't pretend. It's written all over your face. You men are so ridiculous!" She stormed out the door.

"Sally!" he called after her. "Sally wait...can't we just talk?"

She stopped next to her horse. "You have one minute. I gotta get this horse home." Steam billowed off Darkling's hide, white apparitions in the blackness of the night. She felt just as steamy as he looked.

Tom sighed. "I was staring at Vivian because—well, actually I can't tell you that right now. But also, her...boyfriend? There's something not right about that guy."

The thing was, she believed him. Because she felt it too. There *was* something not right about Zach.

She was about to say so, reluctantly, when Tom's phone rang. He took it out of his pocket.

She said, "I have to get up early, excuse me." She tightened Darkling's cinch, got ready to mount up, and waited half a second for Tom to stop her.

But he didn't. Instead, he answered his phone.

She got on and rode home in the dark.

* * *

VIVIAN WOKE UP, STARING STRAIGHT up at cheap woodgrain paneling.

She had slept here. Again.

She couldn't believe it.

Strangely, she was extremely relaxed, almost comfortable in this tiny bed —not even a double, some kind of odd size mattress that only truck campers had, wedged in next to his warm body.

She thought back again, savoring it like a delicious piece of dark chocolate. Remembering the part before they'd fallen asleep in each other's arms.

But something troubled her. She lifted his arm, wriggled out from underneath it, and stood up, looking for her clothes.

She had a brief fantasy of inviting him back to her house. Maybe for the weekend, maybe longer? He could be a...house boy.

She looked at him again as he slept.

I could take you away from this life, this camper. I could pay for your tattoo removal. You could still work, for fun. You could cook for me, and take care of me.

During my inevitable decline.

Nope, scratch that.

She grabbed her shirt and one of her boots. It was next to his boot, both of them covered in mud, the little pieces between the treads starting to dry and fall out onto the floor.

She got down on her knees and groped under the bed for her other boot, and hopefully her pants.

When he'd invited her back here for a nightcap, she couldn't resist. But now, she needed her freedom again. Something felt wrong. This was all wrong.

She reached further under the bed, her hand hitting his other big construction worker boot, and peering under, she saw a stack of folded maps, an old-fashioned compass...

There it was. She snagged her boot, far underneath the bed, and pulled it out—to find him staring at her with one eye.

"Oh! Good morning," she said, unsure why she had startled so easily. Maybe because he hadn't moved at all, hadn't rustled to let her know he was awake.

"Running off again?" he asked, with a sly smile.

"Yes, I'm afraid so. I have to feed my horse."

He grabbed her hand. "You know...I rode a few horses here and there, maybe I could help you—I mean, you all want to keep searching for this girl, right? Got an extra horse?"

"I only have the one," she said, not sure why that filled her with relief. Maybe because non-horse people always assumed riding a horse was like riding a motorcycle. As long as you pushed the right buttons and pulled the right levers, you could do it. Not so.

He sat up. "Well, maybe I could come along—hey I could get a mountain bike. That would be fun."

She smiled as she put her boots on. "Yes, it might be."

There was a pounding on the door. Her heart rate soared.

He pulled on a t-shirt, noticed her shrinking against the wall, smiled like he was laughing at her, and held up the covers for her to climb under. She did. She didn't want to be caught dead here.

"Just a second!" he called. He put on his jeans, and pulled his boots out and stuffed his feet into them without tying the laces.

He opened the door. Sunlight, fresh air, and Gorda's voice floated in.

"Have you gotten your ID and Social yet?"

"Uh, no. I'm still working on it. Sorry."

"It's been over a week," Gorda said firmly. "What's the hold up? I thought you said you could call your mom and just get the number? That's all I need, we can work on the photo ID later—"

"Yep, I've just been a little preoccupied."

"Yeah, I can tell. You left early last night, right when I needed you."

There was silence, she hoped not because Gorda was looking inside the trailer.

Gorda spoke again, and her voice was even lower than usual but more authoritative. "I don't like being strung along. I gave you this place to stay because I really need the help, but I can't keep paying you under the table. We gotta get above board, man."

"Alright, yep, I'll take care of it today. Thanks."

He climbed back inside, and as he closed the tiny door behind him he said, "Fat bitch," under his breath.

Aaaaaand that's why I don't take charity from anyone—or give it, Vivian thought.

"Sorry 'bout that," he said, running a hand through his hair. Too bad he was so handsome. "Guess I can't offer to make you breakfast today. Unless it's back over at your place?"

She flung the covers off, and stood to leave. The maps had come out from under the bed when he grabbed his boots, and she slid on them as she whirled around.

"What were you doing there? Last night?"

He put his hands up. "Whoa. What is this, gang up on the dude day? Haha." He reached down to gather up the maps.

She didn't laugh. "Were you following me? Is that why you wanted to know where we were searching on Thursday? Why you so conveniently showed up at the nature preserve?"

"I thought maybe you'd need lunch when you got back from your ride. Something about you makes me want to pamper you. I'm sorry if that offends you." He stood and tried to kiss her.

She pulled away from him.

How she wished she could go back in time. Before she'd seen his tattoo. Before she'd had to feel sorry for him.

But she was the one to feel sorry for.

"You were looking for your next place to squat," she said. "Right? Once the 'fat bitch' kicks you out?"

He didn't answer, and in not answering, she got her answer. She left.

She couldn't believe she'd left Apache home all alone for that guy.

* * *

THAT EVENING, THE EXCLUSIVE INTERVIEW with Deirdre Boyd, conducted by Jackie Page, up-and-coming investigative reporter, aired on Channel 9.

The interview had just been shot that day. Deirdre was frazzled from being up all night on the mountain, and worse, couldn't tell Jackie that she'd seen Samantha Austin, alive. The whole thing had been a tiring minefield of questions she wasn't allowed to answer.

Walt had taken the younger kids to a movie, Rebecca was at work, and she settled into the couch to watch, alone except for the dogs, Buck and Granger. She couldn't stand watching herself onscreen with anyone else around.

Here it was. She cringed as the news music came up.

Jackie was standing at the chained-up gates of Paraiso as the sun set.

"I'm Jackie Page, bringing you our exclusive interview with one of the heroes of October's deadly wildfires."

Helicopter footage circling the plateau showed the two burned houses and other foundations, everything as black as the tarmac on the streets.

"Deirdre Boyd was a completely ordinary, salt of the earth, unremarkable woman. Just your typical suburban wife and mother of three."

Suburban? I'm not suburban, thought Deirdre.

"The only thing special about her was that she loved to ride."

A photo of Deirdre on Bowie, from when she was much younger, popped onto the screen. It had been the most recent photo she had. She didn't have any of her on Scarlet—she hadn't owned her that long, and didn't make a practice of having her picture taken.

Jackie's voice continued. "But, when her daughter was snatched by a deadly thug and spirited away to this mountaintop lair, Deirdre Boyd did what any mother would do."

Any mother doesn't have a crazy horse, Deirdre thought, feeling proud of Scarlet, for perhaps the first time. The best off-road vehicle available.

"She leapt into action. Riding her horse, Scarlet's Fire, seen here."

Here they inserted footage of the little stalls out back, and Scarlet snorting angrily at the cameraman, running in circles, and finally backing towards the fence, where the footage switched back to Jackie.

"She certainly is fiery, isn't she? Deirdre rode INTO the path of the firestorm headed their way, and got up to this luxury housing development, and overpowered the man holding her daughter hostage. But, the worst was yet to come, as a 200 foot wall of flame barreled down on them. Earlier today, I sat down with Deirdre Boyd to talk about those events."

It switched to the two of them sitting in the studio.

Deirdre covered her face, then peeked through her fingers at herself on the screen.

"And who was this thug that captured your daughter?" Jackie asked.

"I'm not sure. I'm not at liberty to say," TV Deirdre replied. Watching herself on the screen made her feel like she wasn't really here.

"And what was Brian Bartley really up to on that mountaintop?" Jackie asked.

"That's also something I can't talk about."

"We have information that there was a meth lab, and the whole place is condemned now because of the environmental toxins involved with that."

"No comment."

"So let's get to the action. You were up there to rescue your daughter. You can say that much at least, can't you?"

"Yes."

"And you rode your beautiful Arabian horse up there."

"Yes."

"And what was your plan when you got to the top?"

"I guess I was planning to...figure it out when I got there. All I could think about was getting to Rebecca."

"So the fire swept over, after your fight with the mysterious thug. And you ended up saving not just your child, but the son of the very man who put your daughter in danger, is that correct?"

TV Deirdre didn't answer. *Oh god, I'm an idiot.*

"Deirdre is that correct? That when the fire swept over you grabbed Brian Bartley Jr. and pulled him into the swimming pool with you, your daughter, and your neighbor, Vivian Johnson?"

"Yes that's what happened—except no, that's not what happened. I didn't save Brian Jr."

"So who did?"

Well, it could've been Hector. Or the giant owl. Or Flaco. Or a mountain lion could've carried him like a kitten and dropped him in the pool. Who knows.

"I'm still trying to figure that out myself."

If Brian Jr. was watching she'd have to explain it to him now. Burst his bubble. She hadn't saved his life.

"So, let's get to the current mystery," Jackie said. "Girls are missing in Fairy Glen. And you—perhaps because you know what it's like to have a daughter missing—are aiding in the search and rescue efforts. Is that because you want to help your old friend, Cassandra Hernandez? Do you want to shield her from some of the details of the search that might be, shall we say, upsetting?"

"I guess so. I never really thought about it. I just know we need to find Angela."

"But then, the horrible news came, that her best friend Lexi Marconi was the one that was brutally murdered, and her body burned. The body that you and your friends found on the trails near Lake Hemingway. What do you think the chances are that Angela, Lexi's best friend, the one that she had plans with on Halloween night, is still alive?"

TV Deirdre's chin stuck out. "I think they're very good. The dogs picked up on her scent several days after Halloween. We found evidence of her being on the trails north of Fairy Glen Road, near Seeker's Sanctum." She crossed her arms.

"Mmm," Jackie said.

TV Deirdre sat forward, her face turning red, glowing with sweat from the infernally hot television studio lights. "Besides, I don't believe in giving up."

Jackie Page turned to the camera and addressed it directly. "As you can see, Deirdre Boyd is not a mother to mess with."

Jackie Page certainly knew how to push people's buttons.

Deirdre was still sitting there staring at the TV when Rebecca came home from work.

"Mom, can you mute the commercials please?" Rebecca said from the kitchen.

"What do you have against commercials?" she sniped back.

"Mom!" Rebecca slunk into the room, sighed and put her hands on her hips.

"I'm just saying! They pay for the television!" Deirdre said.

"So do you," Rebecca said, pointing to the cable box.

"But this is network," she said, then gave up and turned off the TV. Rebecca was too young to even know what network TV was.

"Did you record the interview?" Rebecca asked, taking the remote from her and turning it back on. "They didn't show my picture did they? Or say my name?"

Deirdre's cell phone dinged. It was a text from Stephanie.

Brian is asking me a lot of questions now. Maybe you should talk to him.

She threw down her phone and sighed, rubbing her face.

"Who was that?" Rebecca asked.

"Stephanie Bartley. Brian Jr. thought I was the one who threw him in the pool, until this interview aired. I've got some 'splaining to do."

"Oh." Rebecca grew serious. "So do I. I have something important I need to tell you."

Deirdre sat up, ready to listen.

* * *

GINNY MOVED THROUGH THE DARK night. She climbed up from the dry stream bed, towards the pipe corral.

The morning Vivian left the pasture gate open, Ginny had decided to head for the hills. The only thing that had given her pause was leaving Scarlet there.

But there were only so many years left for her. She wanted to roam the countryside.

And besides, she could always come back and visit, which is what she was doing now.

The barn sat in the half moonlight. She nickered softly, and her barn mate stuck her head out of the open door to the corral, even before her voice had died in her throat, then paced boldly over to meet her.

She walked up and put her head over the fence. They nuzzled a greeting, touching noses and sharing scents. Ginny put her head down, close to Scarlet's flank, sniffing through the fence. Scarlet was changing.

She remembered the morning after the fire, after they'd all come up the creek together and into the old lady's pasture. How Apache had nuzzled her, teasing her.

Yes, Scarlet was changed now. There was a quickening inside of her.

Ginny had experienced the same thing, many times in her youth. She would have to keep visiting Scarlet, to guide her on this journey.

They stayed close together for an hour, grazing on the grass on either side of the fence, until the sky lightened and Ginny decided to wander out of the neighborhood, back towards her freedom in the endless, anonymous canyons.

But first, she'd stop at Apache's place, and let him know.

Sunday, November 11

REBECCA HUFFED AND PUFFED. LAKE Hemingway was far to go on a bike, and there was no good way to get there from her house, even from work. Either way there was a giant mountain to go around; to the north, through Pleasant Hollow and the outskirts of Encantadino, or to the south, through Rancho Alto, which she had done today, keeping a watchful eye out for their overzealous security force.

She should've asked Darius for a ride. She should get her driver's license.

She had confessed to her mom last night. Confessed to knowing that Jeremy and Crystal were safe. Or, as safe as two teen runaways in Vegas could be.

"Rebecca, please, you have to tell Detective Goodwin, and after that, you have to tell Stephanie and Brian Jr.," her mom had pleaded.

So, she'd promised she would go see Tom today. And here she was, sweating her life away on the Del Diablo Highway.

At least there were clouds in the sky. It had rained pretty hard again last night, but that wasn't enough, two nights of rain. She looked at the lake, visible now that she'd passed the dam. It was actually kind of pretty, and it smelled fresh from the downpour. Lots of old oak trees, old enough and with deep enough roots that they were surviving the drought.

The houses on the other hand...not so nice, most of them. There was one down below, where she saw a man helping an old woman into his little white car using a walker, getting her out of the house, maybe going to church. Sunday go-to-meeting clothes, a double wide trailer with a shitty little carport out back.

Balding, but not in a too much testosterone way, more like an "I live in my mother's basement" way. Hunched upper back that made his stomach protrude even more. Frizzy red hair down past his ears. Yuck.

He glanced up the hill at her, gave her a hard stare. She stared right back, until the old lady got stuck with her walker and he had to help her.

At Gorda's, there was a fire in the fireplace. This was what passes for a rainy day in San Diego County, so it was an attempt to make it cozy and inviting—gray clouds outside, warm orange light inside, too bad it was suffocating. She ripped off as many layers as she could and still stay decent.

"Detective Goodwin!" she said, finding him among the crowd. "Can we go outside? I'm burning up."

He followed her outside again, and they sat on a cute little concrete bench decorated with a broken tile mosaic, under the giant oak in the dirt lot. "You can call me Tom," he said.

"Okay. Tom."

"Your mother told me you had a statement to give me. Is that right?"

"Yes," she said, all her bravado draining away now.

"Okay." He pulled out a notebook and a pen, slowly, just like he'd approached her and Jeremy up by the quarry the first time she'd met him. So smooth, like he had all the time in the world. He was good. "Take your time," he said, looking down at her. She sat up straighter, but he was so tall he towered over her even in a sitting position.

"It's okay, I'll just tell you." She wrung her hands together in her lap.

"Mmhmm." Tom looked out over the lake, casually.

"It's about Jeremy and Cr-Crystal." Damn, why was her voice cracking like a little pubescent boy? Was it because this was the wrong thing to do, to sell out her friends like this? After all, they hadn't committed any crimes, she knew that for a fact. At least not any big ones. And here she was sitting next to the enemy, about to betray them. "But, first, can I ask you something?"

"Ask me anything," he said, but she knew the way he said it, he wouldn't necessarily answer.

She tried anyway. "What kind of a deal did you make with Jeremy? That day you found us at the quarry, and I left. What did you guys talk about? He sounded crazy afterwards, like he thought he was going to take down his dad or something. Sometimes I don't think he understands things all the way."

"Well. Sorry, I can't tell you that."

She figured. She pulled in a breath, deciding to tell him that Crystal and Jeremy were in Vegas, last she knew. It wasn't that big of a giveaway. It had been since Halloween, really since the 28th when he texted her. They could be long gone, and even if they weren't, Vegas was a big place. They wouldn't find them right away. Crystal was too clever.

Just then, a little white car drove past Gorda's, banking around the sweeping curve up towards the highway. It clicked in her brain—the shape of the little round car.

She hopped up and ran to the edge of the parking lot, checking for the license plate, the one she'd memorized when she'd seen Crystal departing with this loser from WokChikaBok!Bok!

Had he recognized her—was that why he was staring at her as she biked by? She tried to remember if he had even seen her that day. She'd been behind the dumpsters, and she usually didn't attract a lot of attention anyway.

"Dude," she said out loud. "That's Crystal's...*man* friend." She couldn't use boyfriend because he wasn't a boy. But, he wasn't really a man either.

Tom caught up to her.

"You okay? You recognized that man, or that car, didn't you."

"Sure as hell did. That dude's a pedophile. That's what I was going to tell you. His name is John, and he was having some kind of relationship with Crystal. Jeremy was pissed about it." She shook all over with full-body heebie-jeebies.

Tom stared after the car, even though it was long gone, his chiseled jaw in profile, his eyes going all Clint Eastwood as he said to himself, "That, right there, is probable cause."

* * *

As Deirdre walked to Bonnie's house for wine night, she thought about how disappointed she had been in her oldest daughter last night.

She couldn't believe Rebecca had kept it secret that Crystal and Jeremy Bartley had gotten away safely.

But, Rebecca had finally, ten days later, come to the decision on her own, out of guilt.

And today, with a little prompting, Rebecca had set things right by telling Tom. Good girl.

Sally was already at Bonnie's when Deirdre got there, wearing gray sweats and sitting on the couch eating potato chips by the handful.

Deirdre questioned Bonnie with her eyes, and Bonnie glared back like, *"Don't you dare ask her."*

"Hey Sally," Deirdre said. She'd ask about the search for Samantha. That should be a safe topic. Tom had probably gotten his search warrant by now. "How is the search at Seeker's Sanctum going?" Bonnie smacked her arm.

"I wouldn't know," Sally said, staring at the television news.

She sat down next to Sally. "Have you talked to Tom?"

Sally stopped chewing, looked at her and said, "We had a fight."

"About what?"

Sally looked back at the TV and ate another chip.

Bonnie said, "That's not important, Deedee. Anyway, let's just try to enjoy ourselves tonight, we've had enough upset—"

"Where's Lina?" Deirdre asked.

"She's not up to coming over tonight," Bonnie sighed.

"What's up with her and Mike?" Deirdre asked, looking at both of them. Bonnie was Lina's neighbor, so Deirdre figured she'd know the scoop. And Sally and Lina were kind of close...at least, she thought they were.

"I don't know," Sally said. "She told me they're going to counseling. And that's all I can pry from her. She's a hard nut, that one." She took a swig of her rosé. "And she needs to get those horses out."

Deirdre changed the subject to something more pressing. "Well, since you haven't talked to Tom, then you wouldn't know this. Rebecca cracked the case."

"What?" Bonnie said.

"She recognized some pervo that was hanging around with Crystal Bartley. Tom is going to arrest him for Lexi's murder."

"Who is it?" Sally asked, sitting up so fast a chip flew off her sweatshirt.

"Some guy that lives in Lake Hemingway."

Sally said, "I knew it! I knew that guy was guilty, from the moment I saw him. And Tom had to tell me I was *interfering with the investigation.* Just like the other night. First, he asks for help, then, when we give it?" She shook her head and tightened her lips. When the pink had finally receded somewhat from her face, Sally said, "So that covers Lexi. What about Angela?"

Deirdre said, "Well, I don't care if Tom thinks we're interfering, we've gotta keep searching." That got a smile from Sally. "We can still find her and Samantha." *And Ginny,* she added, secretly.

"Dee. Are you *sure* you saw Samantha?" Bonnie asked gently.

Sally said, "Yeah, remember last month when you thought you saw the Black Witch? That was a crock of shit wasn't it?" She laughed, a little too hard.

"Sally!" Bonnie said. "Since when do you swear?"

"Since freaking yesterday!" Sally said. She looked down, and shook her head. "Goddamn that man."

"Okay, that's enough of the wine Sally." Bonnie said, taking her glass from her, after a small struggle. "And, you really do need to go to the eye doctor

Dee," she added, with a disapproving glare.

"She kicked me in the face! How can you not believe me? She was wearing this, like, potato sack dress. Are they keeping her hostage up there? And, I swear I saw someone standing above us, right before Samantha slipped away."

Bonnie shivered, and said, "I'm still not over getting soaked to the bone. It was nice of Zach to bring hot cocoa."

"So, Vivian's quite the cougar," Sally said bitterly.

"Apparently," Deirdre said, thinking of him coming downstairs in Vivian's living room, disheveled, bedhead hair everywhere. Vivian was a woman of endless mysteries.

"When does the pedophile get arrested?" Sally asked.

"Tomorrow," Deirdre said. "Rebecca has to formally ID him."

Monday, November 12

MONDAY MORNING AT SIX, TOM and his cavalry pulled up to John's house.

He'd taken his time getting a good search warrant, requisitioning the proper techs to come with him. He wanted shock and awe, the element of surprise, to put him off his guard, overwhelm him, scare the bejeezus out of him, knock the truth out of him. If only Tom wasn't so law abiding, he would do it with his fists.

He had two uniformed officers do the door pounding, the initial notification, handcuffing of the suspect, and sitting him on the porch while the techs made their way inside the house for a thorough search.

Tom watched for John's reaction. He was wild-eyed, confused, in boxers and a grimy undershirt. He was asking the officers something, asking if they would please not upset his grandmother.

Rebecca had come with them, and was sitting in the protection and anonymity of his partner's car—Scott had a much nicer car, some recent Japanese luxury coupe, and liked to drive it around on duty, whereas Tom preferred the Crown Vic.

Tom got out of the car, yawned and stretched his arms, kicked his legs. He made eye contact with John Davis, waited for the spark of recognition, but didn't react, just leaned back and spoke into his walkie talkie. This part was mostly for effect.

From behind Scott's tinted glass, Rebecca positively identified John as the man who had driven away with Crystal. Scott radioed that confirmation back to him, and Tom put the radio on his belt and pulled a notebook from the car, and walked slowly across the patchy lawn, avoiding the roots of the giant oak tree, which stuck up from the grass like bent knees under a blanket.

He climbed the three steps to the front porch, and took a seat across from the handcuffed suspect, on the same wobbly Adirondack chair he'd sat in the first time here.

"What's going on? What is this about?" John asked.

Tom didn't waste breath. "This has gone from a missing person to a murder. That's why I'm involved. If you cooperate, if you tell me everything, maybe I won't arrest you for the murder of Alexandra Marie Marconi." He allowed some of his real aggression and disdain to creep into his voice.

"Murder?" John's face grew paler. "Oh no," he said, a catch in his voice.

"So, let's cut the bullshit. Tell me about that night, and this time, tell me the truth."

John looked at his feet, what he could see of them over his paunch. From inside, the old woman yelled something, and his head jerked. "Please tell them not to upset my grandmother," he pleaded.

"Tell me the truth, and this'll go a lot smoother. She came here that night, didn't she?"

John nodded. "She did. Lexi came here. She said she had a big date, and she had nowhere to clean up." He looked out at the lake. Scott's car slid away, taking Rebecca back to Gorda's so she could head to school.

John cleared his throat. "Her family's been living in shelters or their car since the fires. I let her use our bathroom." He tilted his head to point inside. "We also had to evacuate for the fire, but luckily...nothing happened." He turned to look at the mobile home, as if to verify it was still standing. "But her family lost their house. Lost everything."

"Did she say who her date was with?" Tom asked.

"No she didn't. But she seemed really excited."

"So, after she cleaned up, what happened?"

"Well, she just took a shower, and then she was in there a long time, blowing her hair dry, getting made up."

"What was she wearing?"

"She was wearing all black, like usual, just a little fancier. Maybe a red top."

"And how did you happen to know Miss Marconi?"

"Uh...she was a friend of another friend of mine." Now he looked nervous. "They'd come over here a few times. It was part of a community outreach program, to sit with my grandma and read to her, so I could go do shopping and things...I really didn't know her that well. I was surprised when she called, but..."

"This other friend have a name?"

"Crystal Bartley."

Tom wrote the name down as if he'd never heard it before. He'd leave that for later. Right now he wanted to know about Lexi.

"So, big date huh? So, she showered. And then where did she go? Her boyfriend come pick her up?"

"No, she was fighting with her boyfriend. He was mad at her, they'd broken up. He didn't want her to go, wherever it was she was going. She just left, on foot."

"What's his name? The boyfriend she was fighting with?" he asked. He was obviously trying to implicate Jason Ontkeep, who had a rock-solid alibi.

"I—can't remember. Sorry."

"And did you know Angela Hernandez?"

"No, never met her. Lexi mentioned her, I think they were besties or something like that."

Besties. What kind of sick fuck talks like a junior high school girl.

"And have you ever met Samantha Austin?"

"No, never heard of her. Who's she?"

"Do you ever watch local news, sir?"

"Not too much, no."

"Samantha Austin is another, local, missing, girl." He emphasized each word, drilling his stare into John Davis' eyes. "As is your other...friend, Crystal Bartley."

John didn't do anything, but started to tremble slightly. That was good. He left him there under guard of the uniformed officers and checked inside. The forensics team were crawling over the place like ants. "It's a gold mine in here, long hair all over the place," the lead tech told him. That was enough for him.

He went back out to the porch, nodded to the officers, who knew what that meant. They hauled John out of his chair and turned him around, while Tom read him his rights. "You're under arrest. Anything you say can and will be used against you in a court of law."

"What about my grandma? Who's going to take care of her—I can't go to jail!"

From inside, the old woman yelled again from the back of the mobile home, this time intelligibly. "There was a fire! On the mountain. A fire!"

Tom finished the Miranda and walked into the back room, where the old lady was sitting up in her bed as the techs searched her room. A social worker was nearby, filling out paperwork. Tom had anticipated the grandmother problem and had notified APS to come out and take care of her.

As he stood at the head of the bed, the grandmother grabbed his hand, and looked up into his eyes. "It was trick or treat," she said, her voice full of girlish excitement. "The kids were all dressed up." She smiled. But then her face changed into a grimace, her hands shook and she yelled again. "There was a fire! A fire on the mountain!" She was pointing to the window facing her bed.

Crouching to her level, he looked where she was pointing. Through trees and power poles, she had one clear spot with a view all the way to the mountainside trail, where her pervert grandson had burned Lexi Marconi's body.

Tuesday, November 13

"YOU DO REALIZE, THAT THREE missing girls—one of whom is dead—have hair in your drain." Tom stood next to the table, looking down at John, using his height to his advantage.

The man, who wasn't that big to begin with, shrunk in his chair.

The hair that the techs had found in his shower yesterday was long, dark, and curly, which matched his story. He'd admitted Lexi had taken a shower there.

But they also found long, straight, light brown hair, possibly Angela's. It was being analyzed now.

And also, someone else's long blond-ish hair, all over the place. Possibly Crystal Bartley's. They didn't have anything to compare that to, unless they took a hair sample from her little brother to check against.

John hadn't gotten a lawyer. He was compliant and submissive, said he'd tell Tom anything, just as long as he didn't have to spend another night in jail. He wasn't cut out for it.

"I swear," John said. "I swear on my mother's grave. Angela never came to my house. And Lexi was there, but she left. I told you all this already."

"Okay." Tom sat down across from him. "You better start talking, because what we've got so far casts a lot of suspicion on you. Start with the phone call."

John sighed. He was sweating. "So, she called me Halloween night, around 6:30. I was handing out candy, and trying to feed Grandma dinner at the same time. She calls, and she sounds...I don't know...hurried, agitated? Asks if she can come over and use my bathroom. I said sure, whatever.

"So she shows up about twenty minutes later. She was in there for a while, using the hair dryer and everything. When she came out, I asked her what was going on. That's when she told me that her house burned down, and her friend had stood her up, and she was going on a job that night and needed to get ready."

He paused.

"Go on." Tom said. Now they were getting somewhere. "What kind of job?"

"I was only half listening, because of the trick-or-treaters, and my grandma, but, they were doing a photoshoot, or a film or something. And they were paying."

"Paying for what?"

"To model, act, whatever. Possibly some kind of acrobatics thing. She was really into that—circus, sideshow, carnival, all that stuff. Last spring, she mentioned she wanted to start training on aerials, but she didn't have the money."

"Aerials?"

"You know, like hanging from the ceiling twirling around."

"Like Cirque du Soleil?"

"Yep."

"So, she was a daredevil."

"Yeah, I guess you could say that. Nothing scared her. Not even going into the woods on Halloween night, with a bunch of guys she didn't know that well." He clenched his fists and took a couple of deep breaths. "You need to find them."

Tom closed his eyes.

They would find whoever did this.

But it wasn't John.

Sure, the guy was a total creep, and he'd throw him back in the lock-up when they were done here.

But Tom could tell John wasn't lying anymore.

The search at Seeker's Sanctum, once he'd gotten the warrant, had been a complete bust too.

Tom was starting to feel like a bad detective. And, to top it off, Sally wasn't speaking to him.

* * *

THE OLDSTERS HOSTED AN INFORMAL memorial for Lexi, in the rec room at Enchanted Gardens Retirement Home.

This was just for her school friends and other acquaintances, since her family hadn't planned the formal funeral yet. They were pretty devastated, from what Rebecca's mom had told her.

Rebecca wanted to pay her respects. The more she learned about Lexi, the more she admired her. She had guts, and spirit. And she wasn't someone who could easily be put into a box. Cheerleader, drama geek, rebel, friend to the unwanted (Angela) and elderly (these folks). Rebecca put her head down. She actually had tears in her eyes. She wiped them away.

But the real reason she was here was to find Lexi's killer. Or at least some kind of clue about who might've done it. And any kind of connection to Angela, and where she might be now. Dead or alive.

Oh sure, Tom Goodwin had arrested John yesterday, and she'd watched, with great satisfaction. At first.

But the longer she watched, the more she could tell, just from looking at the guy, that he was no match for Lexi.

Lexi was smart, and bold, and tough. No way she would let herself get caught off guard by a guy that looked like he could barely make it up a flight of stairs.

Or was Rebecca just fooling herself, trying to imagine that there was a way to keep from becoming prey—prey to the male of the species. If you were tough, smart, fast, strong...was that ever enough? How many women and girls got murdered, all the time, everywhere. No matter how fast or strong or smart they were.

It was so fucking futile.

Darius was sitting next to her. She'd begged him for a ride, since the old folks home was on the far side of town. They could still make it to work almost on time, once they were done here.

He had shown up this morning for school in a dark suit and tie, even though it wasn't *that* kind of a memorial. He was totally overdressed. But he looked so dapper, Rebecca had to talk herself down from crushing on him, just a tiny bit. He was the enemy. No matter how smooth and brown his skin was, how long and black his lashes were, how the other girls in AP English today had given him a second or a third look.

Darius would never murder anyone. She knew that for a fact.

So they weren't all evil.

She heard whispering and looked behind her. The cheer squad had just arrived.

They sat at the back, holding Kleenex, wiping tears, as the stern looking old lady spoke about Lexi and all her accomplishments. She finished with a few Bible verses, then everyone got up and milled around.

She elbowed Darius to get up. They went and got some punch and cookies.

Jason was there, talking to Jen and Gemma and Eric. He was cute, and seemed nice. Don't judge a book by its cover, she told herself. This could be Lexi's killer.

She kept up the ruse that she had known Lexi long ago. She could feel Darius' disapproval, but she didn't care. She introduced herself to Jason.

His face was puffy, like he'd been crying. She felt bad, but she needed information. "So, you were Lexi's boyfriend?" she asked.

"No...I mean, yes, we *were*. But I don't know if we still were. We were out of touch during the fires. Our phones didn't work, school was canceled. My family was staying over on the coast with my grandparents. We'd been... fighting a lot too. When we went back to school last week, it was already Halloween, and she wasn't even that excited to see me."

"Well," Rebecca said, trying to think of something comforting to say. "It makes sense she was distracted. I mean her house burned down."

"What?"

Did he not know this? "Yeah...she and her family were living in their car."

"I didn't know. She didn't tell me." He had a confused and hurt look on his face.

Rebecca felt bad now. "I'm sorry," she said, putting a hand on his arm. She lowered her voice. "What do you think happened?" She was talking about who might've murdered Lexi, but he was so lost in regrets he started talking about what had led to them breaking up.

"Over the summer, she was taking some kind of trapeze lessons or something. She'd take the bus down to San Diego once a week. She asked me for a loan to buy some equipment. But I'm not rich either. I don't even have a car." He hung his head. "She was tired of being poor. She said, 'I'm gonna be famous.' I thought she was joking around, and when I laughed, her face changed. She thought I was laughing at her, that I didn't believe in her. That's when it was all over for us." He started crying again.

She waited for a minute, keeping her hand on his arm, then said, "So, what about Angela?"

"What about her?" said Jason, looking up.

"She was supposed to be with Lexi that night. She still hasn't been found. Is there anything you can tell me? Anything at all that could help find her?"

Jason thought for a second. "Not really. Lexi attacked life, but Angie, sometimes it just seemed like she was waiting, in the background." He paused. "Even the black hair on Halloween didn't help her stand out."

"Black hair?" Rebecca said.

"Yeah," he said. "She came to school on Halloween dressed as a witch. Jen touched her hair and realized it wasn't a wig, and they all started squealing.

It was like they had a new respect for her. But the weird thing was, it didn't look...unnatural, you know? It looked like she was meant to have dark hair."

This was major news. She wanted to throttle him, and Jen, and whoever else had seen Angela that day. Why hadn't they thought to tell anyone about it?

She tugged Darius' sleeve, and they went out to the parking lot. She pulled out her phone and called her mom. It went to voicemail.

"Mom! Angela had black hair. She dyed her hair for Halloween!"

As she said this, the BMW from Lexi's vigil cruised by. The glint of a camera lens showed through the tinted windows in the back seat. Then it was gone.

Eric was waiting at his car. He gave them the evil eye as they went by. "Darius, hold on." She went over to him.

"Who are those guys? What did you say to them at the vigil?"

Eric said, "Those are those dudes that filmed that Blair Witch rip-off last year and got a million views. I told them to get lost."

Jen and Gemma had walked up.

"Your friends?" Gemma looked at Rebecca like she wanted to punch her. "From nursery school?"

"No, I don't know them!" Rebecca said. Jason was there now too.

"They were filming this. Probably working on their next fake documentary," Eric said.

Jason looked sick. "Oh my god." He put his head in his hands.

"What, Jason? What?" Gemma asked, bouncing up and down and looking urgently at him.

"That was one of the things we had fought about," he said. "Lexi told me she was collaborating with a guy, who just happened to have a new BMW. I said, 'what the fuck do you mean *collaborating*?' And she said, 'Exactly that. Collaborating.' Like dead serious." He looked at the driveway where the BMW had just left the parking lot. He clenched his fists and swallowed hard.

"What school do those guys go to?" Rebecca asked.

Eric said, "Del Sol, I think. I'm not sure, maybe private school, some of them. Maybe Obispo Prep in Costa del Mar."

The Catholic school. The one that cost more than Harvard.

"How did Lexi meet them?" Darius asked.

Jen sighed. "Lexi—she's hard to explain. She knows—she knew everyone, it seemed like."

So, Rebecca thought, Lexi knew everyone. But nobody really knew *her*.

Wednesday, November 14

THE NEXT DAY, REBECCA AND Darius stopped by his house in the few minutes they had after school and before work.

"Hello Rebecca!" Mrs. Fariz said, a surprised look on her face.

"Hi Mrs. Fariz. Nice to see you," she called as they dashed past her.

"So nice to see you. Can I get you anything to drink? Or eat?" she called after them.

"No thank you!" Rebecca yelled, as she followed Darius down the hall into his room and closed the door.

Darius turned on his computer, and offered her the desk chair. He sat on the corner of his bed nearby. They watched the progress bar travel across the screen as the computer started up.

"Come on, come on." Rebecca thrummed her fingers on the desk.

"Darius?" A tap on the door. "Are you two okay in there?"

"Just watching a video Mom! We'll only be a minute!"

Darius' family actually had real internet, unlike her house where just downloading an email took forever. They searched for and found the Blair Witch ripoff, which was titled, nonsensically, *The Silence of the Dams,* and hit play.

But instead of the video starting, they now had to wait through several annoying commercials.

"There's ads! Since when do they run ads on people's videos?" Rebecca said, disgusted.

"Since last May," Darius replied.

She let out a frustrated sound. "Come ON!"

She really hated ads.

There were ads for LipoCrush, Jolly Janitors, and even the "finest in luxury living, at Paraiso."

Seriously? They were still advertising Paraiso? Someone was asleep at the wheel. Just because Brian Bartley was a fugitive who'd escaped the country, didn't mean his executives shouldn't be taking care of the corporation. She shook her head and tsked.

She focused on the stuff below the video while they played. The user name was UrbanLegendary. "Look how many views it has. 1.2 M? Does that mean million? Fuck. How much is YouTube making on this thing?" Rebecca said.

"It's not just YouTube," Darius said. "They pay the users too. It's called monetization. Okay, here it is." The video was starting up.

They leaned towards the screen. Four guys came into view. Rebecca recognized two of them, from Lexi's vigil.

"Look at these douchebags," Darius said.

The video was shaky. It was almost dark, so it was really hard to see, and the unbalance made Rebecca feel sick.

"Where are they?" she asked. "Is that Del Diablo?"

The video showed their feet, lit by the camera light, going down a trail.

They were laughing and joking, teasing each other that they'd be scared shitless. Their dialogue sounded stilted.

Then, there was a scream from off camera.

"What was that?" one of them said. The camera flew around, just darkness and white faces.

"This shit is making me dizzy." Rebecca stopped the video.

"What else happens?" Darius asked.

She scrubbed through the rest of the video in fast forward.

Legs walking fast like Charlie Chaplin, more trail lit by a single flashlight, then, the camera swung up and around, outlining the shape of a dam.

"Yep, Lake Hemingway," Darius said.

She let it play. The boys were climbing up something concrete—the lower part of the dam.

"That's where the dogs picked up Angela's scent," Rebecca said.

The boys then went inside, into a big cavernous space.

"How many people have died here?" one guy said.

"Parker, look at this!" another one said.

She and Darius sat forward as the camera swung around, and a spotlight illuminated some massive paintings. It was like cave art, but modern.

"Nice," she said. She didn't know that was there.

"This, this must be the witch's lair," the Parker dude said. These guys were in no danger of winning an Oscar.

Another fake scream. The camera whirled around again.

"Ugh. It's giving me a migraine." She hit stop to give herself a break and started reading the comments. Stuff like 'totally sick brah' and 'made me sh*t my pants.'

She hadn't seen anything that terrifying, unless you were a complete sucker for a jump scare.

"Darius?" Another knock at the door. "What's that screaming?"

"Nothing Mom! Hey, I'll watch the rest later," Darius said. "We need to get to work."

"Okay, let's go," she said. "No, wait!" She grabbed his arm. "Look at this." Down to the side of the video were other related or recommended videos. "The Gray Girl. By FrightKnight. Look how many views that one has," she said, pointing. It said 120k.

"It's got a ways to go to catch up to Silence of the Dams," Darius said. "But, not bad. And look, it's only 38 seconds long."

"Let's watch it." She clicked on the video, and was shocked to see Fairy Glen Road, right where she had been biking last week before she turned to go to Jeremy's house.

The video was in slo-mo, shot through a dirty windshield, and she watched as the car took a curve, and right there, crossing the road was..."The Gray Girl!" she said. "What the..."

It was a young woman, dressed like a pioneer, except no fancy calico, just head-to-toe gray. The video had the quality of the famous Bigfoot footage, especially after the girl saw the car and started running towards the side of the road, looking behind her once. She disappeared into the undergrowth.

That was the end of the video. Rebecca felt the hair on her arms stand up.

"Darius!" called Mrs. Fariz through the door.

"Well, that was ten times creepier than that other video," Rebecca said, getting up.

"No kidding," Darius said. "That wasn't fake."

"You've gotta promise to watch the rest of the dam video tonight," Rebecca said, as he opened the door. His mother hopped out of their way. "Sorry, Mrs. Fariz. That's D-A-M. Haha. See you later."

Darius grabbed her arm and pulled her out the door.

* * *

THAT EVENING, VIVIAN WENT TO yoga at Morgan's house.

She usually avoided going on Wednesdays, which was Fairy Glen Residents Only Night, but she was starting to get used to the ragtag crew of local horse ladies, if only for entertainment value.

She walked into Morgan's serene, plant-filled entryway, kicked off her shoes, went into the living room and rolled out her mat.

There, in front, were Lina, Sally, and Bonnie. No Deirdre so far. But she was always late.

Sally was saying fiercely, "...and he said to me, there's something not right about that guy—"

Bonnie turned and smiled at Vivian, all crinkly blue eyes and silver-gold curls. "How are you?" she said, forcing the rest to turn around and see her.

Sally was still scowling. An awkward silence descended.

"It was so nice of your...friend to bring us hot chocolate," Bonnie said, and smiled again. Did that woman ever say anything *not* nice?

Vivian simply nodded at them, and folded herself into Lotus to wait for Morgan.

But, maybe Bonnie wasn't just being nice. Maybe she was dropping a big old hint. About Zach.

Because really. Why had he been at the search? Why was he so interested in finding this girl?

Plus, he had started at Gorda's *after* the girl went missing.

And the biggest mystery of all: why had she been so easily swayed by something as simple as a man bringing her hot chocolate?

The lights dimmed halfway, and Morgan entered in her bare feet, long limbs swinging. She wore white yoga pants and a sky blue and white tie-dyed tank top. She was always so relaxed. Maybe because she made so much money on something as seemingly spiritual as yoga.

Morgan sat on her little round pillow at the front of the class. "Good evening everyone."

They were the only ones here, besides old deaf George, who'd just now walked in and was creakily unrolling his mat and lowering himself to the ground, slow as a tortoise.

Morgan began the class.

When they were in warrior pose, Vivian kept thinking of Zach, his tattoo, how he'd been forced to join a gang in prison.

If she didn't provide enough info to the DEA, she might end up in prison too. Could she hack it? Would they put her in federal lockup, and was that any nicer? If you were a female white collar criminal, was it at least...livable?

The other alternative was to go down shooting.

Visions of slow-mo gunfire, like scenes from a Quentin Tarantino movie, played in her mind. First Bill. *Bam!* Right in the head. Then Ted. He'd get it in the kneecaps first. Make him suffer a little.

She made a note to clean the guns her father left her, maybe tonight. Or...

maybe tomorrow. Her dad had instilled in her, never touch a gun if you've been drinking. And she had already started, before coming here.

She breathed out, twisting her body into the next pose. On the other hand, if Martha Stewart could survive prison, she sure as hell could. There must be ways to procure what one needed while on the inside.

After class, after they'd all lain in shavasana in the dark for many minutes, Morgan turned the lights back on. She looked at her students. "How are we tonight?"

The three horsewomen in front answered, all at once. They stopped, and started again, one by one.

"It's so tragic about Lexi Marconi," Bonnie said.

Lina turned around and waved imperiously to Vivian to come to the front, and she reluctantly scooted closer to the cabal.

"We're still searching for the other girls," Sally said. "Every time we go out riding."

"DeeDee thinks she saw Samantha up on the hill, on Seeker's Sanctum land," Lina said.

"Really?" Morgan said, and looked into the distance. "By the way, where is Deirdre tonight?"

* * *

DEIRDRE TURNED ON THE DOME light and looked at Angela's flyer again. Last seen taking the bus to the mission, where Deirdre was right now, sitting in the Bronco waiting for Teresa.

Her heart had soared yesterday when Rebecca told her about Angela's hair being black. She called Tom and told him, and he'd let slip that the hair found at John's was light brown, undyed. Meaning she probably *wasn't* there on Halloween with Lexi.

The girls could've shared a hairbrush so many times that their hair was all intermingled. Which means they weren't necessarily together that night.

Deirdre had wanted to jump up and dance around for joy, because there was still hope.

But, even after an update to Angela's hair color went out on the news last night, complete with a computer alteration of her picture to give her black hair, there were still no new leads.

She looked at the flyer again. Missing since 10/31/2007.

Halloween had been on a Wednesday. Why hadn't she noticed that before?

Wednesday night services seemed like a throwback to the olden days—

who has time to go to a church on a weekday? But then again, I go to yoga class religiously on Wednesday nights, I could just as easily be going to church, Deirdre thought.

And there were a surprising number of people here. The way Deirdre figured it, some people have habits and routines that you can set your clock by.

And maybe some of them had been here that Wednesday too, and seen Angela.

She got out of the car and looked around the parking lot for Teresa.

There she was. Deirdre stuck a hand in the air and waved to her, and they met up and went inside, just as mass was starting.

Teresa elbowed her, trying to show her when to kneel.

Deirdre nodded and whispered, "I was raised Catholic. It's just been a long time."

"So you're not Catholic anymore?"

"Well, once a Catholic, always a Catholic, I guess." She shrugged, then to her dismay, groaned loudly as she knelt. That ride on the mountain last Friday—not to mention getting kicked in the face—had left her aching and sore. She folded her hands, which was awkward with her cast, to pray for a miracle.

After mass, they went out the side door, to the little courtyard where they'd sat under the tree the first time Deirdre came here, on Day of the Dead.

Deirdre looked to the right. Just leaving through the wrought iron gate, were two women in black dresses.

The gate swung shut behind them.

"Let's go look at the grave," Deirdre said, and started walking towards the gate.

"O-*kaaaay*," Teresa said, drawing out the last syllable of the word. She obviously wasn't convinced about Deirdre's quest, but she was going along with it.

Once they got partway out to Cheryl's grave, Deirdre realized how dark it was, and how cold—she hadn't brought a heavy enough jacket, because it was damp too, the kind of damp that seeps through your clothes and into your bones.

She looked at Teresa, who pulled her heavy shawl tighter around her. "You okay?"

Teresa nodded. "Let's just hurry," she said, pulling out her phone and using it to light the way.

When they got to the grave, Teresa shone her flashlight on the stone.

"That was Angela's mother," Deirdre said.

"So young!" Teresa said.

She spotted the two women—it was the same two old women she had seen exiting the church that day she was talking to Teresa out by the big tree. They must be regulars. She nudged Teresa.

The old women finished visiting their grave and walked back towards the church, towards Deirdre and Teresa.

Teresa stopped them and showed them photos of Angela, and at first they shook their heads, but once they said her hair was black now, they looked more closely and then one of them nodded and said "Ahh. Si. Yes."

They spoke mostly Spanish, so Teresa was doing most of the talking, but Deirdre understood almost everything.

"Oh yes, Indian girl. Beautiful hair," the older one said.

They had seen her meeting a man.

"They met at the grave," the younger one said.

"So, he approached her...?" Teresa asked.

"No, he was there first," the younger one said.

Which meant, this man knew the grave? He knew the grave that Angela would be looking for. How?

"Did she talk to him?" Deirdre asked in Spanish.

"Yes, we saw them leave together later. We were sitting on the bench waiting for the bus."

Angela had left with an unknown man. That was bad news.

"What did that man look like?" Teresa asked them. "What about the car?"

They gave two wildly varying descriptions, and began arguing with each other.

But what they could agree on was that he had sandy or light brown hair that was in need of a haircut, a little wavy, and was wearing jeans and a black overcoat. Broad shoulders, a curved back. "Como un mono." Kind of like an ape.

"He had one of those chains hanging out near his belt...the ones that attach you to your wallet," said the younger one.

And for the car, all they could really remember was that it was an older Japanese car, one with a loud exhaust and square trunk. One remembered it being burgundy, one remembered it being black, but faded to gray from the sun.

Sounded like the car that she'd seen in Vivian's driveway. Millions of them around. Japanese cars just keep running, long after the paint fades and the miles add up.

Zach's car. The new barback at Gorda's also had a wallet chain, she remembered when he'd come in to apply for the job. And he obviously was not naturally black haired, she'd noticed that the first time she met him. What was his natural hair color?

But she shook her head. It couldn't be him, could it?

"Lo siento, yo penso they were familia," the oldest woman said, with anguish in her eyes. Deirdre understood her Spanglish.

"She looked so happy," the older one said in Spanish, with Teresa translating. "If she had looked scared we would've intervened."

"Gracias, muchas gracias," Deirdre said, holding her hands and looking into her eyes. "You've helped enormously."

"We will keep them in our prayers," the younger one said.

Deirdre turned to Teresa. "Can you ask them to come make a statement to the sheriff?"

And, if it was who she thought it was, identify him.

Teresa turned around to ask them, but they were gone, into the foggy night.

The flesh at the nape of Deirdre's neck prickled. Then she shook with a full-body chill.

She called after them in a shaky voice, "Yes, please ladies. Keep her in your prayers."

Wherever she might be.

* * *

AFTER THE SNAKE BIT ANGELA, a huge white owl had descended and covered her with his wings, protecting her, like she was a little owl baby in a nest.

He lifted her, and she flew over the valley, higher and higher, over the asylum, over the lake, straight up dizzying heights, sheer faces of granite, and craggy peaks, until she landed, defying all physics, at the very top of a towering mountain.

There, she'd spent uncountable hours, innumerable days, infinite minutes.

Now, singing infiltrated Angela's dreams.

White wings, singing...where was she?

Was she dead? The thought jolted her. Was this the afterlife?

She struggled to regain awareness.

She woke in the dark. It was hot. There was smoke, drifting upwards, like a soul escaping.

Maybe she was in the other place.

She peered above herself, into what should've been the sky. As her eyes adapted, she could make out the lines of branches curved overhead, not far from her.

She was in some kind of a tent, dome, or handmade shelter. A small fire burned near her feet, releasing its smoke through a tiny hole in the roof. To her right was a short doorway. Outside, the gray of a coming dawn. The singing continued, one male voice, but words she didn't know.

The massive pain of her swollen foot felt distant and disconnected, like it belonged to someone else. She tried to look down at it, but she was completely covered by a blanket.

She heard rustling, outside the dome, and she was suddenly full of fear again. Now she was a captive, and she couldn't walk, and...

A shape darkened the doorway. She threw the blanket off of her and tried to scramble to her feet, but couldn't. She dragged herself backwards with her arms, but they collapsed underneath her. She started shivering.

"No child, don't fear." A man's voice, trembling and quaky, but still strong. A very old man. The shape moved inside the tent, shuffling and clucking like a mother hen. "I've brought you something. Here, drink."

He held out a bowl of sorts, looked like it had been hand carved from a knot of a tree, and then polished smooth. When she didn't take it, he set it down and stayed still, perhaps sensing that she was terrified. She tried to see him.

The first thing that materialized out of the darkness were eyes. Large, round, too large for his shrunken face. A peculiar reddish brown.

His leathery skin seemed to have wrinkled around his shrunken skull and down-pointed, prominent nose. White hair surrounded his head in a fuzzy globe.

"Child. You're hurt. This will help you heal."

"A snake bit me," she said.

"Yes. Drink this, and flush the poison from your body." He picked up the bowl again and came closer. She didn't move away as he placed stacks of folded blankets behind her, to help her support herself in a sitting position, and covered her up with the blanket she'd thrown off. He handed her the bowl again. "Drink. I will dress your wound."

She took the bowl, and took a tentative sip. It smelled awful. It tasted like sour berries and dust. While she drank, he unrolled the blanket from her leg, unwrapped the linen bandages. She was shocked to see her leg about twice its usual size, red and purple. She was surprised the skin hadn't split open, like when you leave a hot dog on the barbecue too long. But somehow she wasn't afraid.

"Who are you?" she asked. It was a question that was obvious, hanging in the air.

He put something cool and wet over where the snake had bitten her, on her lower calf. Her boots were gone. What else was gone? She panicked for a second. What was she wearing? Her camisole and underwear, under the thick woolen blanket that smelled like a dirty dog.

Yet still, she wasn't afraid. He pressed the cool compress onto her wound, then wrapped newer strips of bandage around her leg with surprising swiftness before he turned to her.

"You and I are kin," he said. "Now, drink."

She drank the rest of the foul-smelling liquid and handed the bowl back to him.

"You will sleep. Don't be afraid, I will protect you. Wherever you go in your dream world, remember that. You don't need to come back until the snake poison is all gone."

She was already lying down again as he said this. He tucked the blankets around her in a warm embrace, and then his shadow slipped out the doorway and the flap closed her in, as she slid down, down, into welcome darkness.

Thursday, November 15

IT TURNS OUT, THE CHILLS Deirdre got last night at the mission were not just from seeing the old ladies seemingly vanish into the mist.

They were also because she was coming down with the flu. Bad.

That cold, rainy night on the mountain had thrown her immune system for a loop, and now she was down for the count.

She at least had enough energy to call Tom and tell him about the ladies at the mission, and her theory about the barback, before she sunk into a deep sleep last night.

Justin was home all week and next. Stanton Academy, unlike normal schools that take two days off for Thanksgiving, instead took two weeks so that travel to other parts of the country would not be undertaken during the busier Thanksgiving week. Justin, being his kind, level-headed twelve year old self, had made breakfast for the rest of the family this morning, which she had heard them eating, with absolutely zero appetite of her own.

Deirdre flipped impatiently in the bed, unable to get comfortable. She couldn't get up and do anything, and yet she so wanted to be doing something, even helping Walt, who she could hear outside dismantling the barn, with Justin and Brian Jr.'s help.

She turned on the TV. On the 11am news, there were interviews with people who were coming forward with sightings of the black-haired girl still dressed like a witch a few days after Halloween.

The first was an interview with a trucker that drove Angela back to Encantadino from the desert.

Deirdre sat up. What was she doing in the desert?

The male reporter, who looked like he just graduated junior high, was asking, "Why didn't you tell the Border Patrol checkpoint that you had the missing girl in your truck? Why did you hide the girl?"

The truck driver, who had bulging eyes and thinning blond hair said, "I just wanted her to get home."

"M-hmm." The man-boy thoughtfully scrunched his brow and put a pencil to his lips.

The truck driver nervously filled the silence. "She seemed old enough to do her own thing. She just really wanted to get home. I didn't want to spook her. I picked her up in the desert. You know what happens to people that get lost in the desert?" He lifted his lip.

"And yet, you could ask the same thing about young girls who hitchhike in semi-trucks..."

The phone rang. It was Cassie. "Are you watching this?" she asked, a tremble in her voice.

"Cass..." she said, but said nothing more as the truck driver continued, "—you know, we get a lot of hitchhikers on the road, runaways."

Cass's pained voice came over the line. "Why was she in the desert? Trying to find where her mother died? What happened out there? I think that driver is lying, he did something to her, just look at him, he's a weirdo, you can tell. Or maybe...maybe she really did run away." Cassie burst into tears.

"Oh, Cass, you shouldn't be watching this. Okay? Turn it off. I'll—I'll call you later, and check on you." She hung up, feeling like a piece of garbage. She was reaching the exhaustion point with supporting her friend.

She looked back at the TV.

Now, there were interviews with the employees of the Diesel Diner, the desert cafe. The waitress remembered that there was a girl, then she was gone. "Didn't even touch her burger," she said, and described the man she was with. "He was tall, kinda cute. Sandy, longish hair, kinda greasy. Rude, too." She didn't remember what the girl looked like, except scared.

"Then why didn't you do anything, you cow!" Deirdre shouted. She muted the rest of it; a long string of sightings, people coming forward for their one minute of fame.

She sighed and lay back down, staring at the ceiling. She was so tired.

The fever made her skin hot and dry, which reminded her of her ride up the mountain during the fire. That had been less than a month ago. No wonder she was tired.

Not to mention, her cast had gotten wet last Friday night and was starting to get flexible, which she was sure was not a good thing for a broken bone. But she would just be careful with it. No more riding, not until she was well. No more looking through forests for disappearing girls.

"Mama, did you read the chapter I marked for you?" Clara bounced into the room, went to the nightstand, and pulled the book off to look. "You didn't read it yet, did you?" she said.

It was Clara's newest obsession, *The History of Fairy Glen*, an old, out-of-print book that she had checked out last week from her school's library.

"No honey, I didn't. I'm sorry. Why don't you read to me?" she said.

"Okay." Clara hopped onto Walt's side of the bed, sat back against the pillows with the big book, and went into her reading voice. "The reason that the wee folk are depicted in drawings as small, is that their natural world is actually much larger than ours. Therefore, they look small in comparison. But do not be fooled. Fairies are the same size as we are, and fickle and capricious, so beware of crossing one..."

"That's not really in there Clara, you're just making that up."

Clara giggled, but continued in her bubbling voice. Deirdre closed her eyes and drifted...

She entered a forest of outsize trees.

Every leaf was like a patio umbrella to her. Under the leaves, she took shelter from the rain.

Oh, it felt wonderful, and tropical. They really needed this rain. A spout of water came down from the tip of a leaf above her. Rainwater, fresh and pure.

The rain subsided, and she walked further into the forest. She kept walking along the path until she came to a clearing.

In the clearing, bathed in pure bluish white light, in soft focus from the recent drizzle, was a white mare.

Ginny.

She was young and beautiful. Her flesh round and filled out, muscle quivering under her silky hide. She looked straight at Deirdre, then spooked and ran, trailing rainbows.

"Oh!" Deirdre said it as she woke, slick with sweat and completely disoriented. She must've fallen asleep.

Walt was talking softly to her. "Sweetie, Morgan's here."

She looked up at his face. There was sawdust in his mustache, and she wiped it off for him.

He said, "She wanted to give you something in person," then whispered, "Sorry I tried to keep her out." He stood up. "Clara, come help me and the boys."

Deirdre lifted her head, which made her eyeballs hurt. Morgan appeared in the doorway, her hair up in a bun, dressed in a white trench coat.

"Is it raining?" Deirdre asked.

Morgan stepped into the room. "Not yet!" she said cheerily. She was carrying a canvas tote bag and started digging through it. "I brought you some stuff to help you get over this flu. Echinacea, lavender, eucalyptus, that should help you sleep—"

"Speaking of sleep," Deirdre got up on one elbow, "I just had the wildest dream. It felt real."

Morgan pursed her lips and sat on the edge of the bed. "Oh yeah? Tell me about it."

"I was in this giant rainforest, and then I saw Ginny, except she was young and filled out again. She looked good! But then it was like she was blaming me or something. I saw it in her eyes."

The vision slipped away. Still, the lingering guilt plagued her.

In the dream, Ginny was young, like when little five year old Angela had ridden her, ten years ago.

Arabs were notoriously youthful. So Ginny at nineteen had been in the prime of her life. Just old and smart enough to be trusted with a little kid, one that had already gone through a hell of a time.

But since then, had Deirdre done everything she could for Ginny?

Ginny had gotten swaybacked and her muscles were stringy, but Deirdre always thought of it more like Jack LaLanne, like a tough but strong old man. The flush, filled-out look of youth, replaced with sinewy elegance.

She couldn't afford endless supplements, but she did make her a nice, hot, beet pulp mash every night, with extra carrots.

But maybe if she had given Ginny supplements, if she had been stronger and faster, she could've outraced the firestorm.

"I don't think she was ever at Mrs. Fey's house," she said to Morgan. "I think she burned in the fire." She burst into tears—howling, uncontrollable blubbering, that caught her off guard.

Morgan hugged her and rubbed her back.

Deirdre sat up, grabbing a tissue and getting herself under control. "I'm sorry I haven't come to yoga all month."

Morgan shook her head. "Yoga means never having to say your sorry." She paused. "What else was in your dream?"

"Well, it was like a strange world of gigantic plants and ferns."

"Really?" Morgan sat up straighter. "And did you see anything, other than Ginny? Any other animals or...people?"

"No, I think I woke up too soon."

"Well, here's a little tincture." Morgan pulled a dropper bottle out of her bag. "This might help you get back there. And whatever you do, trust what you see."

She put a dropperful onto Deirdre's tongue. "Sweet dreams," Morgan said. "I have a mission of my own."

She smiled and left.

And now, taking her place at the doorway, was Brian Jr.

"Hi Mrs. Boyd," he said. The bright sunny boy she'd met last month was so different, so serious now. Poor kid.

"Can I talk to you?" he asked.

She nodded, and Brian walked in.

"If you didn't save me, who did?" His eyebrows twisted up on his smooth, twelve year old forehead. He was so young, just like a puppy or a kitten or something. She didn't want to hurt him, more than he'd already been hurt.

She thought, and thought, and finally the only explanation that made any sense came to her.

"Your brother and sister."

"Really?"

She nodded, smiling. "You must be so glad to hear that they made it out of the fire, right?"

"What?" He screwed up his mouth and backed up. "I didn't hear that. I mean, I'm hoping they did, but...Jeremy's car was completely burned—" He hiccuped, and stopped talking.

Oh crap.

Rebecca! Rebecca hadn't told Stephanie and Brian. Had she even told Tom?

Oh God, she felt really strange. The tincture was kicking in. She lay back in bed. "Brian, you shouldn't be around me, I have the flu. I'm not making sense. Go, go. We'll talk when I'm better."

Too bad Deirdre couldn't keep her eyes open. Because it was Rebecca that needed a good talking to right now, wherever she was.

* * *

"So what was the rest of the movie?" Rebecca asked Darius, as they got in his little Honda after school.

"Just jump scares, like you said." He pulled out, and instead of going to WokChikaBok!Bok! he headed for the freeway.

Not only had Darius watched the rest of the video as promised, he'd also tracked down the usernames on MySpace, and correlated them to the filmmakers' real names and where they went to school.

"So, like what was the plot though?" she asked.

"No plot," Darius said. "Just someone—couldn't tell if they were real or fake—hanging from the ceiling. And then they flashed some lights, and it wasn't there anymore. Then vice-versa. Lame."

"1.2 million views lame," she said.

He laughed. "Some cool murals inside the dam though. I know those guys were not responsible for that. A real artist was."

"Maybe we should check it out sometime," she said.

He looked at her. "You like hanging out in strange structures, huh?"

"What?"

"I mean, what happened between you and Jeremy? Didn't he take you up to Paraiso before...everything happened?"

"Darius. Let's focus on our mission."

"I am focused. Hell, I'm missing Academic Decathlon practice for this."

"And I'm missing work. Your dad's gonna be mad at me."

When they got to Obispo Prep in La Jolla, Darius pulled into the parking lot. About half the cars in the student lot were still there, even though school had let out an hour ago. In the field, lacrosse practice was in progress. Over on the track, runners were doing sprints.

"What's the plan?" Darius asked.

"Drive around, look natural," she said. "I'm looking for the BMW. If nothing else, I'll get the license plate number."

There were so many BMWs though, and they all looked the same.

"Damn it!" she said.

"Time to give up?"

"No, keep going. There's a few more rows."

He swung the car around and went down the last row.

"I don't know," Rebecca said, losing her certainty that they'd find something here. "There's no BMWs in this row."

"Wait!" Darius said. "Act cool." He pulled into one of the empty spots. A group of lacrosse players passed by on the walkway in front of them. One of them gave Darius' car a funny look.

"Maybe you should've gone to the carwash first," she whispered, sinking in her seat.

"No, they see I don't have a parking permit," he said. "They know we're intruders. But I thought I recognized one of them from the movie."

"Which one?"

"The limping one. I think that's Parker." He looked like the typical rich asshole antagonist in an eighties movie.

This guy hadn't been at the vigil, or the memorial, at least not that she'd seen. They watched as he shifted his gym bag and pulled out some keys.

"Day-um!" Darius said, when he clicked the keys and a silver sportscar chirped and flashed. He popped the trunk and put his bag in.

"What?"

"That's a Lotus. Several leagues above a Beemer." Darius' eyes grew wide.

"Put your tongue back in your mouth dude," she said to him.

She angled the rearview mirror to see Parker. He was getting into his car, she didn't have much time.

"So, follow him?" Darius asked. He started the engine. "Or is it too risky...hey!"

She was already out of the car and striding towards the Lotus. The driver's side door was closing. She scooted over faster and said, "Heeeeey Parker," in what she hoped was a flirtatious, girly voice.

He looked up from the driver's seat. His face was a little off-kilter, no smile, just deadpan. "No fans," he said through clenched teeth, and shut the door, started the engine, and pulled out.

* * *

ANGELA WOKE UP COVERED IN sweat. She threw the blankets off her, trying desperately to breathe. The fire was dead, no more smoke, just a few hot embers glowing.

But now, frigid dry air assaulted her skin, like shards of glass pelting her. She broke out in full body tremors, the sweat turning to ice water. She reached desperately for the blanket again, but after a few moments of shaking under it, her teeth chattering, she was blazing hot once more.

Exhausted by ten more rounds of this, she slipped away finally.

She flew again. She met Lexi, a thousand feet above the dam, at Lake Hemingway.

"Finally, you show up where you were supposed to meet me." Lexi floated beside her, on the edge of night and morning, the edge of life and death. "You missed my first and last performance. My big debut. That was my surprise for you. I hope it was worth it."

Below the still surface of the lake, a shape slithered through the dark water.

They dropped down and stood outside the ruptured chain-link. Angela handed her the lost lipgloss.

Lexi took it and swiped some onto her lips. It was dark purple against her skin. When had she gotten so pale?

"What happened to you Lexi?" she asked.

Lexi pressed her lips together, rubbing the lip gloss in, then made a kissy face. "This is what they call OOBE. Out of body experience. Astral projection," she said.

Lexi had studied that too, tried to get Angela to meet her on the astral plane in the middle of the night. Angela figured it was finally working. It was kind of cool, but now she was losing her patience.

"Lexi, answer me. We need to go home. Where are you?"

"Oh, you know, I ran away and joined the circus." She laughed.

Angela was not amused. "Seriously Lexi. Tell me."

"Seriously? Okay." She looked down. "You know that lioness you saw?"

"Yes..." Now, Angela wasn't sure if she wanted the answer.

"There's a reason you didn't see the male lion. It attacked me and the boys. At the asylum. Three of them ran, scared, and the lion attacked me and Parker." Lexi clenched her teeth, balled up her fists. "Parker cried like a little boy, and the lion ripped his testicles off, then his arms and legs, one by one. Then his head." She was really acting it out, eyes wide, looking at something that wasn't there, making claws with her hands. "I jumped on the lion's back and pulled him off, then he turned on me, but I fought. I fought him. I broke his jaw."

Lexi breathed out, relaxed her fists. She looked at Angela and smiled, a lurid, purple grimace. "I survived."

Friday, November 16

THE CAT JUMPED ON THE bed, and Deirdre woke up with a start. She threw the covers off of her, looking at the ceiling in the dim night, then at the clock on her nightstand, which read 2:48 in glowing red numbers.

She had an uneasy feeling, more than just her sickness. She had slept all day, but hadn't dreamed a thing, just blankness. Complete oblivion.

She put her hand out, and felt nothing but empty, flat bed. Then she remembered, Walt was sleeping on the couch because she was sick. Now she desperately wished he was here next to her.

She shivered, and pulled the sheet back on, her eyes heavy-lidded. She closed them, drifting down into sleep once more.

The sound of rain and running water came back to her.

Now she was walking through some kind of tunnel—a corrugated steel drainage tunnel, like the one near the asylum. She stopped and listened for traffic sounds overhead, but all she heard was rain. She continued, moving towards the light, towards the rain. Step by step.

She put a hand out to balance on the wall of the tunnel. But it gave under pressure and she gasped and pulled her hand back.

She put out her hand again, carefully, looking closer. The tunnel was... alive.

Was she in the maw of a giant beast?

She touched the ribs, ran her hand up the side, traced the veins coming out of each one, which branched into endless fractals of capillaries.

Recognition kicked in. She was inside a curled leaf.

She hurried towards the light. The sound of rain lessened, then stopped.

She stepped out, into the rainforest. Soggy peat bounded back with each step she took. She began to run, and the steps made her bounce like the astronauts on the moon. She was invincible, unbreakable, leaping up so her head touched the underside of the enormous ferns.

It was so cool here, fresh and wonderful. There was the creek ahead.

As she got closer, she could see it was a raging river, miles wide. Beyond, on the far bank, was a lush forest, not coastal scrub like her home territory. More mountainous, alpine.

Across that river was where she needed to go, to find Ginny. She knew it.

But how would she get there? The river got wider the longer she stared. Suddenly, it all felt hopeless. She was shrinking smaller and more insignificant with each breath.

Now the river looked like an ocean, endless and impassable.

A winged shadow fell over her. She clutched herself into a ball, but it was too late, a bird's giant talons wrapped around her shoulders...and lifted up. Screaming, she saw the ground beneath her zoom away, down down down.

She screamed again, but then realized it didn't hurt, and stopped.

She was suffused by a buoyancy, carried along by the mighty wings as if they were her own.

This is what it was like to fly.

Then she heard something. It was a soft nicker, the same sound Ginny made when her hay was coming in the evening, when her eyes went all doe-like, and she was content.

"Ginny?" Deirdre called out. Below her now was pine forest, and peaks of snow-capped mountains, and crystalline lakes.

Far below, she saw a horse, only the size of a lizard, miniaturized by her altitude. It was running on a trail.

A white horse.

Ginny.

She was stretching her neck, pumping it with her gallop, her mane streaming back. On and on she ran, leaping occasionally as if for the pure joy of it, kicking her heels out behind her.

Deirdre floated up higher now, even though she wanted to follow.

"No," she said, trying to stay down, but it was no use, like trying to stay underwater, she felt herself rise up, and up and up, and soon she was above the clouds.

"Ginny! Find Angela!" she yelled, and then everything was white.

* * *

WHEN SALLY GOT OFF WORK at noon, she left her office and went to the courthouse library again.

It was Friday before Thanksgiving, and the library would be closed all next week. She was running out of time.

She'd gotten the adoption records unsealed, seen Angela's birth certificate. But there was no father listed, so she'd have to do some more digging.

She could pull Cheryl Sandman's birth certificate, do a records search to locate any family she could track from that, and also pull up prior addresses and credit records for Cheryl.

That would be a good start.

About an hour later, she'd exhausted her search. Cheryl Sandman didn't have a birth certificate, at least under that name. Might be some kind of alias, or a married name, but there was no record of a marriage.

However, Sally did find credit records, which were almost always reliable. Bills follow you everywhere.

Cheryl's last known address was close by. Like really close by, in the southwestern part of Encantadino. Which was only a small detour from her normal route home.

She picked up her purse and headed for her car. She didn't have to worry about picking Emily up—school was out this week, so she was at home.

On the drive, she thought about Angela, who was only a few years older than Emily. With Angela's best friend dead, what were the chances she was still alive?

Cheryl's old address was in a large apartment complex of patchy beige stucco. Two stories, with outer stairways with white wooden railings, a little peeling paint here and there, but it was decent enough.

She parked her car in a visitor's spot and got out. She put her hands on her hips and arched backwards as she looked around, stretching. Good thing she had an active hobby like endurance riding. And good thing her job was part-time, otherwise all that chair sitting in the DAs office would make her ass twice as huge. Secretarial spread, they called it.

There were still some nice bushes and landscaping. It wasn't completely dilapidated. A little rundown, yes. But not scary. Rent was crazy high anywhere in California. Sally was lucky she still had her house, her property, that she and Paul had bought back when things were normal-priced. And now that she was single, she was lucky she could still make the mortgage payments.

She thought suddenly of Tom, and a chasm of longing and regret opened inside her. Why had she been so hard on him? And what was he doing now? She refused to call him so she had no idea if he was getting close to finding Angela.

She looked around for apartment 302. She saw it, up the stairs, the front door looking down on the parking lot.

This is where little Angela had lived, before the fateful night that her mother got murdered. Murdered in the desert, a hundred miles from here. Sally had a moment of self-doubt. Would visiting the apartment actually tell her anything? Maybe this was a complete wild goose chase.

Nope, it was worth a shot. What else could they do?

She climbed the stairs, and knocked on the door. No answer. Of course—it was the middle of the day. The people that lived here were probably at work. And it's not like they'd know anything about whoever had lived here ten years ago.

She started slowly down the stairs. A gust of wind picked up her skirt. She tucked it down, looking at the sky. Typical autumn sunshine, but there were clouds rolling in.

Below, in a little courtyard next to the pool, was a swingset. A young woman with two toddlers was swinging them, tucked safely in their little seats that surrounded them like diapers. She smiled, remembering when Emily was that little. She walked over, her heels clicking on the concrete, and the woman looked up.

"Hi," Sally said. She realized she had an advantage. People weren't afraid of women. It must be so much easier to investigate. "I'm trying to track down an old friend that used to live upstairs, ten years ago. Is there anyone in this complex who's lived here that long?"

The woman straightened up. "Yes, actually. Betsy. She's over there, in 112." She pointed to a door across the drive.

Sally went over, knocked on the door, and the old lady let her in. She invited Sally to sit on the couch. She had a good memory, knew exactly who Sally was talking about.

"Handsome rogue. Beautiful Indian lady."

"Indian?" Sally asked.

"Yes." Betsy straightened her skirts and cleared her throat. "Native American. From the tribe up north."

"Do you remember their names?"

"Cheryl was the woman. The man's name was Travis. One night a whole bunch of police showed up—oh yes, it was Halloween night, that's right—and the next day they were all gone. Never found out what happened. Cute little girl. She was dressed as a little lion that night. She and her mother had come by trick-or-treating earlier in the evening. I don't remember her name though...hmm..."

Sally looked out the window from her seat on the flowered couch. She had a perfect view of the front door of apartment 302. "Angela," she said.

"Yes!" said Betsy. "It was Angela."

"So what did the cops do when they came?" Sally asked.

Betsy said, "Well, I think they took him away. But, the girl and her mother..." She lifted her palms to the heavens. "Who knows? They were just gone."

An arrest. That was something she could research, she had an exact date and address, an actual concrete event. If only she was on speaking terms with Tom, he could look it up.

Luckily she still had a few hours of the day left. She could go back to the courthouse for more research. Secretarial spread be damned.

Sally stood up. "Thank you. You've been so helpful."

Betsy said, "You're very welcome. Oh, wait! I remembered something else. Oh, it's probably nothing, but...at around 3am, the fire alarms went off. There was smoke billowing out of the apartment, and when the fire department came, they found something burning in the oven. A pie."

* * *

Morgan finished her baking, packed it up, and drove her white Jaguar out of Fairy Glen and through downtown San Amaro Hills.

At the stoplight, she saw a few of her clients—well maintained women who were chaperoning their children out of school, walking them home.

This whole planned community was designed to be walkable, like a place from the 1950s, like Leave it to Beaver. She smiled and waved as one of the women recognized her. There was a slight nip in the air, so they were wearing sweaters, tights and Ugg boots, their long, straightened, glassy hair streaming in the blustery autumn currents.

They were, to quote the home decor plaques, Too Blessed To Be Stressed.

They had all day to go to the beach, the mall, the spa, the gym—even to her place for yoga—before picking up their children and then cooking healthy organic meals in cozy brand new kitchens. It was good for business to have so many potential yogis so close by. But she did miss the empty hills that had been here before. The newness of this place left her cold.

And also, quite a few of her clients had started paying late, or forgetting to pay altogether.

There was, despite the relaxed California vibe, a palpable undercurrent of fear. As if at any moment these moms could turn feral, baring their fangs and fighting for their lives.

The light turned green. After passing the town square and the elementary school, she turned and drove through one of the more expensive subdivisions, a newer one with hardly any occupants, until she reached the start of Seeker's Sanctum Road, where the pavement changed visibly.

Here, at the threshold, she paused, put the car in park, and put a ward over herself. Seeker's Valley was powerful, and that could be good or bad.

When she was done, she patted the basket of home baked cookies in the passenger seat, chuckled to herself, and continued down the road.

At Seeker's Sanctum, they buzzed the gate open for her. She had an appointment.

Morgan was no stranger here. She'd been to their weekend open houses, and a few of her friends had held events, retreats, and classes here. She much preferred the homey nineteenth century white clapboard church down in Pleasant Hollow, that the spiritualists had lived around in their hand-built cottages and tents. However, there was absolutely no reason why she wouldn't eventually want to run an event here at Seeker's Sanctum. No reason at all.

She met with the event coordinator. He was a tall, stout young man with the look of a teenager, but eyes that held ages of wisdom.

He showed her all around the retreat center—the auditorium, the bunkhouse, the bungalows, the dining hall.

The sheriffs had already done a complete search of the place, after Tom Goodwin got the warrant, based on Deirdre Boyd's eye witness account of seeing Samantha on their property. The sheriffs didn't find anything. But that didn't mean Morgan wouldn't.

She knew from what the horsewomen had told her that the girl was seen on the hillside, in a little stone house. That house and the trails surrounding it had also been searched, but sometimes searching—truly seeking someone —meant more than the physical cataloging of a place.

She spoke for a while longer about a fictional overnight retreat she'd like to run. "A ceremony...a sacred ceremony that has been misunderstood, misappropriated, and monetized improperly in recent years." This one, she said, would be the real deal. But it was for a very small group, and they wanted absolute privacy and time in nature. "There may only be a handful of people attending. My goal is not to make money, but to aid in the enlightenment of those who seek the truth." This, she said with conviction, because this part was true. "Is there anyplace more...remote?"

He looked about to say something, looking from side to side, but then pressed his lips into his mouth. Morgan found that body language was often quite literal. He ate his lips so as not to speak.

She added quickly, "It doesn't matter if it's rustic—in fact, the more rustic the better."

His eyes went side to side as if deciding, and he finally said, "Let me show you our olive groves and paths."

They walked out through the main gates, across the dead-end road, to a chain-link fence topped with barbed wire, where he opened a locked gate. They went through, into a labyrinth of hedges. There was only enough room to walk single file, so she let him lead. They got higher and higher, and she turned to look at the valley behind her. If nothing else came of it, it was good cardio.

Finally, when they were almost to the top where she'd be able to see over the hill to the other side into Fairy Glen, he stepped off the trail, through some more tall bushes, and came upon a tiny stone house.

"This was a shepherd's cabin, long ago. We left it as it was, to honor the history."

She stepped inside. There was a view to the north of Seeker's Valley, and to the west, over the hills, to the ocean.

"Very nice," she said quietly. "Could we sit for a while? I like to absorb the ambiance of a place."

"Certainly," he said, with a smile. He felt much more relaxed here than he had on the retreat grounds. "Let's go outside, here." He stepped through the doorway towards the view of the valley to the north. Outside was a stone bench, and they sat in the shade. She took a drink from her water bottle, then pulled two cookies out of her purse.

"Baked fresh this morning!" she said playfully, and handed him one.

He looked almost embarrassed, but took it with shining eyes. "Thanks!"

"We needed sustenance after that hike, right?" she said, kicking off her Birkenstocks and sitting cross-legged on the stone, gathering her skirt around her legs and feet. It was beautiful up here. The sound of birdsong, the fresh coastal wind sighing through the sagebrush.

Why would they keep a girl hostage here? It didn't make sense. She took another bite of her cookie. He'd eaten half of his, and they sat in easy silence, looking at the horizon.

Turning to him, she suddenly realized she couldn't pull off this charade; didn't want to.

"I'm sorry Matthew. I'm not here about a retreat."

He looked at her, surprised. "Oh?"

She confessed to him that she was looking for Samantha. They were communing now, truly communing, with nature, with each other, by sharing the sacrament of the baked goods.

He confessed that the girl was here, seeming to be relieved by the unburdening. "But we were sheltering her, not holding her hostage."

"Why?" she asked. Why would an established religious retreat center take the risk of doing anything with a minor?

"We were granting her temporary asylum." He sighed, folded his hands, and explained. "Her family belongs to a religion that believes things contrary to what we believe."

"What do you believe?"

"We believe that people have autonomy, and self-direction, and all people are sacred and should be protected and honored."

"And their religion doesn't believe that?"

"Not unless you think marrying twelve-year-olds is 'honoring' them," he said, a touch of bitterness creeping in. "I must admit, I convinced Raymond to take this on. He didn't want to, but I felt a special connection...a personal responsibility to make things right." He looked in her eyes. "I grew up under the same system. I escaped that life. I wanted to help her escape too."

Morgan placed a hand on his. His eyes were full of compassion. "Is she still here?" she asked.

He didn't answer, but said, "Her parents put a price on her head. A bounty. So other people will help hunt her down."

She said, "I won't compromise her. I want to help."

He sighed. "She's still under our protection, that's all I'll say. I won't let her go back to her parents. However—" he stood up, so she couldn't see his face. "She can't remain here indefinitely. Her conscience is weighing on her."

"Her conscience? She hasn't done anything wrong has she?"

Matthew turned to look her in the eye, and the babyish-ness was gone from his face, replaced by determination. "If she testifies, how can we guarantee her safety?"

"Testifies? About what?" Morgan stood up.

There was a long silence. Then he spoke. "She witnessed the murder of that young woman."

Morgan put a hand on her chest. *Oh Lord.*

A clap of thunder rolled over the hills from the east.

* * *

ANGELA EMERGED FROM A CLOUD. She looked for Lexi, momentarily panicked when she didn't see her.

Then, Lexi spun down from a greater elevation.

"What happened to you Lexi?" she asked again. Maybe this time she'd get an answer.

Below, in the gray water, she saw the massive creature again, sliding through the depths near the dam.

"There's Ernie," Lexi said, smiling down at it. "You know, the reservoir at the top of Mount Richardson is connected to this one with underground pipes. They pump water up there. That's also how Ernie's babies get up there." She did a triple flip in the air.

"Lexi! Stop pulling my leg," Angela said. "Let's go back."

"Come with me." Lexi pulled her further down.

They flew down to the entrance of the dam again. On the shores of the lake, the white horse watched, eating grass, just keeping an eye on them. Lexi opened the gate and pulled Angela through and they went inside, into the tunnels with the murals.

Angela tried a different strategy. Maybe appealing to Lexi's desire for fame would make her want to go home. She said, "You're the girl that fought off a lion. You'll be a legend. 99.9 percent of missing girls just get raped and offed by pedophiles. You've got the best story. When should we go back?"

Lexi was silent for a bit. Then she said, "My family didn't even report me missing for two days." Her voice was like lead. When Angela saw her face lit by the Christmas lights in the tunnel, she saw sadness. She couldn't remember ever seeing Lexi sad. Mad, yes. But not sad.

"But, that's because you've run away like fifteen times."

"You go. Go home without me. Cassie really loves you." Lexi always called adults, even their teachers, by their first names, as if she were their equal. "What do you think she's feeling right now? She's probably going out of her mind with worry!"

"I don't wanna think about that," Angela said. "I'm not going back without you."

"You've got it good, and you don't even appreciate it." Lexi laced her fingers and flexed, cracking her knuckles. "Besides. I lied. I didn't fight off a lion."

"You didn't?" Had Angela imagined the pack of African animals? "What happened then?"

Lexi looked up. "Parker...Parker wouldn't pay me. I'd told him my fee up front. But when it came time to pay up, he said, 'Oh, I didn't bring any cash.' Then he tried to say that I should be paying him, because by being in his stupid movie I'd get famous.

"Yeah. I drag all my equipment out on this long-ass hike in the middle of the night on Halloween, and then risk my life doing some death-defying stunts in an old building that's falling down? And what do I get for it? Exposure, he says. Exposure. For all my time, practice, costs, risks, blood sweat and tears. 'I don't want your exposure,' I said to him. 'I want my money. They money we agreed on.'" Lexi was agitated, her voice getting louder.

"Then he comes towards me, like, as if I was going to *sleep* with him or something, for payment. I said 'No way, that wasn't the deal. No fucking way dude. Now give me my fucking money, like we agreed on.'

"He comes at me again, all smooth and suave like I just needed a chance to change my mind, to decide I wanted to fuck him."

"God, what an asshole," Angela breathed. "What'd you do?" Angela had never been in that situation. She wondered what she would do.

"I told him to back off, but he kept coming at me. He threw me down, and then I started yelling, and he started choking me. I fought him, but...he was stronger.

"Then they all came running back to see what happened, and he told them I'd gotten tangled in my silks.

"But then...then he convinced them all, somehow, because he's just the golden boy, that they had to get rid of the *evidence*"—she rolled her eyes and made air quotes—"or else they'd all get in trouble. Pussies. That's what they called me after I died. The evidence. Watch too much frickin' CSI."

Angela felt a tear run down her face. "We're never going home," she said, "are we?"

Lexi ignored her. "They burned me up. They burned my—my perfect body," Lexi said with anguish, gesturing up and down her equally perfect ghostly body. "With my own white gas from my fire poi, no less."

"You're dead," Angela sobbed. "It's my fault! I wasn't there with you. I killed you Lexi. I killed you." Tears washed down her face. The reservoir below was filling up with her tears.

A thousand unspoken words passed between them, like always; their language, the closeness of best friends, the way they were almost psychic. She would never have that again.

"Lexi," she said. "I'll miss you." Those words were weighted a thousand times, heavier than gold, pulling her down towards the dam, the water. She'd drown.

Rain started falling, pulling her further down, pelting her.

Lexi followed and pulled her up by the collar.

"Eh, what can you do? I'm dead. You on the other hand, are still alive. You'll get to learn how to drive, and go to prom...and man, why'd you kill me Angela?" she said with a wicked grin. "You gotta make it up to me. You gotta live. I mean really live. For me."

* * *

Sally searched arrest records for 10/31/1996 and cross-referenced the apartment address. There. She found it. Travis Baker, arrested on Halloween night for the burglary of a pawn shop in Hemet the week before.

She scanned his details: 25 years old, blond hair, green eyes, 6'1", 185 lbs.

She clicked on the icon to load his photo.

The mugshot downloaded at a glacial pace. First the hair appeared, a short haircut, messy, light brown. *Hmm. Wouldn't really call that blond,* she thought. Then the eyes came in. Something caught in Sally's throat.

Those eyes. Very familiar. The nose was there now. "Oh my god!"

Before the rest of the face loaded, she was running out of the library, desperately dialing Tom's number, her purse and attaché case bouncing as she ran in her heels.

It went to his voicemail, and she yelled into the phone, "Tom, you were right about Zach! Meet me at Gorda's!"

She was halfway there by the time her phone rang.

She explained to Tom what she'd found, and said, "I'm going there now. We need to find out if he's seen Angela. Why would he be hanging around, trying to help find her, but not want anyone to know who he is?" she said, speeding up. It wasn't rush hour yet, but traffic was starting to clog the streets anyway.

Tom said, "Wait. Sally, don't go by yourself. I don't want to spook this guy. Sally?"

She was racing down the main thoroughfare that would turn into Del Diablo Highway, concentrating on driving. She focused in on Tom's voice again, listening over the sound of her engine revving. He was saying, "...after all, we don't know what he's done...so far, he's only guilty of going by an assumed identity, possibly violating terms of his parole. It's best for me to talk to him. Besides, he could be dangerous."

She sped up and barely made a yellow light. Now the road narrowed to one lane each way and swung down towards the lake.

"Sally? Can you hear me?" Tom said.

"Just...just hurry!" she said, and hung up. She needed both hands for the wheel now. It was starting to rain.

When she got to Gorda's, she parked and ran inside, past the restaurant and into the bar. She wasn't sure if he'd be there, hadn't thought through what she'd do. Her eyes darted back and forth. Nobody here except two construction workers at the end of the bar, and Gorda wiping down the other end of the bar. The construction workers, who'd probably gotten rained out of their jobs and decided to start happy hour early, turned to check her out.

Although on second thought, they weren't checking her out. The stare was a little too deadpan. She must've looked panicked, and she was wet from the rain. They probably wondered what was wrong with her.

She ran to Gorda, who was stocking liquor bottles behind the bar. "Is Zach here?" she whispered hoarsely.

Gorda turned around and took stock of her. "No, not yet. He comes on at four. What's going on?"

Sally leaned over the bar, closer to Gorda. "He's not who he says he is." She stopped to catch her breath.

Gorda's eyes widened. "I knew it!" she said.

"He was in prison."

"Well, I knew that," Gorda seemed to relax. "I've given lots of ex-cons jobs. He told me that up front."

"No—he's Angela's father."

Gorda's mouth, lined in perfect red lipstick, dropped open. "What the hell? Why isn't he helping find her then?"

"He's hiding something. He's hiding who he is. The question is, why?"

Gorda threw down her bar towel. "Let's find out," she said ominously, and marched into the back room.

"Gorda, wait!" Sally yelled. She followed her into the storeroom, where she saw the back door closing. She ran towards it, and out into the back parking lot. She didn't want Gorda finding out anything before she did.

She spun around, trying to see where she'd gone. "Gorda!" she called. The back parking lot sloped up, towards the thick fairy oaks and underbrush that covered the strip of land between the restaurant and the highway. There, at the top edge of the lot, a branch was swinging.

She ran towards it and ducked under the branches.

"Gorda, wait!" she said again, catching her breath as she came out in a small clearing.

What was this?

A truck camper that should've been in the bed of a pickup, but was set up on cinder blocks instead, stood in the clearing.

Gorda was sticking a key in the lock of the little door at the back of it, ignoring the rain. "I knew he was hiding something from me," she said, as she pulled herself inside the camper.

Sally followed her into the tiny, wood-grained space. This must be where Zach was staying. Rain was beating on the roof, their breath steaming in the small space. "You shouldn't be here...he might be dangerous," Sally said. "I'll search, you go back to the bar."

"Bullshit. This is my place, he's just sleeping here."

A quick look under the bed revealed hiking boots, a compass, and binoculars. "What is this map for?" Gorda said, pointing at the ceiling.

Sally craned her neck to see. Taped to the ceiling was a large map of Fairy Glen. She stood and peered up at it in the dim light, then pulled out her cellphone and turned on its flashlight. Each spot that they'd searched on horseback was marked in some way.

She pulled the map off the ceiling, put on her reading glasses, and looked at it more closely.

On Fairy Glen Road, just north of the parking lot for the nature preserve, was a small scrawl in black ink that said "Ang" with a slash of an X in red marker on the road, then a line, up and up to the spot where the other gals had found that backpack and feathers.

Gorda was pulling more stuff from under the bed. Printouts of Google satellite, newspaper clippings, and some other printed pages. "Hey," Gorda said, pulling out the binoculars. "These are night vision goggles."

A chill came over her. He was hunting his own daughter.

"Gorda, you have to get out of here. Tom is on his way—" Sally started dialing his number as she folded the map and stashed it in her purse.

They stepped out of the camper.

Just then, Zach ducked under the branch and walked into the clearing, his long arms loose, strolling like he owned the place.

He saw them and startled. Sally narrowed her eyes.

When he recovered, he said, "Hola amigas! Que pasa?" He put one hand up for a high five from Gorda. Gorda put her hand on her hip.

His smile faded, and he put his hand back down slowly. "Why are you going through my stuff?" Anger changed his face. "Hey...you-you can't come in here without notice. What about tenant's rights!"

"What's up with all these maps?" Gorda asked, holding up a handful of them. Looking like she could smack him with the stack.

"I like to hike."

"In the burnt wilderness?" Sally asked. He looked at her, as if seeing her for the first time, and a cold wave spread through her midsection. She held her phone at her side, hoping that Tom had picked up and could hear.

"Have you gotten your ID yet, *Zach*?" Gorda asked, saying his name sarcastically. "From your mom in...where was it? Idaho? Indiana? Or Iowa? Or was it Illinois? You've told me at least two of those. Do you remember which ones? Because I do." Gorda's black eyes were flashing, her cheeks flushed with anger underneath her rouge. Sally wanted to step between them, but thought better of it.

"I don't have to listen to this. I could report you to the Labor Board. Just go ahead and fire me. I'll get my stuff and move out right now." He maneuvered around them and reached inside the camper.

Gorda said under her breath, "Oh you're fired alright—" But then she sucked in her breath and backed up, her hands in the air. He was pointing a small revolver at Gorda. "A fucking gun! Are you kidding me? How in the hell did you buy that with your prison record?"

"More like who did you steal it from?" Vivian said, emerging from the trees.

Everyone turned to stare at Vivian, who held out her hand and said, "My father gave that to me. Give it back."

Zach's face was immobile. Sally could tell this was a crucial split second. What would he do?

Sally was trying to judge whether she could reach him with a karate kick —she'd taken martial arts back in the eighties—when Tom stepped from the undergrowth, aiming a huge revolver at Zach. He held it easily, almost casually. She'd never seen him carry a gun before. Suddenly, she feared for him.

"Zach. Put it down now," Tom said. It wasn't a command so much as soothing, fatherly advice. He might as well have called him son.

"His name's not Zach, it's Travis!" Sally said.

Zach turned to her, pointing the gun in her direction. Tom started towards him, but Zach arced the gun back over to aim at Tom.

Tom stopped and backed up a step, but didn't lower his weapon.

Zach's eyes widened, and his teeth showed like a cornered animal. She looked at his finger on the trigger of the little gun, attuned to any movement.

Zach didn't do anything for a full second. Then he twitched. Sally squeezed her eyes closed, thinking Tom would surely be shot dead, but there was no gun blast. Footfalls, scuffling, and the sound of grunting and bushes cracking...

She opened her eyes, and both men were gone from the clearing.

She looked for Tom, but he was already running towards his car. He pulled the radio out of it and called for backup.

When she caught up she said, "How do we find him now?"

"*WE* don't. Stay here Sally!" he roared.

Sirens whooped, and red-and-blue lights lit up the rain out on the highway.

Tom ran through the bushes after Zach.

Saturday, November 17

SALLY GOT UP EARLY, SADDLED Darkling, and rode to Vivian's house, where she pounded on the door until it opened.

"Okay, show me where this old lady lives," she said.

She showed Vivian the map, the one she had kept tucked in her purse last night after the sheriffs had searched the little camper, while the manhunt was going on across the street and up the side of Mount Richardson.

Sally didn't feel guilty about keeping the map because she could always give it back afterwards. She could claim it was all so upsetting she forgot she had it.

"It has some stuff circled on it, and notes, and I'm thinking Mrs. Fey might know about it, since she's lived here forever."

Vivian just nodded, and went to get Apache ready.

They rode far up the creek, crossed through a stand of cedars, and came out into a lush, grassy clearing shaded by the tall trees and the steep slopes of Mount Richardson. There was a tiny cottage, complete with a curlicue of smoke coming up from the crooked stone chimney. It looked like a painting from the Thomas Kinkade store in the mall come to life.

They tied up the horses and went inside, where Vivian introduced her to Mrs. Fey.

"So nice to meet you. I've heard a lot about you," Sally said.

Mrs. Fey was welcoming, and offered them breakfast. "Put your horses in the pasture out back while I make it," she said, bustling around the kitchen. When they came back in she said, "My, what a beautiful horse you have!" to Sally.

Darkling was a beauty—a dark, almost black, bay MorAb. He got comments everywhere she went.

Part of what made Darkling so beautiful was the conditioning; the exercise, nutrition, and rest program she adhered to that made his muscles sleek and his coat glossy.

"Pretty is as pretty does," she said. "That horse could just as easily go a hundred miles as ten."

Mrs. Fey stopped from her cooking and looked at her. "*Really?* Hmm. Quite interesting. I'll keep that in mind." She went back to frying whatever she was making for breakfast. Sally moved the teacups to the side and spread the map out on the old lady's kitchen table so she and Vivian could look at it.

"So, he marked it here, where he must've seen her, sometime around the day that Deirdre went searching at the asylum." She looked up at Vivian. "You know, that really pisses me off! He was just lurking around Gorda's to pick up on what we were doing and where we were searching."

Vivian swallowed. "I saw him that day. I thought he was looking for me."

"Well, now you know better." Sally said. Vivian still looked uncomfortable, so she said, "Hey, better to find out a guy's a loser sooner rather than later, right? Now, back to the map. What I found on here was something else. See this mark here? It's pretty close to where we are now, and I think it says 'G'father Tree'. What do you think that means?"

Mrs. Fey put their plates on the table, over the map. "Grandfather Tree," she said.

"What is that?" Vivian asked her. As she listened to the old woman talk, Sally dug into her breakfast. She sensed they might have another long trail ride ahead of them today, and she would need the fuel.

* * *

THE LONG, PRE-DAWN DRIVE to the prison was Tom's penitence.

Penitance for being headstrong and foolhardy. He flinched from his bruised ribs as he took a regretful breath.

Tom had led the massive search last night up the side of Mount Richardson, to the west of Gorda's. But it seemed that Travis Baker had a knack for disappearing into the woods, just like his daughter Angela.

When they'd searched Travis' trailer, they found printouts of news articles about Cheryl Sandman's murder, and maps of the desert where it had happened. Which lined up with the stories of the waitress and the truck driver. He'd taken Angela to the desert, but she'd escaped from him. And now he wanted her back.

He had to admit, Sally was onto something when she was researching Angela's parents. And he should've taken Deirdre Boyd more seriously when she'd told him her suspicions of Zach.

So, taking a cue from Sally, Tom had decided on a new way to attack the mystery of Angela's disappearance. Instead of in the present, in the past. Back in time.

Tom did all the security mumbo jumbo at the entrance, parked in the cool morning fog that smelled of the nearby cow pastures, and walked to the guard house, where he showed his credentials and passed through the sally port into the prison.

The fluorescent lights were jarring on his sleep-deprived eyes. He waited for the guards to pull Eddie out of his cell and bring him into the private room. He watched as the man—tall, salt and pepper gray hair, rugged and sinewy—was seated, his manacles left in place.

Tom looked at his notes.

Edward James was serving time for the 1996 murder of Angela's birth mother, Cheryl Sandman.

The circumstances had been horrific. Her body left beaten in the desert, her car destroyed, torn apart.

So, Mr. James had been looking for something that night in the desert. Just like Travis still was.

The kid was left high on a ledge. Thank God some ATV riders had found her the next day, or she wouldn't have survived. Thank God it was November, and a cool enough day in the desert. She was LifeFlighted back to Paloma Hospital in Encantadino. She survived.

Eddie was picked up at a nearby Border Patrol checkpoint. His face was scratched, and he was high on methamphetamine. It wasn't hard to put two and two together, especially once the dead woman was found.

For the trial, Eddie had a public defender, and there was DNA evidence. He'd pled down to avoid the death penalty, but was still in for life.

Tom went into the room.

He sat, facing this man, a man who had left a kid to die in the desert, after killing her mother.

And instead of telling him what he thought of him, Tom offered a deal.

"If you cooperate with us, we can see about a reduced sentence. Think of that. You could maybe get out while your dick still works. What do you know about Travis Baker?"

Eddie raised his eyebrows, and looked pleased. "Travis was a cheat."

There had been an anonymous tip, Halloween night, fingering Travis in another burglary that had taken place the week before. Tom took a chance that it was Eddie.

"So, you tipped off the cops about the other burglary you'd done with him. The pawn shop?"

Eddie didn't respond at first. The man's face was cruel. Anyone who could murder a young mother and leave the kid in the desert was human scum. He tried to keep the opinion off of his face, keep it neutral. He waited. Prisoners were often eager to talk, even just to appease the boredom.

"Travis did a job, that night. He had the loot from it, and I wanted it. Simple as that. I'd done all the work, casing the place, figuring out how to do it. The cops picked him up, but before I could get there, the bitch took it. She hid it somewhere. I thought she had it on her, but—" He left it unfinished, and shrugged.

"What about the kid?"

Eddie said, "What about her?"

"The kid was there. Do your buddies inside know that? What did you do to her?"

Eddie raised his hands, clanking the chains. "Hey, I didn't even know there was a kid. Not until the trial. So don't go accusing me of that kind of shit."

"Fine. Say I believe you. You gotta give me more."

"More?" Eddie scowled, his forehead screwed up in knots from using all the brain power he had. "Like what?"

"Save me some computer time. I can look it up, easy enough. Halloween, 1996. Unsolved burglaries." Tom leaned back in his chair. "But it's more interesting coming from you. What was the job?"

"Okay," Eddie said. "Easy enough. An estate jewelry store in old town Encantadino. There was this display window, of orange and black stones, all Halloween decor and stuff. All expensive, all valuable—let's see. There was fire opal, garnet, topaz, jet, ebony. And one very, very expensive, fancy vivid orange solitaire."

"So, he busted the display window? Smash and grab?"

"Oh, hell no. Too risky during the day, and they always put that shit inside at night. It was in the safe. Very tricky burglary. Cat burglary, they used to call it. I taught him everything he knows about that. And about jewelry. He knew safe cracking. His old man taught him, I think he said. These old buildings are full of security gaps, potential ways in. He slid through the ventilation shaft, and cracked the safe. We were supposed to divvy it up. But he tipped them off about me, an anonymous tip about the job we'd done the week before. They arrested me the day before Halloween. Just like he planned, so he could take it all."

"So you turning him in was what, payback?"

"I told you. I didn't turn him in."

"Right." Tom stood up.

He would double-check the details of the crime, see if he could track down the store owner, and get more information. He turned to leave.

As the door buzzed open, he heard Eddie behind him, saying, "Hey! When do I find out about getting out of here?"

Tom smiled and didn't answer.

As he drove, he thought about what Eddie had told him.

These were just a few of the thousands of silky fine threads; the loose ends of cold-cases, so-called 'solved' cases, and disappearances.

Often one just needed to shift perspective, to zoom out a little in order to tie them all together into the larger tapestry of a crime.

Now he knew what Travis wanted. Somewhere out there was a very valuable stash of jewels, presuming nobody had found it in the intervening years.

And Angela might be the only one alive—if she was still alive—that knew where.

* * *

"*WHAT DID YOU FIND?*"

"Huh?" Angela mumbled. Her tongue was thick but her eyes opened surprisingly easy. The white puffy halo of hair was above her in the darkness. Rain beat a snare drum on the lodge. "Here, drink. But before you forget, what did you find?"

He placed the smooth bowl in her hands, and she took a tentative sip. Fresh water. She gulped, and almost choked, because she was remembering now.

"Lexi. Lexi. I'm so sorry." Anguished tears drenched her face, and she fell into the old man's arms, sobbing and sobbing, for minutes, hours, until nothing else came.

She pulled away and looked into his face. In it she saw hers, and for the first time, her mother's.

"Grandfather," she said, and pulled him close again, laughing through her tears.

"You may call me that."

He led her out of the hut. She wore the blanket like a poncho.

It had rained, and the ground was damp, mist hanging in the air. They were surrounded by pine trees. She'd never seen pines around here before, they must be up high.

A small campfire was out in the open of the small clearing, and a stone house, if you could call it that, seemed to merge with the wall of smooth gray granite behind it. It looked smaller than her bedroom.

She walked past it to a break in the circle of pines, and when she looked down, her breath vanished from her lungs. They were at the very top of the mountain, the height was dizzying. The valley below looked like she could hold it in her hand.

He stood beside her, waiting for it all to sink in. She looked over at him. He was so small. His skin was red brown, burnished where it wasn't wrinkled. His eyes were so surrounded by folds of skin that she couldn't see them now. His white brows were outrageously fluffy.

She remembered the strange, yellow-brown eyes peering at her in the hut. She saw it behind her now, an upside down dish shape, like a tall UFO, but made of long flexed branches woven together, filled in with strips of bark and pine needles.

She looked back at him. "I remember," she said.

She remembered him, lifting her when she was only a baby, high above, how she'd giggled, felt like she was flying. That was it. But it was enough.

A spindly white horse, hip bones poking, came out of the trees.

"Do you know that horse?" Angela asked.

He nodded. "She's a good old gal."

Angela looked down at her leg. The bandages had fallen away on their own. There was an angry red area surrounding the bite, which was still covered in the chalky poultice. But the swelling was almost gone, her leg was almost normal size again. She'd walked out here without pain.

He tossed some hay to the horse, who began munching it off the ground near the edge of the trees.

"Come, sit down. I've made breakfast," he said.

"How do you survive here?" she asked.

"Acorns, pine nuts, rabbit, quail." He gestured around him. "There is plenty."

They went into the stone house, sat down, and he served her some kind of baked squash filled with seeds and berries and grains. It was delicious. They talked for hours after breakfast was done.

"My home was in the high valleys." He pointed to the east. "But we were evicted. Mexicans and Spaniards, even though they came here and claimed that they owned the land, they at least let us stay in our villages. But when the white man got a grant, the U.S. government didn't see it the same way. They forced us to leave. Sent us down the mountain, to the mission. That's where the rest of my family stayed. That's where you come from. But really, you belong to the high valleys. That's your home too.

"I could not abide. I came here. I couldn't be on my mountain, so I found another one. One that nobody else wanted. One that nobody could force me off of."

He imparted their entire history to her. And she remembered everything. Finally, he went to a stone in the fireplace, removed it, and pulled out a package.

"I can't go down the mountain with you," he said.

"I'll stay here then," she said.

"No. You must go back. You need to be with your family."

"You're my family."

He walked to the single, warped glass window, and looked out into the yard.

"Maybe she'll take you," he said.

The white mare was still outside, waiting for her. It was time to leave.

* * *

MRS. FEY FINISHED TELLING SALLY and Vivian the legend of the old man on the mountain.

"Some associate him with the white owl. But he's known as Grandfather to most people."

"Have you ever met him?" Vivian asked. "Is he even real?"

Mrs. Fey frowned and tilted her head. "Well, the tree named after him isn't far from here. They say he took it as a sapling from his old home and brought it here and planted it. The owl is sometimes seen there, and it became known as the Grandfather tree. But that isn't where he lives." She smiled at them both. "Finish your tea, dears."

Sally and Vivian drank. "We have to get going," Sally said. Her phone rang. It was Tom.

"Sally, I'm driving home from CMC. I'll be back in a few hours. Look, I'm sorry I wasn't interested when you were looking into Angela's past. You were onto something. So I went and interviewed the man who killed her birth mother."

Sally sat forward. "And?"

"The story is, Travis stole a bunch of jewels on Halloween night. But when the cops came to arrest Travis, it was for a previous burglary. They didn't know he'd just gotten home from committing another one. They didn't search the apartment, because they had no reason to. The loot from the previous burglary had already been recovered from his partner, Eddie, who had confessed to the crime and cut a deal by ratting out Travis. Because of his cooperation, Eddie was out on bail by that evening, and killed Cheryl the next morning."

"So..." Sally said, trying to piece it all together. "When the cops came and took Zach—I mean Travis—away, Cheryl was left home with Angela and... a bunch of jewelry?" She scratched her head. "The old lady at the apartment complex said that after the cops came, Cheryl left with Angela. She thought they were probably going to post bail or something, or go stay with a relative. But maybe..."

Tom said, "Yep. Angela knows where it's hidden. Eddie killed her mother because she wouldn't tell him where it was. It's still out there somewhere."

"We're going out on another search for Angela." She didn't tell him about the map she still had.

"Be careful. Travis could still be out there somewhere. I'm calling Scott right now to come over there and go with you—" She hung up before he could finish.

"Let's go," she said to Vivian.

* * *

GRANDFATHER GAVE ANGELA THE SMALL wrapped package. "Your inheritance."

"What is it?"

"You'll have to see."

He put a blanket on the mare's back, wrapped a huge leather strap over it and tightened it gently around her barrel. Then he tied the package to the strap with a strip of leather. It balanced on the mare's withers.

"Is that what my father is looking for?"

He didn't answer.

He led the horse, who wasn't wearing a halter or bridle or anything on her head, to a knee-high stone in the yard. Angela understood. She had already put her clothes back on, which Grandfather had washed and dried for her, even her boots, although the one on her right foot was unlaced to accommodate the swelling.

She got up on the stone, mounted the horse, and looked down at her grandfather, who looked even shorter now. His puff of hair stirred in the cool breeze. He gathered his wool poncho around him, then let out a yell and slapped the mare's rump.

Before Angela could say goodbye or start crying, they were racing through the pine trees, and it was all she could do to hold on.

* * *

DEIRDRE FLOATED IN HER FEVERISH dream world again. From the white clouds she descended and searched the piney forests far below for Ginny.

There! There she was again. Through the dark green, a white streak. Running on the trails, this time the opposite direction. Towards home.

And someone was on her back. A girl, a girl with faded black hair streaming out behind her.

She watched as they descended the alpine heights, through grassy mountain meadows, and down treacherous rocky outcrops.

Now, they were down in the rainforest, the giant rainforest. Ginny looked as small as a mouse. Deirdre got closer. Ginny approached the tunnel. She slowed. Hesitated.

"Ginny, keep going. Keep going, that's the way home. Go on girl! Go through the tunnel!"

Deirdre woke up, gasping.

It was so frustrating to be this weak, to be incapable of going out and searching.

This past week, Cassie had disintegrated into grief, slowly losing faith that Angela was anywhere to be found.

But, despite what she'd told Morgan, Deirdre couldn't believe in her heart that Ginny was dead. She couldn't give up hope. She groped for her phone on the nightstand, and picked it up to call Sally.

"You have to keep searching for Angela!" she said. "I know she's out there."

"We're already out looking," Sally said. "You were right about Zach. We came to this tree that was marked on his map, but I don't see anything around."

"You need to go up to where you can cross under Fairy Glen Road, there's a big tunnel, like a drainage pipe, but big enough to ride through. That's where she'll come out. And she'll be on Ginny."

"Ginny?"

"Don't ask, just believe me," Deirdre said.

"Okay," Sally said. "Tell us how to get there."

* * *

ANGELA WAS ABLE TO BRING the horse to a walk once they left the pines and entered the oaks.

They traveled carefully through the forest of dispersed, gnarled tree trunks, under the shade of the huge canopies. There was no trail, but the horse had a sense of purpose and walked confidently onwards, through the dry crunchy leaves.

Something about the horse's walking stride went to Angela's core, to her memories...

"Wait a minute. I know you. I know you!" she said. The horse's ears flicked back at her, but it kept walking, steadily, rhythmically, down the slope.

She remembered this horse. An animal that had carried her out of the depths, out of the blackness when she was little, when she was stuck in a doorway between her former life and this life.

Maybe she was stuck in another doorway now...maybe there really was such a thing as knowing too much. About her father, about her mother.

You could never un-know it. Unless...you died?

They came to the tunnel.

Part of her wanted to stay in this peaceful world, outside the strife, the greed, the wanting. In this gray, lifeless, deathless place.

But she couldn't.

"Come on." She clucked to the horse, put her calves against its flanks.

The horse weaved from side to side, put its head down, snorted. It rubbed its face on its front leg. It bent its neck around and sniffed Angela's foot. But it wouldn't move forward.

"Let's go," Angela said. "It'll be okay. It's better to be alive, than..." she looked behind her, "...in limbo."

The pointy white ears flicked. "Come on," Angela said. "Please?"

The horse lowered her head, and sighed, and went into the tunnel. Blackness surrounded them, and the horse hesitated, trembling.

Angela put a hand on the horse's neck, felt her mane, full of little spiral tangles.

"Ginny," she said, remembering her.

And Ginny lost her fear of the dark, walking confidently through to the other side. Into the full color world.

They reached the creek. There were large boulders sticking out of the water. Some had places to stand, but the rest were jagged, or round and slippery, and she considered how to get across, while the horse just continued downstream like she knew exactly where she was going.

In the distance, women's voices were calling. Shouting. Shouting her name.

Oh my god! Her stomach fluttered with relief. She would be found, she would be saved. She would find the boys that killed Lexi, and make them pay.

"I'm here!" she called out. "I'm here! By the creek!"

She guided the horse to cross over, and they stepped in at the top of a little waterfall, and got halfway across. The splashing of the water covered any sounds.

Were the women still there?

She stopped in the middle of the rushing creek, and listened. Yes, they were still yelling her name.

One of the voices, bossy sounding, hushed the other one. Angela used the space to yell again. They were far away. Hopefully they could hear her.

She called out, "Help! I'm here!" but her voice was so weak.

Yell louder! Put your whole body into it! Lexi said.

Angela took a deep breath, all the way down into her belly, puffed up her chest, raised her arms to the side like wings, and prepared to yell again.

But on the other side of the creek, a dark figure stepped out of the trees.

The mare startled, and Angela lost her balance. With a yip, all of her breath left her. She grabbed for the leather strap around the mare's chest, but ended up breaking her nails as she slid to the ground, landing painfully on the rocks. The skittish horse backed away, snorting.

"We meet again." It was her father.

He moved towards her, lifted her by the arms out of the cold rushing water. "Gotcha." He started patting her down. "You found it, didn't you? Give it to me you little bitch."

Her voice stuck in her throat. He shook her and put his face right in hers. "Where is it?"

He wrenched her arm so hard she screamed, and he covered her mouth. She tried to kick, but the pain from the snakebite took her breath away.

With his hand still over her mouth, she struggled to breathe, as she fell into the water. On the other bank, from her upside down perspective, she saw the legs of the white horse, still there, dancing back and forth. It neighed, a trembly sound.

Then, she couldn't see or hear anything, she was underwater, cold water going up her nose...she thrashed her head back and forth, but just swallowed water, breathing some in. It hurt.

He yanked her up, his voice in her ear now, growling and hot. "I wondered, why were you crawling all over this stupid mountain? Then I remembered. Your mom was always talking about this place. She probably hid it here. Somewhere out here." He lifted his face away from hers and his eyes rolled around, taking in the trees and the forest canopy surrounding them. He looked back at her. "Am I right?"

She sputtered, and gasped, pulling in air. "The horse...it was on the horse —" she said.

He looked around. Ginny was gone. Rage contorted his face. "You dumb —" His hands were wrapped around her neck now, squeezing.

She grabbed his hands, but they were too big and strong. She was so close to getting home...she couldn't die now...

Then there was an ear-shredding whistle, high and sustained.

Something crashed through the woods, came splashing into the creek, hooves grinding like thunder on the river stones.

A huge, dark shape swirled above her. Travis' head flew to the side, his hands releasing her throat. She fell on her back into the creek, then scrambled a few feet away, choking.

She heard him fighting, getting killed by stamping hooves.

"No!" she screamed.

No matter how much he scared her, he was her father. She didn't want him to die.

She struggled to her feet. "No!"

There was a big dusky-colored horse on the bank of the creek. A tall woman sat astride him.

They entered the creek and squared off with Travis as he struggled and stood up, dripping water off him.

"Zach, give it up," the woman said. She was terrifying. Silvery fierce and sharp and brutal. Her horse, muscular and darkly tarnished, danced with Travis, facing him as they circled each other, splashing in the creek.

"Hey!" he said, suddenly smiling at her and raising a finger in the air. He looked frightening—fake black hair stuck to his face, red bruised eye swelling, bloody nose. "Hey Viv. Babe. Listen, all you gotta do is find that white horse..." He pointed the direction Ginny had gone. "We'll be rich!" His eyes gleamed as his smile spread. He was missing a few teeth now, and blood spilled out of his mouth.

Angela hid her face, unable to look at him for a moment. Then she looked back up.

A figure appeared from the trees on the other side, behind Travis.

It was the Gray Girl! The real one. She was wearing a long gray dress, a bonnet, and carrying something long by her side.

Travis and the horse were still circling each other. The woman wasn't going for it. She had left the reins loose on her horse's neck and was slowly coiling a length of rope in her hands.

"Vivian, come on," Travis said, like she was being unreasonable. "I had you pegged from the minute I saw you. You're not like other chicks. You're special, you're a rebel. You're a criminal at heart. Just like me."

She was silent. Her face said everything. He watched it change, and the fear showed.

Travis stared at the horse lady another few seconds, then whirled around to run.

But instead got hit in the face with a heavy branch, and splashed down into the water again.

The Gray Girl looked at Travis, then back at the object in her hand, like she couldn't believe she'd done that.

Just then, another dark horse came out of the woods. The rider jumped off, busted out a *"hi-ya!"*, did some karate move, and she and the other lady wrestled Travis' arms behind his back and tied him up.

Angela looked at them, laughing. Then her knees gave way, and she crumpled into the water.

When she opened her eyes next, she was near a road, there were flashing red lights...

The next thing she saw was the inside of an ambulance...

And finally, the emergency room, where Cassandra saved Angela's life—for the second time.

* * *

ON THE RIDE HOME THAT day, Vivian decided to take a different trail, one that went past an old friend's place.

Laura had lived at the house on Orfila ever since she divorced Brian Bartley. Vivian hadn't seen or talked to her in...how long had it been?

She rode Apache straight up the driveway and ground-tied him in the yard. She was still shaking, the adrenaline not quite out of her system. Might as well do something else brave while it coursed through her veins. She knocked on the door.

Laura opened it. Her mouth fell open. "Hi." She still looked the same.

"Hi," Vivian said.

They stared at each other for a second.

Laura set her jaw. "I miss Jeremy."

"So do I," Vivian said.

"Deirdre Boyd told me he used to visit you," Laura said. "A lot. Wanna tell me about it?"

Inside, over cups of coffee spiked with brandy, they talked—about everything, starting with the day's upsetting, but ultimately triumphant, events.

Vivian summed it up. "Apparently I have horrible luck with men. First I slept with him, then I tried to kill him."

Soon, her shakes were gone, and she was laughing as they reminisced over old memories together. And somehow they were less painful with the retelling.

They were talking about Brian Bartley now.

Vivian said, "You know, he only cheated on you with Tanya to make you jealous. He was trying to win you back."

"Win me back? We were still married!" Laura laughed and took another sip. "He didn't have to win me back."

"Well, he *thought* he'd lost you. To me. Brian accused me of being a svengali."

"Oh that's ridiculous! I made up my own mind. If he wanted me back, all he had to do was stop being a criminal. But he didn't want to. That was more important to him." Laura sighed. "So, it had nothing to do with you. Don't blame yourself. He was always so jealous of you. It was really... unbecoming."

Vivian said, "You were his lost queen. When you moved to Fairy Glen, he made it his mission to surround you. First San Amaro Hills, then Paraiso."

"Oh, now you're being completely ridiculous. No more brandy in that coffee or I'll have to take away your...reins?" She cracked up. Vivian remembered how much she loved Laura's laugh.

Eventually, they went out to the yard to say goodbye.

Laura took her hand. "Come to Thanksgiving, here, with Joe and I," she said, looking into Vivian's face.

Joe, the dentist. "Oh, thanks, but...no." She turned and picked up Apache's reins. "I have plans. But thanks." She looked at the house, its perfect lawn, it's easy comfort. She didn't want to mess that up for Laura.

Laura put her face in her hands.

Vivian thought at first that she was overreacting to her turning down the turkey day dinner invitation.

But then Laura said, "It'll be our first one without Jeremy." After a minute, she lifted her head again, and said, "You know, I saved all of Jeremy's child support in a college fund."

"Keep it. He'll come home. He can still go to college."

"No. No, I'm tired of sitting and waiting," Laura said, shaking her head. "I have a better idea of what to do with that money."

Vivian raised her eyebrows.

"You'll see," Laura said. She smiled, walked to the front door, waved goodbye, and went inside.

Sunday, November 18

"SO, DID YOU FIND THE Gray Girl?" Angela asked, taking another bite of pumpkin pie from the hospital tray.

"The gray girl?" Cassandra said. She was just getting off her shift, and kicked off her shoes and laid down flat on the other hospital bed.

"You know, the one that hit Travis with the log."

"Oh, Samantha! She was here last night for a checkup, but she's fine... well, she has a condition, but overall she's not hurt. I can't talk about that, I'm breaking HIPAA."

"Wait, Samantha?" Angela said. "I thought she was dead? I saw flowers for her on the side of the road."

"Well, everyone thought that too, for a while, until..." Cassandra came over and sat next to Angela, brushing her hair out of her eyes. "I'm so sorry about Lexi, sweetie."

"I know Mom, I know. It's okay."

"I'm here if you want to talk about it," her mom said. She yawned, and climbed back onto the other bed.

They watched TV for a while, and when Angela looked over, Cass was asleep.

"Well, I see you've eaten everything!" said the cheery night nurse, who came in to check on Angela. "Oh, sorry!" she whispered, pointing to Cassandra sleeping. The nurse took her food tray and left the room.

Cassandra had worked tirelessly to tend to all of Angela's injuries. She was well on her way to recovering from her head wound, rattlesnake bite, dehydration, and malnutrition—which she had just put a big dent in, by finishing off the open-face turkey sandwich and pumpkin pie dinner.

It was fake jiggly turkey, on white bread with boxed mashed potatoes and gelatinous pale brown gravy. And the pie? Well—it's hard to mess up pumpkin pie. But it can be done.

Despite everything having an artificial, slightly congealed quality to it, it made her feel happy and content, and best of all, full.

Angela's throat still hurt from her father choking her. All the muscles in her neck were strained, and the tissue felt tender and bruised.

But, the Gray Girl had given him a worse injury, and the two ladies on horses had finished up the job.

Earlier today, as soon as she was feeling well enough, Mom and Detective Goodwin brought in her yellow backpack. The witch hat was there, and the granola bar wrapper. And the Simba.

Detective Goodwin had told her straight, everything he knew about her father and his crimes.

And she told the detective everything she knew about Lexi's death, which wasn't much. Just a name and an injury. She hoped it was enough.

When he left, Cass had asked, "What's up with this Simba? Where did you get it?"

Angela reached out and took it, looking at it up close in the daylight coming in the hospital window. "He gave it to me, when I first saw him at Cheryl's grave."

Her mom said, "You know, when you came into the ER that day, the first time I saw you, you were in a little Simba onesie. That's probably what kept you from freezing to death in the desert overnight." Cass's eyes were questioning, probing. Like maybe Angela could remember something then. But she didn't.

Cass said, "You know, he's downstairs. On floor three." Cass had stood up then, giving her a look, like she trusted Angela to make the right decision for her. "There's an armed deputy outside the door, and he's chained up. You can say whatever you want to him." Then Cass had left to finish up her shift.

Angela should've known to trust her mom to tell it to her straight. She wasn't hiding anything about her former life all this time, she was just as clueless as Angela was. All her mom knew was that she'd been a traumatized little four-year-old brought into the ER.

Angela looked at her mother now, curled on her side under the blankets, snoring softly, her nursing clogs abandoned on the floor, her hands folded under the pillow.

She turned the stuffed toy over in her hands, contemplating it.

Suddenly she threw the sheets off and marched into the hallway, into the elevator, and hit the button for three.

At his door, the deputy looked at her, and tilted his head to tell her it was okay to go in.

He was sleeping. He looked like shit.

A light brown scruff of five day growth covered his black and blue face. He had bandages around his head, covering his dyed black hair, and around his torso.

She went and stood next to him. IVs came out of his tattooed arms, and handcuffs locked him to the bed.

He opened one puffy eye. "Hey Ang," he said, all normal as if nothing had happened.

She was mute.

He raised his eyebrows. "Well? What?"

Her voice caught again. Then, suddenly, it broke free. "How did you get Simba? If you went to jail that night, how did you get my Simba? Did you kill her?"

"It's just a shitty toy from the thrift store!" he said. "But it got your attention! See, I remembered you liked the Lion King. It was all you'd fucking talk about some days." He smiled, and laughed, then winced and started coughing. "Ow. Ow." He closed his eyes and put a hand to his ribs.

He was full of shit. She understood now—that was the only thing she ever needed to know about him.

She left and went back to her floor, and climbed back into bed.

Her eyes got heavy. It was probably the tryptophan, from that turkey sandwich.

She pressed the button to lower the head of the bed, and closed her eyes, and listened to the sound of Cassandra snoring.

But before she fell asleep, she remembered her mother, and finally she could see her face.

Angela's mom was going to make her favorite dessert, pumpkin pie.

They'd just gotten back from trick-or-treating around the other apartments, with Angela dressed as Simba. She also carried her Simba, even though Mom tried to tell her it didn't make sense. "You're carrying a stuffed animal of yourself?" she'd asked, laughing indulgently.

"This is my son," Angela had said.

Now they were back inside, out of the cold night air. Her mom went into the kitchen and started pulling bowls out of the cabinets and a pie shell from the freezer.

"Make it from my pumpkin Mommy!" Angela had gotten her own small pumpkin at nursery school today, and drawn a jack-o'-lantern face on it with Sharpie.

She had desperately wanted to cut it up, like the one her mom made yesterday, carving into the big orange pumpkin that was bigger than a basketball, slicing out the top for the lid, cutting spooky eyes and a mouth full of jagged teeth. It was outside their door, with a candle burning inside. But her teachers said they were too little to use knives.

"It's the wrong kind of pumpkin sweetheart. Canned is the way to go. Don't forget that! When you're older, you can bake your own pie."

Angela was sad. She wanted to turn her pumpkin into a pie.

Her mother touched her nose, and she looked up, into her mom's face.

"You know what we can do with your pumpkin, and it'll be really good? Roast the seeds!"

"Okay!"

She took Angela's pumpkin and cut it open for her. Angela didn't like that stupid little pumpkin anyway. She happily plunged her hands inside it and pulled out the guts.

They sorted through the stringy insides, separating out the seeds, which they spread on a baking sheet, and then her mom popped it in the oven.

The phone rang, and her mother picked up. She moved busily around the kitchen while she chatted, her long, dark brown hair swinging behind her, the long curlicue cord of the phone trailing after her.

Angela got up on the couch and laid back against the brown corduroy. Soon the air would smell warm and cinnamon-y.

With her slimy, pumpkin gut-covered hands, she grabbed her plastic pumpkin and dug around inside, pulling out the Snickers and Krackles and Butterfingers, Smarties, Skittles and Starburst...

She looked over at her mother, in the kitchen, who stopped talking for a minute, looked at Angela, smiled, and blew her a kiss.

Monday, November 19

TOM WALKED INTO THE INTERVIEW room.

Parker Metfield sat in the chair, next to his father, a bigwig executive on the board of YouTube.

Parker didn't say anything, didn't move his mouth when he talked.

"What's wrong, here?" Tom pointed to his own mouth and face, as if he didn't know.

"Lacrosse injury," his dad said.

Angela had told Tom this, that Parker would have a broken jaw. "Lexi told me," she said. He hadn't believed her. After all, Parker's jaw would've been broken the night Lexi died, when Angela was kidnapped in the desert. So how could she know?

However, she didn't know Parker's last name. That, he'd gotten from Rebecca and her friend Darius.

He hadn't believed any of it, up until they'd gotten a confession from one of Parker's friends, which led to a search warrant for the Metfield house this morning, where they had taken Parker, with his wired-shut jaw, in for questioning.

The search had also recovered three hard drives full of video.

Once the techs had gone through it all, he and Scott watched the video from the night in question.

In the meantime, Parker and his dad were sticking to a story.

Now, it was time to challenge it. He sat down and went through their story with them.

"So, she was performing when she fell and choked right? That's what your two friends, uh...Kevin and Trevor said."

"Yeah. That's right. Kevin, Trevor *and* Blake. They all saw it happen." Parker had to force his words out through closed jaws.

"But we didn't find any video of that on your hard drives. Plenty of her performance. She was truly talented. But nothing of her falling and choking. I wonder why?"

"It happened when she was warming up," Parker said through gritted teeth.

"Warming up—*after* her performance? Huh." Tom got up and paced back and forth twice. Then he turned to them. "You know what I think?"

"Whaddya think, cowboy?" Parker's father sat back in his chair, put one hand on his hip. The arrogance spread across his face.

Tom had to turn away and get control of his emotions. Once he did, he turned around and kept his face neutral, but energized his voice, trying to knock the privilege out of this kid and his dad, scare them a little.

"I think you tried to have sex with her and she turned you down, so you got mad."

Parker's face went gray. His father's smile faded.

Tom continued. "How dare this 'valley trash' turn you down, right? You were doing her a favor. Gracing her with your presence."

Parker shifted in his seat, looked away.

"You thought she owed you. Right?"

"That's not it," Parker said, his words forced out through his closed mouth along with bubbles of spit. "She wanted to get paid. I didn't have any cash on me. I told her I'd pay her, I—I just didn't have it on me right then. She came at me. I was defending myself!"

"Parker! Don't say anything else. You hear me?"

"But Dad!" He started crying, whimpering like a little boy.

"Parker, shut the hell up!" his dad said. His face was crimson. "Interview over. We want a lawyer."

Tom didn't need to say anything else. A warmth spread through him as he stood and left the room.

In the hall, Raymond Bower from Seeker's Sanctum stood with a circle of people around him: Matthew, the young guy that worked for him; Morgan, Sally's yoga teacher; and two lawyers, a man and a woman.

In the center of the circle was Samantha Austin. She was young, only thirteen, with dark hair in two braids. The long dress and bonnet were gone. She wore overalls that she didn't look quite comfortable in, and a striped sweater underneath.

It was good to see her alive.

"Hi Sam, I'm Tom," he said, and put out his hand. She shook his hand and smiled shyly. "I hear you have something to tell me." She nodded.

Raymond put a hand on his back, and with twinkling eyes said, "I'll see you around."

"Thank you, sir." Tom took his hand, and they exchanged a look of understanding, before Raymond walked down the hallway towards the front door.

The rest of them went into another interview room. Samantha and her lawyer sat at the table, and Tom sat across from them.

Sam opened her mouth to talk, but her lawyer interrupted. "Only questions about what she witnessed that night. No other topics," she said firmly.

"Agreed," Tom said.

Sam looked at her lawyer, who nodded and patted her hand, and then proceeded to tell him what she'd seen.

She had gone to the asylum, on Halloween night. "I wanted to practice singing. But when I got there, there were a bunch of teenagers, so I hid and watched. I figured they would leave, and then I could sing. That building has great acoustics. The main hall? Yeah, awesome sound." She smiled so all of her braces showed. "Like the Mormon Tabernacle. I went there once, when I was little. It sounds like angels in heaven."

"And, what did you see, Sam?"

"I was mainly watching *her* that night. There were four boys. They all had cameras, they had a couple of big flashlights. But, once she started performing, I couldn't take my eyes off of her. She was all lit up, hanging from the bell tower on this long, red fabric, playing this music that sounded like hammers and bells, and she was so brave and free. Like I want to be.

"She did it over and over, twirling around and spinning. Like she was flying. The boys were yelling at her, telling her what to do, when to do it over again.

"But then, when it was done, the music shut off, and they were talking...I saw two of the boys leave, using their flashlights to hike out of there. I was waiting for them all to leave. She inspired me so much, you know? I just really wanted to sing then, so I couldn't wait for them to leave. But next thing, I heard her start yelling. They were out behind the building. She was pointing a finger in his chest, making him back up, walking towards him. So she's poking his chest and all of a sudden he grabs both her arms and twists so hard she flies to the ground. I thought, maybe this was part of a scene for a movie? I don't know. The last thing I wanted to do was ruin a film shoot, so I didn't do anything. But then it stayed real quiet. Like, I thought they'd do another noisy part of the shoot again, but it was just quiet. So, I went back to—"

Her lawyer put a hand out to stop her.

"—well...I left. I came back again, the next time I could, about a week later. I wanted to see if she was...dead. Or if I was imagining the whole thing, but I..." she cried. "I got scared. Someone was at the asylum, and I ran. I didn't know where to go then. But I found Matthew." Her lawyer made a resigned face, but this time didn't stop her from revealing that Seeker's Sanctum had been harboring her. "He kept bringing me food, and he got me a little tent to stay in, and a phone so I could call him. I was still scared, because I'd heard wild animals in the dark. And then, he told me the bad news. The girl really was dead. I'd watched her getting killed. Just stood and watched, like a spectator. He let me stay in the stone house, but then, that rainy night, some ladies found me. I didn't want to go home, so I ran away again, to the forest. Back to the asylum." She winced. "Can you tell that one lady I'm sorry for kicking her?"

Tom couldn't help but smile. "She forgives you."

Samantha breathed out, looking relieved. "After a few more days out there, I kind of gave up. I had finally decided I just had to go home, go back to my parents, when I saw a beautiful white horse ride by, with a girl on it. I followed them, but then by the time I caught up to them at the creek, that guy was choking her, trying to drown her. I...I had to do something this time." She looked up at Tom, desperate for approval or validation. "I had to do something to stop it."

Tom looked in her eyes and said, "Sam, you did the right thing."

After the interview, Samantha's lawyer stopped and talked to Tom in the hall. "Sorry I couldn't let her say more. It's a child abuse case. You understand."

He nodded. "I got what I needed. Will she have to go back to her parents?"

The lawyer shook her head. "No. Until the case is decided, she's under protection." She tilted her head at Morgan and Matthew, both dressed in white, who were waiting down the hall.

Samantha came out of the bathroom, took a long drink from the water fountain, and dragged her sleeve across her mouth. Morgan and Matthew flanked her as they walked out of the sheriff's station.

"She's in good hands," Tom said. He and the lawyer nodded goodbye, and he turned and walked down the hallway to his third interview of the day.

It was with Blake Jennings, a friend of Parker's, and one of the boys that had been there that night.

Blake, AKA FrightKnight, UrbanLegendary's rival on YouTube, had stayed behind after the other two boys left that night, and unbeknownst to

Parker, filmed what happened after Parker shut off his camera.

Blake's lawyer was working on a plea agreement with the DA, according to Sally. In exchange for handing over the video and testifying against his friend, they would only charge him with a misdemeanor related to concealing the body, which had a maximum sentence of a year in county jail and a $10,000 fine.

It didn't sit right with him. Why hadn't the kid stopped filming and done something? Unlike Samantha, he had been right there, he knew what was happening, and he was a big, strapping teenager. He could've done something, and he chose not to.

Tom hoped the DA wouldn't go for the plea deal. After all, they already had an eye witness willing to testify in court—Samantha. And Blake should pay for what he'd failed to do, just like Parker should pay for what he did do.

He opened the door and walked in, knowing his work on this case was far from over.

Friday, November 23

THE DAY AFTER THANKSGIVING, DEIRDRE rode double with Clara along the creek to Mrs. Fey's.

California weather around Thanksgiving was always glorious, as far back as she could remember. They'd had much needed rain earlier in the month, but the past week had been mild and sunny. The aquamarine sky contrasted with the rustling gold maple leaves.

Up ahead, she spotted Vivian on Apache. He whinnied, and Vivian gave her a salute. "Happy Black Friday," she said. Was she joking? It was hard to tell when someone was so serious all the time.

The horses touched noses, for a long while, until Vivian said, "Don't let them do anything funky. Come on."

They rode abreast along the wide dirt trail.

"Black Friday," Deirdre mused, shaking her head. "I'm riding because I don't have any money to shop." She covered Clara's ears and whispered, "I don't know what I'll do about Christmas this year. Plus, we just got the tax bill for our property."

"Why don't you rebuild already?" Vivian asked, as they went down to single file, with her in front, to weave through the trees. "The money you pay for rent could go to that. Why pay taxes on one place, and rent someplace else?"

Deirdre looked into the distance. "We're trying. It's not that simple." She held Clara closer as Scarlet stepped into the water under the bridge. Her eyes welled up, remembering how Ginny had so steadfastly led Scarlet across the creek here the first time.

"Well, I'm sure being injured and spending all your time searching for lost girls doesn't help with the income situation." Vivian said. "When does the cast come off?"

"Another two weeks. I can't wait." The cast was so itchy now she was half tempted to tear it off herself. But she wouldn't. "So, what did you do for Thanksgiving?" she asked.

"What I always do on Thanksgiving. I rode," Vivian said. She smiled—a rare occurrence.

When they got to Mrs. Fey's, they turned Apache and Scarlet out into the pasture and went inside the house.

"I saved Thanksgiving for today, so we can all celebrate together," Mrs. Fey said.It smelled delicious. A turkey sizzled in the oven. "It's almost ready."

Deirdre doubted if she could eat more turkey, but then again, they had gone the easy route yesterday—a complete meal picked up from the grocery store. Some home cooking sounded good.

Clara and Peter went into the backyard to play.

"Any luck finding Cotchee?" Deirdre asked.

Mrs. Fey sighed sadly and shook her head.

Cassie and Angela showed up next. Angela ran up to Vivian and gave her a big hug.

Vivian looked perplexed. She laid an elegant hand on Angela's head, and said, "There there."

Sally, Lina, and Bonnie came, and they all chatted until the meal was served.

Angela told them what little she remembered.

It had been Halloween. She was dressed as Simba from the Lion King, and they'd come back from trick-or-treating around the apartment complex. She was counting out her candy.

Her dad had come home, in a rush.

"After he did the burglary," Sally whispered. She nodded.

She'd been so happy to see him, and he was dressed for Halloween, all in black with a mask on, holding what looked like a pillowcase full of candy. She'd followed him into the bedroom swinging her plastic pumpkin, while her mother was talking on the phone with a friend, having just put the pumpkin pie, Angela's favorite, into the oven.

In the bedroom, he'd shown her the jewels. Sparkling orange, reflecting rainbows. "Pumpkin diamonds," he'd said, and put one ring around her tiny finger.

The doorbell rang, and she ran happily to get it. She opened the door, not realizing trick-or-treaters could be so tall. Her mom had scooped her up, and the sheriffs swooped in and arrested her dad.

Once they were gone, she showed her mom what her dad had been doing in the bedroom. Her mom took her for a ride in the car, late at night, someplace close by.

"Then, we went back home to pack, but when we got there I think my mom saw someone waiting for us. So we left again, and she drove into the desert." She put her head down. "He must've followed us without her realizing it, or maybe she did. Maybe she was trying to lose him, by turning down that desert road."

"You don't have to finish honey." Cassie put a hand over Angela's. They all knew what had happened then.

Dinner was served. They all sat around the small table in Mrs. Fey's kitchen.

Over turkey, Angela raved about Sally and Vivian's bravery.

"He was choking me, and then I got water up my nose," she said. "Then this big black horse came. It was you," she pointed at Vivian. "And you knocked him down."

"My horse isn't black," Vivian said. Angela frowned.

Sally said, "Mine's sort of black, but I didn't get there until after Travis attacked you, remember?"

"Sounds like you two work pretty good together," Deirdre said to them.

Sally said, "Well, we split up to cover more ground, and each had our safety whistle, since our cell phones didn't work out there. Plus, a whistle is just faster."

Vivian said, "Yes, but I didn't have time to pull out my whistle—"

"Who wants pumpkin pie?" Mrs. Fey said, standing up from the table. "Made from real pumpkins!"

"Oh, that's my favorite, Mrs. Fey," Angela said.

"And I don't even have to grow my own pumpkins!" she said, bustling around the kitchen, putting pieces of pie onto plates. "There's a wild pumpkin patch, out in the forest." She set a plate in front of Angela.

"Is that close to here?" Angela asked.

Mrs. Fey put a hand on her shoulder. "Yes. Just out there, through the cedar grove, and across the creek aways. I can show you, if you like."

Outside, a quavering whinny pierced the air. Deirdre sat up. Scarlet squealed.

Deirdre ran to the window, and there, on the other side of the pasture fence, was Ginny.

"Oh my God, catch her!" Angela said, and jumped up and ran outside. Deirdre was already out there. She caught a glimpse of Ginny's rump disappearing into the trees.

"Ginny!" she yelled. She grabbed her halter and lead rope, ran to Scarlet, and pulled her out of the field.

"I'm going after her!" she yelled, leaping onto Scarlet's back, which surprised even her, especially since she was heavy with food.

She gripped Scarlet with her legs and cantered into the trees after Ginny.

* * *

ANGELA BENT AND PICKED UP the leather strap and woven blanket that lay in a pile where they'd fallen off of Ginny. She smelled the blanket, and remembered her grandfather.

She wrapped the blanket around her. The leather strap had broken, but it was still long enough to use as a belt, and she buckled it around her waist to keep the blanket wrapped close and tight around her.

In the grass lay the other, broken off piece of the strap. And, still tied to it was the small bundle wrapped in soft deerskin. She gasped, picked it up, and held it to her heart.

"This is my inheritance," she said, turning around to see the women watching her.

"Well, come inside and open it up," said Mrs. Fey.

They went inside and Angela laid the bundle on the table, untying the lace that held it.

What treasures, what secrets to her family history would this hold? She unrolled it.

Fluffy white down feathers. This must be padding, she thought. She carefully scooped them to the side. What else? A skinny glass vial, full of gold glitter.

Was that it? She hadn't really been expecting the jewelry, the stuff that Travis had been looking for, that Sally and Detective Goodwin had told her about. But still. Anything would've been better than this. Even Halloween candy.

She pushed the feathers around on the table. In amongst them were pale, dried up seeds.

"Hmm." Mrs. Fey picked one up. "Pumpkin."

Angela stared at the jar of glitter. She remembered the tree, Lexi hanging over her, dropping glitter in her face. The tree that the pumpkins grew under. She pocketed the jar of glitter and left the rest on the table.

"Mom, I need to take a walk." She headed for the door.

"I don't want you going alone," Cassandra said, stepping forward to block her and putting an arm around her. "I almost lost you once out there," she whispered.

"I'll go with her," Mrs. Fey said. "It'll be fine."

Angela hugged her mom. "We won't be gone long. I promise I'll come back."

She and Mrs. Fey walked together through the tall cedars, along the creek, over a fallen log, and to the meadow where the old, twisted, cartoonish looking tree grew.

There, among the gnarled roots, was the pumpkin patch that Angela had slept in.

She turned to the old lady. "You brought me that bread and cheese and apple juice, right?"

"Yes."

"Why didn't you bring me back? Turn me in?"

"Your journey wasn't complete. You still had farther to go."

"Was that just a crazy old man on the mountain? Or was that my grandfather?"

"What do you think?"

"I'm not sure." She looked down at the little jar of glitter. "Why does he have glitter? Why did he give it to me?"

"Glitter?" Mrs. Fey laughed, her head thrown back. She took the little jar from Angela and held it up to the sunlight. "That's gold, my dear. And I should know, I've seen enough of it. I had a few gold miner sweethearts in my youth."

Angela tried to imagine her young, and couldn't.

"You stay here dear, I'm going to do a quick little look around for my missing cat."

"Okay," she said, and sat down next to the tree.

* * *

DEIRDRE FOLLOWED THE TRAIL INTO the woods that Ginny had taken. It ran along the creek, then came back out of the trees. She realized she was now on the far side of Mrs. Fey's pastures. A white shape moved, across from her where a uniform line of tall trees marked the end of the pastures.

She and Scarlet took a shortcut straight through the abandoned field, jumping over a few fallen fence boards, and got to the tree line on the far side.

A sound, something up ahead of her, hoofbeats. But they were off-kilter, slightly inept, stumbling. She knew Scarlet heard it too.

They cantered again, up a small hill and over some rocks, and when they paused at the top of the rise to look down, it took her breath away. Below was a swirling spring, its banks carpeted in moss, fairy ferns sprouting from between cool gray rocks, and surrounded by trees so tall she couldn't even see the mountain anymore, could barely see the sky.

Wow.

She stopped and marveled at the sight. Scarlet was breathing hard. Deirdre started breathing again, and asked Scarlet to walk down to the water.

Maybe this was how the Fey's pastures stayed so green—it wasn't magic after all, not that she'd ever thought that.

Underground water. Of course. It was everywhere. Abandoned wells from the time before the water company was set up, before the reservoirs, before man re-routed the goddamn mighty Colorado herself, dotted the landscape. She'd seen them but never really thought about them.

But this...this was bubbling right out of the ground. No drilling, no well, no reservoir necessary.

A white shape flitted on the other side of the swirling pool. "Ginny!" she shouted, knowing that a horse doesn't come to you like a dog, but wanting to try it anyway. Scarlet whinnied, long and loud, her belly vibrating against Deirdre's legs. Deirdre followed up with one of her famous two-fingered whistles that even made Scarlet jump.

Ginny stopped, and looked over the pond at her as if saying, "I'm a little too old to fall for that trick."

"Ginny," she called, her breath turning ragged with emotion. "Come home baby."

Ginny put her head down, snorted, blinked, then turned and ran into the trees.

* * *

ANGELA SAT, VERY STILL, UNDER the pumpkin tree, while she waited for Mrs. Fey to come back.

It was so peaceful here, now that she knew her father was locked up, and she was safe. A flock of wild turkeys crossed the meadow, not paying her any attention.

She took the vial out of her pocket. So, the glitter was actually gold. But she'd been to the mountains, to the gold mine tours. She knew that little jar wasn't worth much.

She heard rustling in the bushes behind her, and turned around, saying, "Did you find your cat?"

But it was Lexi.

She came and sat down next to Angela.

"How are you?" Angela asked her. She wanted to touch her hand, but knew she couldn't.

"I'm okay. Still pretty pissed." Lexi pulled out a blade of grass and chewed on it. "Trying to get over it." She looked up at the sky. "I just can't believe it."

"I can't either," Angela said. "How did you even know these guys?"

Lexi sighed. "I knew Parker a long time ago. He went to my church when we were both little. I think we even had Sunday school together. Since then his dad got rich, started some software companies, and all that. Moved to the coast.

"I ran into him at our church one day, a few months ago. He was there with his Grandma and the rest of his family. He was checking me out, like I would go for a douchebag like him." She laughed. "But, when he told me he was making money as a video producer, that got my attention. So he took me out to eat, and he tells me about this job.

"They were doing another film, Blair Witch style, at the asylum. Talk about cheesy. But they were paying.

"So I said, yeah, I'll do your little horror show, dark circus thing. That's right up my alley. Just do me a favor. Keep the camera steady, at least when I'm in the shot.

"He says, 'Yeah. Of course, whatever you want.'"

"So what kind of performance was it?" Angela asked.

"That was supposed to be the surprise! And you *will* see it for yourself. When you bust those guys for me."

"It's already happening," Angela said.

"Good." Lexi looked around, at the trees, the sky, the mountains. "I wouldn't mind staying here for a while. It's a beautiful place. Come back and visit me, will ya?"

"I will. You can count on it."

"Well, time to go."

"Really?"

"Yeah, you know." Lexi looked down and kicked some dirt with her toe. "I got shit to do."

Angela said, "Hey...I don't know if it works like that, but if you see my mother, tell her I said hello."

"You mean Cheryl?" Lexi smiled. "I will. Love you." Lexi leaned in to give her a peck on the cheek, but then stopped, smiled, blew her a kiss, and started walking away. But she couldn't just leave, she had to throw one last zinger over her shoulder. "Oh, yeah. When you come back to visit me, bring a shovel."

"A shovel?"

"That treasure you've been looking for? It's right under your ass."

Angela looked underneath her. The treasure? It was here?

When she looked up, though, Lexi was gone, and there was a man with a rifle standing at the edge of the clearing. Her heart leapt into her throat.

His face was painted, he wore military garb, night vision binoculars hung from his neck and his gun was complicated—black and shiny with a big scope on top.

She stood up, and screamed. Mrs. Fey came bursting back out of the bushes.

The man looked just as frightened as she was, the whites of his eyes glowing in his camo-painted face. He put a hand out. "Sorry ladies, didn't mean to scare you. I'm a hunter. Got a permit and everything." He fumbled in one of his vest pockets.

A small helicopter rocketed over them, and they ducked.

"Gotta get going," the man said, looking at the helicopter, and touched the brim of his camouflage ballcap.

"Be on your way then," Mrs. Fey said. "Off with you." She waved her hands, like she was shooing a mouse.

He looked ashamed for a second, then jogged across the meadow and into the brush, following the helicopter's path.

Under her breath, Mrs. Fey said, "And good riddance!" She turned to Angela. "We should get back now. Your mother will be worried."

But then she focused on something behind Angela. Her eyes grew wide and she gripped Angela's arm.

Angela whirled around, expecting...she didn't know what. Another hunter? Her father coming after her? A lion?

But instead, she saw an enormous black housecat, winding itself casually around the tree trunk.

"Cotchee! There you are!" said Mrs. Fey.

She hurried to the cat and scooped it up in her arms. It started purring so loud Angela swore it drowned out the sound of the helicopter retreating deeper into the valley.

The cat watched Angela over Mrs. Fey's shoulder with slowly blinking, neon yellow eyes, as she followed the old lady back home.

* * *

ANGELA AND MRS. FEY BROUGHT Cotchee home, to the delight of the other women who had already made short work of cleaning up after the meal.

Deirdre came back, disappointed, on Scarlet.

"You didn't find her then," Bonnie said, walking outside to greet her.

"I found her, but she wouldn't come back!"

"At least you know she's alive. She's alive!" Bonnie said, and hugged her.

As Deirdre put Scarlet back in the pasture, Apache was running around, snorting, as the helicopters flew low over the valley, weaving back and forth.

"What is that racket?" Vivian asked, coming outside and peering up at the blue sky.

"Oh, they're hunting," Cass said.

"Hunting?" Mrs. Fey said.

Bonnie said, "For the wild animals. They hired hunters with tranquilizer guns. There's a bounty for each animal. I just hope they don't hurt them."

Cass said, "The park officials didn't believe Angela's story about the lion. Either that, or they didn't want to admit there was a lion on the loose. They told her she must've seen a mountain lion."

Lina folded her arms and nodded. "Mmhmm. What did I tell you? It's a coverup."

Mrs. Fey took Cotchee inside and they followed. She scolded the cat, and poured a saucer full of cream for her.

Eventually everyone went home, except for Deirdre, Clara, and Vivian.

"I can't leave yet, Apache hates helicopters," Vivian said, draping her long thin body over the couch and smiling at Peter. She was starting to look pretty comfortable here.

"While you're still here..." Mrs. Fey went to the sideboard, slid out a drawer, and pulled a sheaf of papers out. "That nice young woman stopped by again."

"Nice? You mean the process server that you wouldn't allow on your property?" Deirdre said.

"Well, she's just the messenger. No need to punish her. She brought another letter from the county."

"Show it to me." Deirdre read it. "Back taxes...in the amount of...*what?* That's baloney! How can they charge you millions? Last month they said you didn't even own this property. Now you owe millions in back taxes?"

"Damned if you do, damned if you don't," Mrs. Fey said with a shrug.

"But, how will you pay?" Deirdre looked at the paperwork, trying to find a parcel number, any other information.

Mrs. Fey turned and smiled. "I don't get around that well any more. I was hoping you and your friends could look into it for me."

"Sure, I'll try. Maybe Sally can find out more, she works for the county. But I think what you need is a lawyer."

Vivian said, "The question is, do you want to prove you own it and owe millions? Or prove you don't own it, and get forced off?"

Deirdre said, "In the meantime Mrs. Fey, if Vivian and I both pay you board, that might help you pay for a lawyer, or start a payment plan on your taxes."

"Deirdre, I told you. I don't want to keep him here." Vivian stood up. "I'm leaving, before it gets too dark. Thank you very much for dinner, and for...everything else." She nodded awkwardly at Mrs. Fey and Deirdre, and went out back to get Apache and get the hell out of there.

Mrs. Fey followed her outside. "Vivian? I could use your help," she called to her.

Vivian grabbed Apache's saddle and bridle and marched towards where he was grazing in the pasture. Dusk was settling, and bats flew helter-skelter in the clear, darkening sky above the trees.

"I'm not a lawyer," Vivian said, as she tightened the girth. "Talk to Sally."

"I don't need a lawyer. I need an apprentice."

Vivian laughed. "I'm a bit old to be an apprentice, don't you think?"

Mrs. Fey ignored her. "I seem to have too much work to do, and I'm falling behind. I might be getting too old. And my transportation is...well, it's been acting up."

Mrs. Fey paused, then looked up into her eyes. She had a cloudy cataract over one eye, half visible in the dusk. "You're quite a good rider yourself."

"You've never seen me ride," Vivian said, turning to mount up.

"Oh, yes I have." The old woman's voice sounded different, strange.

This whole conversation was getting strange.

Vivian turned around. "When? When did you see me ride?"

The old lady, in her normal voice now, but with a knowing nod, said, "You know. You saw me too." She smiled, and said cheerfully, "Think about it and let me know. Have a good trip home."

She stroked Apache's nose while Vivian got on, then waved as they rode away.

* * *

REBECCA'S EYES WERE SLEEPY FROM the buzzing fluorescents overhead, and she rested her chin in her hands on the front counter of the restaurant.

The drive-thru had been busy, full of Black Friday shoppers dazed from the shopping malls.

But now it was almost time to close down and lock up. It was windy and cold outside, and everyone had already come and gone for the night, she could sense it—she could always sense the last customer, like she could always tell the last kernel of corn to pop in the microwave before the bag scorched.

Except, damn. There was the chime of a car in the drive-thru. One last kernel to pop.

She got on the headset. "Welcome to WokChikaBok!Bok! Can I take your order?"

"I'd like to speak to you about something," a woman's voice said. It was distant and faint.

Rebecca was taken aback, then said, "Uh, this is a drive-thru, ma'am?"

No answer. Next she saw a white SUV pull up to the window. Great. Late night crazies. What was she, a radio shrink? At least she was good at giving people the brush off. If it was Billy, her gullible and innocent coworker, he'd be stuck there smiling and nodding until whoever it was had told him the story of her twenty-two Persians and one Pomeranian.

She opened the window, ready to send them away. There was a Hispanic man, very serious, in the driver's seat. He pulled forward. The backseat window rolled down. A young woman, about twenty-five or thirty, with a subtly made-up face and long, caramel-highlighted hair smiled at her and stuck out her hand. "Sorry this is awkward. I'm Stephanie Bartley."

"Ohhhh." She took her outstretched hand. It was long fingered, soft, and manicured. "Nice to meet you."

"Brian Jr. says a lot of good things about you."

"He does?" The kid didn't even know her.

Stephanie nodded. "And I hear you were quite the hero. Along with your mom of course."

Rebecca shook her head. "No, I wasn't a hero. I had to be rescued."

"But you were brave. And smart."

What was she trying to get at? "Okay, I guess I was."

"I have a proposal for you that I think you'll be very interested in. What time do you get off work?"

She looked over at Darius, who shrugged. He didn't care, she was bored, and now she was curious what this lady could possibly propose to her. "I can leave right now, if it's that interesting. Let me grab my bike."

Stephanie was waiting in the passenger seat of the white Land Rover when Rebecca wheeled her bike around to the front of WokChikaBok!Bok! The Hispanic man got out and helped her load it in the back, then she got in the backseat.

"This is Luis," Stephanie said, once they were all enclosed by quiet *thunk* of the hermetically sealed doors.

"Hi, Luis. Nice to meet you," she said.

He met her eyes in the rearview before they pulled out onto the main road. "Mucho gusto."

Stephanie turned. "I figured we can talk at my place, okay? Luis can drive you home when we're done."

Rebecca said, "Okay." She was dying to know what this was all about. Whether she'd accept a ride home from someone she didn't know from Adam in the middle of the night, she could decide later. It was a full moon, plenty of light if she wanted to ride home the back way, over the hills.

Nobody spoke the rest of the drive. They followed the winding Rancho Alto streets, deep into the curvy labyrinth of the oldest part of the—what was it, Rancho Alto? Not a subdivision, not a town, definitely not a community. An enclave? A city-state?

"Wow!" It just popped out of her mouth when Luis turned onto the driveway. Ahead of them lay a monstrous house, lit up in the moonlight.

No, it wasn't monstrous, she took that back. Because as they drew closer, it had pleasing proportions, a certain charm to it. Unlike some of the newer construction going up everywhere, it looked like a house—like a home.

Stephanie spoke to Luis. "Brian Jr. is asleep, so don't open the garage." He pulled around the circular drive near the front door and parked.

After Luis helped her from the car, Stephanie took the keys from him, and said, "Thanks," softly. He nodded and said goodnight and walked away from the house. Horses neighed in the distance, followed by yappy dogs barking.

It was only then that Rebecca saw Stephanie was using a cane. "Can I help you?" she asked.

"No, I'm fine. Thanks."

Stephanie hobbled to the front door, which was under a portico lit with warm yellow lanterns, and let her in.

"We can go into the office."

Rebecca's mouth hung open as they moved from the entry hall, through the living room, which had a few dim lamps on. The ceiling was high, everything was wood or white plaster, there was a huge stone fireplace. She followed Stephanie through a door to the right of it.

The place looked like a monastery, or a wizarding school—heavy old wood and leather, hammered wrought iron. Her Converse squeaked on the saltillo tile as she followed Stephanie, who was moving pretty slow, giving her plenty of time to look around.

"I love your house," she said, as Stephanie gestured for her to close the door. Stephanie sat behind the huge desk and Rebecca sat in a leather wingback chair in front of it. She could tell her eyes were huge, and tried to put them back into a more normal expression. "When was it built? A long time ago?"

"Not that long. 1920. It was one of the original homes in Rancho Alto, designed by Lily Bancroft herself. She was the architect in charge. She worked for a big firm, Harlow and Swanson, but they were down in San Diego, and back then it took most of a day to travel down there. Her bosses really trusted her, she pretty much had free rein up here. She made this place —Rancho Alto—what it is."

"Really?"

"Yes. Does that surprise you?" Stephanie smiled, lighting up. "You know the main community house is named after her. Back in the day, people ordered custom homes and stayed there while they were being built, playing golf and living the socialite lifestyle. Things were so much more—genteel I guess—back then. When you couldn't just hop in a car and drive forty miles for the hell of it. I feel like with the slower pace, more got done. More meaningful stuff anyway. Things were built to last. Like these walls," she gestured around the room. "San Amaro houses are built of cardboard compared to this." She laughed. "But don't ever quote me on that. I'm still VP of the development corporation. My board would have my hide." She exhaled, rolled her eyes, like she didn't even want to get into how screwed up that whole situation was.

"Do you know where your husband went?" Rebecca asked. She was dying to know what happened to Mr. Fireproof McMansion/meth cooker. She remembered him on his knees, begging the cartel dude.

"He can go to hell as far as I'm concerned. He put my son in jeopardy and he was too arrogant to even know it until it was too late." Stephanie breathed out. "He's in Mexico, last they know. He's a fugitive."

"Oh."

"So, let's get right down to it. I want you to find Crystal, and bring her home. Laura wants to know that Jeremy is alright, know where he is. If you can bring him home too, all the better. We figured we could kill two birds with one stone here." She pulled open a drawer in the desk.

"Laura? Jeremy's mom?"

"Yes. The first Mrs. Bartley."

Rebecca had just figured ex-wives and current wives didn't talk to each other. But as the two surviving spouses out of three, maybe they shared a bond now.

Stephanie pulled an overstuffed envelope wrapped in a rubber band out of the drawer, and laid it on the blotter.

"And Crystal?" Rebecca said. "She's not *your* daughter, right?" Rebecca's unspoken question to Stephanie was, *why do you care?*

"She's my step-daughter, and Brian Jr.'s sister. She lived with us when I was first married. She didn't like it here, so she went back to live with her mother, Tanya." Her face puckered for a millisecond. "Brian liked it better here. With me," she added quietly.

Then she looked at Rebecca intently. "You know Crystal, right?" She turned in her chair and Rebecca saw what was behind her—a large formal photographic portrait in a carved wooden frame, apparently waiting to be hung. It was Stephanie, with Brian Jr. when he was much littler, and...Crystal? She looked like a semi-normal little girl—almost happy. She was about eight years old in the photo.

Next to that was a similar sized picture frame, facing backwards.

Rebecca stammered, "I only know Crystal a little. A very little. How am I supposed to find them?"

"I think you can figure something out. But Laura and I, we're prepared to...underwrite the endeavor." She sat back in her chair, a cold, appraising look on her face as her eyes passed over Rebecca, head to toe. "The only problem is, you don't drive."

"*That's* the only problem? Not the fact that I'm sixteen?"

"I think that gives you a distinct advantage. When you find them, tell Crystal she's got this"—Stephanie waved around the room, the house—"to come home to. Tell her, her little brother misses her terribly." Stephanie's eyes got a little shiny. "Tell Jeremy his mother will welcome him with open arms, that he can live with her and she'll take care of everything."

"Wait wait wait. I haven't agreed to this yet. I have school, I have work. What do I get out of this?"

"Come with me," Stephanie said. "I think I can change your mind."

She grabbed the envelope and limped to the door that led into the garage, and flipped on a light. Inside was a black sporty coupe, a blue Cobra —even Rebecca, who didn't care about cars, knew what a Cobra was—and over on the far wall, a shape covered in a drop-cloth that could only be one thing.

They walked over to it. Stephanie pulled a corner of the cloth, and it slipped over the shape and fell to the ground.

Rebecca's eyes popped. It was love at first sight. She looked at Stephanie. "I'll need cash."

Stephanie handed her the envelope. "It's covered."

Six Weeks Later

LEXI'S GRAVE WAS ON THE top of a green hill. There was a view of the high school in the near distance, through the morning mist, and all the orange and lemon groves in manicured, dark green rows beyond it.

Angela had missed her best friend's funeral, so she was here now, paying her respects. Even though she knew Lexi lived on, in some other place.

The January breeze was chilly, wafting her hair. It looked lame now— growing out light blondish-brown, but the rest was still black from Halloween. Turns out, semi-permanent dye was more permanent than she thought. She couldn't decide whether to keep it dark, bleach it light, or cut it all off. So for now she had a hard stripe where her natural roots ended and the dyed part began.

"Whoa, I like the hair!"

It was Jen behind her.

Gemma ran up, her breath misting in the cool morning air. "Oooh. Yeah, if you keep growing it like that, you'll look like that chick from Berlin." They all looked at her. "You know, the eighties band? Maybe you'll start a trend."

Angela couldn't imagine ever starting a trend. But stranger things had happened.

Jason and Eric walked up.

"Ever thought about trying out for cheer?" Gemma asked.

"Or Drama?" Jason added.

Angela just smiled. She had a different discipline in mind. Aerials.

Eric said, "Come on guys, let's give her some space." He gave her a hug, and she hugged him back. She could see why Lexi loved this guy. He gave great hugs. "We'll wait at the car," he said. "Give you a ride?"

"You guys go ahead. I'll walk."

"Okay, suit yourself!" Gemma said.

"See you at school," Jen said, and smiled at her.

Jason put a hand on her shoulder as he passed, and she knew he understood. She needed time alone with Lexi.

When they were gone, Angela pulled Simba out of her backpack. She was done with him for now, so she was going to leave him here, on Lexi's grave, to symbolize her fight. Even though she didn't fight a lion, she had fought. And she would live on.

She turned and looked back at Lexi's headstone, reading the dates.

Was it really just coincidence? First her mother, then her best friend. Both had met their fates on the day after Halloween.

But Angela? She had survived twice. Once when she was four years old, and again, more than a decade later. It made her want to celebrate life, to really live, as Lexi had told her to do.

And speaking of that, Angela had a hard decision to make. Would she use the buried treasure to help her and Cassandra, the Marconis, or Samantha's legal fund? Or, maybe Mrs. Fey?

She wondered if her first mother had purposely buried the jewels with pumpkin seeds so that she could find them again, or if it had it been accidental, in the hurried panic of that fateful night. Either way, she didn't have to dig it up yet. She knew it was there, and nobody else did. It was safe, like money in the bank. Probably safer. She could decide what to do with it when she was ready.

She looked at Simba one last time. "Well buddy, this is it for us. We've had a wild ride." She gave him a little squeeze. But—there was something hard inside.

She looked closer. There was a tiny hole in the seam in his tummy.

She stuck a finger in, and wriggled it around in the stuffing. And when she pulled it out, a sparkling, pumpkin diamond solitaire ring was around her finger.

This one was just for her. This one, she'd keep.

Apparently, even as a toddler, Angela had also been—as her dad called her—a sneaky little bitch.

Just like her mother.

She smiled, and started the long walk to school.

Epilogue

LEXI'S VIDEO LIVES ON.

Performing aerials on her red silks, in the asylum, to Depeche Mode's *Black Celebration*, the live version, blasting from her boombox.

Trust Lexi to dig up a badass, twenty year old song.

Someone had synced a quality version of the song over it, but they'd mixed in her triumphant yips and howls from the original audio.

She was beautiful, strong, and free. She really could fly.

It gave you chills to watch it. Every single time.

At first, Depeche Mode's record label tried to take it down for copyright infringement. But when the band heard about it, they granted use of their song and made a substantial donation to Lexi's family. That, plus the ad money from her video, and the money taken from Parker's suspended YouTube account, went to Lexi's family. It was enough for them to buy a new house, although that was poor compensation for losing her.

In the months to come, Angela would go to Lexi's murder trial every day.

The first day she sat in the front row, behind Parker, and looked him in the eye as he came in and sat down. Then she leaned forward, and said, "Lexi is making more money dead than you ever will alive."

And when Samantha Austin came to the trial testify to what she'd seen that night, Angela sat where Sam could see her. When she looked scared on the stand, Angela caught her eye, and told her, without words, that she could do it. She could speak up, speak out. She could do anything she wanted to.

There was nothing to be afraid of.

This is the end of November's Missing
Keep reading for a sneak peek of what's to come in
December's Barren
Fairy Glen Suspense, Book 3

December's Barren

THE GASOLINE FUMES DISTORTED REBECCA'S view, echoing the heat mirages she'd been chasing this last leg of the trip. Sunblasted desert, everywhere she looked. A limitless horizon only punctuated by barren mountains.

If she wasn't careful the tank would overflow.

She pulled out the naked metal gas nozzle—so weird looking when she was used to the big rubber covered California ones. But wait, wasn't she still in California? Whatever. She screwed the chrome cap back on the bike's shiny red gas tank.

Inside the dusty store, the guy took her ten, gave her five and some coins back.

She looked hungrily at the peanut M&Ms, but stuffed the change in her jeans pocket.

"Bathroom?" she asked.

The guy, who looked like he'd been there since the Pleistocene, just pointed out back. No smile, no thank you. Poor customer service. But then again, if you needed gas, what choice did you have?

She hoofed it across a forlorn parking lot, weeds cracking it into hexagons of asphalt, nature taking hold again.

December, and it was still hotter than Hades out here. Her black clothes magnified the heat, but as a goth in a hot climate, she was used to sweating her balls off. Once she was back on the bike, the wind would cancel out the heat.

The bathroom was a typical gas station bathroom. Not clean, but not obscene either. She stepped inside and bolted the door, relieved herself, splashed some water on her face, then looked at herself in the unbreakable funhouse metal mirror.

"What are you doing Beck?" she whispered.

His name for her.

Jeremy and Crystal were the only ones that called her that.

When Stephanie Bartley had asked her to come to Vegas to find them, she hadn't been convinced at first.

But when Stephanie pulled the dropcloth off, she'd changed her mind.

Brian Bartley had a brand new shiny motorcycle in the garage, with like, 75 miles on it. He never even rode it.

"Do you have a license? Know how to ride?" Stephanie had asked her, as Rebecca was looking it over with wide eyes, reading the name on the side of the tank. Ducati.

"No and yes—my dad took me dirt biking a lot. No on the license."

Stephanie had nodded her head, and then hobbled to the back of the garage where she took an old canvas tarp off of another bike.

"This one's not registered, not on the books. I don't think it's even freeway legal. It's a 125."

Rebecca looked at it. It was red, and, while not a muscular beast like the other one, it was still cool, in a retro way.

"The Ducati is for when you bring Crystal home. Consider it a bonus. Call when you find her, and I'll send a car."

Stephanie gave her the keys to the Yamaha and some spending cash. She also gave her a fake ID. "Only use this responsibly. You've got a suite at the Luxor. I figured that was your style."

"My style?"

"Because it's all black."

Rebecca was still looking at herself in the metal mirror, wondering what the hell she had been thinking when she'd put her hand out to take the keys and the money.

She cleared her throat. "What are you doing Rebecca?" she said, louder this time, calling up the voice of her mother.

As if in response, there was pounding on the door. She jumped and squeaked.

"Occupado!" she shouted, surprise turning into anger.

"No bathing allowed!" snarled what she assumed was the crustacean from behind the cash register.

"Excuse me?!" she shouted back, indignantly.

"No bathing, no shooting up, no turning tricks."

Rebecca flung the door open. "Do you see anyone else in here with me?"

What an asshole. But then, she saw his black teeth, the gleam in his eye, and why had he followed her out here? She'd been in here less than five minutes. Her anger went icy. His bulky form blocked the door. She was alone with this pervo who was showing undue interest in her bathroom habits, and there was no one around for miles. Nobody to hear her scream.

"I'm done anyway," she said, and pushed past him, breaking into a run. When she reached the shade of the overhang, she jammed her helmet on, swung her leg over the Yamaha, put the key in the ignition, and kicked over the starter.

It sputtered and died.

She couldn't see the guy, the building was in the way. He could be coming right around the corner any second, could reach out his grimy paw, grab the collar of her leather jacket, and pull her right off the back of her bike as she tried to drive away.

She stood up and dropped down on the kickstarter again with her entire 95 pounds of body weight, while juicing the throttle with her right hand, just enough, not too much. The bike roared to life. She chucked it into first and peeled out of the gas station onto the frontage road, revving high up through the gears, not daring to look back.

When she got to the highway onramp, she finally relaxed. "Adios, Zzyzx, you shithole."

Thanks For Reading

I hope you enjoyed November's Missing!

It would mean a lot to me if you could rate and review it on Goodreads or Amazon. Just a few lines and a star rating will help other readers discover books they love!

Continue the journey into Fairy Glen by joining my mailing list. Get a map of Fairy Glen and news about future books. Sign up at valeriepower.com

The Fairy Glen Suspense Series:
October's Fire
November's Missing
December's Barren *Coming Fall 2022*
and 9 more books to complete the 12 book series,
one for each month of the year

Acknowledgments

I'd like to thank:

My husband Bruce Cartier, for being a constant inspiration and steadfast support

Sharon Doar-Toth and Mary Mathews, for their book midwifery

And my family and friends for their encouragement along the way

About the Author

I'm a lifelong horse lover and California native. I've had a varied career that includes photographing pearl farms in Asia and running an underground performance art circus. My husband and I now live at our off-grid homestead in the high desert of San Diego County.
Visit me on the web at valeriepower.com

Made in the USA
Las Vegas, NV
29 April 2023

71314897R00156